Cartel Rose

The Cartel Brotherhood

Sabine Barclay

OLIVERHEBERBOOKS

There's no shame in struggling with mental health challenges.

Find me writing Historical Romance as Celeste Barclay.

Happy reading,
Sabine

The Cartel Brotherhood

Chapter One

Leisel

"No! No! No!"

This cannot be happening.

"Anne, what's wrong?"

I look over at my assistant, Johan, and shake my head. I shift my attention to the man who just walked into the conference room. He prowled—fucking prowled, not walked—into the office as though we're here to serve him. As though this is his investment firm.

It's not. It's not even his country.

"He's half an hour early, and my computer won't connect to the network. I knew I should've brought my own instead of relying on this old piece of shit. It's updating."

"Use mine."

"Thanks."

I watch as Jorge Diaz turns toward my office, and our gazes lock. The man is beyond gorgeous...and he knows it. The arrogance rolls off him in tsunami size waves. He's so damn sure of himself.

Smug bastard.

"If you keep scowling like that, you'll give him the wrong impression."

"More like the right impression. He's here to tank the deal I've worked on for the past four months. It's been a house of cards since the beginning, and he's about to flick the bottom cards out from under everything."

"You can't be sure of that, Anne."

"Maybe not, but it wouldn't be the first time his family's done shit like this. Swooped in and fucked over everyone in sight."

The Diaz family is one of the wealthiest in the world. It's no secret that wealth comes from more illegal enterprises than not. They're originally Colombian, so take that for what it is. They're narco-traffickers. I'm certain of it. No court has ever proven it because evidence and witnesses get lost on the way to trial. They're that powerful. With their home now in New York, their power and influence reach around the world.

Right now, it's reaching into my German office and wrapping itself around me, threatening to strangle me.

"Here. I pulled up the presentation. I'll come with you and connect it to the projector while you schmooze. That's what Americans say, right?"

"Yeah."

I hate schmoozing, but it's an integral part of my job when I'm trying to get companies to invest millions—even billions—in each other. I wanted to be an analyst and stare at numbers all day. I enjoy putting the puzzles together as I watch market trends and company valuations. I enjoy creating investment plans. But my father insisted I be front and center. A pretty face and a brain that works. I never should've let anyone know I'm competent.

Nepo-baby.

I've been called that plenty of times. It wasn't nepotism that got me into Oxford to read PPE—Philosophy, Politics, and Economics. It wasn't nepotism that got me into the Wharton School of Business for my MBA. If nepotism benefited me, I wouldn't be walking into a conference room to shake hands with Jorge.

I inherited my father's Germanic height, so I'm five-eleven. I look most men in the eye. A lot of them don't appreciate it. I also inherited his blonde hair and green eyes. People have complimented my looks my entire life. I know it's made life easier many times, but it's also meant that—combined with the nepo-baby label—plenty of people underestimate me. I've learned to use that to my advantage, but it still stings.

Jorge turns as I enter the room and flashes me a smile. It's polite but reserved. His hand dwarfs mine when we shake, and that's saying something since I don't have man hands, but they're bigger than plenty of women. He has to be at least six-three, six-four. I wonder if everything is proportionate to his height and ridiculously broad shoulders.

The man is fucking *en fuego*. On fire.

Like insanely hot.

It's even more obvious now that we're standing in front of each other.

"Welcome, Mr. Diaz. On behalf of Schlossberg & Sons, we appreciate you coming to Frankfurt."

And Sons.

Doesn't exactly leave much room for me, but I'm still the Chief Operations Officer and second-in-command.

I don't appreciate him sending my father an email two days

ago announcing his impending arrival. We definitely didn't ask him to come. But here I am schmoozing.

"Thank you, Ms. Schlossberg. I know this was a last-minute imposition, and I apologize for the inconvenience. I'm certain you rearranged your schedule to indulge me."

That's unexpected.

"It's all right. We're happy to accommodate you."

Fuck.

I internally wince.

I sounded like a complete bitch. He just apologized, and I threw it back in his face. People say the Germans can be—brusque. Apparently, I'm proving that.

His lips twitch as though he'd smile, but that wouldn't fit with his commanding presence.

"Anne, everything's ready to go."

I forgot Johan was in here, setting everything up. The man is quieter than a church mouse. He also works harder than just about anyone I know. He's completely unflappable, so perfect in a crisis. I rarely get rattled, but if I do, I know I can count on him.

"Thank you, Johan. Please have Alex bring the tray. Mr. Diaz, would you prefer coffee or tea?"

"Just water, please."

I twist to look at Johan, who slips out of the room.

"Ms. Schlossberg, I know I'm early. I wished to speak to you before everyone else arrives."

This feels as ominous as a partner saying, "we need to talk" right before a breakup.

"Please have a seat."

I gesture toward the table and chairs. He walks to the seat directly to the right of the chair at the head of the table. My chair. I force myself not to scowl when he doesn't stop where I assumed but at mine. I'm unprepared for him to pull it out for me. It's on wheels, so he steps aside and pulls out his own seat. The one I thought he'd choose. He doesn't sit until I do.

Old world charm.

His parents must've drilled that into him because it's as though he gave it no thought. He twists in his chair, so he can face me more easily. My gaze takes in his permanently sun-kissed skin, milk chocolate eyes, and five o'clock shadow. He fills the chair with his athletic build, and it's clear he's all bone and muscle. The man didn't skip leg day.

"Ms. Schlossberg, my uncle sent me as the Diaz Holdings forensic accountant rather than my other uncle who's a financier. We have reservations about the valuation you sent. I hoped you could explain it to me, please."

Please.

It's difficult to be in a snit with someone with impeccable manners. However, I struggle not to narrow my eyes when he insinuates I made an error in my analysis.

"What part of the valuation concerns you?"

"All of it."

My chin notches up, and I know I'm looking down my nose at him. It's a reaction I've honed over the years when I feel someone's underestimating me. He's going to argue the company he wishes to invest in is worth less than I proposed.

"Perhaps you could be more specific. Please."

I can be polite too. I swear I can.

"This company is a dolled-up shell corp. Kutsenko Partners currently owns the real holding. That's what we wish to buy. The numbers you reported are vastly under the true value. They only include the shell, which is an asset. But it's not what we want. I suspect it was Pasha Kutsenko, not Sumiko Kutsenko, who sent you the information."

I neither confirm nor deny.

Now he does smile. He knows I'm unwilling to give more information about my client than I must.

"The information Pasha provided made your estimation correct but incomplete. I believe you knew Kutsenko Partners withheld vital records, yet you prepared the offer anyway. Not only that, you submitted it to us."

"Mr. Diaz, I did my own investigation. Kutsenko Partners owns the company that once held the asset you want to invest in. It no longer does. They sold it five months ago, which you already knew since we began the negotiations four months ago. Your suggestion that they still own it is inaccurate. The Kutsenkos offered the historical data as a courtesy."

He smirks, and I think he'd have snorted if it weren't rude.

"If you say so. Your firm's commission increases substantially if the larger deal goes through. We're buying the shell corp and the parent company."

Presumptuous ass.

We're buying.

No, you're not. The parent company isn't for sale.

"Unfortunately, that's not an option. Heidemann Labs is what you hired us to invest in, not buy. Heidemann BioTech isn't for sale."

"With the Kutsenkos, everything is for sale at the right price. Before Diaz Holdings will conclude the Labs' purchase, we'd like you to do a more thorough valuation that includes BioTech. If it's what we expect, then we'll proceed with the offer to Kutsenko Partners. If they won't agree, we'll acquire it by more hostile means."

"A takeover is beyond our purview. A corporate lawyer would be better suited to handle such a transaction. We manage investments. If you'd like to include Heidemann BioTech in your portfolio, we'll happily set that up."

Jorge sits back in his seat as he listens. He appears entirely relaxed, but I sense he's coiled like a snake, ready to strike. I don't trust him.

"Perhaps your father's available."

I force myself not to curl my hands into fists I want to slam into his chiseled jaw. That was an utterly dick move, and he knows it. He's baiting me.

"He is not."

"Then we'll save everyone else the time of coming in here for a meeting that won't happen now."

He rises and buttons his suit coat with just as much suaveness as he unbuttoned it before sitting. I stand as well, but I'm not as ready to leave.

"Mr. Diaz, an ultimatum is premature. We can do the valuations, but we cannot represent you for the takeover. That simply isn't what we do. We can formalize your investment in the Labs, so you hold the majority shares. Once you have those, you can pursue the BioTech sale through your attorneys. Your uncle made it clear from the beginning that your company wants to invest in Heidmann Labs. However, announcing you wish to buy another company is not only unexpected but infeasible."

"Ms. Schlossberg, it may have been unexpected, but very little in business is infeasible when you have the capital my family does. How long will you need to redo the Labs' valuation and include BioTech? I'm in town until tomorrow evening."

I blink at least three times before I answer. He's unreal.

"You know the first valuation took three months. I spent weeks on each division and its projects to create the composite for the entire company. Heidemann BioTech is six times as large as the Heidemann Labs. Do you expect me to finish this by tomorrow?"

"Definitely not. If you can provide me any preliminary

information by noon tomorrow, then Diaz Holdings will complete the investment in the Labs. You can submit your full report on BioTech when it's ready."

He's holding the original deal hostage.

He just demolished the house of cards with one flick of his fingers. Just what I feared.

He offers me his hand, which I accept. It's warm without being clammy just like before, but now it feels as though it singes me. He reaches into his inside breast pocket of his suit coat and withdraws a leather cardholder. He hands me his business card, but I don't look at it. I observe him instead.

"I'd like to meet with you tomorrow."

"I can email you whatever I find."

He shakes his head. "It'll be faster if I can review the data printouts in person. If this room is available, I'd like to request its use, please. The large table will make it easier to examine everything. It'll save you time if I do. If I don't like what I see, then there won't be any need for you to spend more billable hours on this project."

"Are you always so—"

The other senior partners' arrival keeps me from asking if he's always so presumptuous. Probably just as well. The six other men and women file inside and move to their usual seats. Something about Jorge shifts. I glance over at him, and any humor I saw during our conversation is gone. It's like a wall dropped into place, and he's more than just reserved.

"I'd hoped to save your colleagues the interruption, Ms. Schlossberg. I'll leave you to explain my early arrival and departure. Have a good day."

He offers a brief greeting to everyone as he heads to the door. We're all left staring at his back. His very broad back that tapers into a perfect triangle. How many times have I thought about his shoulders? Far too many fucking times.

I think even my eyelashes are tired. I was up all night working on the stupid fucking numbers for Heidemann BioTech. I spoke to my father, who watched the entire meeting from his office a floor above mine. We have cameras in the conference room, so he can observe without being present. It hardly thrilled him, but he accepted my limitations and appreciated how I diffused the situation. He understands Jorge backed me into a corner. He's sent me lunch, dinner, and breakfast since he knows I've been here since yesterday morning.

The last document's printing, so I'm headed to the C Suite bathroom that includes a shower. My sister brought me clothes an hour ago on her way to work. I grab the toiletries I keep here, and the garment bag and head down the hall.

"Anne?"

I stop and look over my shoulder at Johan, who's hurrying toward me.

"*Ja.*"

"*Herr* Diaz just called. He said he'll be here in fifteen minutes." Mister.

"What the ever-loving fuck?"

Johan jerks back, his eyes wide. I never swear in front of my employees, even if I swear up a storm in my head. Jorge's brought it out in me twice. I glance at my watch and realize it's nearly noon. It's way later than I expected. My sister was here nearly three hours ago not an hour. I had my office door shut and blinds closed all morning, so nothing would distract me, and people knew not to knock. I thought it was around nine not eleven forty-five.

"Show him to the conference room. I should be ready just before he arrives."

My hair will be wet, but I'll be there. I dash into the bathroom, already unbuttoning my blouse's cuffs. I hang the garment bag as I work the buttons down the front. I strip faster than I ever have and jump in the shower. The water's barely warm before I'm done. It's one of the fastest showers I've ever taken. I brush my teeth and run a comb through my hair before pulling it into a French braid.

I wrap the long part into a bun at my nape. I force myself to calm before applying my eyeliner. My hand is a little shakier than I'd like, but I get my eye makeup on without fucking up. I hurry to put my blush on before spraying perfume and putting on deodorant. I'm still a little damp across my back—didn't I towel off completely or am I sweating in my haste?—so my top sticks to me as I tug it down. I pull on my trousers and slip on my shoes as I fasten my pants. I collect my belongings, toss the towels in the basket, and head out.

I slip into my office as I watch Jorge enter the conference room just like he did yesterday. I ditch my bags and struggle into my suit coat. I'm a fucking hot mess. I snatch the stack of papers off the printer and grab my laptop—which is working today.

"Good afternoon, Ms. Schlossberg."

Jorge extends his hand as I shuffle things in my arms, so I can return the handshake. I can feel the restrained strength. He could crush mine if he wanted; instead, he returns my firm grip with one that matches. Not too hard, not too soft. Just right.

I'm fucking Goldilocks.

Papa Bear.

Where the fuck did that thought just come from?

Lack of sleep because he's an asshole whose demands caused me to stay at my desk all night.

"Hello, Mr. Diaz. Let me spread out these papers, and you can review them at your leisure."

One of the junior assistants, Alex, knocks on the open door and sticks in his head. *"Tee oder Kaffee, Herr Diaz?"*

We've been speaking English, but the question is easy enough to understand that I don't bother interpreting.

"Water, please."

He didn't stick around long enough yesterday for Alex to bring anything. The young man has a fire under his ass as he hurries to the office kitchen. I don't know if Alex is Jorge's type, but it's obvious Jorge is his. The man practically drooled. I hope he doesn't get any in my tea.

When I shift my attention back to Jorge, he's watching me rather than Alex. His intense gaze makes me want to squirm. When he smiles, my panties want to drop. Good thing I'm wearing a snug thong. He's so fucking gorgeous. His charcoal suit, steel gray shirt, and cobalt tie look like they were each made just for him. His suit is impeccably tailored, and he's freshly shaven. His hair isn't gelled, but it stays in place as though it doesn't dare defy the style he combed. I feel barely put together considering I was still in the shower like five minutes ago.

As I set out the documents, Alex arrives with the drinks. Johan enters to take notes, and the VP of Accounting, VP of Development, and CFO arrive on his heels. I sense more than see Jorge stiffen.

"Hallo." He steps forward and shakes the two women's and one man's hands.

Our CFO, Brunhilde, is a battleax just like her name implies. I got a pissed off email from her this morning about Jorge backing out of the deal. She didn't blame me, but she made it clear she expects me to fix it. She's thirty years older than me and remembers when I was still in pigtails. Usually, she's more deferential, but sometimes, I think she still sees me as that little girl. She definitely squeezes Jorge's hand harder than the rest of us did. He just smiles wider at her.

Except it's not the same smile he's given me. It doesn't reach his eyes. There's a coldness to them now that wasn't there when it was just the two of us. He's retreated like he did yesterday when the partners arrived. I don't get it, and I don't have time to.

"Ms. Schlossberg, you said you have the data for me."

"I do."

I finish spreading out the various reports with my written findings at the end. He reaches for that first and skims it before sweeping his gaze over each pile. He pulls out a chair for me before pulling out his own. The others went around to the far side of the table. He waits until the women sit before sliding into his. Daniel, the VP of Development, was nearly sitting when Jorge lowered himself into the chair.

He nods as Brunhilde asks him a couple questions, but his attention's focused on the paperwork he reviews. I watch him circle and underline various things. He turns to me a few times to ask insightful questions. He makes notes in Spanish along the margins with the pen he withdrew from his suit coat. He summarizes each report on the back of the first page.

Thorough.

Like German auto designer thorough.

When he sits back, he nods to the three executives across from us before he turns his chair to face me. He's definitely not as warm to me as he was when we were alone yesterday and today. I wouldn't have described it that way until I watched how remote he became. I don't get it. It's not like he was flirting with me, then got serious with others around. He's just shut off now. It makes little sense to me. He still has a commanding presence. I don't think that'll ever go away, but he's more an observer now.

"Ms. Schlossberg, we still have a problem."

Chapter Two

Jorge

My problem is the hard-on that's about to tent my trousers if I don't get it under control. How Anne didn't notice it yesterday is beyond me. If she did, she certainly never let on.

Anne.

She doesn't look like an Anne to me. I'm not entirely sure what an Anne would look like, but that just doesn't work for me.

Not that she'll let you call her by her first name after the way you fucked her over.

Fucked her.

Fucking-a.

Now that thought's definitely distracting me.

"Mr. Diaz, what problem could you have with Ms. Schlossberg's work?"

The woman across the table looks like she wants to throttle me. *Frau* Ogre—Mrs. Ogre doesn't have the same ring—over there practically crushed my hand. I didn't expect her to be a world champion arm wrestler. She must be with that grip.

Even though it's Brunhilde Spindler who spoke, I keep my attention on Anne.

Definitely not Anne.

Anneliese is better. It's what's on her email signature. It's a beautiful name that fits her.

"It's not Ms. Schlossberg's work. It's impeccable and impressive for so little time. The problem is Kutsenko Partners heard about our plan and sold Heidemann BioTech when the Japanese markets opened this morning. Since I'm certain the leak didn't come from my family, there's only one place it could have."

I observe her for any reaction to that news.

Guilt?

Regret?

Superiority?

Surprise?

Nothing but distrust.

I would've preferred any of the other emotions. It bothers me that she doesn't trust me. Not that she should. But I've been forthright with her from the start. I haven't lied—though I could've plenty of times. I may only be trustworthy with my family, but I've done nothing to earn her distrust.

Yet.

"Are you accusing us of something, Mr. Diaz?" Anneliese's tone could splinter ice.

"Is there something of which to accuse? I thought it was an observation."

"A thinly veiled observation. You think someone in the office leaked to Kutsenko Partners that you wanted to get control of Heidemann Labs and Heidemann BioTech."

"Want, Ms. Schlossberg. That hasn't changed. Diaz Holdings will still get what we want. But we'll use a different firm to get there."

I push back my chair and sweep my gaze over the four dumbfounded expressions. Like hell my family's using a company that runs to our nemesis and tells them our business. I don't give a flying fuck if it was one person or everyone under this roof. I'm pissed I flew all the way to Germany for this bull-shit. I knew Schlossberg & Sons wouldn't handle the sales, but I wanted to see their reaction. I also wanted to see what their valuations would be.

Anneliese's work matched what I did a month ago. I'm impressed with what she assembled in one night. She must've been at it all night. It's rare I feel this strange emotion nipping at me. I believe most people call it guilt.

Guilt for making her work for the past eighteen hours. Guilt for setting a task I assumed she'd fail. Guilt for having her watch me examine her work with a fine-tooth comb when I knew all along it didn't matter. I was genuinely curious about the data, and once I realized how well she'd done, I couldn't stop myself from reviewing it all. Morbid curiosity I suppose.

She's glaring at me like I'm the biggest douche in the world. I probably am, but it won't change my mind about her firm. I'm certain it wasn't her. She wouldn't have worked this hard to blow it all. Whoever did this didn't think we'd find out, but they had to know the possibility existed.

"Mr. Diaz, is there anything we can do to make this right?"

The man sitting directly across from me looks like he's about to have a full-blown panic attack. Good.

"Your firm's broken my family's trust. Once gone, it doesn't come back—without a price."

"Price?"

I shift my attention back to Anneliese when she takes the

bait. I nod, and I know she's bracing herself for my next demand.

"I want to know who leaked the information."

Four sets of eyebrows shoot straight up. They assume I'll bump the person off. Do they think I'll kill the person in the middle of the office with everyone watching?

"We can't give you that type of information."

"Ms. Schlossberg, I'm probably not the only client this person's divulged information about. That's a problem for you to solve. This person ruined a multimillion-dollar deal, which I now have to explain to my uncle. That's a problem I shouldn't have to solve. Your firm has always had a pristine reputation. It's unfortunate my uncle sent me since I'm the chatty one in the family."

I'm not. Not even remotely. I'm trying not to have my own panic attack sitting in front of four people. I loathe being the center of attention. I hoped showing up early yesterday would allow me to avoid speaking to more than one person. I expected to have others show up to this meeting, but it's not any better than the surprise yesterday.

Thank God for anti-anxiety medication.

"Who will you chat with?" Atila the Hun—I mean, Brunhilde—glowers at me, so I smile.

"Whoever wants to listen. The Kutsenkos already know your firm can't be trusted. They benefited from this, but they'll never do business with you. I'm certain I'll run into Dillan O'Rourke at my brother's upcoming wedding reception. Salvatore Macinelli will be there too. I still have stops in London and Zurich before I head back to New York. Perhaps you'll come up in conversation."

Anneliese hasn't shifted her attention from me once since I confronted them. She's trying to assess how serious I am and what the quantifiable damage will be if I tell anyone, let alone the two people I mentioned by name. I know she understands how fucked her company is now that the Kutsenkos won't use them again. How does she think we heard about them in the first place?

It doesn't surprise me when Gunter Schlossberg, Anneliese's father, enters the room. His already ruddy complexion looks like he's about to have a stroke. He's a mountain of a man. Burly is the only word to describe him. He's as tall as I am at six-four, but he has to be at least forty pounds heavier than me. He's easily two-eighty, and it's not flab. He's not in his prime, but it's obvious he stays in shape.

I stand, scooping up all the papers as he approaches me. He tests me as he shakes my hand, but my grip is just as punishing as his. His gaze hardens when he accepts he's met his match.

"Mr. Diaz, I expected your uncle Matáis. It's a pleasure to meet you."

Since this is a major transaction, normally it would be *Tío* Matáis who'd handle this. But he's in Tokyo for his own set of investment meetings. Since this deal required more forensic accounting than usual, it fell to me to handle it.

"The same. My uncle speaks highly of you."

While my words are encouraging, my expression is not. I frown and furrow my brow. I spotted the cameras yesterday, so I know he watched my meeting with Anneliese and this one. It makes me wonder if he's the one who snitched and prayed I wouldn't find out. I doubt it. He's not dumb enough to think I'm so stupid I'd believe it was a coincidence Maksim sold the company we ultimately wanted. Not on the morning the deal to invest was supposed to go through.

Maks and his brothers were happy to unload the companies as long as they weren't to my family. They know my cousin's wife is a chemist who'd have taken the struggling biotech company and made it into a powerhouse since she knows what's up from down. None of the other families have a scientist in-house who could accomplish that. We have two. My cousin Pablo and now Florencia.

"I see you've reviewed Anneliese's work, but I don't see our contract."

"You won't, and you know why, Gunter."

His right eye twitches when I address him by his first name since he used an honorific and my last name. He's probably thinking I'm a presumptuous little fuck.

"Please explain since I want to be certain I understand."

I point to the camera on the wall beside the projection screen. It looks like it's the switch to raise and lower the screen, but I've installed enough cameras to know what I see. I cock my left eyebrow as I stare at Gunter. Anneliese shifts next to me. I want to look at her, but I can't. I have to maintain my focus on her father.

"Jorge, does your uncle know your decision?"

I flash a smile that makes him narrow his eyes even more at me. They're practically slits now.

"*Tío* Matáis is in Tokyo. He woke me to tell me what happened. Neither he nor I enjoyed waking *Tío* Enrique to bring him up to speed. Both of my uncles agreed without hesitation when I told them we're withdrawing from the deal."

Fuck him for treating me like a kid who ran to tattle.

This isn't an "I'm taking my toys and going home" move.

This is "there's not a fucking chance in hell we'll do business with a company engaged in corporate espionage." At least not a company that isn't engaging in it on our behalf.

"You may not get Heidemann BioTech, but you can still invest in Heidemann Labs. Kutsenko Partners no longer owns either, so they won't be an impediment."

The VP of Development looks entirely too hopeful as he speaks to me from across the table. I can't even remember the man's name, but he looks at me like a beagle hoping I'll take him for a walk around the block.

"We're no longer interested." *Please take us off the list.*

I feel like I'm speaking to a telemarketer. We've gone off script, and he doesn't know what to do short of begging to close the deal.

"I seriously hope you will reconsider this decision since we can continue just as originally planned."

Gunter doesn't sound desperate, but I recognize the look in his eyes. I've seen it on hundreds of men. I don't exaggerate. Between photos from the past, interviews—if you will—I've conducted on my own, and the general appearance so many men have when they see or hear about *Los Diaz* anywhere in the world, I know what desperation looks like.

I cock an eyebrow rather than respond with words. Anneliese shifts next to me, and I swing my gaze toward her.

"Mr. Diaz, we will investigate what happened. We take the integrity of our firm seriously. We do not condone any breaches in our security."

As I watch her, her forthright gaze tempts me to believe she's innocent. As much as I want to look back at her father to see his reaction, I keep her pinned in place, assessing her body language as I continue to observe her. She doesn't flinch or withdraw. She doesn't become defensive. She remains assertive. Finally, I look away and refocus on Gunter. It wouldn't surprise me in the least if he's the leak. I skim my gaze over the other three executives in the conference room with us.

"I'll be in touch."

That's as much as I offer before walking out, dismissing them just like I did yesterday. I make my way directly to the town car waiting for me. As soon as I've given my driver instructions to take me back to the hotel, I slip inside. Since the privacy glass is up, I once again search the vehicle for any bugs.

This isn't one of our private vehicles in our fleet back home. When I'm certain no one can listen, I call *Tío* Enrique and *Tío* Matáis.

"What did you discover?"

Tío Matáis is usually pretty easygoing, but he's pissed this deal blew up. He rarely lets things bother him except for business. Anyone who stands in his way or fucks around with our family soon finds out just how unforgiving he is. Just because he works in an office now doesn't mean he has any less training than the rest of us.

He earned his position as one of *Tío* Enrique's most trusted advisors when they were still in college. That's when he met *Tía* Catalina. His family has been connected to mine in Colombia for a few generations. He grew up in a Cartel family, but no one else in his family ever became part of the *jefe's* most inner circle.

It was his business acumen and his propensity to be overprotective of *Tía* Catalina that caught my abuelo's attention. While they were only dating, he made sure some men who went to university with my *tía* understood how untouchable she was—is. It proved how much my *tía* meant to him. It was the first step to him gaining my family's trust.

Once *Tío* Enrique and *Tío* Luis spent more time with him, they realized he's an asset to our family. They also discovered *Tío* Matáis's father trained him to be ruthless. While he doesn't go on missions with us often, he does when he has to. He never has to be asked twice.

"Jorge, who else is available to us?"

I know *Tío* Matáis means what other investment firms could we work with. I rattle off a list of five other names. They're companies in Berlin, Zurich, and Geneva. There are plenty here in Frankfurt I can check too. We want to expand our holdings anyway and make more legal inroads here in Europe.

"Since I'm already over here, it would be easy for me to meet with any of them, *Tío*. Do we continue to target the Kutsenkos, or do we find businesses that are unaffiliated?"

It's *Tío* Enrique who responds this time since he knows I directed the question to him.

"Both. We look for any viable opportunities. If ones come up that aren't connected to the Kutsenkos but are advantageous, we pursue those. However, they're not off the hook yet. Dig deeper."

"*Sí, Tío.* I think our best bet is to go with König Corporate Finance in Zurich. But I'll do some more investigating before I set up meetings with anyone."

Any company willing to name themselves "king" must have some confidence in their account managers. Family name or not, that sets the bar high.

I hang up with my *tíos* just as we arrive at my hotel. I knock on the window, letting my driver know I'm ready for him to open my car door. I head directly to my room and re-examine the printouts Anneliese gave me. I carried them out with me after gathering them when Gunter entered the conference room. He probably saw them before the meeting. But just in case he hadn't, I didn't want him to catch sight of any notes. I'm uncertain whether he speaks Spanish. I didn't sense Anneliese did while I reviewed the papers.

I turn on my computer, then head into the suite's bedroom. I change out of my suit into jogging pants and a t-shirt. I've worn suits almost every day for ten years. I hate them. They're too constricting. I'd much rather be in athletic clothes than feeling like I have a noose around my neck.

My computer is awake and ready to go by the time I sit down.

Not only am I a forensic accountant, but I'm a licensed stockbroker. I check the numbers in the Asian markets. It's still too early for the U.S., so I check some trends I've seen with companies that caught my attention when I took notice of both Heidemann corporations. I analyze the numbers until I'm certain there are ten potential companies of interest. I check to see who represents them and create a dossier on each. I look for all information available about these companies, which means doing as much digging as I can.

But I know when I reach the limits to my skills, so I send an encrypted email to my oldest brother, Joaquin, since he's our chief intel gatherer. My brother's response is almost immediate. He promises to have more information within the next two days.

As the youngest of three, I'm a mixture of the most patient and impatient person in my family. There were always two people ahead of me to learn and do everything. I was always impatient to catch up. I learned patience because eventually my turn would come, and from watching them, I was often better than them.

Today, the impatient side wins out. I tap my fingers on the table beside my laptop, but there's nothing for me to do now but wait.

What could she possibly have to say? I'm propped up against pillows on my hotel bed in Zurich, and an email from Anneliese just came through. It's been three days since I walked out of her office, rejecting her firm. My brother sent me a slew of information last night just before I went to bed. I took a preliminary glance at it to see if anything needed immediate attention.

I'm reviewing everything now. There're definitely some

prospective companies to invest in. The Kutsenkos own one of them, just like I suspected, but it certainly took Joaquin digging to confirm it.

I click on the new email, surprised by the warm greeting. It immediately makes me suspicious.

Dear Mr. Diaz,

I hope this finds you well, wherever your travels have taken you.

I've been thinking about you and regret how things turned out. I hope you've had time to reflect on what I gave you and can see what a good fit we are, even if our initial plans won't work out. I've been investigating who jeopardized our relationship. While I can't disclose anything from within my firm, I can tell you we are steps closer to rectifying this situation. I hope you'll reconsider your decision to leave us.

Respectfully yours,

Anneliese

I reread the message as my lips twitch. Maybe something got lost in translation, but there's certainly plenty for me to read into. It tempts me to respond with an equally innuendo-filled message. While she might not have meant for it to come across as flirtatious, I certainly will.

Chapter Three

Liesel

Oh. My. God.

This man is unreal.

I can't believe—*actually, yes, I can*—he's that fucking presumptuous.

The email from Jorge is flirtatious at best, scandalous at worst. I read back through mine, already knowing what it says, having read it five times before sending it. I wrote it in English since I'm completely fluent and have been since grade school, but I translated it back into German just to be on the safe side.

Nothing about Jorge Diaz made me think he was the flirtatious type. I think he's the most attractive man I've ever seen, and I'm sure others agree, considering Alex asked about him twice. But he didn't show any interest in me.

Alex's curiosity made him my number one target for investigation. Turns out he's just a horny young man who is certain Jorge isn't interested in him either. But Alex didn't mind looking and making jokes even if he couldn't touch.

I can't force myself to close the email. Instead, I read it yet again.

Dear Ms. Schlossberg,

I am very well, though I am having to be creative about how I stay warm here in Zurich. I hope you're not suffering the same. We can't consider a future relationship if one of us is frigid. I'm willing to come around to the idea of working with your firm, but I will only agree if you are my sole point of contact. Unfortunately, your company's poor choices won't go unpunished. If both parties consent to a new arrangement, your firm will take 0.5% rather than the initially proposed 1% fee. Rather than the standard 20% profit share, you will accept 15%. These are non-negotiable compromises.

I look forward to your response.

Sincerely Yours,

Jorge

"Anne."

I look up from my computer to find my father looming in my doorway. He states my name as though he's not interrupting me. He'd never consider asking if I was in the middle of something. Time stops when Gunter Schlossberg demands your attention.

Without shifting my gaze, I click on the browser tab and close the email.

"*Ja, Papa.*"

He walks to my desk and crosses his arms as we continue in German.

"Have you spoken to Enrique or Matáis?"

"No. I just received an email from the younger *Herr* Diaz."

"We're not dealing with someone who storms out in a tantrum. We will only communicate with Enrique or Matáis."

Now I'm annoyed.

First, Jorge insists I be the only point of contact. Now my

father insists I only communicate with Jorge's uncles. I'll talk to whoever the fuck I want to.

Who's having the tantrum?

"Papa, the younger *Herr* Diaz agreed to consider working with us again. However, it's at a lower commission."

"Lower than one percent?"

"Yes, but not below what's standard. He'll agree to half a percent."

"Ridiculous. And I suppose he wants fifteen percent for the profit share."

Did he read my email?

It wouldn't surprise me if my father commanded IT to route all emails to him before going to employees.

"It could be worse. He could've suggested ten."

My father's left eye narrows. He doesn't care for my forced pleasant optimism. We both know it doesn't come naturally.

"No. We aren't some non-profit charity. We run a business to make money. There will be other clients. Unless you hear those terms from Enrique or Matáis, I refuse."

I curl my toes in my shoes since I can't curl my fingers into fists without him seeing. He tries my patience on the best of days.

"Papa, even with the deal changing and the percentages lowering, we stand to make more this quarter than we have in the last three. This is too good a deal to pass up. We're fortunate the Diazes are even considering returning to the table. They could tell everyone in the finance world what happened. They could blackball us, making it so no one trusts us. No one hires us. Then where would we be?"

"You catastrophize."

I lean back in my seat and stare at him for a moment before cocking an eyebrow.

"You look like *Mutti* when you do that."

He should know. My mother's been giving him this look for nearly forty years. My father blusters while my mother conveys everything with a single expression.

"Fine." He concedes and unfolds his arms but shakes his head.

"Papa, it's for the best. He and his family are right to be angry. *Someone*—" I raise the other eyebrow. "—disclosed that confidential information. Stop while we're still ahead. I'll email him and let him know we'll accept the new terms."

"This is on you, Anne. This is your account. If anything goes wrong, I'll only be looking at you."

My father turns away and walks to the door, but before he can leave, I have more to say.

"Don't set me up to fail again, Papa."

He looks over his shoulder at me, his expression harsh. Mine now matches his.

"You didn't fail, Anne. You won. Make sure Jorge understands that."

He walks out, shutting the door behind him. He has a fucked-up way of thinking of victory. He nearly destroyed the deal, tests me to see if I'll stand up to him, then considers getting the deal regardless of the lower commission a win.

I suppose today the glass is half full.

Dear Mr. Diaz,

Normally, we wouldn't accept such reduced terms. However, we acknowledge we're responsible for the precipitating events. We accept your proposal and look forward to working with you. My assistant will forward the required documents for your review and signature.

Respectfully,

Anneliese

There.

Nothing to misinterpret about that.

I reach for the phone to tell Johan to send the email I requested he prepare as soon as my father left my office. I could see him working on it through my office's glass wall. Before I can hit the intercom button, a new email appears in my inbox.

That was way too fast.

Dear Ms. Schlossberg,

Your response pleases me. I believe you're making headway with this deal. I'm prepared to deliver on my promise now that we've handled that part of our business. Shall I come to you? I can be in your office tomorrow morning.

Sincerely Yours,

J

An email shouldn't affect my pussy, but it does.

Fuck me.

Like, *please*, fuck me.

As though the email itself wasn't grossly informal at best, he signed it with just an initial. That feels—intimate. I'm in a committed relationship and live with my boyfriend. Nothing should be intimate between me and another man. I shouldn't have any thoughts about another man fucking me. The image of him undressing me and fucking me against a wall is more intense than the part of me that remembers I've always been faithful in relationships.

I refuse to reply right now. Instead, I buzz Johan and tell him to send everything to Jorge. I barely catch myself and remember to call him *Herr* Diaz. German business culture has relaxed over the past few decades, but we're still German. Punctuality, professional appearance, hierarchy, and honorifics still matter in many workplaces. They certainly do here. I can't imagine a single employee calling my father Gunter to his face.

I address him as *Vater*—Father—when we're in public. Never Papa. I doubt he'd respond if I did.

I wait until it's time for me to leave, then I send my email.

Dear Mr. Diaz,

I have meetings all morning, but I am available between 13:00 and 15:00. Please let me know what works best for you.

Respectfully Yours,

Hmmm.

A

I have no meetings in the morning. I just don't need him to believe I want to see him first thing. I won't appear eager. I'll appear busy but willing to fit him in.

Good God. That sounds dirty.

But true.

Fuck my life.

"*Hallo, mein Liebling.*" Hello, my darling.

"*Hallo, Bastian.*"

My boyfriend wraps his arm around my waist, and I lean in for his kiss. It's open-mouthed but appropriate for public. I rest my head against his chest, and after a long day, it's familiar. I relax, and he gives me a squeeze. He adjusts my hood against the wind as we pull apart.

"How was your day? I missed you last night." Bastian slides his hand into mine after he opens the restaurant door.

I wait until he steps beside me before I answer. "The same as usual."

"Too long and too stressful. What did your father do today?"

I shoot him a rueful expression and am about to shake my head when I recognize a face among the diners.

What the fuck is he doing here?

Jorge.

Who the fuck is she?!

What the hell was that visceral reaction?

As though he senses me, Jorge looks up from his dinner partner and meets my gaze. He nods and shoots me a quick smile before dismissing me and turning his attention back to his—date. I can only see the woman's profile, but she's stunning.

Sophisticated.

Clearly wealthy.

Beautiful.

And older.

I didn't take Jorge for the cougar type. Then again, I didn't take him for the flirtatious type either. But those emails...

If he's with someone, he definitely shouldn't have sent ones that provocative.

And you have a boyfriend and loved every minute.

I turn away from Jorge and return my focus to my boyfriend.

Yes, boyfriend. Fucking remember that.

"How was your day, *mein Schatz?*" My sweetheart.

"Eventful."

I barely hear what Bastian's telling me as the maître d' leads us to a table. He takes us directly past Jorge and the gorgeous woman who's laughing at something he just said. My fucking luck. Our table is next to his.

Fuck my life.

I get to watch him flirt with another woman all night. I get to examine why that bothers me until I make myself neurotic. And I have to pretend to care what Bastian says when I normally genuinely do.

"Good evening, Ms. Schlossberg."

"Hello, Mr. Diaz. I'd like to introduce you to Bastian Klauss. Bastian, this is my firm's new client."

Jorge and the woman both rise. The men extend their arms, and I notice Jorge's hand dwarfs even Bastian's, who's just over six feet tall and built like what you'd expect a sturdy German to look. He played rugby at university. Bastian doesn't flinch, but I can tell Jorge's squeezing his hand tighter than Bastian expected. Jorge appears completely casual as he does it.

"Ms. Schlossberg, Mr. Klauss, this is my mother, Luciana Diaz."

Mother.

His mother?

There isn't a chance in fucking hell this woman is in her late fifties at the youngest.

I look between the two of them, and I can see the resemblance now. Talk about an amazing family gene pool. I doubt she's had any work done. She's just naturally that breathtaking.

My gaze meets Jorge's, and he appears to fight the urge to smirk.

"It's lovely to meet you both. Funny running into you here."

Luciana's comment forces my attention away from Jorge. Frankfurt is an enormous city and is the financial capital of not just Germany but central Europe. There are easily hundreds of restaurants in the city, yet we both wind up here. It's not near my office or any hotel they're likely staying in. This place isn't exactly out of the way, but it's more of a local choice.

"Small world." What the hell else do I say?

"My parents used to come here whenever they were in town."

Jorge's explanation leaves me with more questions. *Used to? Were in town?*

Why the past tense? Doesn't Jorge's father travel with his

mother anymore? Why did they come to Frankfurt? Was it business for one or both of them?

"That was a long time ago."

There's a wistfulness to the woman's comment, and it makes me think she has fond memories of this place, but they're tinged with sadness. As though she catches herself, she turns to me and smiles.

"We don't want to keep you from your dinner."

"It was nice meeting you both." Bastian offers them a nod before pulling out the chair that will force me to face Jorge throughout the meal.

"Enjoy your meal, Mrs. Diaz, Mr. Diaz."

"It's Jorge, Liesel."

He's standing beside me as he adjusts his mother's seat for her. I barely hear him.

Liesel?

That's not my name. Liese, maybe. But not Liesel. The English equivalent of my name is Anna Elise, not Anne Elizabeth. All three can be diminutives of Elizabeth, though, so it's not beyond the realm of possibility.

Did it suddenly get warm in here? The heat rising along my neck tempts me to fan myself with the menu. This is definitely *not* the place to do that. Am I too young for a hot flash?

"What are you in the mood for tonight?" Maybe if I get the conversation going with Bastian again, I'll forget about the brooding man sitting three feet from me.

"I think the *rouladen*. What about you?"

Stuffed meat.

So *not* what I need on my dirty mind right now.

Especially not when they serve the dish with potatoes.

"The *spaetzle*." I love the micro-dumplings here and the braised beef that goes with them.

"Jorge's *Weiner schnitzel* looked good too."

For the love of all that's holy. The universe is fucking perverted and cruel.

I only know the slang meaning for wiener because of my time in the U.S. for grad school. Bastian probably doesn't since he went to university and med school in Berlin. I don't need any more reasons to think about Jorge's cock. Certainly not when his mother is sitting practically elbow-to-elbow with me.

Thank heavens for small mercies when Jorge and Luciana finish their dinner halfway through Bastian's and mine. They say goodnight and leave. I was so aware of Jorge I practically ignored Bastian all evening. I feel like a bitch.

We've been together for two years, so he's used to nights when I'm too tired to hold up my end of the conversation. I know he thinks that's what's happening right now. If only it were. My mind is plenty awake. It's jumping all over the place from the impending contracts to Jorge's appearance and voice. Then it hops from my father breathing down my neck to worrying about what Enrique Diaz will do if the investment falls through after all this shit. I dread facing one of the world's most powerful men. Jorge is already intimidating. I don't want to imagine what his uncles are like.

"Are you ready to head home?"

Bastian helps me with my coat as I twist to look over my shoulder. His face is so familiar, and it still melts my heart when he smiles at me. I turn toward him and slide my arms around his waist.

"I love you." I practically blurted that.

"I love you too. Ready?"

I nod and let go. I face the door, but not before I take one last look at Jorge's empty chair. I picture his smirk when I realized he wasn't on a date like I am.

Our weekly date night. Something you could set your Bavarian clock by.

Cuckoo.

It's time I pulled my head out of my ass.

Bastian wraps his arm around my waist as we head to his car. I used our company car service to get here because I knew I was going home with Bastian.

Easygoing, reliable...predictable Bastian.

He's loyal—like a spaniel.

Jorge...

He's a fucking Rottweiler. Handsome to look at but ready to tear you apart.

Chapter Four

Jorge

"That was a lovely—and unexpected—meal you treated me to, especially since you *loathe* going to crowded restaurants where you know people."

My mother glances at me nonchalantly as she slides into the town car. I grimace as I walk around to the other side. I make sure my expression is relaxed once again before I get in.

"What are the odds you and your broker should choose the same restaurant when it's such an out-of-the-way place?"

"Her boyfriend may have picked it. I know you've always liked it. You reminded me about it before I came on this trip. It's a lucky coincidence I'm back here in Frankfurt, and you had to be here for your own meeting."

My mother is a corporate real estate shark. Like a great white with fangs, not teeth. She hadn't planned to be here, but *Tío* Enrique asked her to visit an office complex that's just been built. It went way over budget, and the owner is about to lose the property. *Mamá* is here to assess whether it would make a good headquarters once we acquire both companies I'm here for and add a second biotech lab to the holdings.

We'll pay the overage the current owner can't afford, which is still less than the amount he's already paid. We'll get it at a relative steal since the guy can't take another foreclosure after he's already had two businesses fail in the past three years. He claims *Mamá* is here to strong arm him. She told him she's offering a gift, and that he'd be rude to refuse it.

"It's a lucky coincidence *you* picked the same restaurant."

"I suppose so."

She wants me to admit I knew Liesel—that just slipped out, but now it's stuck—was going to be there. Why admit something she already knows? That was my argument when I wouldn't confess to things as a kid. It didn't get me out of shit back then, and it won't get me out of the shit I'm in now. I didn't know they'd seat them next to us.

That's what I fucking get for thinking I could kill two birds with one stone—enjoy dinner with *Mamá* and unnerve Liesel. I got exactly what I deserved—heartburn. I hate crowded restaurants. I hate crowded anything, anywhere. I didn't think my mother's favorite place would be so busy during the middle of the week.

Mamá knew I was trying to listen to their conversation. She frowned at me once, and I knew she understood exactly what I'd done. Made me feel guilty as shit until she grinned at me. I didn't want her to think I used her memories with *Papá* to stalk some woman I barely know. From her knowing expression, I'm as much like *Papá* as my family always tells me. Except he didn't want to crawl out of his skin when he had to make nice in public.

"Jorge, she's intelligent, observant, tolerant of you—and taken."

I meet her gaze and won't look away until she laughs and

shakes her head. She looks up at the ceiling of the car, but I know she's looking beyond that.

"Estebear, see what you did? You're still a bad influence."

She's talking to *Papá*. She does it aloud to tease my brothers and me, but I know she often speaks silently to him. She says he's always with her. Her avenging angel. She was always Lucy to him, and he was Estebear to her instead of Esteban.

It reminds me again that I came up with Liesel for Anneliese. I don't know why. I hadn't heard the name Liesel since I was like fifteen. *Mamá* trapped Joaquin, Javier, and me into watching *The Sound of Music* with her—a movie that still plays an intermission in the middle!

"Don't blame, *Papá*. You're the one who insisted I introduce you."

"I didn't say a word about that."

"You didn't need to, *Mamá*. I knew."

She giggles, and it makes me feel better. She's the baby among her siblings, and she's the funniest of all of them. But both of my *tíos* and my *tía* laugh a lot too. There's too much in our lives that brings sadness and pain. When we can find joy— or at least a reprieve—we take it. It's why I invited *Mamá* to dinner once I knew we'd both be here. Finding the restaurant Liesel planned to eat at was just the cherry on top.

"That wasn't just some new guy, Jorge. They've been together a while."

"I could tell."

I don't need reminding. I knew she was involved with someone from the background check Joaquin ran before I left New York. When nothing came up on him, I didn't ask for more information. I knew I'd meet him tonight since I hacked her calendar. It didn't make it any less annoying having to smile and be polite to the *cabrón*. Asshole.

He's probably the nicest guy in Germany, but he's with her, so he's a *cabrón*.

"She's not a toy."

"*¡Mamá!*"

The woman exasperates me!

"You aren't the type to break up a happy home, Jorge."

Not my fault if I break up an unhappy one.

"I don't plan to."

"Even if she were available, you can't let her get close to you unless it's for good."

"I know, *Mamá*. Even if you and our *tías* and *tíos* didn't warn all of us, I would know that. I've watched *Tío* Enrique, Javier, and Pablo all meet their soulmates. I've seen all of them question whether they were selfish to fall in love and bring women into our world. I would *never* bring anyone near our family if I weren't sure I could trust them for the rest of my life."

She pats my knee. "*Bueno.* Do you have time for breakfast tomorrow? I have a meeting at nine."

And just like that, she changes the subject. She won't belabor the point. She doesn't have to. She knows her voice is in my head where it will stay until I have the Atlantic between Liesel and me.

"Yes, I'll hit the gym at six but only go for an hour and a half. I'll be back upstairs and ready by eight. Should I come to your suite?"

"Sure. It'll only take fifteen minutes to get to the *idiota's* office. From the tremor in his voice on our call today, the meeting shouldn't take long."

"Then we can have lunch before I go to Schlossberg & Sons." I enjoy my mom's company.

"I'd like that. You've been busy lately."

"It's March and nearly tax season." It's my most creative time of year.

"I know. Doesn't mean I don't miss you."

"I was at your house a week ago, and you complained I cleaned out your fridge."

"I don't blame you for that. That was you and Joaquin."

"Humph."

I cross my arms and pretend to pout. She slides her arm through mine and leans her head against my shoulder. I know she misses my brothers and me now that we don't live at home. All of us stop by at least once a week just to annoy her. We leave our shoes strewn in the middle of the foyer, our suit coats tossed on the sofa, and dishes stacked in the sink—for an hour.

Then we clean up after ourselves because we still fear her.

I know she's not exactly lonely without *Papá*, but she is alone. *Tío* Enrique has *Tía* Elle. *Tío* Luis has *Tía* Margherita. *Tía* Catalina has *Tío* Matáis. *Mamá's* a widow.

She'll never remarry. Not even the slimmest chance exists. She says *Papá's* spirit is always with her, so she doesn't get lonely. But my brothers and I still don't enjoy knowing she rattles around her house with no one else there most days and every night. Even now that Javier's married, the three of us go over there for dinner together at least once a week. We go separately too. Now Javier brings Madeline when she doesn't have a rotation as a midwife at a hospital.

"You shall trip over that lip, *mijo*."

"You always say that, and I haven't yet."

As the youngest of three, I've perfected the pout. Doesn't get me anywhere, but I'm good at it. She chuckles and lets go as we pull up to the hotel.

I'm on the side with the curb, so I get out first. My gaze sweeps our surroundings as I button my suit coat. When I'm certain it's safe, I offer *Mamá* my hand. I wrap my arm around her shoulders because it's chilly tonight and as a shield. We thank the driver as we hurry inside.

Alone, I don't worry as much about myself or *Mamá*. But I never want her to be a target because she's next to me. My brothers are the same. We can be a smidge overprotective. She calls it suffocating. We remind her the apples didn't fall far from the tree. Not her tree or *Papá's*.

She's nearly a foot shorter than my brothers and me and slight boned, but she's deadly. Like as in she cut off a guy's *huevo* and sent it to his wife with a bow on the box because he was part of the plot that killed my father. She swung the first machete that made a head roll when my *tíos* caught the three brothers who murdered my father. They did it in front of my brothers and me when I was eight, Javier was nine, and Joaquin was ten. She ordered Diaz Cartel men to drop the men's heads into Bogotá traffic to be pushed around and run over by cars like soccer balls. She had their bodies strung upside down from the busiest bridge in the city.

"Que sueñes con los angelitos, mijo." Dream of little angels, my son.

She's been telling Joaquin, Javier, and me that since we were born. I close my eyes for a moment as she stretches, and I lean over for her to kiss my cheek. I hug her tightly enough she thumps my back. Something I've been doing since I was twelve and outgrew her.

"Te quiero, Mamá." I love you, Mama.

"Te quiero también." I love you too.

I wait until the suite door closes, and I hear her bolt it and swing the bar. I nod to the men guarding her door as they shift into place after giving us our privacy. I head down the hallway to my suite, greeting the men outside my door.

I felt my phone vibrate in the elevator and checked the screen. Joaquin texted me. I pull out my phone and unlock the screen, reading as I take off my coat and tie. I stop with my pants halfway down as I read the last sentence.

JOAQUIN

They leaked the deal again.

I click the link to an article that outlines our investment plan and hints at our intention to take over both divisions of the Heidemann holdings.

What the ever-loving fuck?

I bet the Kutsenkos are loving every minute of this. We're supposed to be sticking it to them, not the other way around. This pisses me the fuck off.

I look at my watch and notice it's a few minutes after eight. Even I have some boundaries. I can't call Liesel. I sure as fuck am not calling Gunter, that lying sack of shit. He did this. What's worse is he knows it'll put his daughter in my crosshairs. What game is he playing?

"Guten Morgen, Fräulein." Good morning, miss.

Liesel narrows her eyes at me.

Was it something I said? Like using the now antiquated—even bordering on offensive—greeting for an unmarried woman.

Was it my showing up before she even arrived at the office? I'm leaning my left shoulder against the wall with my right ankle crossed over my left and my right hand in my pocket.

"Guten Morgen, Herr Diaz." Good morning, Mr. Diaz.

"Wir müssen über Ihr anhaltendes Problem mit der Vertraulichkeit sprechen." We need to speak about your ongoing problem with confidentiality.

The only accent I have when I speak German is German. It shocks the shit out of her.

Of course, someone in my family speaks the language of a country where we do frequent business. I speak French and German, just like *Tío* Enrique. Joaquin speaks Mandarin, Vietnamese, and Cambodian. Javier speaks Japanese and Korean. *Tío* Luis and Alejandro speak Brazilian Portuguese and regular Portuguese. Pablo speaks Russian and Italian. Since we've all lived in New York or just outside the city in New Jersey, we even have healthy doses of Yiddish.

We're all native Spanish speakers. Only Pablo and Alejandro grew up in the States. The rest of us came from Colombia at varying ages from teen to adult. A Spanish accent flavors everyone's English—when we allow it.

"Speaking German with a voice like a foghorn certainly won't help."

Liesel practically hisses at me. I don't think I spoke that loudly, but she glances at the employees walking over from the elevator. I reach past her and open the office suite's door, holding it for her. She heads straight to her office, unlocking it with a code she shields me from seeing. I shut the door behind me as she whirls around.

"Did you hack my calendar?"

So, we're going there, are we?

"That's quite the accusation."

"That's not a denial. That's a diversion. Did you?"

"You assume I took my mother to dinner to spy on you."

"Silence is consent, so I will take your evasiveness as an admittance."

"If I wanted to spy on you, Liesel, I wouldn't sit out in the open. I also wouldn't be halfway through my meal when you arrived."

I wasn't spying. I was watching in plain sight. And it was

her fault we were halfway through our meal because she was late.

"And it was fate that we had tables next to each other."

"It was." Not bending the truth on that.

I walk closer, and she moves to put the desk between us. I cock an eyebrow. Her scowl eases as she silently admits she knows I'm not a physical threat.

"If anyone should be lobbing accusations, it should be me toward you for corporate espionage."

"Espionage? That's outrageous. What do I stand to gain from your family walking away? I don't consider my professional reputation and that of my family's firm being ground into the dirt a gain."

"You may worry about your professional reputation, but your father doesn't. At the very least, he should care about the company's."

I watch that strike between the eyes. She practically jerks back but catches herself. I practically crumble into ash from the way she's glaring at me. But I shall always be a phoenix—even if it's my older brother who's named Joaquin.

"This company has been around since long before you and I were born. It's doing just fine without you or your family."

"For now."

"Are you threatening me, Jorge?"

The way she says my name. She tries for condescending, but I take it as a challenge.

"Liesel—"

"That's not my name."

"Liesel—"

"*Sei nicht begriffsstutzig, Jorgito.*" Don't be obtuse, little Jorge.

No one's called me that since before my dad died. An event like that ages a kid.

I grin, so she can't see how the nickname rattles me. It was special when *Papá* said it. *Hor-he-toe.* I refuse to allow an argument with this spitfire to taint that memory. Just the opposite. I could get used to it—though no one's said there's anything little about me in nearly thirty years.

Her blend of German with the Spanish is hot. Her pronunciation tells me she isn't a Spanish speaker, which begs the question how she knows the nickname. But it reassures me she didn't read my notes. Not that it matters since I wrote nothing she would've understood even if she was a fluent speaker. It was my shorthand.

"I'm not threatening you. I'm pointing out the obvious. By now, half the corporate world has read the news. They'll know my family didn't intend that to go public. They'll know the information came from within your organization, not mine."

"Because our employees don't fear us like yours do you?"

She steps around the desk, no longer hiding from me. Ballsy. She's only safe because she's a woman.

"If that's what you believe, then you know the risk you take with that accusation."

"I'm not accusing you. I'm pointing out the obvious."

I shrug as I slide my hands into my pockets. Not that I need them, but the two knives are always a reassuring presence.

"It was nice almost doing business with you, Liesel."

"And if I can prove the Kutsenkos sold the companies to their own shell corps? That you could still buy them from them? Out from under them?"

That gets my attention.

"Can you?"

"Yes."

"How?"

"Confidential."

She has the most expressive eyes. They're windows to her

soul when she opens the blinds. They can be blank when she wants them to be, but they can hold a wealth of messages when she allows it. They're mocking and challenging again.

I slide my hands out of my pockets, so my suit coat falls back into place. I don't need her seeing what she does to me as my dick twitches. What I wouldn't give to nibble at her plump lips while pinching and twisting her nipple until she whimpers with need. What I wouldn't give to spin her around and fuck her ass against her desk.

The lurid images dancing through my mind aren't encouraging my cock to behave.

"Liesel, even if you could prove that, why would I ever trust you?"

She practically bares her teeth at me when I use my pet name for her, but her eyes—they tell me she likes it.

"Because it wasn't me."

"No, it was your father. Your boss and the owner of this company sold a story that cost us millions in potential revenue. As long as you work here, you're as untrustworthy as everyone else."

"If I'm so horrible, leave."

"I didn't say you're horrible." *You're magnificent when you're angry.* "But you're guilty by association. That's what makes you untrustworthy. Leave this firm, and I might believe you."

Chapter Five

Liesel

Leave this firm, and I might believe you.

Pick the Handkäse mit Musik, and you might not be hungry.

It's a heavy, sour milk cheese with a raw onion vinaigrette that makes it—pungent. It's called "the music" because of the flatulence it can cause. Considering the knots in my stomach, it might be a fitting metaphor.

"I'm no more likely to leave my family business than you are yours."

His expression darkens, and I wonder if I've pushed too far. It's no secret my father agreed to get into bed with a cartel when he accepted the Diazes' inquiry.

Into bed.

For fuck's same, Anneliese, stop making everything sexual.

"Are you always trustworthy, Jorgito?"

I'm probably slipping the noose around my own neck right now, but I can't help the extra dig.

"No."

I'm left waiting for more, but he says nothing else. He watches me for a moment before turning around and walking out. He doesn't even bother to shut my door. I watch him head out of the office suite, leaving that door open too. The elevator dings, and he disappears.

Poof.

Gone.

I'm left staring until I catch myself because people are looking into my office and watching me. I connect my laptop to the dock and sit down. No one can see what's on my screen—or what's not. I hope I look like I'm intently reading something. Instead, I'm gazing blankly at my computer. The part where he blatantly admitted he's not trustworthy—that sparked curiosity and dread. That entire exchange rattled me.

"Did you hear me, Anne?"

"Hmm? Sorry, Bastian."

"You're even more distracted than usual."

Fuck.

"I thought I saw someone I know, but probably not."

We just walked into the grocery store, and I could've sworn I saw Jorge in the parking lot. I know he wasn't there, but I could have sworn...

"Do you want me to get the pork loin and steaks?" Bastian's question draws my attention back to him.

"Yes, please. I'll get the fruits and vegetables."

We have the same conversation every time we come to the store. As though something's going to change after shopping together nearly every week for the past six months we've lived together. I rarely notice, but it seems asinine today.

It's nine-thirty on Saturday morning. Where else would we be?

Normally, I like our routine. It's reliable.

But as I watch Bastian walk away, the predictability reminds me of how I thought of him as a spaniel. It's not a complimentary comparison. I doubt he'd appreciate it. It makes me think of an elderly married couple, and that hardly excites me when he and I are barely thirty.

Is it sweet or boring?

I used to think it was the former. Now I'm leaning to the latter.

I head to the right while Bastian's still to the left of the store's entrance. I glance over my shoulder, something unsettling me. I see nothing strange, so I head to the cabbage. How very German of me. As I place two heads in my *Einkaufswagen* —shopping car—I consider what else I need to make sauerkraut.

Haus frau.

That's what I feel like. A housewife. It doesn't give me the warm, fuzzy contentment I got when Bastian moved in with me. I don't intend to give up my job—I can't since I'll inherit the firm—but I liked the idea of a happy home with Bastian.

It's not like we're unhappy. I don't know what the fuck's gotten into me except for a piss-pour mood for the past three days. Everything's irritated me since Jorge showed up to my office five hours early. Papa and I nearly got into an argument in his office after Jorge left. We saved it until I went to my parents' house that night.

The fight was epic.

I thought he might have a stroke from how red his face got. I thought I was having a heart attack from how hard mine was beating. I nearly quit, and I think he nearly fired me.

Poor *Mutti*—Mama—knew not to intervene, but she tried

for a calming presence. She's the only reason we weren't screaming at each other. I don't know that I've ever been that livid or my father's ever felt he had to justify himself that much. I'm getting heated just thinking about it.

I turn my shopping cart to avoid an older woman's, and I spy a dark-haired man with his back to me. He seems familiar, but I can't think of anyone—except for Jorge—who'd fit his description. He walks away after picking up a bunch of bananas.

I follow him.

But I can't spot him once I get near the crowded cheese counter. Fuck the French. We produce more cheese than them, and it seems like every person in Frankfurt is getting theirs from this store right now.

"You only got the cabbage?"

I shift to see Bastian approaching me.

Fuck.

"Yeah. I just thought about getting some Limburger and didn't want to forget. I'll go back for the rest of the produce."

He buys the lie. He loves the stinky cheese, and he knows I hate it. He thinks I'm doing it just for him. It's the first cheese I spotted when I looked at the display. I sweep my gaze around the parts of the store I can see, but I don't spy the man who reminded of me of Jorge before Bastian and I go back to the produce.

"Watch out."

I barely skirt the trash can my sister points out. I already tripped over the curb a mile ago. I blamed that on an untied shoelace, so we needed to pause our run, anyway. It gave me a chance to look around. I'm fucking certain this time.

I saw Jorge.

"You're in la-la land, Anne."

I definitely can't tell my sister who's really living rent free in my head. I can tell her part of what's distracting me.

"I know, Heidi. My mind's still locked on the argument Papa and I had again right before I left work yesterday."

Bastian and I had a great weekend together. I pushed Papa and Jorge out of my mind, and I enjoyed time with my boyfriend. Then Papa burst that high when he stopped me when I arrived and told me he wanted to speak to me. I got to dread the conversation all day. He did that on purpose.

"*Mutti* said the last one was really nasty."

"It was. We barely kept ourselves from saying things we couldn't take back. He's put me in a shit position with other clients now that they know information doesn't stay secret with us."

"You're certain Papa's the one who leaked it?"

"He's all but said the words. If it wasn't him, he ordered someone to do it. I can't figure out who. I had Michael comb through the server to see where every email for the past two weeks came from and went."

I'm certain he thinks less of me now that he's surely read my exchange with Jorge. At best, he thinks Jorge's a pervert.

"The IT guy Papa hired, so you'd break up with him?"

"We weren't serious. We were friends who thought we might be more. He and I both know he's better off as the head of our IT department than being my boyfriend."

"True. And you wouldn't be with Bastian if you were with him. Bastian's definitely the better of the two."

Yes, my sweet pediatrician boyfriend who works for Ärzte ohne Grenzen e.V. It's the German division of Médecins Sans Frontières—Doctors Without Borders. We met two weeks after he returned to Germany after a year in Burkina Faso. He's leaving in two months for six months in Eswatini. I had to look that one up. It's formerly Swaziland—a small country bordered by South Africa and Mozambique.

He's off to save children in dire poverty, and I'm fantasizing about a narco-trafficker.

What the fuck is wrong with me?

"He is amazing. I'm lucky I met him."

"You're lucky my boyfriend is your boyfriend's best friend."

I struggle not to flinch. I don't need the reminder. We pass the mark where we usually speed up for a mile, so I push us to where neither of us can speak comfortably. There's a curve in the Main River that allows me to look back at the trail we're running in Grüneburgpark.

That man has to be Jorge.

There's a guy with the right height and build to be Jorge, but the hat with a brim makes it impossible for me to tell. His head's lowered against a gust of brisk spring air. Germany forgets spring is supposed to start in March, so it's only in the mid-fifties today. After my time in the States, I think in Fahrenheit and Celsius—which confuses the hell out of my family. I have a beanie on to cover my ears since the wind's cold.

This is a large and well-known park and only about a ten minute jog from some of Frankfurt's best hotels. I suppose it's not a stretch for Jorge to come running here. However, I'm disconcerted that he was at the same restaurant as Bastian and me. I still suspect he was at our grocery store—at least ten miles from any hotel he'd stay at. Somewhere luxurious I'm sure. Why's he still in town? I haven't seen him or heard from him in nearly a week.

The man I spotted fades into what must be a club since there're about fifteen people running together in a pack. I can't see him or even the other runners as the trail straightens again.

"You trying to set a personal record?"

Heidi's practically panting as we get to the next marker where we slow to a more comfortable pace. She's faster and has more endurance than I do. She runs slower than usual when we go out together. If she felt like that was a hard pace, I must have been practically flying.

"Just trying to keep up with you, *Schwesterlein*." Little sister.

"I like it better when you run like *eine Greisin*."

"I'm only two years older than you. I'm not an old lady!"

"Your creaking toes would say differently."

I elbow my sister as we continue to run, and she pretends to stagger sideways before giving me a playful shove. We enjoy each other's company more than we did as kids. We bickered but never got into real arguments—our parents would never allow it. We had little in common until we both went away to college. I'd learned to live with my homesickness in Britain, so Heidi would call me whenever she wanted to leave the States and go back to Germany her first year. We got closer then.

"Do you and Friedrich want to come over for dinner tonight?"

I check my watch. With the pace I just set, I might have time to treat myself to a pastry on the way to work.

"I'll ask, but I don't see why not."

We reach our cars parked side-by-side. A quick hug, and we're both off. As I pull out of the lot, I can no longer doubt the man is Jorge. He's looking right at me.

He's stalking me.

I didn't see his face at the grocery store, yet he let me see him while I was running with my sister. Coincidence could explain the park, just like dinner. But I've sensed him everywhere.

I just haven't seen him again.

I went out with some girlfriends last night, and I'm certain he was at the restaurant and then the bar. I felt like someone was watching throughout dinner. I tried to inconspicuously look around, but I didn't spot him. I just knew.

I tried to walk past him at the bar as though I was on the way to the restroom, but he blended into the crowd. I don't get how since he's a big guy—tall with massively wide shoulders. He could've been an American football player in college for how muscular he is. He may have been nice to look at but knowing he's watching me is creeping me out.

"Anne, we can wait for your rideshare to show up."

I'm out on the town for a second night in a row—such a wild life I lead. My friend Marie is the mother hen in the group. She always tells us not to walk alone at night, to always share our location when we get rides, and not to drink anything you didn't see the bartender open. As though, at our ages, any of us have forgotten. But we know why she's that way. We visited her in the hospital after she was attacked and assaulted in college.

"Thanks, but I'm all right. The sidewalk is still busy, and it's well lit. I'll wait until they pull up directly in front of me."

"If you're sure..."

"I am, Marta."

Marta's Marie's sister, so she's just as vigilant. She's the one who called the rest of us and told us what happened. I flew back from the England. It taught me to be far more cautious, so that's why sensing Jorge around me is freaking me out. I'm pretty certain he came outside when he saw us gathering our coats. He's lurking somewhere around here.

My friends take off as I jam my hands in my pockets. It's

extra brisk tonight, so I have my chin tucked against the wind. I'm still watching my surroundings, but my head isn't on a swivel.

Motherfucker. Grrr.

My ride just pulled past me despite me waving. My hand just got warm. I watch him stop a block away. I wait for reverse lights, praying he doesn't decide to circle the block and leave me out here longer. I definitely don't want him to leave.

Of course, I tell my friends I'll wait right here. Fucking hell.

When the driver does nothing, I hurry up the block. As I cross a narrow street that's more like an alley, I notice a shadow against the wall I approach. I can't tell what it is, but it could definitely be a person. I sprint to the waiting car. I hear someone step out behind me, but I don't look back. I don't want to give them the time to get closer. Tonight's not the night to confront anyone.

My heart's pounding as I practically slam the door.

"Anneliese?"

"Ya."

I twist to look back through the rear window as the driver confirms who I am. I watch a man in front of a couple walking away from me. I can't tell anything about him besides there's a person ahead of them who's taller than most. I suppose it could be Jorge, but this has to be too much even for him.

Do I have a genuine stalker?

Do I think way too much of myself to believe I do?

Would he really go to such extremes to see if I'm the leak?

If it is Jorge, why?

I sit back with my eyes closed as I calm myself. By the time I reach my home, I'm not terrified. Unnerved, yes. Ready to panic, no. I thank the driver and get out. I look around for anything unusual. It's my normal quiet neighborhood. I head toward my building's front door as a car inches out of a parking spot.

That's odd. At this time of night, you'd expect someone to come home, not leave.

As I prepare to put the fob against the pad, I turn back to look at the vehicle. The car's windows appear tinted darker than usual. I step into the lobby of my apartment building and let the door close. The car drives past slower than it should, as though the occupant might be watching me.

I'm going nowhere alone unless it's the middle of the day, and the sun is shining.

Chapter Six

Jorge

I couldn't bug Liesel's phone—not only wouldn't my cracked moral compass allow it, but it also wasn't practical—so I bugged her office. Amazing what a low-wage maintenance worker will do for an extra two thousand euros.

I don't have confirmation yet, but Liesel could still be the leak.

Who does Liesel works for?

If it isn't her, then maybe a conversation I overhear will give it away.

"Johan, I'm going to run a couple errands. I'll be back in a bit."

I listen to Liesel speak to her assistant through the intercom. I turn on the car's engine as I wait for her to emerge from the building. I haven't transformed my hotel room into some evil lair or covert government spy headquarters. But I am stalking her.

I fully admit that. Hell, I let her see me again yesterday, so she'd know I'm watching her.

Some of it is for my enjoyment. I acknowledge that and have no problems with it. She's beautiful, and I'm hot for her.

However, most of it is because I know her father is the leak, but I want to know what she's doing about it. I suspected there was another party involved that wasn't a news outlet. Eventually, she'll go somewhere or do something that'll give it away.

In the meantime, I'm learning her routine. This way I'll know when she deviates from it. The pastry after her run was unusual the first morning I followed her. She runs with her sister every week morning, then goes home to get ready. She goes directly to her office from her apartment. However, her sister wasn't with her today.

I saw her boyfriend come home in scrubs a few days ago, but I'd already learned he's Superman in a lab coat. He couldn't be more different from me. He saves lives while I—don't. Though I've never harmed a child who wasn't a peer before I moved to the States when I was eleven. Just the opposite.

I focus on Liesel as she walks outside rather than letting my mind wander to Bastian or how I donate my time and money when I'm not being a monster.

She looks around before crossing the street. She doesn't wait for a rideshare to pick her up or take another mode of public transportation. She stays on foot. I turn off the car and hurry to follow her. The sidewalk's crowded, so I blend in. I'm also tall enough, and so is she, that I don't lose sight of her.

I observe her duck into a fast-food restaurant and walk up to the counter. There aren't enough people in there for me to go unnoticed. I pull out my phone and appear to make a call. I say nothing, so I could be on hold for all anyone knows.

It doesn't take long for a sandwich, large fries, and a small drink to appear on a tray she carries to a table in the corner. She unwraps the sandwich and closes her eyes for a moment before taking a bite. Even from a distance, I can tell she relishes it. She snags a couple fries before her next bite of her sandwich.

Comfort food.

She came here not because she was pressed for time but to indulge in a guilty pleasure. She savors this rather than rushing to inhale it. She clearly favors the fries since the sandwich and soda are a normal European portion—tiny by American standards—but the fries could feed two people in Germany.

She likes salty things.

You fucking perv.

I glance at my watch, and she's been inside for nearly twenty-five minutes. It only took five minutes for her to get her food. If discovering fast-food is such an indulgence for her wasn't so intriguing to me, I'd be bored and wishing she'd hurry. She disposes of her trash, so I turn away from the restaurant and walk two doors down. I assumed she'd head back to her office, so I walked in the opposite direction. Instead, she's turned toward me. I duck into the store—a children's boutique —and wait for her to pass me.

"Guten morgen."

Damn. The sales associate is evaluating how much she thinks I'll spend. I'm dressed too well to come across as cheap. I sweep my gaze around the store and frown.

"Entschuldigung. Falscher Laden." Sorry. Wrong shop.

I step back on the street and nearly miss Liesel turning left at the end of the block. My long stride and broad frame mean people step aside for me. I can't follow her as she jaywalks to cross a busy road. She'd notice me as she keeps looking both ways. She heads to a bench in a park as she pulls out her phone. She sits in the middle of an open bench, making it difficult for anyone to share it with her. She lowers her head as though she's reading something on her phone.

I cross the street with the crowd at the crosswalk and circle around to observe her from behind. From the way her shoulders move, she's doing some kind of breathing exercise rather than engaging with something on her phone. I creep—because that's what I'm being—closer. Her eyes are closed. The irregular breathing rhythm tells me she's not asleep. Not that I think she'd ever make herself so vulnerable in a public place.

I squelch my instinct to run to her when someone bumps into her as she stands. It's hard enough to knock her backwards until she's sitting again. I don't like that.

She says something, but I can't hear her. It looks like she was muttering rather than speaking to the *cabrón*. I notice a piece of paper on her lap at the same time she does. She looks in the man's direction before unfolding it. Her head jerks up, and she practically jumps to her feet. She heads in the man's direction, and I'm on the move too. I won't let her confront whoever that was. From the way the man carries himself, he isn't someone's lackey. He's trained.

When the man ducks into the U-Bahn—subway—station, she stops. She has limits to how far she'll chase him.

Good.

I've angled myself, so she won't see me unless she knows what to look for. She crumples the paper as she shoves it in her purse and makes her way toward me. I cross the street ahead of her and once again step into a shop. This one is busy, so I don't worry about a sales associate approaching me before I can get back outside and continue following Liesel.

She squares her shoulders and lifts her chin before breezing through her office building's door. She's back to being self-assured and in control. I'm back in my car making a real call.

"Joaquin, any updates on the leak?"

"I haven't heard anything you haven't. Any thoughts on who that was?"

I know Joaquin's been listening too since he texted me to say he couldn't sleep, so he was going to monitor her office.

"No, not yet. Who do you think's behind this?"

"The better question is who isn't? There are plenty of people who'd like to fuck us over and fuck over the deal. Namely Maks, but it's not like Salvatore and Dillan aren't close behind on that list. It could be Tommaso in Boston or Gareth in Trenton. It could be Jean-Peter in Montreal."

The list goes on for people overconfident enough to think they rival us or people who're delusional enough to aspire to rival us. They're like a train of ants. Where there's one, there're plenty. They follow each other blindly until we crush them under our Italian leather shoes—the only Italian thing good enough for us. Sometimes it takes spraying bug killer—a spray of bullets—to make people realize we're the apex predators.

"Where'd she go on her errands? Did you hear someone go in and out of her office?"

"No. I stopped listening when I followed her. She got some food and then went to sit in the park. I think she wanted the time alone. But someone dropped a note on her lap, which she crumpled up and shoved in her purse."

"Good thing she didn't notice she has a second shadow."

"Yeah. Good thing."

I roll my eyes because he can't see me. Joaquin and Javier are giving me a hard time about her. *Tío* Enrique just wants me to finish up and come home. As far as my *tío's* concerned, I'm more interested in Gunter's comings and goings than Liesel's. My brothers didn't need to guess. *Mamá* told them.

"I'd ask how much longer you're going to keep this up, but I suppose I need to water your plants again."

"It's not like you don't steal tomatoes every time."

"I don't steal. I accept payment in kind."

I snort.

I cook with the tomatoes. He puts a dash of salt on them and eats them like apples. Disgusting and messy.

"Just keep my petunias alive, will ya? You underwatered them last time. They were as shriveled as *los huevos de un viejo*." An old man's balls.

"Wah wah. I'll go tonight."

"*Gracias*." Thank you.

"You need to come back just so you can weed your garden. It's like the Amazon followed you here."

I have a private greenhouse on my building's rooftop. Perks of owning the entire place.

"After this trip, I'm ready to lock myself up there for a few days."

"That bad?"

I hear the worry in my brother's voice. I didn't mean to make him nervous.

"It's just annoying more than anything. A little uncomfortable at times but nothing I'm not used to."

Anxiety blows.

But I've had it since I was a kid. Price I pay for what I witnessed with my dad and other shit that happened to us when street gangs thought three young boys and a gorgeous, widowed mother were easy targets. I stabbed someone for the first time five months after my dad died. A guy tried to grab me. Javier was there, and he killed him. He was barely ten, and I was still eight.

We stayed in Colombia for three years after my dad's murder, then it got too bad. We moved to the States to keep my mother, brothers, and me safe. But by then, the damage was already done. I hate crowds, and I hate being the center of attention. Therapy helps, but it's never gotten rid of all the flashbacks.

"Let me know if you need anything, *manito*." Little brother.

I know Joaquin means more than just intel.

"I will. I'm going to get some work done while I wait for her to head home."

"*Te quiero.*"

We speak at the same time before hanging up.

I can appreciate Liesel's usually a homebody because so am I, but she and Bastian are fucking boring to stake out. They take turns cooking, which I can see most of until one of them closes the blinds when it gets dark. I can see the TV flicker, and sometimes Liesel's office light is on. Their lights go off at ten, practically on the dot. The bedroom lights flick on for ten minutes while they get ready for bed. I hate thinking about what happens after that.

It's the same routine every night except for Wednesday when they seem to have their date night and twice when Bastian was on call at the hospital. Those were the nights she went out. Three long nights outside their apartment made me confident they stay in until Liesel leaves at six for her run with her sister. They vary their routes, but they stick to three places. I head back to my hotel at eleven, and I'm back in Liesel's neighborhood by five-thirty.

I've been at this for two weeks. I'm definitely a bona fide stalker at this point. This isn't just about observing a potential threat to my family's business. This is about a smoking hot woman I want to bang. I'm jerking off too often to pretend I don't want her.

I haven't let her see me again since the two times in the park. I can tell she senses I'm nearby, though. She might think it's the man who threatened her, or maybe she's guessed it's me. Either way, she looks over her shoulder more each day. She's taking a company car everywhere, so she's never alone.

Considering the note the guy dropped on her lap in the park, I'm glad she's with someone when she's out and at home. Bastian's hint of cauliflower ear tells me he wrestled or played rugby. It reassures me he can defend her. It's the only thing he has going for him.

I hate thinking I scare her, but it's a necessary evil to protect her and my family—and indulge my fantasy.

I'm a sick and twisted fuck.

All I can say in my defense is I've never stalked a woman before. I've followed men around and terrorized them when they've crossed my family. But I've never been a woman's shadow before.

First time for everything.

It's not just her looks. I'm still listening to her office. If I weren't learning anything, I would've headed home already. Her father's poked around her office three times. From the way she mutters the next morning, she's aware. I find Alex, the junior assistant or whatever he is, the most problematic. He snoops for the sake of snooping. As best I can tell from the bugs I planted in his apartment and on his phone, he isn't selling the information. He sleeps like the dead, so I didn't just put mics and cameras in his place like I did the entire Schlossberg & Sons office, I got to his cell phone too.

Johan's clean as a fucking whistle. He's as boring as Bastian. I had a couple of my guards follow him a few times. They reported he's tried to find out from some friends at other brokerages if we went with them, but beyond that, he minds his own business. My kind of guy.

Sounds hypocritical, but what the fuck Schlossberg & Sons does is now my business after they fucked us over. I know it was Gunter, but the douche who's called Liesel is pushing her harder to get us back on board. She's still standing her ground against him while I drag out the negotiations. I've glimpsed no one else surveilling her, but that doesn't mean he hasn't found other ways to track her. I can't get to her phone to be certain.

I have boundaries even I won't cross, so I haven't been inside her home. Maybe the *carechimba*—face of a vagina—doesn't have those limits. Maybe he's seeing things I'm not. I *don't* want to see her in bed with Bastian. Sick fucker if he is.

"*Hola, Tío.*"

I can't ignore *Tío* Enrique when he calls, even though it means I have to turn down the feed from Liesel's office.

"*Hola, sobrino. ¿Algo nuevo?*" Hello, nephew. Anything new?

"*Nada.*" Nothing.

I can't lie because I'll have nothing to show. I know what's coming as we continue the conversation in Spanish.

"Any reason for you to stay?"

"I still haven't figured out if Anneliese or someone else is working for a rival."

I catch myself with my *tío*. Maybe my brothers have told him my pet name, but I've been careful not to let it slip.

"You can keep monitoring her office from home. You don't need to remain in Frankfurt for that. Drop a tracker on her car and the ones in their company fleet. Come home."

Grrrrrrrr.

"And if something comes of the guy who dropped the note in her lap? I have the Atlantic between us before I can do anything to him." *For her.*

"We have people in Frankfurt who can keep an eye on her. You've been gone nearly a month, Jorge."

"*Lo sé.*" I know.

I nearly snap at my *tío*, but I mutter it instead. That's not much better. I sound petulant rather than pissed. Neither will fool him.

"There's something about her, isn't there?"

Fuck my life.

"I don't know. Maybe."

"Your *mamá* says she has a boyfriend."

Fucking-a.

"She does. It's not like I've asked her out."

"No. You're just stalking her."

Fucking hell.

"Monitoring the situation."

"Sure, *sobrino*."

"Are you ordering me home?"

I screw up my nose. Not the right choice of words or tone. *Fuck me.*

"Do I need to?" *Tío* Enrique's tone isn't quite ice, but an arctic blast is about to blow through.

"My intuition says there's still something to learn here."

There's a long pause. My *tío* never pauses to think something over. He's likely ten steps ahead of me already. He pauses to make you want to shit yourself.

My phone pings, and I know I have another call coming in. I recognize the number.

"*Tío*, Anneliese is calling. I have to go."

"*Está bien.*" All right.

I don't wait for him to say more before I click over.

"He—"

"Jorge, help!"

Chapter Seven

Liesel

"I'm on my way, *chiquita*."

I hear a car alarm beep, but it barely registers with me as I stare at the amputated hand in a box on my desk. I barely shifted my gaze away from it long enough to find Jorge's business card and dial his number.

"Jorge, I need you. Hurry."

"I'm coming. I'm almost in the building."

There's silence for a moment, then I hear the elevator ding. He must've practically run to the elevator. It feels like an eternity before I hear his voice again.

"I'm coming into your office right now."

The blinds on my glass wall are shut, but my door is open. I see him step through the office suite's doorway as I snap the lid shut on the box. It's only now that I think about the type of package sent to me. It's not a regular shipping box. It's more like a gift one with a lid that flips open. I can't handle looking at it any longer.

He enters my office without knocking, shutting the door behind him. I feel like I can breathe again. The tightness in my chest eases only a fraction, but it's enough to keep the panic at bay.

"What happened, Liesel?"

His voice is soft yet commanding. It allows me to focus on something specific rather than the way my mind raced a moment ago. I point to the box and look away. He lifts the lid but says nothing. I hear him close it again, and his hands gently cup the outside of my arms.

"Is that your father's?"

I nod. "The ring. He's never taken it off."

Jorge offers me a tight smile. I'm gazing into his eyes, but not everything registers. It's as though my brain is in a fog. He pulls me against him, and I shudder. I hunch, so I can listen to his heartbeat and feel his heat seeping into me. With his arms wrapped around me, I feel protected. But it doesn't last long since I pull away and look up at him.

"How did you get here so fast?"

I guess some things are becoming clearer to me. I suspected he might've been outside my building, but I wasn't sure. I told myself that's why I called him and not somebody else, because I knew he was nearby. But that's not the entire truth. I feel safe with him. Only him.

He watches me as he fires off some text. I can't read what he's writing, but his thumbs are going a mile a minute.

"Liesel, you need to come with me to my hotel."

I shake my head.

"Liesel, I'm not asking you. I'm telling you."

"I can't go there. I have to..."

What the fuck do I have to do? I don't even know.

"Have to what, Liesel? You called me for a reason. Because

you knew I'd know how to handle this. You didn't call anyone else, just me."

"How can you be so certain of that?"

Because I need you to be.

"Because I'm standing here, and no one else is already here, and I can tell no one else is coming."

"I still can't go to a hotel with you."

Some sense of propriety permeates my rattled mind.

"Do you fear me? Do you think I did this?"

My mouth drops open as I shake my head vehemently. "If I thought you'd done this, I wouldn't have called you."

"Exactly. You know you can rely on me."

My brain seems to clear with that one word. Rely.

When has a Rottweiler ever been reliable? I suppose reliably defensive of its family and territory. I'm not his family, but am I now some type of territory in a syndicate war? I lick my lips in nervousness but shake my head again.

"Can't you make this go away?"

"Not until I know what this is. I need to find out where your father is and whether anyone else is in danger."

"My mother? My sister?" The panic is back.

"I don't know yet, Liesel. That's what I have to find out."

"How will you do that?"

"I need to get you somewhere safe in an environment I can control. Then I can sort all of that out."

"Can't we do that somewhere I already know?"

"Liesel, are you afraid of appearances if someone sees you going to a hotel with me? Is that why you're hesitant?"

I can't do much more than nod. I know I should've called Bastian, but he's barely a thought. Today is his day off, so I know he's at home. I could've gone straight there. I could've called him from the car. I could've called Jorge from the car. I don't know what else I could've done. I'm making excuses now that I remember my boyfriend.

"Liesel, you are coming with me to my hotel. Do not argue, little one, or I will spank you."

My head jerks back, shocked at Jorge's words, but it's clear he's unwavering in that promise.

"I'm not a child."

His gaze sweeps over me, and I think he likes what he sees. I think he can tell it intrigues me, and I hate that.

"I never thought you were, but I will spank you if you disobey me."

He scoops up the box and ushers me toward my office door. It's not until we step out of the suite that his hand hovers at my lower back. I can't help the shiver that courses through me. The gesture is possessive and protective.

I like it way too much.

No man has ever done that before. I'm certain he felt my reaction because now his hand presses against the top of my hips as we enter the elevator. He positions me so that his right shoulder is slightly in front of me. It looks like we're standing side by side, but it would only take one step for him to shift and block me from anyone entering the elevator. Fortunately, it doesn't stop until we get to the ground floor.

He ushers me toward a vehicle as he uses the fob to pop open the trunk. He opens the front passenger door first and holds it open for me. I slide in and twist toward him, but he gently closes the door before walking around to put the box in the trunk.

A pang of guilt strikes me as I think about my father's hand rattling around in the trunk by itself. It seems so inhumane. But I can't picture sitting here with the box in my lap or between my feet like it was Thing from the *Addams Family*.

I nearly jump out of my skin when he opens the door. I

hear my name, but I don't react. Another moment of mental paralysis strikes me.

"Liesel."

He rests his hand on my thigh and gives it a gentle squeeze. When I only turn my head to stare at him, he reaches across me and snaps the belt into place, adjusting it so it doesn't rub against my neck before he puts his own on.

"Thank you."

That's the last thing either of us says until we reach his hotel, which is blessedly only a couple miles away. We're there in ten minutes. We pull into the hotel's underground parking garage, and he backs into the spot. It dawns on me this must be a strategic move in case he should ever need to leave somewhere in a hurry. That's both frightening and reassuring, as though I need any more complex or conflicting emotions right now.

"Stay in the car until I come around to your side."

I nod. He gets out and goes to the trunk, retrieving the box. I remember it struck me as odd when I arrived and found it on my desk after lunch. Johan said he didn't see who delivered it because he'd also gone out to lunch.

Jorge opens my door, and I unfasten my belt. He offers me his hand, and I gladly take it. It's warm and dry, which makes me worry mine might be clammy. But if it is, he doesn't seem to notice. It's reassuring the way it's so large it practically swallows mine completely. He lets go entirely too soon, but his hand goes back to the small of my back once he's pressed the elevator button. When we step inside, he angles us the same way he did the last time.

It shouldn't surprise me he's in a penthouse suite. When we step off the elevator, I notice the men outside his door. They must be his guards. I refuse to look weak in front of anybody since I trust no one but Jorge right now. I lift my chin and push my shoulders back and look straight ahead.

Jorge unlocks the door, but before I can walk fully into the suite, his arm goes out in front of me, blocking my way. He places the box on the entryway table before looking around the room. He pokes his head into the bedroom before tilting it. I suppose he can see into the bathroom from there. He does the same thing with the other bedroom.

It reassures me as much as it frightens me. Doesn't he trust the men outside the door? Aren't they there to keep anyone else out?

"Liesel, old habits die hard. Unless it's someone else in my family sweeping a room, I'll never be comfortable without looking around. It's not a reflection on my men so much as proof that my uncles' ingrained their training in me."

My mind is clearer than before Jorge arrived at my office, but my ability to speak hasn't fully returned. I feel like a bobblehead when all I do is nod. He returns to stand before me. He reaches past me to shut and bolt the door, then he places his hands on the outside of my shoulders just like before he hugged me in my office. His hold is light, but it bolsters me.

"You're safe with me, Liesel. I promise."

That forces a choked laugh from me. "If you were a safe man, Jorge, I wouldn't have called you."

His gaze intensifies as it sweeps over me before returning to meet mine. "Safe with me, *chiquita*, not from me. Obey me, and we won't have any problems."

Even in a moment like this—when I'm terrified for my family and confused about what the fuck is happening—he can make my pussy ache with a look and a few words. He tempts me to reply with "Yes, sir," but I remain quiet.

"Would you feel better if I ordered you a cheeseburger and some fries? Would it distract you for a bit?"

Wait. A cheeseburger and fries? How does he know I like those? That they're comfort foods. They have been since grad school.

He's been following me. I suspected it, but that confirms it.

Panic rises from the tips of my toes, churning in my belly, making my chest burn, and brain scream *"RUN."*

My gaze sweeps around my surroundings. I want out. Now. There's no way I can make it to the door with him near it. I edge around him, and he watches me. It's not like he's the predator, and I'm the prey. But he observes me intently. It's as though he knows what I'm thinking, and he's indulging me. That irritates the fuck out of me.

I consider running to a bedroom and locking myself in. If I bolt, he'll catch me. Instead, I ease my way toward the far wall. It gets me farther from the door, but it'll allow me to see everything in front of me. It'll keep one side of me protected.

"Liesel, stay away from the windows."

It's a command he expects me to obey. I should. But I need space from him. I'm not thinking clearly yet, so all I know is I want distance.

"Liesel."

I ignore him and back up, not taking my eyes off him. He allows me to—until I step in front of a window. He crosses the floor between us before wrapping his arm around me. He pulls me against him, turning us, so his back is to the window until we move away from it. I stare at the tie knotted in front of me, and my mind flashes to it loosened with his shirt's top button undone. It's hard to imagine him being that casual.

You saw him on your run. You didn't imagine it. He wasn't in a suit then.

His gaze dips to my lips, and I think he might kiss me. I shouldn't want him to. I've been around other attractive men since I met Bastian. None of them have tempted me. Jorge does.

When he lowers his head, I'm ready to tilt mine back. Before I can, his hand draws back and spanks me.

"Ow!"

I attempt to jerk away, but his arm is a steel band. Completely inflexible. My next strategy is to pull my arms up between us and push, but I can't move them in time. He expects that and pins both arms to my side. He widens his stance before I can stomp on his foot. I try to lift my leg to knee him in the balls, but he spins me around. Then I'm lifted off my feet as he carries me to the sofa.

I struggle against him, trying to headbutt him and kicking my legs as he walks. But it isn't enough. He's sitting, and I'm across his lap as I continue to fight. His hand lands across my ass again, and it burns like I just stuck it in an oven. His broad hand finds a new spot with each swat.

"Jorge, stop! Stop! I didn't agree to this."

"I warned you in your office. You came with me. You consented."

"I didn't. I didn't think you were serious."

"What made you think I would jest during a situation like this?"

"I..."

Nothing about him or this is humorous. I told him I wasn't a child when he threatened to spank me, but I didn't refuse. The idea even intrigued me, but that was before he lit my ass on fire.

"Stop! I agreed to come with you. You scared me."

"Because I offered you a cheeseburger."

He nails one across my horizontal crack, pushing me forward on his lap. My clit rubs against his thigh, and my body has an entirely different—but not entirely unexpected, to be honest—reaction. I bite my lip to keep from gasping. He'll know it isn't from the pain since I haven't done that. Panted, yes. Gasped, no.

I catch myself not fighting as hard. I don't want him to know this isn't such a horrible punishment after all. I stomp my feet and kick. He slaps the backs of my thighs, and it stings. I try to pull my hands free, but he manacled my wrists with his hand, pressing them against my lower back. I squirm, but it's to gain relief from the ache he ignited in my pussy. It's to rub my clit against him again.

He abruptly stops and helps me to my feet. His expression tells me he guessed what I was doing. But he still wipes the tears away that I couldn't stop. When his arm wraps around me, it's no longer to pin me in place. It's holding me up.

"You know how I know you enjoy cheeseburgers and fries. You did nothing to confront me or call me out about it. You may fear the things I do, but you don't fear me, Liesel. You wouldn't let me call you that if you did. You wouldn't have come with me. You'd be screaming the house down if you feared me. There are any number of people you could've called, but you called me. You may loathe me right now, but you trust me. You need to let me protect you. If I tell you not to do something, it's for your safety. I don't know who this is or what they're capable of and willing to do. Don't stand in front of the window again. Do you want a soda to go with your food?"

He punctuates his sermon with a kiss on my forehead as he lets go of me. I'm dumbfounded. Everything he said is true. I agreed to all of that because I trust him. I don't understand what's going on. I'm way out of my depth with this. I may have been unprepared for his punishment, but I deserved it. I think my mini freak out was justified, but I didn't need to endanger myself while having it.

My ass hurts like a motherfucker, and my pussy's less than

thrilled with me too. It wanted things my head's forbidding. I want to cling to him and beg him for relief. I wouldn't say no if he rubbed lotion on my ass right now. But I wanted him to kiss me earlier. I wanted him to do it again a moment ago. I want some part of him to ease the need that pulses between my thighs. I'm a fucking horrible girlfriend—to another man.

I watch as he walks to the hotel phone and presses a button.

"Ich hätte gerne einen Cheeseburger mit Pommes, bitte." I'd like a cheeseburger with fries, please.

His German is perfect. Despite his Spanish accent that flavors his English, he sounds like a near native German speaker. I figured he knew some, but I didn't expect him to be fluent. Yet another surprise I'm not sure how to handle.

He turns to me and raises his eyebrows.

"Eine Cola light, bitte." A Diet Coke, please.

I wait for him to order something for himself, but he doesn't. Instead, he hangs up.

"I need to make some calls. Get comfortable. One of my guards will let the waitstaff in."

Chapter Eight

Jorge

I rub my palm after I shut the bedroom door. I made my hand hurt from spanking Liesel. Or maybe it's touching her that burned. But once I started, I couldn't stop.

Not true.

I absolutely could've stopped if she insisted, but her objections were half-hearted at best. It wasn't like I spanked her indiscriminately, just spanking her as many times as I could before my hand hurt. She got twenty-five, which I know is a lot. I didn't do it out of anger. I did it as a punishment and to prove a point. I don't think she noticed the last fifteen were far lighter than the first ten. Her ass already hurt by then.

She needs to understand I take her safety seriously. I'm unwavering in my promise to protect her, even if it's from her foolish or mistaken choices. She needs to understand my will is unbendable. I'll consider what she has to say, but when I decide something is for the best, she won't beg or argue her way out of it.

I noticed how she rubbed her cunt against me for the last few spankings. I bet she was wet by the end. I kept her as close to my knees as I could without her falling off my lap, so she wouldn't feel how hard I was. Her ass is perfection. Perfectly round, soft to the touch but firm when she clenches. My dick wants me to bend her over the sofa and fuck her from behind.

She may be attracted to me, but she has a boyfriend. One she lives with. It was a moment of weakness for her during an already stressful time. I only added to it by spinning her world around with a spanking. But I'm certain she wanted me to kiss her the first time I drew her against me in the suite's living room. I think she would have accepted it the second time too.

"*Tío, nosotros tenemos una situacion.*" Uncle, we have a situation.

I'm certain my *tío* Enrique doesn't want to hear that after he greets me.

"*¿Qué pasó?*" What happened?

We continue in Spanish. As far as I know, Liesel doesn't speak the language. Maybe she picked up some while studying in the U.S., but she's not fluent. I don't want her to understand anything she overhears. I ordered the food as much to comfort her as I did to occupy her.

"Gunter's hand showed up in a box on Anneliese's desk. She recognized his wedding ring."

"Were you there when it arrived?"

"No. I was in the area when she called."

"Convenient."

He knows I didn't just happen to be there. The drawback to my generation being carbon copies of his generation is that they know what we're thinking before we even formulate the idea.

"I brought her to my suite. I don't know what's going on,

but if a courier can deliver a package like that, then she's not safe there."

"Do you believe whoever's the leak is responsible? Do you think they killed Gunter?"

"Either is possible, but I'm not convinced. You know what Gunter's brother is like."

"True. Gunter may be pompous, but he always came across as harmless compared to Clyde Schlossberg. Joaquin, check if Clyde is at home in Munich right now."

I knew I was on speakerphone from the sound quality. I guess at least one of my brothers is there. I figured my *tío* just wanted to be hands-free. It's Alejandro who speaks next, so my cousin is with them.

"We've never worked with Clyde before, but Sean has. It was back when he was dating Nicolina. Remember? Her brother—shitbag that Ewan is—was trying to do a deal with them up in Boston. Sean fucked him over with that to get back at Ewan for being a douche to Nicolina."

"Yeah, and the O'Rourkes made a killing off the goods they stole from Ewan. They invested half through Clyde, so he still made a profit. It wasn't what it was supposed to be, but Clyde knew not to bite the hand that feeds him."

The gang's all here. That was Pablo. I'm sure Javier will have something to say soon.

"Gunter doesn't seem that smart."

Javier's an introvert just like Joaquin and me, but he generally just doesn't like other people. At least not ones outside our family. He's an old soul—by sixteen, he was a jaded misanthrope.

"It wouldn't surprise me if he pissed someone else off enough for them to do this. Joaquin, I still need your help. Did you make any progress?"

"Not yet."

I swallow my aggrieved sigh. "I'm not prepared to reveal to Anneliese that I tapped her office phone. If I ask her about anything I've heard, she'll know."

"And when it comes out, she'll be pissed."

"Yes, Javier. I know." *Fucking Captain Obvious.*

"Snippy."

Fuck being the baby of the family. Javier's barely a year older than me. Hell, Joaquin's barely a year older than Javier. At twenty-one months apart between Joaquin and me, we probably could've all been in the same grade.

"Until I have some certainty about what's going on, I'd rather she fears the unknown than panic over inconclusive speculation. I don't want to leave her alone here to search for her father. I need help tracking his last known whereabouts. If we can narrow down where he might be, I'll send men to check it out. I need to get her mother and sister here too."

"And her boyfriend?" I hear the humor in Javier's voice.

"I don't know if he's on shift at the hospital or not. I won't call him away from that unless I confirm he's in danger or poses a danger to those around him."

I sure as fuck don't want to watch him holding and consoling her. I'll rip his fucking lips off if I see him kiss her.

"I'll call as soon as I have something. I'll start digging online. I'll also call *Tío* Matáis to see if he knows anything about Clyde or has heard anything about Gunter."

"Thank you, Joaquin."

Tío Matáis—Alejandro's dad—is on his way to Hong Kong today. I'm glad I came here in his place, but that's because I'm a glutton for punishment. I want a woman who's already taken, and now I have to help her discover who chopped off her father's hand.

Fuck if this isn't some eighties mystery TV show shit.

Murder, She Wrote meets *Friday the 13th.*

Fucking *Kojak,* but I'm not bald. Though Telly Savalas looked like he could've been in a syndicate.

If anyone knows shit no one in the international finance world wants made public, it's my *tío.* He knows shit about *everyone,* but not everyone gets to know him. Anyone who's unaware he represents Diaz Holdings wouldn't guess he's linked to narco-traffickers. Hell, they wouldn't know he is—was —I guess still is—one. He maintains a clean image to make people feel safe investing. Those investments often go through shell companies we control without them knowing until a merger or acquisition. His last name is Dos Santos—All Saints —so he must be harmless.

I practically snort at my thought.

No one would believe that.

"Do you need one of us to meet you?" *Tío* Enrique's voice pulls me back to the conversation.

"No thanks. For now, I can handle this. If it looks like I can't, I'll ask for help immediately."

I won't endanger Liesel if I can avoid it. I don't think my dick's so big that I'm less of a man if I ask for help. I even ask for directions—sometimes.

"All right. Keep me posted, Jorge."

"I will, *Tío.*"

"*Te quiero.*"

There's a round of "I love you" before we say goodbye, and I end the call. I look at the bedroom door. I heard the food arrive, then it went quiet for a moment before Liesel turned on the TV. I brace myself to go back out there since I have no news. With a deep inhale, I rise from the bed where I perched. I hang up my suit coat and fold my tie, placing it on top of the dresser before I head back to the living room. I unbutton my cuffs and roll up my sleeves.

I fucking hate suits. I truly do.

Liesel watches me as I approach. Her gaze follows my movements, and I see curiosity as parts of my tattoos peek beneath my sleeves. I'm not covered in them, but I have several.

I have what looks like a sundial over my heart. Where there should be numbers, there are initials. Twelve o'clock has an E for Esteban. My father—when he was alive and now his spirit—has always been my north star, my guide.

One and eleven o'clock have Js for Joaquin and Javier. They stand beside *Papá*. There's M for *Tía* Margherita at two o'clock, and P for Pablo at three o'clock. Four o'clock has J for Juan—I have mixed feelings about covering that with the initial of any wife I might have. Five o'clock is L for *Tío* Luis.

Six o'clock—directly across from *Papá's* E is *Mamá's* L. When I'm lost and get turned around, *Mamá's* always the one who puts me back on the right path.

Seven o'clock is M for *Tío* Matáis, and eight o'clock is A for Alejandro. Nine o'clock is C for *Tía* Catalina. Ten o'clock—directly over my heart—is E for *Tío* Enrique. He's the head of our family, and mine beats for them.

Mamá didn't let go of me for a solid five minutes the first time she saw it. I feared I pissed her off since it's a sizable tattoo, and it was my first. Instead, she cried happy tears when I explained its meaning. My *tías* were misty-eyed, and the men were silent—the macho way to handle being choked up.

"Did you learn anything?" Liesel's slow to stand from the sofa after she puts her tray on the table.

"Not yet. I asked my family to help."

"I called my mom."

She looks hesitant to tell me. She's worried about how I'll react.

"What did you tell her?"

"Nothing about this. I asked for a recipe. She sounded completely normal, so I don't think anyone's holding a gun to her head. I called my sister too. She was walking into a meeting and said she'd call me back."

"And Bastian?"

I struggle not to grimace at the thought of him. His name is an unpleasant taste in my mouth.

"It's his day off. I tracked his phone. He's at the apartment."

"Did you speak to him?"

Nervousness flashes across her face as she shakes her head. She talked to her mom and sister but not her boyfriend.

"Why not?"

"Because he can tell when something's wrong, even when I try to hide it."

I fight the urge to clench my fists.

What do you expect from a boyfriend she's serious enough about to live with? That's the way it should be.

These emotions spinning around in me are becoming a nuisance.

"What time do you usually get home? When will he be expecting you?"

I know the answer to that, and I know she knows I've been following her. But I don't want to unnerve her even more by giving that away. She glances at her watch. It's nearing four o'clock. Juan o'clock according to my chest.

"Around six."

"I doubt I'll have this solved and handled in two hours."

Her gaze sweeps the living room and toward the second bedroom before she looks at me again. Her eyes narrow.

"Will you follow me home and drive past my apartment building just to be sure you know where I am?"

I cock an eyebrow to appear mystified by what she's accusing me of.

Why would I follow her anywhere or drive past anywhere

since she's not leaving this fucking suite until whoever did this is dead?

"You terrified me that night, Jorge."

"If I were such a threat, such an ogre, why'd you call me?"

"I didn't say you were either of those. You still scared me. How fucked-up am I to turn to my stalker for help?"

She wraps her arms around her waist, and she appears to shrink into herself. The enormity of this situation just hit her again. I shove my hands in my pockets to keep from reaching for her like I did earlier. But her lip trembles at my rejection. I approach her slowly.

"It was dark, and you couldn't be sure who it was. That kind of situation should scare you. It should keep you aware of your surroundings and not take your safety for granted. I think the idea of me following you makes you feel safe. You don't like it, but it's sprouted roots in your mind. You know I wouldn't be there as a threat. You know I'd protect you."

"Just admit what you did, Jorge. Stop speaking in hypotheticals when we both know it's real."

I don't admit to crimes.

"You're certain it's the truth, so you don't need me to confirm what you're sure you know."

"Being evasive doesn't endear you to me."

"Should I be dear to you, *chiquita?*"

My gaze sweeps over her, lingering on her mouth. I'm not trying to seduce her. I'm trying to distract her.

"Don't do that."

"Do what?"

"Try to distract me. Skirt the truth by putting this all on me."

"Am I distracting?"

"Stop flirting with me. I'm not a toy."

"I'm not playing with you."

Her cheeks flush with the innuendo. She turns away from me and sits on the sofa again. She ate half the cheeseburger and most of the fries. She picks at the ones that are left, but they look soggy.

"Liesel, you need to have your mom and sister come here. We need to explain what happened."

"I know we have to tell them, and being here with your security detail is best. I just don't want to be the one who has to."

I sit beside her and cover her hands on her lap with mine. She doesn't object, so I don't pull away.

"I'm here to do this with you. Tell them a client offered you a night in a suite as a gift of gratitude. Does your boyfriend work tomorrow?"

"Yes."

"Say he can't make it because of work. Make it a girls' night. Tell Bastian the same thing. We explain once they're here. We do *not* want them to involve the police or tell anyone else. That's what'll happen if you give even a hint that something's wrong."

"All right."

She retrieves her phone from her purse which is on the dining room table behind us. She unlocks it as she returns to the sofa. She looks at me before pulling up her contacts as she sits. She calls her mother first. I follow along with their German since Liesel has it on speakerphone.

"*Mutti, ein Kunde hat mir ein Dankeschön-Geschenk gemacht. Es ist eine Suite in einem Fünf-Sterne-Hotel.*" Mom, a client gave me a thank you gift. It's a suite at a five-star hotel.

"*Das wird ein schönes Vergnügen für dich und Bastian.*" That'll be a nice treat for you and Bastian.

"*Er kann nicht kommen, weil er morgen eine Superfrüh-*

schicht hat." He can't make it because he has a super early shift tomorrow.

They continue in German as they go back and forth. I sense Liesel's getting frustrated. I rest my hand on her thigh, and she relaxes beneath my palm.

"Save it for another night."

"I could, but I really hoped you'd come with me today. We can order room service and just be together. I'm going to invite Heidi too. Work's been extra complicated recently. You know that. It would be nice to have you around right now."

Her mother hesitates, and I grit my teeth.

"All right. I'll let Papa know."

Liesel flinches before tears fill her eyes. I watch her take a breath before she responds.

"You'll need to leave him a message."

"Okay. When should I head over?"

"Can you pick Heidi up on the way? She should be done with her meeting by now. I think she can slip out early. I'll call her when we hang up. If you don't hear from me, it means she's ready."

"Okay. Love you."

"Love you too, *Mutti.*"

I like the informal diminutive for *Mutter*—Mother. It'd be sweet if things weren't so fucked-up.

She hangs up and presses another contact. She keeps this call on speakerphone too as she speaks to her sister in German.

"Hey."

"Hey. Guess what I got."

"What?"

"You sound rushed. Can you talk right now?"

"Yeah. I just went to the restroom, so I'm walking back to my desk."

"Okay. A client gave me a night at a suite."

"In exchange for?"

Liesel glances at me before looking straight ahead at the TV which I muted as she called her mother.

"Nothing. It was a thank you gift. Bastian has to work early tomorrow, so I decided to invite you and *Mutti* to join me. It has two bedrooms. If you snore, I'm kicking you out to the sofa."

"Such a welcoming invitation. You're the one who kicks in her sleep."

I swallow my laugh. She scowls at me before she leans to whisper in my ear.

"Not since I was like ten."

She sits up, surprised how close she got to me. It's like she didn't expect to confide a secret. Her warm breath against my ear was faint which made it erotic as hell. She turns her attention back to her sister.

"*Mutti's* on her way to pick you up unless you can't leave yet."

"Um—that gives me about half an hour. Yeah, I can come. I won't have an overnight bag though."

Liesel turns to me in a panic. Neither of us thought about that. We'll sort out what they need for the next few days once we get past sharing the news.

"Don't worry about that. Just be ready for *Mutti*."

"Okay."

"I'm going to send *Mutti* the hotel name and address right now."

"Thanks for the invite. I'm picking out the unhealthiest thing they have on the menu."

Liesel's face flashes a pained smile before she plays it off. "We can order two. It'll be good to have you here. See you in a bit."

"See you. Bye."

"Bye."

She hangs up and puts the phone on the armrest to her right. She wraps her arms around herself, and she appears so lost. I slide my hand across her back until it cups her shoulder. I nudge her, and she leans against me. She rests her head on my shoulder.

"Jorge, what are we going to tell them?"

"Do you want me to do it?"

"Yeah. But it should be me. They'll already be upset you're here once they find out you're—"

"A man in your suite who isn't your boyfriend."

"That too. Once they know who you are."

"A potential investor."

"That won't convince them to have faith in you. We have to tell them who you are."

"No, they'll automatically assume this had to do with my family doing business with yours. It might, but it might not. They'll fear I lured you all here. They'll insist upon leaving, and they'll insist upon calling the police. One of them might slip away to do it even if we convince them to stay. Right now, I'm an obscenely rich businessman who has unlimited resources at my fingertips because of that wealth."

"That'd be true even if you weren't in a cartel, wouldn't it?"

"Yes."

She leans away to look at me more easily. She studies me before she nods.

"What if they've killed Papa and are going to send him to me in boxes? I'm not at my office to receive them. Did they follow us and know to send anything here?"

"Whoever this is, is watching you. They knew to deliver the package while you were at lunch that way you couldn't ask questions."

"My assistant was away from his desk too."

"They know the significance of your father's ring and that you'd recognize it immediately."

"Will they send more of him here?"

"I don't know who this is yet. I can't give you an honest answer—not even speculation—about what will happen next."

"A ransom?"

"I doubt it. This isn't about money. At least, that's not all of it. What can you tell me about the note dropped in your lap at the park?"

Chapter Nine

Liesel

That wasn't the question I expected next.

I narrow my eyes at him but squinting shoots a burst of pain between my eyes and up through my forehead to my scalp. I'm too exhausted to deal with that on top of everything. I'm completely drained suddenly, and I still have to brace myself for my mother and sister's arrival.

I exhale before looking at Jorge. "There's not much for me to tell you. It just said 'we're watching you.'"

"What does that mean?"

Anger flashes in Jorge's eyes despite how the rest of his demeanor remains the same as it was. Reassuringly calm. I think he wants me to know he's not okay with any of this, but he won't lose his shit to keep from scaring me. He softens his tone before he speaks again.

"Liesel, I don't like any of this, but I don't blame you, and I still respect you."

I can't help the shudder that escapes. I didn't expect that

reassurance, and I didn't expect how much it would mean to me.

"Thank you. I've been trying to make the best of a bad situation, but everything has just gone from horrible to catastrophic."

"Do you believe whoever was responsible for the note is behind this?"

I'm not prepared to tell what's been happening, but I may not have a choice if the people who've been watching me are behind my father's disappearance. I do my best to skirt explaining its meaning.

"I believe it's entirely possible, but I truly don't know."

I watch Jorge to see if I can get any hint about whether he thinks I'm right, but his expression now is entirely inscrutable. I don't know what he's thinking. The glimpse into his thoughts a moment ago evaporated. I suddenly feel cold and alone despite how he still has his arm around my shoulders. I feel goosebumps form on my arms from his remoteness.

"Is there anything else you can tell me to give me any hints where to look?"

I twist to look at Jorge better before I continue. He pulls his arm back, and I regret shifting. Now I really feel untethered. All I can do is shake my head. If I knew who was behind everything that's gone wrong in the last couple years, I would tell him.

"*Chiquita*, what's going through your mind right now?"

"It's just that I never imagined I'd wake up one morning to find my father's hand on smy desk after lunch. Or that I'd be dealing with some secretive phantom who seems to know far more about me than I know about him. It's all terrifying, and I don't know what to make of any of it."

As I watch Jorge, I consider my other clients and business contacts. I'm not withholding anything about the mystery messenger or who could have my father, but there's so much more that I'm not prepared to share yet. I nearly jump out of my skin when my phone rings. I show Jorge the screen before I swipe to answer in German.

"Hi, *Mutti*. Are you almost here?"

"Yes, we just parked. Can we come straight up to the room?"

I glance over at Jorge, and he nods.

"Yeah, it's actually the penthouse suite."

"That's exciting." I hear my sister chime in with her voice slightly muffled.

"We'll be up in a few minutes."

I end the call and drop my phone in my lap. "My mom and sister will freak out when they see your guards at the door, or they'll believe they wound up in the wrong place."

"*Chiquita,* my men will let me know when your family steps off the elevator. We can wait for them."

"Should I answer the door, or will they let my mom and Heidi in?"

"You can answer the door."

"Where will you be?"

"I can stand over by the table, or I can stand behind you."

"Um—"

I sweep my gaze around the living room, trying to decide what's best. I feel like the moment I stand, my knees will knock together, so I want Jorge close. But that won't set the right tone for their arrival. I look at the box on the entryway table. I've studiously ignored it ever since we arrived, but its presence has lurked in the back of my mind throughout my conversations.

"We can't leave the box by the door when they arrive because eventually we'll have to show them. I don't want them to think I just put it there as a convenience when I came into the suite of a man who isn't my boyfriend."

"We'll move it over here to the desk, and we'll see how things go before we decide whether to show them."

"I can't keep this from them."

"*Chiquita*, I'm not saying keep what happened from them, but do you really want your mother and sister to see what you did?"

I shake my head, but my shoulders sink.

"Jorge, my mom will demand to see it. And my father's wedding ring is still on his finger. She deserves to have that back. And what do we do with it? I mean, it's flesh and everything."

My stomach cramps.

"We have a little while longer before we have to do anything with it to avoid it being even more unpleasant."

I cock an eyebrow. Unpleasant? That's how he would describe what's going on? He certainly has a stronger stomach than I do.

"What will we do?"

"Not 'we,' *chiquita*. My men will make sure what needs doing gets done to keep it safe."

"You won't just throw it out, will you?"

I think I might vomit.

"No, Liesel, that isn't what we'll do."

My brow furrows. "Do you need it for something? Is that why you'd preserve it?"

"For starters, that's your father. I would never just throw him away. And I'm not sure what we may need going forward. I certainly won't do away with anything."

It's only a few minutes before Jorge's phone pings, and he looks toward the hotel room's door. I shove my phone in my pocket, and Jorge takes long strides to the entryway table. He picks up the box and hurries to take it over to the suite's workspace. I watch him take a place standing beside the dining room table.

I run my hands up and down my thighs, fearing they must be sweaty. I open the door just as my mom raises her fist to knock. Heidi is just behind her left shoulder, peering at me before shifting her gaze to the bodyguards. But mom's focus is unwavering on me.

"Anneliese, who are these men?"

I step aside, opening the door wider. "Come in, *Mutti*. I will explain everything."

We may speak German, but her tone doesn't need interpreting. I inhale as my mother and sister walk past me, and I close the door behind them. Jorge steps around the table but doesn't approach. Instead, he greets them in German.

"Hello, Mrs. Schlossberg, Ms. Schlossberg. I'm Jorge Diaz."

I watch my mother's face to see whether Jorge's name means anything to her. I see no hint of recognition, but the confusion remains. Heidi stands beside me, shifting slightly to bump our arms together. It's subtle, so our mom doesn't notice. But Jorge's gaze meets mine for a flash before he smiles at my sister, then looks back at my mother.

Heidi and I have been nudging each other like that since we were young children and wanted to communicate without our parents noticing. I glance over at her, and I know she wants to blurt out, "what the fuck is going on?" I don't need her lips to move to hear her voice screaming in my head.

"*Mutti*, Heidi, Jorge is a potential client of mine. *Mutti*, you may recall Papa and I disagreed about their deal. Jorge is part of an influential international family. Something happened today, and I asked Jorge to help because I'm confident he has resources available to do that."

I shift my gaze to Jorge, hoping he'll pick up where I left off. I can feel a lump rising in my throat, and I'm not sure I can continue speaking without bursting into tears. He offers me a reassuring hint of a smile before he continues in German just like I did.

"When Anneliese returned from lunch today, there was an alarming package on her desk. She called me because she didn't know what to do. I believe being here together is the safest place for all three of you. The package Anneliese received made us aware someone assaulted your husband, Mrs. Schlossberg. I don't know the extent of it, and I don't know where he is right now. That means we know he's been gravely injured, but nothing beyond that. I am using all my available resources to answer those questions."

Jorge tries his best to be gentle as he explains what happened earlier. I can tell he's struggling not to make light of the situation while not causing my mom and Heidi to panic.

My mother turns toward me. "What does he mean by assaulted?"

I open my mouth, but I can't form any sounds. I shake my head and look back at Jorge. He steps closer and is within arm's reach. I want nothing more than to burrow against his chest, but there's positively no way I can do that with my family around.

Heidi leans forward. In a man, it would be an aggressive posture, but she's shorter than I am, so it certainly doesn't appear threatening when it's directed toward Jorge.

"What the hell does that mean?"

Each word is clipped. I practically feel the fear and anger vibrating off of her. I know I can't be a coward right now. I have to speak up.

"Heidi, *Mutti*, like Jorge said, when I came back from lunch today, there was a box on my desk. I don't know who delivered it or where it came from, but..."

I take a deep inhale and gather whatever resolve I can muster.

"It was Papa's hand. I know it was his because of his wedding ring."

A heartbeat of silence greets my announcement. Then all hell breaks loose. I can barely distinguish my mom's voice from my sister's. They're demanding answers to questions neither Jorge nor I have. I know we told them we didn't know more than once, but it's understandable that they want them now. I want them too.

"Anneliese, where is Papa's hand? I want to see. I want his ring."

I look at Jorge, and he gives a subtle shake of his head. I'm barely hanging on. I'm breathing so rapidly and deeply that my nostrils hurt.

"*Mutti*, I'll make sure you get his ring, but right now it's best if we leave things alone."

"Is it with the police? Why aren't they here? Why aren't they telling us what we should do? Why is he helping you?"

I expected all these questions, and I tried to come up with answers to them in the moments after I discovered the box and knew I needed to call Jorge. Any wisp of an idea has flown off into outer space. Once again, it's Jorge who comes to my rescue.

"Mrs. Schlossberg, I don't know how much of your brother-in-law's business you know. But he has made friends and enemies with men and women who want nothing to do with the police. Men and women who punish people for involving the police."

"What the hell is he talking about? What does this have to do with *Onkel* Clyde?"

Heidi's more demanding than *Mutti*. I watch our mom, and I know she understands what Jorge means. When I shift my focus to my sister, I know she doesn't.

"What kind of people do you think my father and uncle associate with? What kind of low-life criminals do you think they do business with? You don't even know them."

Jorge is patient and understanding as he keeps his voice soft when he speaks to my sister.

"I know a great deal about your uncle. I haven't done business with him, but I know many who have. He has an unyielding and unforgiving reputation, which has made him incredibly wealthy and successful. However, it's also burned almost every bridge he's walked across. Your father is a tamer version of your uncle, but he has also angered his fair share of people over the years. Several of the clients Schlossberg & Sons have had are ones they certainly never kept official records on. They are ones they certainly don't want anyone to know or ask about. It seems someone your father did business with is angry and wishes to make a point."

My mom's temper is about to explode. "Are you accusing my husband of illegal business practices?"

"Mrs. Schlossberg, I'm not accusing anyone. I've been in investment banking since before I finished high school. I'm a licensed Certified Public Accountant with a Certified in Financial Forensics designation. I became Diaz Holdings' official accountant when I finished grad school. I know what I've seen, and I know what my business rivals engaged in with Clyde. Your husband and brother-in-law have clients with no tolerance."

"No tolerance for what?"

"No tolerance for anything, Mrs. Schlossberg."

It's clear Jorge won't offer more specifics than that. It leaves my mom, sister, and me speechless. As though saved by the bell, we hear his phone vibrate in his pocket. He pulls it out far enough to peek at the screen.

"I need to take this. Excuse me."

He doesn't wait for any of us to respond, instead heading to the bedroom he went into earlier. I'm ready for the onslaught. My mom glowers at me.

"If this happened after lunch—"

She bursts into sobs. Her initial anger and shock give way. Heidi and I both cry along with her. I'd done my best to remain stoic after feeling so numb. Jorge's punishment distracted me, and I know that's part of why he did it. He understood what I needed. Now my mom, sister, and I are adrift and terrified. I need him more than ever as the weight of their fear piles upon my own, crushing me with it.

"Why, Anne? What could Papa have done?"

"I don't know, Heidi. Jorge is right that we have clients with dubious connections. But Papa handles those."

I force myself not to flinch at that lie. It's a half-truth. He oversees most of those. I need to make my own calls that I wasn't clear headed enough to make earlier. But I can't walk away from my family.

Our mom opens her arms to Heidi and me, and we fall into her embrace. Jorge's already consoled me, so I feel like I should be the one doing the consoling. That I should be a shoulder *Mutti* can lean against. She deserves support too rather than having to be the adult in the room while contending with her own fears. But I can't. I simply can't get my shit together enough now that the dam's burst. It was leaking before. Now it's disintegrated.

"*Mutti*, what are we going to do? We don't know that man." Heidi nudges her chin toward the bedroom. "How can we trust him? I don't believe him about the police. Maybe he did this."

I pull away and shake my head. "Jorge is the only person we can trust. If Papa's still alive, and we involve the police, they'll arrest him. He downplayed Papa and *Onkel* Clyde's business arrangements."

"If that were the case—which I don't believe at all—why would a stranger know what's best for us?"

Heidi's livid. The more afraid she is, the more her fear presents as anger. She's been that way since we were kids. She doesn't enjoy feeling emotionally out of control, so anger at herself gets shared with those around her. Fortunately, she's usually fearless. I'd say it's understandable today.

"The Diaz family is among the richest in the world. They have influence in international business across most continents. He and his family have connections all over the place. He can keep this private and can work faster than the police."

"Why is he helping you, Anneliese? Why didn't you call Bastian? You gave us false pretenses to be here." My mom isn't sobbing anymore, but the tears stream down her face.

"Bastian has to work. His patients need him more than what he can do here. I wish I had his shoulder to cry on, but he'd hate Jorge being able to do more than he can. He'll insist we call the police, and I am absolutely certain that is the last thing we should do." I keep swiping at my own tears.

"Why did you lie to get us here?"

"*Mutti*, was this something you wanted to hear over the phone?"

She shakes her head as her face drains of color. I take her hand and guide her toward the sofa. Heidi follows us. I move my tray of half-eaten food out of the way, so I can perch on the edge of the coffee table with my elbows on my knees to look at my mom and sister.

"He's Colombian, isn't he?"

I jerk back at my mother's question. I understand the implications. Heidi's eyes widen, so she gets it too.

"He is."

"This must be his fault. This only happened because he became a client."

"*Mutti*, we don't know that. He's not even a client yet. Even if it were true—and I admit it could be—he's still the only person we have who has the resources and connections to help us."

"What do you mean by resources? Is he going to kill people?"

"Heidi." I hiss her name, fighting the temptation to look over my shoulder in fear that Jorge heard her.

"I told you he comes from an extremely wealthy family that—"

"Sells drugs and murders people."

"*Mutti*, does that matter right this moment if he's willing to pay people to find Papa or pay a ransom for him? We're wealthy, but nothing like he is. We couldn't pay a sizable ransom without liquidating assets. That takes time. We don't keep that much money in bank accounts. If these people demand a ransom, it might be impossible to get that much money in a hurry. Not without setting off alarms. We could wind up with our accounts frozen during fraud investigations. We don't need more attention brought to this."

"No. You don't know what you're talking about. *Mutti*, tell her she's wrong. We should call the police and call the news. Call whoever can help get attention on this. Someone was bound to have seen Papa or might know who took him. They won't know to come forward if they don't see it on the news."

"Heidi—"

"Enough! Stop, Heidi. *Mutti*, she's wrong. Alerting the people who did this that half of Germany's looking for them is a sure way to get Papa killed before they flee."

"Maybe he's already—"

"Heidi, don't say it. Not until we know for sure. We wait for Jorge. If he says call the police or alert the media, then we do. You may not trust him, but I do. Right now, that's all that matters."

Chapter Ten

Jorge

"Hola."

I hope Joaquin has good news because I know things are about to get contentious for Liesel. I hate leaving her alone because all three women will find their shock wearing off soon. Then it'll be fear and anger along with uncertainty and grief. I don't want it to devolve into an argument or any of them acting impulsively.

"Hola, manito." Hello, little brother.

He's been using *hermanito* and its diminutive, *manito*, since Javier and I were old enough to be insulted when he called us babies. *Mamá* scolded him enough that he switched to little brother, and it's stuck for the past thirty years.

"What did you find?"

"Clyde's in Munich. I hacked the airport and the train lines to see if he had any reservations or any last-minute ticket purchases to come to Frankfurt. There are none. He might drive, but it looks like there was no pre-planned trip to Frankfurt, and he hasn't set off on an emergency one either. His car was last picked up on CCTV in Munich."

"Do you think he hasn't heard yet?"

"It looks like it."

"Can you get into his email or his phone records?"

"The email I can hack easily. The phone records would be faster if I called in a couple favors."

"No. Not yet. We keep this among ourselves as long as we can."

"You could call Sean."

"I know. It's not like the idea hasn't crossed my mind a few times, but I don't want to ask that fucker for shit. He'll think I owe him something."

"But if it helps."

"I know."

"This woman—Anneliese, right—must be special. Would you cut off your nose to spite your face?"

Fucking hell that no one can have a private thought in the family. We know each other too well. The occupational hazards of mixing family with business and pleasure. Normally, I appreciate being nearly inseparable from my family—especially my brothers—but right now, I'd like to keep some things to myself.

"I won't. But I'm nervous to let anyone else in this in case we underestimate who's involved. It could be the O'Rourkes getting back at us for potentially hiring Gunter. Maybe they warned him away from us since they've done business with Clyde. If that's the case, I don't want to give them any information. Period."

"Just keep it in the back of your mind. The Schlossbergs have some other interesting clients."

"Such as?"

"A couple Eastern European oligarchs."

"With ties to any particular governments?"

"No. Mostly private industries and corporate monopolies. But it wouldn't surprise me if I found some dubious connections as I dig deeper."

"Are these current or past clients?"

"Both."

I consider what else to ask. "Does any CCTV show Gunter's activities today?"

"Yes. His car appears on the highway near his home. I watched it arrive in the city center, where he parked in the office building's underground lot. I got into the building's security system, and I can see where it logged his keycard swipes. Their internal cameras showed him arriving at his office suite a little after nine. It's the floor above Anneliese's. He went to the restroom at eleven-o-seven. He left the building on foot ten minutes later after briefly returning to his office. The street CCTV showed him turning right and going three blocks down. There's a gap in the coverage. He never passed the next camera. He disappeared somewhere in that dead zone."

"Do you think his abductors knew that would be the spot to grab him?"

"Grab him if he doesn't know them. He might have gone willingly if he knew them."

"True. Any bank or credit card transactions?"

"No. Once I get the phone records, I'll know if there were any inbound or outbound calls or texts. Are you sure you want me to hold off on those?"

I scrub my hand over my face as I stare at the door. I can hear the women. Their voices are raised, but they aren't yelling. They're definitely not chatting. I need to get back out there.

"Get them. What did the office cameras show when the delivery person dropped off the box?"

"Anneliese left for lunch before Gunter. She went to—"

"Skip that part. I already know."

"Because you've been parked outside her office building every day since you returned to Frankfurt."

"How about you pass judgement on me after I find who dropped off a hand?"

"They were in a hooded sweatshirt. They had it up, covering their hair. It looked like a woman, but I can't be sure. Whoever they are, they knew where the cameras are in that building. I saw them arrive on the footage. They stood out because of their casual clothes along with the box. Anneliese's assistant came back after the delivery but before Anneliese."

"Is there anything else?"

I don't like it when anyone in my family pauses before answering a question. It's not that they're thinking of an answer. They're deciding how best to present it.

"I haven't found specifics yet, but you need to speak to Anneliese. She's got questionable connections too."

"You can't drop that bomb without more specifics. What does that mean?"

"I told you I have none. Not yet, at least. I just hack the accounts. I don't interpret the data. I'm going to send you several financial statements. After you review them, if you need me to get you into anything, let me know."

"Fucking hell."

"Pretty much."

"When can you get them to me?"

"I'll send them now."

"Fuck." I release an aggrieved huff. I close my eyes before exhaling deeply.

"What now?"

"My laptop is not only out there with the women, it's also next to the box that has Gunter's hand in it. I can't walk over to get the computer without drawing attention to the package. I haven't heard any screaming, so I don't think Anneliese's mother or sister have seen it yet. Once I'm out there, it'll only lead to a ton of questions about why I only came out to get the computer before heading back into the bedroom."

"Do either of the women know about our family?"

"I didn't get the impression they do. The mother is aware that at least some of Gunter's business wasn't entirely aboveboard. But I doubt she knows details."

"For what it's worth, I don't think Anneliese knows what her father's been up to. But that may be because she has her own secrets to keep."

"Can't you give me a hint?"

I'm fighting my impatience. I'm certain my brother's doing the best he can, but it doesn't quell my growing irritability.

"She has a separate encrypted email account that isn't for work, but it's about work. I haven't backtracked far enough to see who's sending her emails, but there are plenty. They use no names, and there's nothing definitive enough to raise legal red flags. But you and I know what language we're looking for."

"Is it someone intimidating her?"

I'll kill a motherfucker.

"Not now. Maybe it started that way."

"She's a willing participant?"

Was I wrong to trust her after all? I'll still help her, but I won't forgive her.

"I wouldn't say that either. They're too vague to tell. I checked her digital calendar for some dates and times mentioned, but there's nothing showing meetings or travel that match. You and I know we're both far less suspicious than

Javier is about everything, but we also know when to listen to our intuition. Something is off, Jorge."

"All right. Thank you. I'll figure this out. Once I've had a chance to review the documents and speak to Anneliese, I'll get back to you."

"Morning, noon, or night, *manito. Te quiero.*" We've pledged that since our dad died.

"Te quiero también."

I hang up and lock my phone before shoving it back into my pocket. When I return to the suite's living room, I find Liesel sitting on the edge of the coffee table as she tries to reason with her mother and sister. All three are crying, not that I can blame them.

I've been calling her Anneliese instead of Liesel, and it feels odd. I'm worried Liesel will slip out one of these times. My family might understand, but hers definitely wouldn't. I don't need an irate boyfriend to deal with right now.

I focus on the box and my computer. They're on the desk behind where the women sit on the sofa. It appears untouched from when I put it there. There's no way I can get the laptop without them guessing what's in the box. Liesel rises when her mother and sister's attention shifts to me. She hurries to me as I approach the three women.

"Anything?"

"My brother's going to send me some documents to review."

I keep my voice low, but I dart my gaze to the desk then back to Liesel. Her eyes widen, band thankfully, only I see her reaction. She understands what I meant.

"I don't know what to do."

She mouths the words, and she looks more fearful than she has since I arrived in her office. I offer her a half smile before looking at the other two Schlossbergs.

"It's approaching dinnertime. If you get hungry, you can order whatever you'd like. I know you didn't plan to be here overnight, so if there is anything you need, we can order those too."

"Overnight?! We aren't staying here. We only waited because Anne said you might have information." Mrs. Schlossberg stands and reaches for her purse.

"*Mutti*, you need to stay here. We don't know if any of us are targets too. We don't know what else they might do. None of us are going back to unguarded homes. Jorge doesn't have that many men to spare."

I do, but I'm not confessing that. I'll have to fly them in from Brussels or Amsterdam. I may need those men to retrieve Gunter or whoever did this. I might need them here to protect the women if someone decides they're the next targets.

"Mrs. Schlossberg, I understand how you—"

"No, you don't. You could never understand."

Her anger is reasonable, but it won't get us anywhere.

"I was eight years old and leaving the movies with my father and brothers when I watched a man murder my father. I understand all too well."

That lands like a ton of bricks. I didn't expect it to go over well. My father's execution-style murder is no secret since it happened in broad daylight on a street in Bogotá. My brothers and I begged our dad to take us to a movie. We really wanted to see it, and we knew he'd let us have all the snacks *Mamá* wouldn't. We had stomachaches by the time we left, but it was —at that point—one of the best days ever.

Papá and our guards sensed something was wrong when my brothers and I couldn't. I was only eight. Javier was nine, and Joaquin was ten. What did we know back then? *Papá* herded us into an alley so we could have our backs to a wall, and no one could sneak up on us. There were two snipers and a guy on the ground. The snipers picked off our men, but one of our guards shot the man on the street and a sniper on a rooftop.

When our armored SUV pulled up, *Papá* shielded us as we ran to the vehicle. I was the closest to him and the lightest. He practically threw me inside. I scrambled across the seat as Joaquin crawled in behind me. *Papá* had just slammed the door shut behind Javier when blood splattered the window.

Neither my brothers nor I remember much of what happened after that. We remember *Mamá* somehow managed to have all three of us on her lap when we got home. She couldn't speak. She just rocked us and kept kissing our heads. I remember we all cried a lot. The next thing I remember clearly was the funeral. The next day my brothers and I went to New Jersey to stay with *Tía* Margherita, Pablo, and Juan. *Tío* Luis stayed in Bogotá.

It wasn't until years later that Joaquin, Javier, and I learned what *Mamá* did to avenge *Papá*. Heads for soccer balls. After all I've seen and done as a Cartel member, in a fucked-up kind of way, I couldn't be prouder of *Mamá*.

"I—I never imagined. I'm sorry." Mrs. Schlossberg can't meet my gaze.

"I didn't tell you that to make you feel worse. I want you to know I understand what it's like to wake up to a normal day only to have it turn into the worst one of your life. My family is exceptionally wealthy, so we've faced many threats over the years. We have safety protocols in place. We did the day my dad died, and it still happened. It wouldn't have if we hadn't been out in the open. The men who killed my father knew the only way to succeed was to attack when he was with my brothers and me. That he would protect us before himself. I don't want anyone to use you to inflict more suffering. I need you to stay here for now. It's a place my men and I can protect. No one can get up to this floor without us knowing about it first. We can control what comes in and out of this suite. I can't promise the same if you leave."

"Why did that happen?" I can barely hear Heidi's question, but I expected it.

"My family is just as ruthless as your uncle. We've burned as many bridges as we've built. Not everyone has the patience to wait for a rival to retire. Not everyone works harder to make up for money lost during a bad deal. Some people want retribution and have the means to get it."

By some people, I mean us. My family. We've made careers out of retribution.

"Does that mean you do illegal things too? That's what you said about *Onkel* Clyde."

If you only knew a sliver of it, Heidi.

"I've done things others don't approve of." *Like law enforcement and most countries' judicial systems.*

"Can you do things to get my husband back?"

I look Mrs. Schlossberg in the eye when I answer. "I will do everything possible to get him back."

I can't promise I will. He could be dead. I don't want to promise to get his body back dead or alive. That wouldn't inspire confidence. I give them the best I can offer.

"*Mutti*, Heidi, do you want any dinner? I already ate."

"That was your food? You ate?" Heidi's nothing short of accusatory.

"You know how I handle stress and fear." Liesel's defensive, but when she looks at me, I see her embarrassment.

"Not right now, *mein Püppchen*." Little doll.

Her mother offers her a weak smile, turning the attention away from the argument that's about to erupt between Liesel and Heidi. I can imagine what Liesel probably looked like as a young child. It's a common enough endearment, but I bet it fit.

I watch Liesel's body relax when her mother calls her that.

She steps forward, and her mother hugs her. Silent tears trail down Liesel's cheeks, and her mother's eyes water. I wish I were the one holding Liesel. I glance at Heidi who looks left out. Their mother must sense it because she opens her arms to her other daughter. The three of them cry, leaving me feeling useless but determined.

Chapter Eleven

Liesel

My mom, sister, and I stand huddled together as we cry again. For the first time in years, it's not Bastian I want to turn to. It's not even my mother. It's a man I barely know. The man who stalked me, for lack of a better term. But he was nearby when I needed him. It tempts me to wonder if this is some fucked-up situation he concocted to force me to rely on him. It's a twisted thought that leaves my mind as quickly as it came.

While the three of us hug, Jorge slips around us and grabs his computer. I'm silently grateful he could without drawing any attention to himself or the box. He's discreet when he places it on the dining room table and sits. He flips it open and clicks on several things. While he does that, I burrow against *Mutti*. I wrap my arms around her and my sister. I don't know if I'd cry like this if it was just Jorge with me. I wonder if being around them amplifies my emotions. I was calm with Jorge. He kept me distracted.

Now my mind jumps from one horrific scenario to another.

I can't make it stop. I envision my father chained to a chair, bloody and beaten. I imagine his mutilated body coming back to us piece by piece in the gift boxes for months. I picture him returning to us as if nothing happened except for his lack of a hand. I even try to convince myself that they stole his ring and stuck it on someone else's hand. That he's really fine, and this is all a diabolical hoax. That certainly seems the least plausible.

"You should call Bastian and have him come here." My mom's words intrude on my wayward thoughts.

"No. There's nothing he can do. His patients need him more than I do."

I try not to flinch as that sounds horrible, especially since we're in this suite because I insisted upon relying on someone else—some other man. It sounds like I don't care about my partner—the man I planned—plan—planned to marry. There's something inherently wrong with me because my boyfriend isn't who I'm turning to.

Was there already a crack in our relationship that was previously invisible? Or did meeting Jorge do that?

I've reacted to his physical presence in a way I haven't since meeting Bastian. I didn't even react to Bastian as strongly as I did Jorge. Now I'm leaning on Jorge and have confidence he can protect me when I don't believe that about Bastian. I know he'd try, but he doesn't inspire the same confidence.

Maybe he should be here in case my father arrives and needs medical attention. That would be reasonable, but I'm not motivated to call him. Excluding Jorge from my rationale, I don't want to explain why this might be happening. I don't want Bastian to know the things my father got into. What I've gotten into. I'd like to think he'd understand, but I'm not convinced he would.

"Shouldn't you tell him something happened?" Heidi pulls away from us. "I have to tell Friedrich."

"No!" My answer's too emphatic.

"You may not want your boyfriend, but I want mine."

"Heidi, it's not about wanting or not wanting Bastian. The more people involved in this the messier it will get."

"Do you think Friedrich would do something to keep Papa from coming home?"

"No. I think he'd ask the same questions Bastian would, and they're ones we can't answer."

Her gaze darts to Jorge. "Or ones you just don't want to."

"That's right. I don't want to answer why I'm certain a potential client I barely know has a better chance of solving this than anyone else."

My words are harsher than I intend. I don't look at Jorge because I know how unappreciative and manipulative they sound. I don't mean them to be hurtful, but they're true.

"I want my boyfriend here to comfort me. You might be fine being alone, but I'm not, Anne."

Jorge rises from his seat and walks around the table. I finally meet his gaze, and I know he understands what I meant. There's no anger, annoyance, or hurt. He accepts what I said with more grace than I have.

"Ms. Schlossberg, I empathize with your wish to have someone you trust and is familiar to you here. But you're sister's right. Involving more people only endangers more people. Until we know for sure who's involved, it's best not to draw attention to you or your loved ones. The best thing to do is to remain here and out of sight."

"You said overnight earlier, but now you make it sound like it'll be longer than that."

"Mrs. Schlossberg—"

"It's Gretel. Formality seems a bit pointless right now."

"And I'm Heidi."

"Thank you. Unless things resolve by tomorrow, it'll be

indefinitely. You can take the two bedrooms, and I'll sleep on the sofa. My mother has a close friend who lives here. I can ask her to go to your homes to gather what you need."

"How will I explain that to Friedrich?"

"We'll come up with something by then. Telling Friedrich and Bastian may be inevitable. If it comes to it, I will get the suite next door, and they will join us."

This suite alone is nearly two thousand euros a night. He's been here for over a week. Now he's saying it could be days or weeks more. He doesn't even bat an eye at the offer.

"Thank you."

It's the least I can say, especially after I sounded like a bitch a moment ago. I look around. It's too early for bed, so the other thing to do is watch TV. It feels wrong to kick back and relax. But what else are we going to do to fill the time. *Mutti* has her own solution.

"Mr. Diaz—"

"Jorge, please."

"Jorge, I'll take you up on your offer of a room. I'm exhausted."

Heidi and I glance at each other. Our mom has reached her limit for being the stoic parent for us to lean on. She needs time alone.

"My room has the en suite. There's a bathroom down the hall. Let me gather a few things, and I'll be out of your way."

I have the most disturbing longing to sleep in the bed where Jorge did. To perhaps smell his cologne on the pillow or sheets. It would reassure me.

"You girls take that room. I'll take the other." My mother offers the better room, but I know Heidi will agree to give her the en suite.

"Is there anything you need? There are toiletries in both

bathrooms, but if there's anything specific, I can get them. I can have three toothbrushes brought up."

Jorge is trying his best, and I can tell my mom and sister appreciate it. I certainly do. The least I can do is express that.

"We would appreciate that. Heidi, do you need contact saline and a case?"

"Yes, please."

"Anneliese?"

I fucking hate hearing him call me that after how he's insisted upon calling me Liesel. I know he's doing it for my sake, but I don't like it. However, I can't explain that away if I just told my mom and sister I barely know him.

"Just the toothbrush for now."

"I can ask my mother's friend to go to your places for fresh clothes in the morning."

"Wouldn't she need to come by here to get our keys?" I wonder the same thing as Heidi.

"She would. I think you'd all like her."

"I think we're all ready to head to bed."

I can tell Heidi's tired, but she also wants to speak to me in private. This is the perfect opportunity. I'm certain she's about to pepper me with questions. I'm as ready as I can be. I've been considering answers to these questions since I arrived here. I didn't really focus on the TV show I turned on while Jorge was in the bedroom on the phone the first time.

Heidi closes the door behind us, and I turn around as she opens her mouth. I shake my head and wave her over. I don't want anybody to overhear us, so we head to the two armchairs in the room near the window. I remember how upset it made Jorge the last time I got near one. I change course, instead sitting on the bed.

"Let's stay away from the windows."

"Why?" Heidi practically barks the question.

"Just as a precaution, I think it would be wise to stay out of sight. That's the whole reason we're all here."

"Really? Because I thought the reason might be partly that you're into him."

My sister knows me too fucking well. There's a searing pain behind my eye that makes it twitch.

"I'm into staying alive, Heidi, and I'm into finding out what happened to Papa."

"Okay, sure, that might be part of it. But it's more than that. Are you fucking him?"

Maybe I'm not as prepared for these questions as I assumed. I expected her to ask if I liked him and whether I wanted something to happen. I didn't expect her to jump straight to that. I should have.

"No. You know I would never cheat on Bastian."

"So, when are you breaking up with him to be with some stranger?"

"Heidi—"

"Don't tell me it's complicated. It doesn't have to be."

"Of course it does. We're in an extreme situation that's both a complete shitshow and a crisis. I don't know what's going on. I don't know if there'll more surprises showing up at the office. I don't know if you, or Mutti, or I will be the next target. I don't know anything about how to solve this. But the one thing I know is that Jorge has been calm and supportive through this whole thing. I know I can rely on him."

"And why is that? Because he's a Colombian narco-trafficker?"

I can't say I'm shocked she asked since I've suspected all along that he might be. But I don't agree with her accusation aloud.

"Are you just making that assumption because he's rich and Latino?"

"No, I'm not. Bad Bunny is a rich Latino, and I don't think he's a narco-trafficker."

The Puerto Rican rapper hardly compares to Jorge Diaz.

"But you assume Jorge is."

"You keep telling us how wealthy he is and how he has all these resources. Why would he have resources to deal with criminals if he wasn't one too?"

"That's a gigantic leap. He might have friends who can work behind the scenes with Interpol or some other agency. It just wouldn't be smart for us to file an official case. Maybe he knows someone who knows someone. Maybe he's able to examine more financial records and understand ones I don't. I may be an investment banker, but I'm not a forensic accountant like he is. Maybe he can discover who's behind this by looking at more of our company's financial records. There's any number of reasons and things he could do without it being about whether I want to jump his bones."

"That's not a denial."

"It's not an affirmation either."

"I think it's an excuse, and I think you're making a massive mistake."

That's still to be determined. "Right now, I'll risk that mistake if it means we get Papa back."

"Don't make it sound like I'm more interested in giving you shit than I am having Papa come home safely."

"I didn't say that you were."

"But it doesn't change the fact that this is all very questionable."

I'm struggling not to lose my temper. I know it's partly a guilty conscience, and she struck a nerve. I wanted to come to her with what's going on, not face a one-woman inquisition.

"No shit, Heidi. I know that too. But my sex life is the least of anybody's concerns right now."

"Look, I don't mean to make you defensive, and I could've started this off a lot better than asking you whether you're fucking him. But there's definitely something between the two of you, and it doesn't exist with you and Bastian. He's a great guy, and I know you love him, but you've never turned to Bastian for confirmation and affirmation the way you do with Jorge."

"This is just an extreme situation where we're way in over our heads."

"True, but it's more than that, and you know it."

I inhale so deeply that my ribs expand. Then I exhale as I gather my wits.

"How I feel about him is confusing. I don't know what to make of it. He's an attractive man who teased me and flirted with me a bit before all of this happened. But even when we were negotiating the deal, I knew he was steadfast and dependable. It's just the aura he's given off the entire time I've known him."

"Which hasn't been very long."

"True, but what I'm saying is also true. He came to help me, no questions asked. He's been kind to all three of us, and right now, he's the best suited person to help us."

"You keep deflecting and moving away from talking about your feelings. There's something between the two of you."

"Maybe—possibly—I don't know—I guess." I'm conflicted.

"Have you kissed him?"

"No. I told you, I will never cheat on Bastian."

"I know, but sometimes the heat of the moment—"

"Absolutely not. You know me, Heidi. You know no heat of the moment would make me forget Bastian or my commitment to him."

"All right then, do you want to kiss him?"

I look away as I nod. "Maybe all of this is just heightened

emotions from this situation. I'm confused, and I'm looking for someone to save us."

"Maybe so, but did you want to kiss him before all of this happened, when you were just meeting with him as a potential client?"

"Well, yes."

I feel so guilty admitting that. I hate it because it makes me sound like a horrible girlfriend, and it makes me sound so unprofessional, but it's true.

"You know you could've called Bastian and had him come here too. He would obviously take off work for this."

"I know that."

"You know I didn't put up as much of a fight about calling Friedrich as I could have because I didn't want to make it more difficult for you with Bastian. But I can't keep this from Friedrich beyond tomorrow morning. He'll expect me home."

"I know, and that means I have to tell Bastian. He can't hear this from Friedrich or from you."

Heidi shoots me a rueful expression before she admits the obvious. "You know they're both going to be livid that we didn't tell them right away."

"I know. Do you think Friedrich will understand if I say I asked you not to?"

"Hardly. It still means I chose you over him. That's not exactly what's supposed to happen in a relationship when we've been talking about getting married."

"Oh, Heidi, I'm sorry. I know you guys have been thinking about it, but are you really getting that much closer to him proposing?"

"Yes, I even considered proposing to him."

"I may risk my relationship, but I don't want to risk yours, *Schwesterlein*." I feel horrible now.

"Should we call our boyfriends after all?"

"No, not yet. I think it's plausible to say we didn't because we wanted to lessen the danger to more people."

"It truly can't go on beyond tomorrow morning, Anne."

"I agree."

"What're you going to do about your feelings?"

"It's too soon for me to tell. I can't make a reasonable decision about anything right now, but I can't help but wonder about this. I've met other handsome men since Bastian and I got together, and I didn't have this kind of reaction to them. I didn't even really have this strong a reaction to him when I met him. It's just visceral. It's like Jorge's a magnet to me."

Heidi offers me a sympathetic smile. "I get that."

"I can't help but wonder, if I can have any type of feelings for someone else, is there something broken in my relationship that was invisible until now? Or did this cause a crack?"

"I can't answer that for you."

If only she could, but I know I'm the only one who can. My sister leans forward and gives me a hug and rubs my back as we cling to each other. We both strip down to our bras and panties and climb into bed.

I thought it would take her much longer to fall asleep, but I soon hear her rhythmic breathing. I know the difference between when she's really asleep and when she thinks faking it fools me. I slip out of bed, watching her the entire time. I put my clothes back on before easing the door open.

I step out and shut it soundlessly. I move across the narrow short hall to the room my mom's in. I put my ear to the door, half expecting to hear her muffled cries, but it's silent. Maybe she's as exhausted as Heidi.

I, on the other hand, still feel on high alert. Maybe it's my personality, or maybe it's because I actually saw the hand and know without having to imagine it, the gravity of this situation.

It surprised me that *Mutti* didn't push harder to see it. Heidi, I think, followed her lead. It's a blessing.

I turn toward the suite's living room, and it only takes me two steps to realize Jorge's been watching me since the moment I stepped out of my room.

"*Chiquita*, we need to discuss your client list."

I watch him and try to look like I'm focused on him when really I'm wondering what he's been reviewing on his computer.

"What about my clients?"

"I'd like to know about the ones that aren't on the company's books."

"I don't work independently."

Fuck my life. What the fuck did he find? I'm not prepared to discuss this shit with him.

"Maybe not officially."

"I can't just do whatever I want. It's illegal to be some unregulated self-contractor."

"That doesn't mean you're not."

"I'm sure I don't know what you mean."

"Being evasive won't protect your sweet little ass. Do you want another spanking?"

Fuck how that tempts me. Instead, I try to muster as much defiance as I can as I stare back at him. He rises from the table and stalks toward me. There's no other way to describe it. It's like watching an elegant panther about to attack its prey. He backs me against the wall but doesn't touch me.

I flatten my palms against the surface to keep from reaching for him. We're looking at each other's lips before our gazes meet again. I think we both want a kiss. I think we're both so tempted, yet neither of us gives in. Instead, he leans forward and whispers in my ear.

"The next time I spank you, *chica*—and there will most

definitely be many more—it'll be bare-assed, but only because you're mine and no one else's."

"That's impossible. I'm with Bastian, and I love him."

"If that's the case, then why did you lie to him so easily today? Why have you rejected every suggestion your mother and sister made to tell him? Why haven't you insisted upon revealing what's happening?"

"Because I took your advice."

"Exactly. *My* advice. Not your mother's, not your sister's. You didn't call him to ask for advice, either. You've been relying on me."

"Was that as big a mistake as it's starting to feel?"

"You don't think it's a mistake at all. You feel guilty that you want it as much as you do. I can tell you exactly what I want."

He leans back, and once more our gazes lock. My eyes are riveted to his mouth as he continues to speak.

"I want to feel your hands on me as I touch every inch of you I can reach. I want to slip my fingers inside you, knowing you're already drenched for me."

He leans forward again; this time his chest barely brushes against mine.

"I want to sink deep inside you and make you cry out my name as you come all over my cock. I want to look down and see your pretty little mouth wrapped around me as you suck me off. I want to taste your clit in my mouth as I make you come."

I fight to keep my breathing steady, but I can't help the rapid rise and fall of my chest.

"You're only saying that to shock me."

"You're not rejecting it, though."

He backs away and returns to his laptop, which he spins around to me. He points to the screen.

"Explain this."

Chapter Twelve

Jorge

Liesel's wary as she approaches me. I see the flash of surprise, then anger before she glues in place her poker face from our meetings. She casts an imperious expression at me. It's easy to tell she doesn't want to discuss what Joaquin uncovered.

"Is that what your phone call was about earlier? Not investigating what happened to my father but looking into me?"

"You know one can't happen without the other. I need to discover anyone with a motive for this. I already know your father and uncle are into some shady shit. I didn't want to believe that about you, but there's a ton we don't know about each other, isn't there?"

"Yet, you think one day I'll fuck you."

I flash her a smile that's let me get away with murder—literally. I may avoid crowds like the plague, but there's tons to learn at busy nightclubs and bars. A little come-hither smile gets me a long way.

"I don't have to think that." I really am a smug fucker.

"Never."

"Sure—"·I flash her that smile again and then become deadly serious. "—but we digress. Liesel, you need to tell me the truth. If you want to be sure we all survive this, then I need to know what's going on. No half-truths, no sort-of-truths, no maybe-truths. All the truth. Who do you work for?"

Her eyes narrow, and there's practically palpable defiance radiating from her. I've seen this a multitude of times since I became an enforcer. It's feigned courage to hide paralyzing fear. She hates that I've discovered enough to ask that question. Her mind's zipping around, trying to figure out how to extricate herself from this conversation. What she can tell me that's enough to pacify me without giving away anything. Too bad for her I'll push until her back's against a wall, and the only way out is to give me the info I demand. That's the only way I'll move aside.

"I see from the transactions that money's being laundered through Swiss accounts. They are disguising it as commissions deposited into your accounts and then withdrawn as income. Except the one little problem is I can also see where it's paying for goods and services provided by a syndicate."

"You could've asked."

"So, you could just lie? Would you have told me the truth? I asked who was spying and was the leak. You didn't tell me the truth about that."

"How could you expect me to? That was about my family's company."

"And look what good it's done you to protect a company that won't protect you."

I stand with my arms crossed and cock an eyebrow. Does she think I'm new? As though I don't understand what's going on.

"You owe me an explanation, Liesel. And as for asking you,

obviously that doesn't work very well, so I had to do some digging on my own. Since I have no concrete evidence—yet—of which syndicate this is, it means you need to explain."

"Is there any credible reason to believe anything you see now has to do with my dad?"

I unfold my arms and appear sympathetic. I hate that it's part of a routine I perfected when I was fourteen and started stirring up shit in our Cartel neighborhood in Queens. In Jackson Heights, my brothers and I would cause trouble no one knew—half the time still don't know—was us. Then we'd show up for the family, offering sympathy before pressuring them into paying protection money to *Tío* Enrique.

"I can't know that until you explain, Liesel."

She pauses, and her shoulders sag. She appears so resigned to misery. It makes my heart ache, a feeling I'm wholly unused to with people outside my family, but one that is becoming familiar to me today. I wish I could make all of this go away for her, make it all better, but there's no chance of that while I'm lacking all the pieces to put together this puzzle. I need her to give me more.

"A syndicate based in Paris approached me, but I think it's a front for one in the U.S. Like you said, there's no concrete evidence who, so I can't be sure."

Immediately my mind jumps to the other three families, especially the Kutsenkos. They've already tried to fuck me out of a deal with the Schlossbergs. Did they approach her months ago? Did they extort her? I want to believe they'd leave her alone and not target her because she's a woman. But we know the old rules no longer apply. Even the saintly Kutsenkos break that promise.

Those fucknuts have always done it. They're just more inconspicuous than the other families. Everybody always thinks they're so angelic, riding around on their moral high horse. But they've used women to do their bidding ever since they rose to power. They only got pissed when it was *their* women who got used. Fucking hypocrites.

"How did they contact you?"

"Someone made a massive deposit into my personal account. Then they sent a follow-up email threatening to report me and that I would go to jail for embezzlement. I tried to track its source and return it, but I couldn't figure out who."

"Don't you know any forensic accountants?"

"Yes, but I didn't want to bring anyone else in the firm into it."

Now that she's begun to tell me what happened, it surprises me how easily she lets the story flow. She's not hesitant like she was before. She's pulling her walls down and allowing me in. I feel even more motivated than ever to protect her because she's finally showing me she trusts me completely. I don't want to do anything to ruin that. It means more to me than I expected it would.

I need my brother to dig back further into the bank records. I suspect this has been an issue for far longer than he and I thought.

"When did this start, *chiquita*?"

"Two and a half years ago."

I can't believe how much rage bubbles inside me. To say I'm pissed someone's been coercing her that long is a massive understatement.

"What did your father have to say about it?"

"I hinted at it, but he always blew it off. I even flat out told him, and he suggested I give him the money."

"From what I can see, you didn't. That's probably one of the best decisions you could make."

"I know. I hate saying I don't trust my father implicitly, but I don't. They knew I spoke to my father about it. I'm convinced someone's secretly listening to my conversations. Their emails mention things they shouldn't know unless they heard me say them."

"Is that how the information about my deal leaked, and you knew about this all along?"

"No. I searched and found the cameras and microphones about two months into this. I was careful to make sure the cameras never saw me get close enough to record me inspecting my office and the conference room. I'd position people with their backs to the cameras and put things in place to muffle the microphones when certain clients came to the office. You were one of them. The camera and microphone my father installed in the conference room remained on. I couldn't shut that off."

She grimaces and swallows as she crosses her arms. It's an unconscious reaction to protect herself. It's our instinct to guard our vital organs when we feel unsafe. She looks away from me as she begins again but soon meets my gaze.

"That leak came internally, and I believe it was my father's assistant. I'm uncertain yet. Everything points to her, but I never found definitive evidence. I don't know if she did it at my father's request or independently."

"What sorts of things have they said in their emails?"

She grimaces again and shivers. I step closer and wrap my arms around her. She tucks her head and burrows her face against my upper chest as she continues her story.

"Mostly they've stuck with business threats of interfering with the various contracts. They've laundered money through my accounts many times, like you said, making it appear as though I purchased goods or services from businesses. I received nothing in exchange. They controlled me by showing me they were one step away from lodging professional ethics claims against me or reaching out to law enforcement. They've been doing this the entire two and a half years."

"How frequently does this happen?"

"Something usually comes in once every couple of months. The longest they've gone without intimidating me is four and a half months."

"Do you have any suspicions about who it is? You said it was a syndicate out of Paris that contacted you, but you really think it might be one based in the U.S.? Could it be the Kutsenkos? How do you know they're supposedly based in Paris?"

"It's a Parisian banking number. It goes back to a lesser-known bank."

"Do you believe they're also laundering money through that account?"

"Yes. I suspect it's passing through several stages before it arrives at its final destination."

"What do you mean?"

"I'm not a forensic accountant, so I could be missing something obvious. I'm inferring all of this. It's the amounts that come in. When it's supposed to look like dividends, it's random amounts. They'll let it sit for a few weeks, then it'll disappear in a series of small transactions. It's as though I'm paying for normal day-to-day items. The deductions appear like clothing stores, the grocery store near my apartment, a cell phone bill. It could be a cleaning service or handyman. They mask them by using actual businesses' names. It's originating somewhere, then it's passing through the Parisian accounts to ones in Switzerland. From there, they've made it look like I'm drawing money from my investments. It goes out through those fake purchases. It has to make it to them after at least that stage."

She shakes her head but shrugs at the same time. "I truly don't know. At this point, I wouldn't put it past anyone, but I don't have a short list of suspects. I know there are syndicates that exist that I couldn't even imagine."

"What makes you think they're American?"

She lets go of me and steps back. Her brow furrows as she considers my question. "The tone of the emails. They're just not written like they'd come from a European."

"What do you mean?"

"Some phrases sound more American than they do French."

"Are the emails sent to you in French?"

"No, they're in German. It's how casual they sound. They're not the correct conjugations for the situation. French has formal and informal types of address. So does German. It's also the idioms in the threats."

"Such as?"

"They used a literal translation of there's more than one way to skin a cat. *Es gibt mehr als einen Weg, eine Katze su häuten.* We wouldn't use that. We'd say *viele Wege führen nach Rom.* They used the literal translation for keep your nose out of it. *Halt deine Nase da raus.* We'd say *Seinen Senf dazugeben.*"

Many roads lead to Rome. The English would be all roads lead to Rome. Even I know they wouldn't use the skin a cat one. The other means to add one's mustard. It means mind your own business.

The men I frequently trade bullets with wouldn't make those mistakes. They're too cosmopolitan, and there are too many people in the various families who speak German. Or they're well connected enough to have a German speaker check their wording.

This speaks to inexperience. It makes me think it's not somebody from New York.

"Liesel, can you show me the first email they sent you?"

Her lip trembles as she nods. She steps forward, but before she can reach my laptop, I engulf her in another hug. Her forehead rests on my shoulder as she trembles. I run my hand up and down her back, and she sighs before pressing her right hand over my heart.

"I know this has all been too much today, little one. I know you're exhausted and terrified, but I need to know all of this."

I try to keep my voice soft, maybe even soothing. I don't want her to feel worse than she already does.

"It is not just all of that, Jorge. I feel like such an idiot, but I've had no one else I could confide in. You know my father didn't support me when I told him I needed help with all of this. He left me to deal with it alone because I knew I couldn't trust him. It's not like I could tell my sister or mother, and I certainly couldn't tell Bastian, so I've just kept this to myself the entire time."

"That's exhausting, *chiquita*, but you don't have to do this alone anymore. Let me shoulder your burden for a little while."

"You're already doing so much for me. I don't know how I could ever repay you."

"*Chiquita*, this isn't a debt. There's nothing to repay. I'm not doing this with an expectation that you return any favors. I'm doing this because it's the right thing to do to help you. You've been adjacent to this world, but now it's sucked you fully in. What else have they expected you to do?"

She releases a shuddering breath. I think she's surprised I suspected there's more. But if they already have her working for them, they'll push until there's nothing left of her to give.

"Insider trading. I received photos of my sister and her boyfriend in Croatia, followed by a demand for information about client contracts."

"They wanted to know where the investments were going, and you obliged them."

"How could I not? They were already extorting me and using my bank accounts. Then they sent me photos of my sister and her boyfriend. These weren't just photos of them at dinner or on the beach. They were verging on explicit. It was obvious these people had a way to see into the bungalow they were staying in."

"Did you tell your father or uncle about that?"

She shakes her head against my shoulder. "At that point, what could they have done?"

"Perhaps your father wouldn't have done much, but your uncle certainly would have."

She leans away from me as she looks up, her hands resting on my ribs. "What does that mean?"

"Your uncle is a major importer of marijuana and cocaine into the German market. He's a man with connections he keeps secret. They're the type of people who could handle this."

She goes positively rigid. "How do you know that?"

"Because as many secrets as every syndicate has, there are just as many that never stay hidden. We know far too much about each other's business. That's why there's never a clear king of the hill. The power balance only remains balanced because it shifts among us so frequently. No one stays on top or at the bottom for too long. My family knows the O'Rourkes retaliated against the O'Malleys a few years ago by stealing a product shipment Clyde was supposed to bring in. I don't know what he's like around family, but he's one of the most cold-hearted, determined men I've met."

We also know far too much about one another's proclivities. As much as we want to think we're different, we're the same. We're all kinky fuckers—literally.

"You said something like that before. I don't remember if you said you've met him. Do you know him well?"

"No, but we've been at charity events together, and I've heard what he's capable of. It's one reason your firm appealed to my family. We didn't want to get into bed with him directly, but we wanted to know he'd be there to secure any deal that might go awry."

"All that time, you weren't really there to interview me. You'd already decided."

"Not exactly. As you know, I very nearly walked away from that deal. That leak nearly cost you a few million euros."

"I know. Was it my uncle who made you give us another chance?"

"No, that was entirely you."

Our gazes lock, and she nods. My forefinger goes under her chin and tilts her head back.

"Liesel, I told you what I want. It isn't some power play to manipulate you. It isn't because we're forced to stay together in this suite. It isn't because I want to torment you or treat you like a toy I'll cast off when I get bored. I know you're serious about Bastian, and that's why you live with him. But there's no denying there's something between us. And I don't for a minute believe it's purely because of desperation that you turned to me."

"Maybe not. Maybe there really is something there, Jorge."

"I'll respect your relationship. I won't do anything to make you a cheater. But you know you want what I said earlier. You want to kiss me. You want to feel me inside you. You ache for it just like I do. You want me to touch and taste every part of you. You want to submit to my dominance."

Her eyes widen to where it must be uncomfortable. It tells me she isn't into BDSM because it shocks her. But she wants that dynamic, even if she doesn't want that type of sex.

"Jorge, I—"

"You don't want me to keep being domineering. But you want me to continue to take the lead. You want to know I'll do more than protect you. You want me to take care of you. You want the weight of the world off your shoulders. To focus on something beyond all this. Even after this, you want to focus on something beyond work and your duties. You *need* someone who understands that."

"Bastian—"

"Might be someone whose company you enjoy. You may love his personality and what he does for you. But you know it's not enough. If that were the case, you wouldn't be attracted to me. You wouldn't be attracted to a man like me if you didn't want this deep down. Maybe you haven't recognized that, but it's there."

"I know." She whispers her response, but I see how conflicted she is.

"I told you I won't do anything to compromise your relationship. But this wasn't a secret between us. It just needed to be said aloud."

"I'm not ready to leave a relationship I believed would lead to marriage and a life with him."

"Believed, *chiquita*. Past tense."

She swallows, and tears well in her eyes.

"I'm not giving up on that future for something temporary. You'll go home, and I'll just be left behind."

I can't demand she move to the U.S. with me, but that's the only way this will work. I can't move here.

"Liesel, I won't leave you behind. I wouldn't suggest this if I didn't see this as something more than a quick fuck."

"You don't live here. I do. I can't uproot my life."

"I know. But I'm not walking away from you if you decide I'm who you want."

Chapter Thirteen

Liesel

My head's spinning. I feel like something sucked all the oxygen out of the room. Being in Jorge's arms is different from any other man I've been with. It's like we've been a couple for ages. It's that normal and comforting. I want the things he said. I feel the way he described. It's visceral. It's intuitive. It's practically primal.

But it doesn't negate my feelings for Bastian. I love him. I live with him because I see—saw—see—the fuck if I know at this point—a future with him. I saw marriage and maybe children in the future. We've talked about that, but neither of us is sure we want them. We were going to discuss marriage when he returned from his next overseas assignment. We want to see how things go during that time apart. Mostly, it's how I do with the separation and being left behind. I was so positive it wouldn't be a problem.

How deeply in love are you if you're aching for another man to fuck you? Aching for him to take care of you just like he said? Wanting to submit to him like he said?

I've never had thoughts of dominance and submission before. Sure, I like it when Bastian holds my hands over my head or gives me a spank or two during sex. But that's playful more than anything else.

If I ask Jorge what he means by that, it'll show it intrigues me far more than it should. That I might consider it. From the way he's looking at me, he knows my innermost thoughts. Ones I don't want him to read.

Yes, you do. You want to feel that seen. You want someone who just knows you. Someone you don't have to explain your feelings to, knowing he'll listen but won't truly get it. It's why you accepted the spanking and crave more of them.

Something about Jorge makes me want to confide my deepest fears. That scares the fucking shit out of me.

What if this is all manipulations?

"*Chiquita*, if I didn't mean this, I wouldn't put all of this on the line. I wouldn't suggest there's more between us because that means bringing you into my life. Bringing you deeper into this world. I wish that weren't the case. But if there were anything between us, it would bring even more danger to your life. I'll do anything to protect you, regardless."

I study his expression. There's an openness in his gaze that's never been there before. I know he's been sincere since we got here. Even his arrogance is sincere. However, what I see now is vulnerability I don't think he'd fake. His life depends on never showing that. Not ever.

The longer I observe him, the more I sense a growing anxiety simmering beneath the surface. He's nervous. He doesn't want me to see that. It's not obvious. I can just tell. I think I see him in a way he doesn't allow others to. Certainly, no one outside his family. It feels special.

"I think I've known that all along. Thank you."

He brushes the back of his fingers along my left cheek. Then he lets me go, and the real world comes rushing back in. I'm bereft of his touch. I'm drifting without mooring when I'm out of his embrace. It's like being dropped into freezing water after being beside a toasty fireplace. The man generates a ton of heat. That alone comforted me.

"Try to get some sleep."

I nod before looking toward the sofa. "You don't have a pillow or a blanket."

"I have some work to do."

"You can't do that all night. You need sleep too, Jorge."

"I will once I'm done. I'll be fine."

"Bullshit. Let me get a pillow and blanket. There's bound to be extra in my room. Hang on."

"*Chica*—"

"No."

My resistance makes him grin. He nods, and I turn toward the bedrooms. I feel like I'm slinking back into my room after doing something I wasn't supposed to. Having another man hold me, try to seduce me—at the very least arouse me—was completely wrong. I know it, yet I didn't stop it. I barely held on to any sense of morality and didn't accept what he offered. His honorable refusal to push us to do more made my heart swell. I gained even more respect for him.

I slip into the bedroom, not quite closing the door all the way, but keeping any light from shining in Heidi's face. I open the closet and find what I'm looking for. I creep out again and walk back into the living room. I leave the bedding at the end of the sofa. Jorge's already back at his laptop. He looks up at me and nods.

"Sleep well, little one."

He calls me that along with *chiquita* and *chica*.

It's presumptuous as fuck.

It's inappropriate.

It makes me happy.

I wish I had a pet name for him. I called him Jorgito twice. It was condescending at the time because I was upset with him. I don't remember over what. But now I wish I had something equally sweet to call him. But that only encourages a connection we shouldn't have. It's already bad enough without fostering it on both sides.

I strip off my clothes and climb into bed beside Heidi. She stirs, but she says nothing. I listen for a moment and know she isn't pretending. She's dead to the world. I take a few minutes to settle my mind, then I drift into dreamless sleep.

"I have to call Bastian, Jorge. It's been nearly a full day. I need to tell him something. Heidi has to do the same for Friedrich. We both called in sick already, so it bought us the day. But our boyfriends are going to wonder what's going on since it's not the weekend."

"I know. You both need to be selective about what you say."

"Can't we have them come here?"

I want to cringe when Heidi asks. We already agreed the less people know, the better. Now she wants to bring two more people into the mix. I guess our boyfriends are already there. I get why she wants to speak to Friedrich. She's scared for us and for him. She wants him to comfort her. But it puts me in a position where I'll have to call Bastian too. I don't want to explain to my mom and sister why I don't want the man I love here. I can't claim it's protecting him when he's safer here than on his own, unaware of the dangers.

Jorge focuses on Heidi, not even glancing at me. "Not yet.

If we make no progress before tonight, then yes, they can come here. I know you'd feel better with them."

I struggle not to wince. I could agree with him, but he and I would know it's a lie. But in this, I have to be the leader. I pull out my phone and unlock it.

"I'll call Bastian first. I'll tell him as little as I can. You stick with what I say when you speak to Friedrich."

"Fine."

Jorge shifts his focus to me, and he looks about as thrilled as he would if he walked in to get a root canal. I tap on Bastian's contact and wait while it rings.

"*Guten Morgen, mein Liebling.*"

"*Guten Morgen.*"

I can't muster an endearment for him while Jorge listens. It feels fake. I've never hesitated before. But once Bastian speaks again, the familiarity reassures me as we continue in German.

"Did you have fun last night?"

"It was good to have *Mutti* and Heidi with me."

"Did you stay up late chatting?"

"Yeah. How was your night?" That is true; it was just with Jorge.

"Lonely. The bed feels awfully big without you."

"Now you know what it's like when you're on rotation."

I can't help but smile. We slip into our easy banter, and the familiarity is even more comforting than I expected. At least, it is until I look up and see Jorge observing me. His expression is impassive. I don't know what he's thinking.

"Are you coming home before work?"

"I'm not headed into the office, actually."

"Why not? You nearly never work from home."

"Something's come up, Bastian. It involves Papa. I don't know the full extent yet, but I think it's better I stay out of the office for now."

"Is it his health? Do I need to call anyone?"

I close my eyes and swallow. I wish it were as simple as him calling around the hospitals to see if he can find Papa. I know he isn't at one.

"No. We're having problems with an angry client. I'm trying to stay out of sight for now."

"Did they threaten you?"

There's a seriousness I rarely hear in Bastian's voice. I know he feels protective of me, but I'm all too aware of his limitations. He's a powerful man, and I'd usually put my money on him in a fight. However, this isn't some bar brawl. He'd be no match for anyone we come across.

"Not me, but they did Papa."

My attention moves to Heidi, making sure she's listening. Her story has to match mine since Bastian and Friedrich are best friends. They'll definitely discuss this.

"Are your mother and sister still with you?"

"Yes. They're going to stay here with me for the day. I'll let you know if anything comes up, and we need to stay longer."

"Longer? Just how serious is this? What does your father say?"

"We're being cautious. He's busy right now, so I haven't spoken to him recently."

I pray he isn't busy being dead. I want to believe amputating his hand is the worst these invisible menaces would do, yet I know that's likely not the case.

"I can switch shifts and come to you."

"No. I don't want to inconvenience you. I'd like you to join me if I don't sort things out by tonight."

"Because you're worried about my safety too?"

"That's part of it. I also want to see you."

I observe Jorge as I say that. It isn't a lie. I want to see Bastian. I want the comforts they can both offer. It's not like I want a three-way, but they both make me feel safe in different ways. That doesn't mean Jorge enjoys hearing me say I want another man here when he confessed what he did last night. I'd feel wretched if I heard him telling another woman he wants her to come over.

"Keep me informed, *mein Liebling*."

"I will, *mein Schatz*." My darling.

I lapse into what I started calling him four months into our relationship. He'd think it even odder if I didn't. I've always been affectionate and usually say the term of endearment without thought. With Jorge watching and listening, it feels forced.

"*Ich liebe dich*." I love you.

"*Ich liebe dich auch*." I love you too.

Heidi's watching me with suspicion as I hang up. She can tell something's up, and it's more than caution while discussing this—situation. I glance at my mom, and she's staring off into space. I walk to her and wrap my arms around her like I have since I was a toddler. She leans against me in a way she never has before. She's looking to me for strength I need to dredge up from somewhere.

"*Mutti*, we'll get through this."

She nods, her head resting on my shoulder. She gives me a squeeze but lingers before pulling away. I guide her to the sofa, and she sinks onto it beside me. I'm only half paying attention to my sister's conversation. It sounds like Friedrich isn't taking it in stride like Bastian did. He's not overbearing, but he's far more protective than Bastian. It's not like he thinks Heidi's incapable, and Bastian doesn't think that about me. He's just more mindful of things. Bastian assumes I'll tell him if I need his protection. I never have, so he doesn't offer.

When she's done, she joins us on the sofa, sitting on the other side of our mom. We both lean against her. She rests her head on top of Heidi's while stroking my hair. My eyelids droop closed, and I exhale. I let myself relax for a moment, feeling better having my mom and sister near me while we're awake. I want to know what Jorge's doing, but I'd have to look over my shoulder to do that. I'm too comfortable, and I don't want to be so conspicuous.

However, the moment's ruined when my phone rings. I slide it from my pocket. There's no name or number on my screen. I rise and hurry to Jorge, showing him my phone. I don't want to put it on speaker in case something's said that'll upset *Mutti* and Heidi. At the same time, I want Jorge to hear everything. He nods as I come to stand beside him. I hold the phone between our ears with the volume all the way up. I think we're far enough away that my mom and sister won't hear whoever's speaking on the other end.

"*Hallo*."

"*Hallo*, Anne."

"Who is this?" The accent sounds American, so I switch to English.

"Santa."

Sick fuck!

"Did you leave me any more gifts?"

"How would I do that with your Chihuahua yapping next to you?"

Jorge. He's neither Mexican nor little. I stand by my comparison to a Rottweiler.

I glance up at Jorge, and his expression is entirely blank. I can't tell if he's insulted, impatient, bored, or pleased these fuckers made contact.

"I don't have any pets." I play dumb for now.

"Ms. Schlossberg, you know who I mean. You're far too intelligent to pull off the dumb blonde act. It doesn't suit you.

You're in a suite with Jorge Diaz. Interesting place to spend the night when your father's missing."

Does he think this was some booty call?

The implication suggests he doesn't know my family is with me.

Would I be here banging Jorge with my mother and sister around the corner?

You were nearly ready to do that very thing last night.

It would've taken little encouragement. I hate admitting it to myself. It feels like a personal failure and a betrayal to Bastian.

"What do you want from me?"

"I'm glad you asked. Your father owes a large sum to people he pissed off because he's kept them waiting. The hand was a warning to get your attention."

"You certainly did that."

"He owes six million euros. You need to pay that amount. *Then* we'll discuss ransom."

If that's true, then Papa's still alive.

"I want proof of life before I do anything."

Jorge nods at my request. His approval makes this a bit less terrifying.

"Demanding anything from me isn't good for your father's health."

"Perhaps, but it's the only condition I have. I need to see my father's alive and well before I give anything."

"If you'd like him to remain alive, you won't be so pushy."

"I'll only give the money if I'm positive he's still alive. If he's dead, I owe you nothing."

I won't give this man jack shit if I don't get my father back. I'll set him up with law enforcement and stand back.

"I'll collect one way or another. How would your mother

and sister feel if I hacked you to bits and sent you to them piece by piece?"

"Let me hear his voice. Send a photo with something that shows the date and time."

"Avoiding the question tells me you didn't like that idea."

"The only thing I'd like right now is to see and hear my father."

My phone pings with an incoming message. I tap the screen and pull up my texts. There's a photo of Papa. A bandage covers his arm, and bruises mark his face. Who knows what they've done that I can't see? Someone's holding a phone beside him. The time matches what I read on my device. The date matches too.

My mom and sister sit in anxious silence as they watch me and hear only one side of the conversation. I nod, and relief visibly sweeps over them.

"There. You have your proof. You will transfer six million into your father's Swiss account."

"I can't move that much money without raising flags all over the place. It'll take me a couple days to get that much."

My gaze shoots to Jorge as panic threatens. I can't possibly accomplish that. His expression goes from blank to reassuring. I can't tell what he's reassuring me about. Will he help me get that money together? Does he know a way to avoid it? Does he have some Black Ops team that can rescue Papa?

"I'll do my best. If I can't get all at once, then consider what I do a sign of good faith."

"Good faith?" The man laughs at me.

"Yes. Just like I consider the photo one. If you're lying to me, you'll get nothing."

"You won't know one way or another since you need to make the deposit *before* I return your father."

The call ends. I stare at my screen, avoiding my gaze

meeting my mom's or sister's. When I've gathered my thoughts enough to not feel my head's a tornado one moment and blank the next, I gaze up at Jorge. When he doesn't respond with a solution immediately, my gaze drifts to the box—or where the box should be. My gaze flashes back to Jorge. He mouths his response, and it makes my stomach twist.

"Mini-fridge."

Oh, God. It's keeping it from smelling as decomposition sets in.

"Do you know the Swiss account information?"

"Not off-hand. I'd need to get into my laptop or my father's. I don't know where Papa's is, but mine is in my office. I only brought my purse with me."

It's not until after I respond to Jorge's question that I realize we're speaking English. My mother and sister both speak it, but not as fluently as I do. They don't use it as often. I don't know how much of the conversation they understood. I assume most, if not all. I'm certain at least *Mutti* did when she stands.

"Are you going back to your office? You can't go alone."

"I don't think we need either computer just yet, Mrs. Schlossberg. If we do, I will take Anneliese. I have men who can stay behind to guard you, and I have ones who can come with me."

"Do you travel with an army?" Heidi's question could be accusatory; instead, it sounds like she marvels at the idea.

"Not quite. But I've been to a few countries on this trip. When I travel for this long, I ensure my men can have adequate time off by having a contingent large enough for them to rotate."

"Smart."

Not that he needs Heidi's approval, but he smiles when she gives it. My family and I look at Jorge, waiting for him to tell us what's next.

"I'm going to call my brother. He'll get into the banks and examine your father's personal accounts. He'll go back through the firm's banking records too. He'll piece it all together. He can also make it look like a transfer's on its way when it isn't. There's not much he can't do with a computer. I'll be right back."

He shuts his laptop and picks it up, tucking it under his arm. He grabs his phone from beside his wireless mouse.

"Mrs. Schlossberg, may I step into your room, please?"

Mutti nods, and he takes off, leaving me to wonder exactly what he means by there's not much his brother can't do with a computer.

Chapter Fourteen

Jorge

I scrub my hand over my face when I get into the bedroom. I didn't let the women see my frustration, but it's there. I didn't recognize the *pedazo de mierda*—piece of shit's—voice. It could be a mercenary, or it could be a syndicate member somewhere who I don't know.

I'm too trained to make the mistake of walking close to the window. I skirt around the furniture and pull the curtains closed. I'll check Liesel's room when I'm done here. They need to know not to open the curtains. A rifle's strong scope or a drone could look straight in.

I sit in one of the room's armchairs near—but not in front of —the window and flip open my laptop. I heard it ping a couple times with emails. I notice Joaquin sent me more information. I see more bank accounts I'm positive Liesel doesn't know about. I'm certain Gretel would know even less. They're only a smidge on the right side of legal.

I calculate as I go along. I've always had a mind for math.

I've always enjoyed puzzles ever since *Mamá* would keep me occupied with the old-fashioned wood ones with the peg pieces. I was barely in preschool before I moved onto the cardboard ones with the large pieces. By elementary school, I was doing puzzles that said they're for eighteen and older. I suppose manufacturers believe it takes eighteen years to build the patience.

I look at equations the same way. They're puzzles that need me to solve for X. Right now, it's who the fuck is terrorizing the Schlossbergs. As I examine the new information, I see if I can find any patterns. I look for data I can string together to make a solvable equation. I find a few things, but they're too insignificant right now. Maybe they'll be worth something in a while.

"*Hola, manito.*" Joaquin answers after the first ring.

"*Hola.* I looked at what you sent me. Nothing stands out right this minute. We got a call from the kidnappers. They sent proof of life. They want six million euros in a Swiss account."

"The Schlossbergs don't have that kind of liquidity. Not without stealing it from clients, and that would be a challenge for them. They'd have to do some serious moving around of their funds that would raise too much attention."

"Do they have any assets they could liquidate?"

"Not quickly."

"I want to put enough in Gunter's Swiss account to make them try to draw on it. That way we can see where they try to take it. There's barely nine-hundred K in there. If I can get it up to a million, Liesel could say it's a deposit before getting more proof of life. That she didn't trust them not to hurt her father once they believed they'd pacified her."

"Liesel?"

Fuck my life.

"Should I air out my tux?"

He knows Liesel means more to me than a passing acquaintance because I gave her a nickname. The men in the Four Families are far too much alike. If we didn't want to murder each other, we'd probably be one big happy commune since all the married couples live in the same two neighborhoods. If we could put aside our egos and join forces, we could rule the world. Since we're so alike, the men in all the families have a habit of giving their woman a nickname. It's usually some diminutive of their real name.

It's possessive as fuck—and sweet as can be.

"How about we get through this and see whether she's interested when her father's life doesn't depend upon me?"

"What about her boyfriend?"

"That's not what I called to discuss."

"But you want to."

I mostly love how my brothers know my thoughts without me having to say them aloud. It's kept us alive in deadly situations. It's also rescued me when my anxiety flares, especially in large social settings.

Another tradition the Four Families have is to invite one another to wedding and baptism receptions. They're excuses to mingle with wealthy guests who preen over their invitation and want to schmooze with each other. Most of all, they want access to the Four Families to score lucrative deals. Being around all those people a few times a year is excruciating.

"Later, *mano*."

"Fine. I checked the usual forums and groups on the dark web to see if anyone put out a hit for him or kidnapping order. I found nothing. There's nothing that hints at Germany. There are a few open jobs in Europe, including ours in the Czech Republic and Lithuania. Pablo just posted those last night. We'll fuck over the Kutsenkos for giving you a hard time. The unclaimed jobs are along the Med and in Asia."

We have an interesting network of colleagues. We contact

some mercenaries directly when we have someone specific in mind. Other times, it's an open casting call. We see who wants the job and decide from there. All the assignments are posted in codes law enforcement still haven't figured out. The encryption changes constantly, and no one's given up details as part of a plea bargain. They'll take their chances with a government's death penalty before they do a syndicate's.

"I snooped around the others' accounts and found nothing pointing in your direction."

The 'others' are the Mancinellis and O'Rourkes since he's already told me about the Kutsenkos.

"What about the lesser ones?"

"I checked Boston, Trenton, Chicago, and L.A. No internal communication within those families."

"Triad? *Yakuza?*"

"Neither. There's some conflict between Hong Kong and Tokyo, but nothing that stands out beyond their usual shipping wars."

"Is this an oligarch?" It wouldn't be a first, and Gunter's done business with some.

"That's what I'm thinking. Someone who's way overreaching. They might be making a play to establish themselves as the head of a syndicate. Or they might want to start one."

"That's usually a doomed experiment."

There are too many longstanding organized crime families and branches. Anyone with an entrepreneurial spirit rarely has the means to elbow their way in. Whoever they try to nudge out of the way already has the means to shut newcomers out. If they don't, then that means the established syndicate has an overlord that'll destroy the interloper. We don't like new kids at school. They sit at a lunch table on their own.

"Do you think they're Russian or from one of the Stans?"

"Possibly."

Whoever this is knows I'm connected to Schlossbergs & Sons. Their insults implied I have a personal connection to Liesel. If they involve me, that means taking on my entire family. We come as a package deal.

"Get me what you can on them. Dig more in Asia too. See if the pissing contest between Chinese and Japanese syndicates is spraying toward here."

"I'm working on it as we speak. What're you going to do?"

"I'll comb through everything you send as it arrives. But I may need to take Liesel to her office. If you can't find the Swiss account info, we'll need her laptop and hopefully her father's. His device is the only way into the accounts."

"And her mom and sister?"

"They'll stay here with some of the guys."

"When does her boyfriend get there?"

"Funny. She and her sister will have to invite their boyfriends over before it gets too late. I can't guarantee the cover of darkness would work in our favor. I want to make sure our guards can see anyone coming. I'll make sure they bring the boyfriends in through the back."

That'll be interesting. I'm certain neither will listen to their girlfriends about staying close to the floorboards for the entire ride. It won't please them to take orders from me. They'll really hate how they're transported if they refuse my guards. I'll cross that bridge when we come to it.

"Do you need anything else, *manito*? You still good on your own?"

"I'm good. But you know I'll contact you and Javier the moment I'm not."

"All right."

"You don't sound like you believe me."

"This is the first time a woman—your woman's—been involved."

"She's nothing to me right now."

He blows out a snort. "Yet."

"*Te quiero.*"

"*Te quiero también.*"

"Bastian, things are worse than I thought. I want you to come to the hotel tonight."

"What's going on? Are you scared to be there with just Gretel and Heidi?"

Liesel's watching me as she speaks to Bastian. Just like the last call she was on, she stands close enough for me to hear when she has the phone between our ears, and the volume's all the way up. Neither her mother nor sister can hear Bastian, only her.

"I'd like you here to be on the safe side. Heidi's going to call Friedrich in a moment. She'd feel better with him here too."

"The safe side of what, Anne? What's going on?"

He's asked twice, and I can tell he's getting testy. Liesel's looking up at me for guidance, I whisper my answer to her unspoken question.

"Say no one's seen or heard from your father, and you're nervous. Something's happened, but you aren't sure what."

She nods as Bastian repeats her name.

"*Mutti* can't get ahold of Papa, and neither can Heidi nor I. We're all getting nervous. It's not like him. If this has to do with work, and I work alongside him, then I want to make sure everyone connected to us is protected."

"And a hotel room is going to do that?"

"A friend of mine with private security is here. We have guards with us. I can explain more when you get here."

"You said Heidi's calling Friedrich?"

Liesel glances over at her sister, who taps her phone screen and puts it to her ear. It only takes a moment before I hear her greet her boyfriend.

"She's talking to him right now. My friend will send cars for each of you. It's really important that you stay down below the window."

"What? Anne, this is insane. You want me crouched on the floor of a car with people I don't know."

"Yes, Bastian. I trust this recommendation. If anyone's been watching my family, then they'll know about you and Friedrich. I want you to get here safely. That means no one seeing you on the road."

"And I suppose we'll be coming up the freight elevator or something."

"Until you have to switch to the guest elevator to get to the penthouse. It'll keep you out of the busy lobby."

"All this cloak and dagger is ridiculous for your father not calling you back for a few hours."

Liesel looks at me for guidance again. All I can do is nod in encouragement because I don't know the douchebag, so I don't know what'll encourage him.

"Bastian, he disappeared before lunch yesterday. *Mutti*, Heidi, and I waited here, but he didn't call any of us or answer any texts. We got worried, so my friend and I went back to my office to get my laptop and Papa's. I thought I might figure out where he went from his calendar. I didn't. It's been more than twenty-four hours. Please just come. We can get into more detail once you're here."

We decided we should get the laptops simply to keep anyone else from accessing them. We made a fast trip during the time most of our employees take lunch. There were fewer people in the office. She slipped in and out with barely any conversation. She said Gunter had an unexpected trip, and she was under the weather but would work from home.

"Have you called the police?"

"Bastian!" She cringes when she snaps at him. "Please just come here, and we'll discuss everything. I don't want to do this over the phone."

"Do you think someone's listening?"

"Yes, Heidi and *Mutti*. I don't want to argue in front of them. Heidi just gave me a thumbs up. Friedrich agreed to the same thing I asked you. A car will be at the hospital for you in—"

She looks over at me, and I hold my hand up.

"Five minutes. Can you be ready?"

"Yeah."

"Go to the service entrance on the north side of the building."

"What? You have to be kidding. Is this a joke?"

"Bastian, just do it." Her frustration's clear in her tone.

"Fine. How will I know who I'm looking for?"

"It'll be a large SUV with tinted windows, and four large Latino men with earpieces."

I explained these details already, so she knew what to relay to Bastian. She warned me he might be difficult, so I was prepared. She assured me she'd convince him to come without a problem once he was in the vehicle.

"What the hell, Anne? Who are these men?"

I bristle at his tone and his words. Liesel shoots me a placating glance, and I grit my teeth.

"It's a potential client who's become a friend. I trust him, and he's offered to help."

"Why would your client know how to deal with this?"

I'm fighting not to lose my patience and snatch the phone from Liesel's hand.

"Bastian, either get in the damn car when it arrives or don't. But I'm not arguing with you over the phone. I'm doing my best to make sure everyone I love is safe, but if you don't want the help, then go home and see what happens."

I cringe at that. But the man doesn't argue again.

"All right. Thank you. But we aren't done."

"I didn't think we were."

She ends the call and drops her phone back in her pocket. If we were alone, I'd hug her again. She looks lost and unsure of herself. Heidi's still on the phone with Friedrich, but her call is going much smoother. Gretel's watching Liesel and me, and I know she's no fool. She senses something's brewing beneath the surface.

"I'm sorry he isn't being more grateful."

"He's confused, and now he knows there's a man involved. Of course, it has him on edge."

"I know, but—"

"It's fine, Anne."

Her right hand fists. She doesn't like hearing me use that name. She darts her gaze to her mother and understands why I did it. When our gaze meets again, she offers me a weak smile before walking over to the sofa to join the other women.

It's twenty minutes before my guard knocks and announces in Spanish that Friedrich is here. I respond in Spanish too, telling him to let the man in. I checked out Heidi's social media last night, so I knew who to expect. He's sliding his ID back into his wallet as he walks in. He looks over his shoulder as he adjusts his suit coat once his wallet's back in place. He looks a bit befuddled after the pat down I know he got.

"Heidi!"

Friedrich rushes forward, and Heidi hurries toward him. He engulfs her in his arms and lifts her off her feet. Neither cares who's around when they kiss. It's not inappropriate, but it's certainly passionate. He puts her back on her feet and brushes hair away from her face. They keep their voices low, but I get the gist of their conversation. He asks if the men outside forced her in here. If they patted her down too.

He looks toward me and asks if she's afraid of me. She reassures him that everything is fine—as good as it can be. She insists we'll explain everything once Bastian arrives. She refuses to go through it twice. At first, I think Friedrich thinks she just doesn't want to be bothered repeating herself. Then he senses it would be too difficult for her to say it or hear it twice.

Liesel introduces him to me, and we shake hands. I sense his hesitation, but there's no resistance. They sit together on the sofa after he greets Gretel.

It's another twenty minutes before Bastian arrives. He looks more ruffled than Friedrich when he comes in the door. He glares at the man who handed his ID back. He recognizes me immediately, and I can tell he's pissed I'm the one here. Did Liesel mention her suspicions about me stalking her?

He pulls her in for a kiss when she hurries over to him. I see her relax against him, welcoming that kiss. It's—sweet. It's not anywhere near as passionate as Heidi and Friedrich's.

It still makes me want to puke.

I noticed Gretel watching me, so I plastered a smile on my face as he walked in. I force my posture to remain relaxed as every ounce of possessiveness in me vibrates like a tuning fork.

When they pull apart, Liesel brings him over to where I still stand near the dining table. We both extend hands, and this isn't the casual but curious greeting I got from Friedrich. He tries to crush my hand, but he's unprepared for my grip. I'm careful since I know he performs surgery when he's on his Doctors Without Borders missions. But I make sure it'll sting for a few minutes. I'm clearly larger than him, so I don't know what made him think I wouldn't be stronger than him.

He hates it. His bearing puffs up like a pissed off peacock. Liesel watches the exchange, understanding what's happening. She's staring at Bastian, the warning clear on her face. She knows—I believe she knows—I won't rescind my help just because Bastian's being a douche. But she doesn't like it.

"Anne, you will explain what's going on. Now."

She shoots me a quelling look. Bastian doesn't miss it, and it only pisses him off even more.

"Who are you? Why do you have guards?" He turns back to Liesel. "Did your mom and sister really spend the night here?"

She opens her mouth to respond, but I cut her off in German. He probably thinks I don't speak the language past the introductions. Surprise, motherfucker.

"This isn't the time to accuse your girlfriend of cheating. It's insulting. Who I am is a venture capitalist and accountant from New York. I have the means to provide private security for you, Anne, and the others. I'm well connected with the best and worst of society around the world. I'm the person who can get answers to what's going on. I suggest you let Anne explain the situation without interrupting. It's been a difficult day and a half for her mother, her sister, and her. Be nice."

I inhale at the end, letting my chest expand to its full breadth. Liesel practically flinches before desire sparks for a moment. Bastian doesn't quite wilt, but he certainly backs down. He nods, so I gesture toward the sofa and armchairs. It's my turn to practically flinch when he sits in a chair and pulls Liesel onto his lap. I sit in the other armchair as though it's my throne.

I'll let Liesel explain as much as she can, but I'm ready to step in if she needs me. I'm certain I will when Bastian pitches an inevitable fit. I sense it. She looks at me, and I nod. I see Bastian's hand tighten on her hip. He doesn't enjoy her deferring to me about anything. He hasn't seen us together long enough to have a reason to doubt her, so he's threatened by my mere presence—hell, my mere existence.

As he should be.

"When I returned from lunch yesterday, there was a box on my desk. I was entirely unprepared to open it and find Papa's hand in it. I'm certain it was his because of his wedding ring. He's never taken it off."

"What the hell, Anne?! You didn't think you should tell me that?"

I clear my throat. My gaze locks with Bastian's, and everyone knows I don't approve of his tone. Friedrich's far smarter than his friend.

"Heidi, did you know this?"

"Not until I got here. Anne didn't tell the truth, but she was wise not to. *Mutti* and I would've freaked out. We wouldn't have handled it well and probably would've made everything worse."

"How could it get worse?"

Bastian's demand earns him an equally scathing look from Friedrich, who lets go of Heidi's hand and wraps his arm around her shoulders. She sinks against him, burrowing her face against his chest. Liesel picks up as though there was no interruption.

"Someone dropped a note in my lap while I was at the park. I didn't understand what it meant, but now I know it was a threat against Papa. It warned me something was coming, and I wouldn't be ready for it. I got back to my office, and there was the box. It was terrifying. I called Jorge because I know enough about his family to understand the influence they have in the global economy. I also knew if I needed resources, he'd have them."

"So, this is about money. We're not without means."

"We don't have six million euros lying around, Bastian. So, unless you've been hiding it under our mattress and didn't tell me, you couldn't help the way Jorge can. It's not about his lending us the money. It's about him understanding the consequences of someone demanding six million. It's about him knowing people who can help us investigate what's going on."

"How docs he know this?"

My turn to talk. The *cabrón* doesn't get to pretend I'm not sitting right here.

"My family is extremely wealthy. We own an international conglomerate with holdings in multiple industries. I have my personally owned businesses that make me independently wealthy. We have connections to people in government and the highest echelons of the business world. Many of them have dubious connections."

He stares at me. Let him read between the lines. I can tell he's about to accuse me of being in a mafia—ahem, no, thank you very much. I doubt he knows how to distinguish the various syndicates. I'm proudly cartel—*the Cartel*—not some shitty little mob or mafia.

Never let the Mancinellis see their name associated with mafia with a lowercase m. They'll be quick to correct you. The only "legit" Mafia is from Sicily—*Cosa Nostra*—but they acknowledge other branches from mainland Italy and "allow" them to share the title. Pompous fucks.

The fucking mob and bratva—they're lucky they're smart enough to spell their own syndicates. Fucking morons across the board.

Liesel gives him a hard stare that makes him back down rather than challenge me. I can tell he's chomping at the bit to grill me or put me in my place. He'll wait until he can get me alone. Fortunately for him, this suite is well lit. Make it a back alley, and it'll be doctor heal thyself.

"My brother is gathering as much information as he can and sending it to me to analyze. I'm a certified forensic accountant. It's my job to examine financial statements and extrapolate what's going on from the numbers on the screen. If there's a money trail, my brother will find it, and I'll follow it back to where it started."

"Why?"

I cock an eyebrow at his sneering question. I watch Liesel squirm before I sweep my gaze across everyone seated together.

"Why wouldn't I? No one here asked to be thrust into this crisis. None of you are equipped to handle something like this."

"And you are? I doubt being rich and knowing other rich people is why you *think* you can handle this."

"Without being gauche discussing money, you need to understand who I am. By the time I was twenty-four, I had more money than you will make in a lifetime. More than all of you combined will make in a lifetime. I'm an astute day trader, and I invest my money wisely but aggressively. I study all potential ventures with a microscope. It means my businesses and investments do extremely well. My uncle is CEO of my family's company. He's led the organization for more than thirty years. My wisdom comes from watching him. He's amassed wealth even greater than mine. When you have what my family does, people get fidgety. They want what you have, and they don't always want to gain it legitimately. We've lost family members to rivals. We've had family members kidnapped by rivals. We take all threats seriously. We take protection details seriously. We don't tolerate anyone coming after people who are important to us."

"And why is Gunter—or is it my girlfriend—important to you?"

"Both. Investing with them could make my family's business close to a billion dollars in the next year. Gunter can't make that deal happen if he isn't around. I wouldn't expect Anne to focus on that while her father's missing. I need them both back to business."

"This is all about money for you?"

"It's motivating. I've witnessed people murdered and had to help rescue others. I wouldn't wish that on most people. I certainly wouldn't wish it on Anne, her mother, or her sister. Mrs. Schlossberg and the Ms. Schlossbergs deserve to have their family complete rather than grief. If I can help them, why wouldn't I? It's the right thing to do for them."

Let the little pissant question that. He'll come across as an ungrateful *carechimba* if he keeps pushing the issue. Without fail, he does just that.

"You've watched someone murdered." Bastian practically scoffs at me.

"I was eight when someone blew a hole through my father's head while he protected my two older brothers and me."

That shuts the fucker up. Finally.

Friedrich intervenes at the right moment. I'm certain he wanted to know the same things. He's just far more diplomatic.

"If Heidi and her family need six million euros, how will they get that? Will you lend it to them?"

"I'm hoping it won't get to that point. We made it look like Anne transferred a million euros to them as a deposit, claiming the Schlossbergs will pay the rest after an updated proof of life. It'll buy my brother and me time to see who goes into the account. It'll take leapfrogging to get back to someone local. It may take even longer if they're only in town for this. We need to hold them off for a while without angering them so much that they lash out."

Friedrich looks down at Heidi before meeting my gaze. "I can get that six million. It'll take a few hours, but I can do it."

I stare at him suspiciously. He matches my gaze, and there's more for us to discuss. But it'll definitely be a private conversation. He's got ties to someone or something. Glancing at Heidi tells me she doesn't know what it is.

"I can too. But I'd like to keep the least amount of money transferring hands as possible. Sums that large will raise red flags if it isn't a merger or acquisition or inheritance. I want this to remain a private family matter."

"Why is that?" Bastian just can't shut the fuck up.

"Because I'd like to keep Gunter alive."

Chapter Fifteen

Liesel

I'm ready to throttle Bastian. He's being jealous, and it's not at all appealing right now. He's never been possessive, to the point that I've sometimes wondered if he even cares. But right now, he's holding on to me as though I'm his favorite toy he's worried Jorge will snatch away from him. I need to end this fucking conversation and let Jorge get back to examining Papa's computer again.

He already went through mine. He found more questionable emails in the encrypted account, which he sent to his brother. Then he got into the rest of the banking information available on my computer. He connected his and mine and ran a program I didn't recognize or understand. He's been evasive ever since, and I want to demand answers.

That attitude won't get us anywhere. Perhaps if we were alone, I could push him to tell me more. But if I do anything like that in front of Bastian, he'll seize the opportunity to interrogate Jorge. I don't need them in a pissing match right now.

What I need is Bastian to stay seated and shut the fuck up and just hold me. His hug almost made the world feel right again, except it doesn't have the same reassurance it once did.

Not after the way Jorge's held me.

Then Bastian tried to pick a fight with Jorge rather than listen to our story. I don't like where his priorities lie right now. It feels selfish rather than caring and understanding—which is what I need—which is what Jorge's been. Even when he's questioned me, I've never doubted his support, whereas Bastian feels like he'll storm out if he doesn't get what he wants.

My stomach's in knots even more than it was before as I listen to the two men argue. My heart breaks all over again, and my head's ringing like a church bell. I am growing more discomfited and annoyed with Bastian as I listen to him going back and forth with Jorge. The latter reassures us all he wants is Papa to live, yet Bastian hasn't asked any questions about whether he thinks Papa's alive.

He hasn't tried to reassure me everything will be okay. No one believes it will be, but he could at least try to be sympathetic, if not empathetic. Jorge watches me, and I can tell he knows I'm getting more and more upset by the moment.

"How about the two couples go to the adjoining suite and get settled in? You'll find everything you could need there."

Jorge's mother's friend stopped by my apartment and Heidi's. She grabbed clothing for all of us before she went over to *Mutti* and Papa's house to gather things for her. Heidi and I gave her a list for our boyfriends. I know that'll freak them both out. Hopefully, Heidi and I can reassure them enough that they see the practicality of it. Otherwise, it'll be disconcerting that a stranger went into our places and rummaged through our belongings.

Heidi and Friedrich follow Bastian and me as we go into the hallway, then next door. I already have the keycard for the room. We look around, and it doesn't take long for Heidi and Friedrich to close a bedroom door. I'm certain they have more to discuss. I lead Bastian back into the bedroom that'll be ours and shut us in.

"Why are you being like this?"

"What do you mean? How am I being?"

"Bastian, the defensiveness. Why are you being like this? Jorge's just offered to help."

"Really? Because he looks like he wants to suck your pussy."

"Bastian, that's disgusting! How can you say something like that?"

"Because it looks like he wants to fuck you into next week."

"You're being ridiculous."

I'm positive Jorge's expression hasn't given that away. Just the opposite. It's not like he's trying too hard to pretend there's nothing between us. His expression and his tone toward me have been just as casual and somewhat impersonal as it has been toward Heidi and Friedrich.

Bastian's seeing things that aren't there, but I suppose he senses it. That or he's trying to stir trouble because he feels insecure. Maybe it's not even insecurity, and it's just he's pissed off that he isn't the center of attention for whatever rescue mission we might devise. Whatever his reasoning, it's pissing me off even more.

"Look, Bastian, you can either support me or not, but I won't argue with you, and I won't listen to you argue with Jorge. He's been nothing but kind. He doesn't have to help us, but he's spent the last two days trying to figure all of this out. He's asked his brother all the way back in the States to give up his time as well. They've both been working nonstop to help us figure this out. If you can't appreciate that, then I don't want to hear you say anything at all. You may not trust Jorge, but you need to be fine with his decisions because it's not your choice."

Bastian gives in with a loud sigh and a shake of his head. I head into the bathroom to get ready for bed. I'm exhausted and just want to forget today existed. Not that I can forget it any better than I can what happened yesterday. My mom, Heidi, and I already had dinner. Jorge picked at his food a little, but he didn't order a full meal like my family and I did. It's late enough, I'm positive Bastian and Friedrich have already eaten as well.

I came in here earlier and unpacked, laying out our toiletries on the counter. It's reassuring to have my toothbrush and my hairbrush. I take care of everything in the bathroom, then head to the dresser and grab pajamas.

"How the hell are those here?"

Bastian comes to stand over my shoulder, peering into the drawer, seeing not only my pajamas, but some of my bras and panties. He also sees his boxers.

"Jorge's mother's best friend lives here in Frankfurt. He's known her ever since he was born. She went to our place and Heidi's to gather things for all of us before she went to *Mutti's*."

"You just let a stranger into our apartment?"

"I did because right now what I want is to be as comfortable as possible. I want clean clothes and clean teeth so that I'm not sitting in my own filth and misery."

Perhaps I'm exaggerating a little, but that's the way I feel. Bastian's only putting me on edge more and more. He huffs but stays quiet for once. He goes into the bathroom and gets ready for bed as well. We climb under the covers, and he tries to pull me closer.

I consider the distraction, but I really just don't have the energy for all of this right now. His tone softens as he whispers in my ear, and I feel myself easing back into what seems normal with him.

"Let me take care of you, *mein Liebling*. You don't have to do anything in return. I'll get you off and hold you afterwards."

His hand cups my breast and kneads it before sliding down beneath my pajama pants and panties. His fingers inch toward my clit, and it feels so familiar to me. I'm enjoying his touch until I remember Jorge's in the suite beside us. My mind jumps to the things he suggested, the way it felt when he spanked me, how wet that made me. My body reacts to that, and Bastian clearly thinks it's his ministrations that are getting me horny. But he whispers to me again, and his German accent just doesn't sound right.

"That's right, *Liebling*. Open your legs for me. Let me get into that tight, wet cunt."

Suddenly, out of nowhere, I finally burst into tears. I haven't cried all day today, but now it's a deluge. Bastian freezes, and I rest my hand on his forearm. After a moment, I draw his hand away.

"Bastian, I can't do this. I feel so guilty thinking about enjoying sex or even just getting fingered while my father's probably being tortured. It just feels so wrong and so selfish."

He kisses my temple and pulls away.

"That makes sense. I thought perhaps I could distract you for a while, but I don't want to make you feel worse than you already do."

That's the kindest thing he's said to me so far, and I finally feel an ounce of reassurance from him. I won't admit it also doesn't feel right picturing the man next door. I know Bastian's a bit annoyed from his aggrieved sigh as he pulls back, but he holds me instead. He curls up around me and spoons me, just like he usually does as we fall asleep. I finally feel like he's the boyfriend I need.

I didn't sleep well again last night, and Heidi and I are barely eating this morning. Starvation prompted us to eat more last night, but reality sets in all over again with sunrise. None of the guys are much better than my mom, Heidi, and me. Everyone just picks at their food.

When I came into Jorge's suite, I could tell he'd barely slept last night. He's been going at it for two nights without enough rest. While Bastian talks to my family and Friedrich, I pull Jorge aside.

"You can't keep going like this. You look exhausted. Did you sleep at all last night?"

"I got in a few hours, but there's still plenty to do."

"You can't keep running on next to no sleep. You'll collapse."

He keeps his voice low as he responds to me, making sure he's angled so nobody can read his lips.

"*Chiquita,* I'm used to running on next to no sleep for days at a time. I'll catch up later."

Hearing him call me *chiquita* makes the world bright again for just a moment. It's the way hearing Bastian call me *Liebling* used to, but at a far greater degree.

"What are you two whispering about?"

Bastian stalks toward us and demands to know what's going on. He continues to pepper Jorge with questions he answers, but Jorge simply won't engage with Bastian, which only makes him increasingly irritated. It's my mom who steps in. She's withdrawn further, and I can tell she grows more despondent as the hours turn into days.

"Bastian, I really don't want to listen to this right now. Stop looking a gift horse in the mouth. Jorge's been nothing but polite and concerned for us. If you're going to pick an argument with him, then you can just go next door because I don't want to see or hear you if you're going to be like this."

My boyfriend turns toward me. "Then, Anne, you come with me, and we'll discuss more while we're alone."

"No, I'm not leaving my mom and sister right now to go discuss something with you I have no answers for."

"You won't discuss why a man brought you to his suite alone and is bending over backwards to help a practical stranger?"

I stare at Bastian for a protracted moment before I lose my ever-loving shit.

"Of course! He's actually useful!"

Everyone stares at me before I realize how horrible that sounds. I walk away from Bastian and Jorge. I need space from both of them, but I pass in front of the window.

"Anneliese, no."

Everyone stares as Jorge barks at me. It's a tone I haven't heard since we first arrived at the suite. I look around the room and know everyone senses something happened with us. Bastian storms off, slamming the door behind him and must march next door because we hear that door slam as well.

I'm so humiliated by his behavior. This tantrum is so unlike him. I'm positive Jorge would never behave like this. He wouldn't give anybody a glimpse into his emotions, and he'd never embarrass himself like that.

Jorge basically comes to my rescue when he suggests everybody sits down again, so we can discuss what he's found. He offers me one of his half smiles that's barely a subtle twitch of his lips, but it's enough for me to know he's still on my side. He walks over to the armchair he sat in yesterday, and I take the one that I shared with Bastian. It's far more comfortable on my own.

"I spoke to my uncle this morning. He's made some calls

as well, and we think we have a lead on who sent the messages, but we aren't positive yet. I need to go out this afternoon and follow up on this. I don't want to make any false promises or get your hopes up because I can't guarantee what I'll find, but I think we might be making progress."

This time he's not being evasive. He's being candid about the limitations to the information he's received. That's the best that I can ask for, all things considered. My mom, Heidi, Friedrich, and I watch TV. It's just ambient noise for us while we're all lost in our thoughts. None of us are really paying attention to the movie while Jorge returns to his work. He admits he has to get some things done while he waits to hear from his uncle.

As the morning creeps closer to noon, I haven't heard the door open to the suite I'm sharing with the others. My mom looks over at me and raises her eyebrows.

"I know. I'll invite him to join us. *Mutti*, he's not usually like that."

My mom didn't ask any questions aloud, but I'm certain she's thinking them. I call him, and he answers on the first ring, barely greeting me.

"I'm headed back to work."

"Bastian, I'd really like you to join us for lunch instead."

I slip into the bedroom Heidi and I used, realizing it's now Jorge's. He continued to let my mom have the bigger of the two bedrooms. I sense another argument coming, and I don't want to do it in front of the others.

"No, I feel useless here. There's no point in my staying when I could be helping people who want it."

That stings. I can't believe he just said that. It's like an alien possessed him. This isn't the man I thought I knew.

"Bastian, if you leave, I won't forgive you for this. I need you right now. If you choose work over me when you're already off, then we're done."

"Anneliese, don't issue me ultimatums."

"Then don't abandon me when I need you."

"You have Jorge."

"What I need is my boyfriend. What I need is the man I'm supposed to rely on and know is at my side no matter what."

"Well, I think you're putting all your faith in the wrong man. You got one photo yesterday and have heard nothing else to prove your father's alive. How do you know Jorge's not lying? He probably caused all of this."

My head might explode because my temper's about to.

"Then all the more reason to stay with me and make sure I'm safe. How can you walk out on me if you think I'm relying on a man who could order my father's hand be amputated?"

"Fine, I'm coming."

When we hang up, I hardly feel reassured knowing he's coming back. Is he doing it because I've guilted him into it? Is he doing it because he truly wants to help? Is he doing it because he believes I'll end the relationship if he doesn't?

As I consider that, I realize I truly will break up with him if he doesn't support me when I need him most. There's a light knock on the door as I head back into the main living room. A guard lets Bastian in. It's clear he doesn't want to be here as he reluctantly enters the suite.

He's scowling and bad-tempered, which makes the rest of us uncomfortable. My mom shifts on the sofa restlessly, and I can tell his attitude's upsetting her. I shoot Bastian a look I hope he understands means he needs to change his attitude. It just earns me a deeper scowl.

"Bastian, if you're going to be like this, then leave. You're not doing Anneliese any good by being foul-tempered, and it's just going to put the rest of us in an even worse mood. We asked Jorge for you and Friedrich to join us because we want to keep you both safe. But if you think you can do better on your own, then by all means, leave."

My mom's words shock me. They're a blessing in disguise, so it's not just me saying the same thing. It makes me feel a lot less guilty for sharing those sentiments. It doesn't entirely surprise me when he leaves in a huff, but that doesn't make it hurt any less. We hear the door next to ours slam again.

So much for lunch. Once Friedrich goes next door to check on Bastian and get some work done, my mom, sister, and I sit together again. My mother turns off the television, and I brace myself for what comes next. I'm certain it's nothing I want to hear, but it's something I should.

"Anne, you know we care about Bastian. We've welcomed him into our family. We've been happy that you found somebody you love and who loves you back, but he's proven today what I've always known about him. He's an inherently selfish man. He always put you first because he wanted something in return, like your time, attention, love, or to be praised by others. He'll do that if he gets something in return."

I swallow back tears, since this is painful to hear, and I know Jorge's listening. He appears preoccupied with work, but he's sitting too close not to hear. She takes my hand and squeezes it as she continues.

"I hate that it's something like this that proves who he really is. I pray we never go through another crisis like this, but better to know now than five years—ten years—twenty years down the road, and you've had to live with this."

I look at my mother, and I don't want to agree with her. I don't want to admit the last two years may have been a mistake, that the future I planned isn't the person I'll really get.

It's difficult to face my mom and sister, especially when I know my sister and Friedrich's relationship isn't perfect.

However, it's a hell of a lot better than mine is right now. Friedrich's been the model boyfriend through this, and not because he has eyes on him. That's just who he is.

I'd love to make an excuse and say Bastian's not great in a crisis. However, he goes to war-torn places and helps children who are on their deathbeds. He faces crises all the time. While those aren't necessarily personal like this is, he keeps his head on his shoulders and leads his medical teams. He does it without throwing hissy fits like he did today.

I'm not sure what to do with everything we've seen. Heidi says nothing, listening to my mom and me talk, but she's nodding the entire time. When my mom finishes speaking, I look over at her, and I want to believe it's sympathy, not pity, in her eyes.

"Heidi, have you felt the same way?"

Now she appears guilty. "Yes, I know Bastian's Friedrich's best friend, but there have been things about Bastian I've observed that I don't like. I've tried hinting at it to you, and it's not like you've shut me down, but you seemed oblivious to it and happy. So, I figured you were okay with how things stand. Friedrich and I have even spoken about it and discussed whether he and I should intervene. We haven't, but I'll be honest. Last night, we agreed that if Bastian didn't start helping you out and being more supportive, we would talk to you separately. Friedrich would tell him to pull his head out of his ass, and I would tell you to consider leaving him."

The weight of the world settles back on my shoulders, and it feels overwhelming to me just as much as everything else has in the past two days. Not only is my father missing, but now my relationship might draw to an end. And not just because of my attraction to Jorge. But because I'm seeing things about my partner I don't like. Things I've been blind to while everyone else around me saw them.

The three of us fall quiet while Jorge remains silent behind us. Another fifteen minutes pass, and I feel my stomach rumble. I run my hand through my hair before turning to the others.

"Should we order lunch? I'm actually hungry."

"Yes. Will you invite him back over?" I know my mom means Bastian.

"Yes. Maybe including him will calm him down a bit."

I doubt it. It didn't work with the first attempt, but I can extend the olive branch. I step into my mom's room in case he picks another argument. I picture the suite next door. It wouldn't surprise me if Bastian packed his things and then sulked, waiting for me to beg him to come back. Even waiting for me to apologize on my mom's behalf.

"*Hallo.*"

"Bastian, will you please join us for lunch? I really don't think you should leave right now. You can stay in the suite if you want, or you can come back here, but it's not safe for you to leave. If you do, you need guards along with you. That'll take men away from guarding us here as well as Jorge when he goes out today."

"Whatever, Anne, I'll take my chances. I'm not staying here to watch you stare at another man and watch him practically undress you with his eyes."

I know Jorge hasn't been doing that. He's been incredibly discreet, so maybe Bastian has picked up on something. Jorge's certainly not being flagrant or even inconspicuous. There just have been no outward signs.

"Bastian, I'm telling you this is not a good idea. If you leave, I won't forgive you for this because not only are you abandoning me in a crisis, but you're now putting all of us at risk."

"Don't bother. Nothing's happened since the day before yesterday. Nobody's approached Friedrich or me."

"You don't know that they aren't watching you, planning something. Something could already be in the works, Bastian, that we just don't know about. You really willing to take that kind of risk just because you don't like that a man is helping me? I thought you were more evolved than that."

"Well, I guess I'm not because as many ultimatums as you want to issue me, I can do the same. You should call the police. You should call your uncle. There're plenty of other options for you rather than having some narco-terrorist on your side. Get him to back off, and we all leave, or else I'm ending it."

Jorge might not be a narco-terrorist, but he is a narco-trafficker. I have no intention of correcting him.

"You cannot be serious right now, Bastian."

"I'm deadly serious right now. Either come with me and have your family leave him behind, and we call the police like normal rational people would, or we're done."

Rage fills me. If I had something handy, I'd lob it across the room. My death grip on my phone is all that's keeping me from hurling it at the wall.

"Then goodbye, Bastian. Pack your shit and get out of the apartment before I get home."

"You don't mean that, Anne."

"I mean it just as much as you meant your ultimatum. Or were you trying to manipulate me into staying with you by scaring me? Because I'm deadly serious right now. If you aren't too, then you played a hand you don't have. You've made your choices just like you said. You can do what you want, and I will too. I won't put up with your selfishness while I also try to figure out what the fuck is going on with my father and keep everybody I care about safe."

I take a breath because my voice is rising with each word, and I know the others can hear me.

"If you can't appreciate the one person who's helping us,

then I don't need you around. That says too much about your character for me to ignore."

It's obvious there were cracks in the relationship already, and this made those fissures open up as though an earthquake ripped through them. We're two tectonic plates rubbing against each other right now, and the pressure has pushed us apart. I don't believe there's any coming back after this without a major scar in our relationship. At this point it is what it is; it was what it was.

Chapter Sixteen

Jorge

I slipped into the other bedroom to make plans for this afternoon. I could hear Liesel arguing with Bastian. I want to throat punch the *caremonda*—face of a penis. I finish my call to my head guard. We've hammered out the logistics as best we can. I close my eyes and take a calming breath. I can't lose my shit in front of the others.

I head out to the living room to say goodbye. Liesel's already back with them. Friedrich came back, but I don't see Bastian. She rises and walks over to me. She glances at the door again. I feel the tension radiating off her as though it's my overcharged emotion.

"Don't worry, Anne. I'll make sure he has men with him. They'll be discreet. He won't know they're following him, but they'll be there if he needs them."

"Are you sure you can spare the men for that?"

"Yes."

I don't hesitate, but I know she's already getting to know me well enough to recognize my various expressions. She doesn't believe I really do, but I'm willing to. Not for Bastian's sake, but hers.

She glances in Gretel, Heidi, and Friedrich's direction before she keeps her voice barely above a whisper. "Please stop calling me Anne. He's not here anymore."

"And your mother and sister? Friedrich?"

"I don't care. It's comforting when you call me Liesel. I need that more than I need their approval."

"What else do you want, Liesel?"

A flush rises along her neck and into her cheeks. She shifts uncomfortably, and I have my answer. I wait for her to admit it. Will she?

"Jorge, I—you know—you. I want you."

"Then you have me."

"Can it really be that simple?"

"Why wouldn't it be?"

She assesses me for a moment, and she comes to a decision. "You really are practical by nature, aren't you? You'll make this happen, won't you?"

"Yes to both. If this is what you want, then you are mine."

"I have been all along, haven't I?"

"Since the moment we met." I want nothing more than to devour her to prove it.

We fall silent as Gretel approaches us. Neither of us is prepared for what she says, but I count it as a blessing.

"Jorge, take care of Anne. It's obvious to everyone. That's why Bastian was so angry. He knows he can't live up to what you offer Anne already. Sometimes it takes months, years to know when you've met the right person. Sometimes it takes only minutes. I don't know how things were when you met, but it's clear how they are now. Anne's never relied on anyone the way I see she relies on you. She's stubborn, so I warn you about that. But she'll listen to you because it's obvious you have her best interests at heart. You're doing far more than you have to. You're doing it for her. I can't tell you how much I appreciate you taking care of her, even if you couldn't come out and say it. Because you're protecting her, you're helping my entire family. Thank you. Be good to her. I don't know what your life is like in America, but I can guess. Protect her there just like you do here."

I'm stunned when she not only gives us her blessing, but she also acknowledges Liesel will likely come to the U.S. with me. I shift my focus to Liesel to see her reaction. She's just as taken aback as I am. She stares at her mother like the woman's sprouted a second head. Then she steps forward, and Gretel wraps her arms around her daughter. Liesel rests her head on her mother's shoulder, and it reminds me of when I do the same with *Mamá*. The world is set back on its axis, and all is right again when she hugs me.

"*Mutti*, I need to speak to Jorge alone."

Gretel nods. She glances at me, and I'm certain she knows part of the conversation won't include words. Liesel and I turn toward the bedrooms, but Heidi steps in front of us.

"I can only guess how things'll stand once this crisis is over. Maybe you'll both realize this isn't right. But I'm certain this is better than life would've been with Bastian. Even if you wind up alone, it'll still be better."

Liesel's lips twitch at the way only a younger sibling could say the last bit. It sounds like me with my older brothers.

"Thanks."

It's bliss when I slip my hand into hers as we walk to the bedroom. Bastian's arrival ratcheted my anxiety nearly through the roof, leaving me worried that Liesel might agree with him. My mind's inclination toward catastrophizing pictured her leaving with him, being injured, or killed. It pictured her rejecting me, both my help and me as a man. I've learned to control these obsessive thoughts that the worst-case scenario will be reality. My mind no longer runs away from me like it did when I was younger, but I still have my moments where my anxiety nearly paralyzes me. I've just learned to hide it. The Academy owes me an Oscar.

I ease the door closed before pulling Liesel back toward me. I press her against the wall beside the door. I rest my hand on her throat, not squeezing, but the possessiveness is clear.

"You earned another spanking, *chiquita*. Do you know why?"

"Yes. I walked in front of the window."

"You did. This time, you will be over my lap with a bare ass. Can you be quiet?"

"I can try."

Her teeth slide across her bottom lip as she considers what's about to happen. She glances down at my hand, then her gaze meets mine. I release her throat as I lean in to claim the first part of her that's mine. Our lips brush together before they fuse. It's only a few seconds in, and it's already the best kiss I've ever had. I cup her breast as my other hand slides between us to cup her cunt.

"Every part of you now belongs to me, *chica*. All of you. Inside and out, top to bottom, back to front. Whatever I wish to possess I will. I will fuck you when I want and how I want. I will make you beg and scream my name. I control your orgasms. They belong to me to give or deny. You will be the only one who gets all my cum. I will mark you—brand you with it. You will wear it and carry it inside your pussy and your ass. I will not share you. You are done with anyone else once you agree to this."

"And you?"

"I just told you that you'll get all my cum. What did you think I meant?"

"If you wear a condom, then that woman wouldn't get it. But they'd still get you."

I observe her. There's a tinge of fear in her eyes, but mostly, it's intentional antagonism. I box her against the wall. I refuse to let her move until I'm ready.

"You have my mind and my body and the one thing no one else has ever had. My heart, *chiquita*."

"You have me. Heart, mind, and soul too—"

She stops, and I wonder if she's considering a term of endearment. She arches her back, offering herself to me. She leans forward to whisper in my ear. We've spoken quietly enough no one could hear us, even with their ear to the door. It's conspiratorial and erotic as fuck.

"I know you'll protect me to your last breath. That's why I turned to you. Not because of your wealth and the resources I suspected you have. I know to the depths of my marrow, you will do anything to protect me. But will you really take care of me?"

"In ways you didn't even know you needed. I will give you everything you need, and I will always endeavor to give you everything you want."

She leans back and swallows as she reads my expression. She doesn't know the whole truth about my family, but she gets some things may pull me away, even if I don't want them to. She accepts this is her new reality when she slides her hands up my abs and over my chest until she wraps her arms around my neck.

"I'll do the same. I want to take care of you too. I want you to know you can turn to me no matter what. I suspect there are things you'll never tell me, and I hate knowing there'll be secrets. But I get it. I hope you'll let me in as much as you can."

The back of my fingers brush against her left cheek before I cup her jaw. I know I could fall in love with this woman. When I gaze into her eyes, I know we understand each other in a way no one else gets either of us. She leans in to whisper to me again.

"I know we aren't alone, but will you take care of my spanking now—Daddy?"

She breathes the last word, and my body's reaction shoots straight to my cock. I never imagined hearing a woman call me that would affect me so viscerally. It's never been my thing, but it is with Liesel. Our lips meet once more, and this time there's no denying we're together now. This isn't a gentle first kiss where we each test the waters. This is a claiming kiss that steals our breath.

"Strip, little one. Slowly."

I back away until I reach the armchairs that force me to skirt the window. I cock an eyebrow, and she understands my silent warning. Her spanking will be way worse if she forgets the very rule she's being punished for breaking.

She raises her shirt up her ribs, baring her creamy skin. I wait with bated breath as the hem grazes her bra. Her arms bend, and she lifts the garment over her head. She watches me as she drops it to the floor. I want to nibble my way from her hip up to her nipple, enjoying each smooth inch. She unfastens her pants, watching me as she lowers the zipper. She's not a professional stripper, but she's certainly put on a striptease before. My cock's throbbing.

She kicks off her shoes before she lowers her pants, letting those hit the floor too. Then she's just in her bra and panties. She reaches back and unfastens the clasp before easing the straps over her shoulders and down her arms, keeping the bra trapped in place. She's killing me slowly. I'm as eager as I was on my sixth birthday for *Papá* to take me on a special just me and him day to see the koalas at the zoo.

The piece of clothing joins the others on the pile before she shimmies out of her panties. This is the last time she'll wear any. Her ass looks good as she turns to let me see the flossy cloth between her ass cheeks before she's naked. She looks over her shoulder at me before turning to face me once more.

"Come here."

A moment's trepidation flashes across her face as I pat my lap. She's less confident than she was a moment ago. Does she fear me seeing her naked close up? Does she only fear the spanking? Is it both being naked and the spanking?

Do NOT catastrophize this and ruin it!

"Don't make me wait. Don't make me come and get you. I'll edge you into next week if you do."

She's horrified by my threat, making me chuckle. Her nipples tighten at the sound. When she stands before me, I tweak both hardened nubs. My hands grasp her hips and tug her forward until I can latch on to the right one. I suck like a starving baby. She moans, and my cock wants to skip the appetizer and get straight to the main course. But we have something to settle between us before we can do anything else. We also don't have that much time before her mother and sister grow uncomfortable.

I guide her over my left leg. I know from the last time that she'll kick her legs and stomp her feet. I wrap my right one over hers, pinning them in place. My hand runs over her ass, squeezing as I go. I love the plush feel of it as I prepare her for what's coming next.

"*Chiquita*, I didn't pleasure you after the last spanking because I already broke the rules of propriety by touching you. But you were already mine, even if I had to suffer through a night of you sharing a bed with another man."

"Daddy, nothing happened. He and I slept. I—I couldn't do anything because I was thinking about you."

I slip my fingers between her thighs, running the tips between her pussy lips. She's already so fucking wet. It tempts me to abandon my original plans, but she deserves the punishment. We both need it to return to our homeostasis. She must accept I set the rules when it comes to her safety, and I'll enforce them however I see fit.

"Normally, I wouldn't let you get off after a punishment—which I hope I don't have many to dole out in the future—but this is our first opportunity to be together. I don't want to miss the chance to see you come because I made you. I also don't want to leave things unresolved."

"Unresolved? You mean horny and miserable."

"Yes. Hold my ankle like you did the last time if you're tempted to reach back. I will spank each side ten times. You will count them. Then you will come when I command it."

"Yes, Daddy."

I groan as I squeeze her ass particularly hard. She squirms, but when I bring my hand down on her right ass cheek, she freezes.

"One."

I spank the same spot a second time.

"Two."

I land a combo on her left cheek then her right. She gasps as she tries to kick her legs.

"Count, *chica*."

"Three, four."

I land two quick ones across both sides.

"Five, six, seven, eight."

I gather cream from her pussy and rub it over her clit, making her grind against my thigh. She'll wrinkle the pant cuff if she continues to clench it in her hands. She whimpers when I pull away, but her back arches when I land the hardest slap yet across her left ass cheek.

"Nine!"

"Shh, *chiquita*. Do you want your mom and sister to investigate?"

"Good God, no."

I land another and another until we reach twenty. She has a light sheen of perspiration along her hairline and between her shoulder blades. Her ass is a bright pink as I feather my fingers over the skin. She shivers before I lift her to straddle my lap. I keep her cunt away from my dick because I can't take the temptation, and she'll leave a stain. I widen my legs enough for her ass to rest between them.

"You took that so well, little one. I'm proud of you for this and for how you've handled everything so far. I hate knowing how you feel, but I do. You never have to ask for my help. You will come to me when you need me to hold you. When you need me to make the world go away for a while. It's my right and my privilege."

"Do I have the same?"

"Absolutely. I want no one else, Liesel. I only want you."

I slip my fingers into her, stroking the inside of her cunt. She swoops in for a kiss, and I'm certain it's smothering her moans as much as it is desire. My thumb rubs her clit until she rocks against my hand, clearly begging for relief. My arm wraps around her waist as I lift her off my lap, my other hand continuing to work her. I lay her on the bed, and she draws her feet up to the mattress. She lets her legs drop open as I drop to my knees. I add my mouth to my ministrations as I work to get her off.

I want us to do so much more, but we're not alone. We don't have much time. I'm certain Gretel and Heidi have guessed what we're up to. I have enough sense not to fuck Liesel, but I don't have the restraint not to get her off again.

"Daddy."

That breathy whisper makes my cock rebel against the constraints of my boxer briefs and pants. I want to thrust into her and come. I want to pound her pussy until she begs me to stop because she can't take any more—then begs me to do it all over again. I want to see my cum drip from her cunt, knowing she's truly mine. The more I let myself fantasize, the more possessive I feel.

"*Sí, chiquita.*"

"So sexy."

"*¿Que?*" What?

"The Spanish. Your accent. It's so se—Fuck, Daddy. Please?"

Her hips buck off the mattress when I slide three fingers into her and caress her G-spot. She moans when my free hand presses on her belly, the added pressure intensifying the sensation. I rake my teeth over her clit before sucking. Hard.

"Come."

"*Ja,* Daddy."

We both lapse into our native languages. Our thoughts are too crowded by instinct to worry about what we're saying. We understand each other without words. Liesel's cunt contracts around my fingers, and I watch her abs flex. Her fingers grip the bedding as her orgasm makes her entire body tense. With her hips off the mattress, I grab her ass, separating her cheeks until my fingers can press against her puckered hole.

"This will belong to me tonight, Liesel. I will fuck your mouth, your cunt, and your ass. You will take my cum in all three places. I will mark your tits with it and brand you as mine."

I watch her to see how she reacts to the dirty talk. She

reaches for me, and I stand. She grasps my shirt with both hands and tugs. When I lean over her, she reaches for my belt. She's frantic as she tries to unfasten it.

"Pick where you want to do it now."

I swallow my groan as I catch her wrists in my hands and pry hers loose from my clothing. I pull her to sit up before I lift her into my arms. I sit where she was just lying, curling her against my body.

"If I fuck you now, we'll get nothing else done today. Plus, your family is waiting for us. We don't need to make it even more obvious."

She glances toward the door. "Do you think they heard us?"

Chapter Seventeen

Liesel

What the fuck am I doing? I broke up with the guy I live—lived —with all of five minutes ago, and I'm already naked with another guy.

He's not just some guy, and you know it.

I may not have technically cheated, but I nearly did. Now, I'm blowing off my mom, my sister, and my dad to get off. I'd blow Jorge if he'd let me.

"Liesel, it's all right to have a few minutes to escape all of this. A few minutes to feel good before facing reality all over again."

I gaze up at Jorge, and I marvel at how he knows what I'm thinking. Maybe my expression says it all, but I don't think so. I think he just gets me. Maybe he's been in so many shitty situations—dangerous ones—that he's learned how to cope with them. Maybe he's learned it's okay not to be in a panic all the time. I don't know, but those explanations make me feel justified. Otherwise, I'm the shittiest person alive.

As much as I want to revel in that escape, we can't. With a sigh, we stand, and I get dressed. We both check our appearance in the mirror. I smooth back my hair and twist to look at the back of my clothes, ensuring I look the same as I did when we came into the bedroom. Jorge adjusts his rolled shirt sleeves for the same reason.

"Are you ready, *chica?*"

"Yes, Daddy."

We head back into the suite's living room. My mom and Heidi smile, but neither of them makes it awkward. At least no more awkward than it already is, since I'm certain they know things have progressed between Jorge and me. We're not a family where parents and children discuss sex lives, but my sister and I have both lived with men. My mother's not ignorant, and I just disappeared into a hotel bedroom with a man for at least twenty minutes.

I do my best not to wince when I sit, but my ass is definitely sore. I can tell my mom and Heidi want to know what'll happen next, but neither of them wishes to ask in case it reveals Jorge and I haven't devised a plan. I'm just about to open the conversation to make it easier for all of us when Jorge's phone buzzes.

He pulls it from his pocket and glances at the door after looking at the screen. He answers, and it only takes a moment for me to realize it must be one of his guards.

"Something's arrived, and it's addressed to you, Anne. I'll take a look before anybody brings it in."

He needs to stop calling me that now that there's nothing to hide.

"No, I want to know what it is regardless."

"I'll tell you the truth, but I think it would be better if I find out first."

"No, we all have a right to know what it is."

He puts the call on speaker, and the guard describes a small package that arrived. Apparently it's barely larger than a ring box. Jorge's expression tells me he believes having this call on speaker is the wrong decision. He wants to shield my family and me from whatever the next shock will be. The guard switches to Spanish without prompt. He speaks so rapidly I can't understand him—not that I speak enough Spanish that I would if he spoke slowly.

Jorge says little more than thank you before hanging up and walking to the door. I follow, but he only opens it wide enough to see out and to receive what the guard hands him. His shoulders are far too broad for me to see around, and despite my height, I can't see over his shoulder to know what he received. I observe his arms move, and I can tell he's opened the package. He nods before stepping away and closing the door emptyhanded.

"Jorge, what is it? What's in the package?"

My questions are more demanding than I intended. I know how rude they sound, but if he received something from Papa, then I want to see it, even if it is grotesque. After all, my father's hand is truly chilling in the fridge right now.

"It was an eyeball."

Before he can say more, my mom screams. He walks purposefully to her and offers her a comforting embrace.

"Mrs. Schlossberg, it wasn't your husband's."

"What?" It's Heidi who asks the question the rest of us are thinking.

"It was a pig's eyeball."

"How can you be sure?" It's my turn to pose the obvious question.

"Because a pig's eyeball has a thicker cornea, and the iris is larger than on a human's. I could tell just by looking at it that the iris wasn't from a human eyeball."

He steps back from my mom, and I realize he has a piece of folded paper in his hand. I move to stand beside him and my mom. We shift to make room for Heidi to see as well.

THERE'S NOTHING WE DON'T SEE.

My gaze locks with his, and I shudder. Queasiness washes over me as I consider the truth of that warning. Before any of us say anything else, my computer pings on the dining room table. I step away and unlock it with my fingerprint.

I really need to remove the biometrics and revert to a password.

I open my email, and there's a folder attachment. "Jorge, I'm uncertain whether I should open it."

Not only do I fear seeing what I might find inside, I worry about a virus or malware being downloaded onto my computer.

"Let me forward this to Joaquin and see what he says. We won't open the folder. He can do that safely."

He taps his phone screen and puts it to his ear as I step aside and gesture to the laptop's keyboard. I watch him forward the email. It must have only rung once or twice when Joaquin answers. Jorge is quick to explain the situation. We wait in silence as Joaquin must receive the email. I can't tell if he's speaking to Jorge or not.

Jorge's watching me, his attention solely on me, even though I'm certain he could tell you how many times my mom and sister have breathed in the last thirty seconds.

"*Está bien. Gracias.*" Okay, thank you.

Jorge hangs up and slides the phone back into his pocket. I notice a new email comes in, and he clicks on it. He opens the folder, and I can't swallow. My gasp escapes before I can stop myself. My mom and sister rush forward. I twist the laptop toward them, and they spy the photographs sent to me.

There are ones from within this room but were clearly taken from outside. There are photos of Bastian and Friedrich being picked up, and even ones of them arriving at the loading dock here. There's a photo of Bastian returning to the hospital.

"How did they get pictures so up close?" All the colors drained from Heidi's face as she speaks.

"Drones. I feared a telescopic lens from one of the other nearby windows, but the clarity through the flimsy curtains tells me the camera was just outside the window. As for the photos of Bastian and Friedrich, it's obvious these people knew to watch them, assuming you'd contact them, or they'd come to you. I've arranged for guards to be with Bastian, so he's not alone."

I nod my thanks.

It's odd to consider the man I'm now involved with providing security for my ex-boyfriend, who was my boyfriend up until an hour ago. Everything about this situation feels like it's either on warp speed or slow motion. Nothing feels like it's happening at a normal pace. Time has taken on a different value than it had three days ago. With photos taken this clearly, the threats escalated.

Exponentially.

"I refuse to risk anyone's safety beyond what's already happening. It's time to have my family come and help. It will take a day for my brothers or cousins to get here. I'd prefer to get all of you out of Frankfurt, but I can't do that immediately."

There's a knock on the door, then it opens before Jorge can say anything. He immediately reaches toward his lower back. We've all grown accustomed to the sight of his gun holstered there since he stopped wearing his suit coat yesterday. He relaxes as Friedrich walks to Heidi and engulfs her in his arms. I knew she was texting him as we waited for the return email.

"Friedrich, I'm going to ask for a couple of my family to join us to help me with this, since things just escalated."

My sister's boyfriend glances down at her before looking at my mom, then me. He appears in two minds whether he should say what he's thinking, but he goes for it.

"My family is from Essen in the West. We've owned a major commercial construction firm for three generations. It means we've created strong business ties to many different groups in our community, employing workers from all different ethnic backgrounds."

My brow furrows as I wonder what he's getting at. I shift my focus to Jorge, but he doesn't appear perplexed like I am, just the opposite. He seems to already know where this is going.

"Friedrich?" It's my sister who asks for an explanation with just one word.

"We have connections to the Camorra."

"As in the mafia? Friedrich, how do you know anybody in organized crime?"

Heidi sounds doubtful, but considering what we've learned about our family in the past two days—and what I'm certain she's guessed about Jorge's—it seems like a bit of an asinine question at this point.

I don't know much about the Neapolitan mafia beyond the organization's name, and that nobody wants to tangle with them.

"Do you remember Maximilian?"

"You mean your best friend growing up? Yeah, of course."

"His father heads the Camorra in Essen. My high school girlfriend's uncle and father are also high-ranking members."

Heidi's surprise registers across her expressive face, but Friedrich shifts his attention to Jorge.

"Like I've said, I can get the money quickly if we need it."

I wait for Jorge's reply as he studies the man who's likely to be my future brother-in-law. He offers an appreciative smile but shakes his head.

"I knew all of that about your family already. My brother dug deeper into your family's background after you made the offer the first time. For now, I'd prefer we not use those connections until I can learn whether they have any ties to Salvatore Mancinelli. The Mancinellis may be *Cosa Nostra*, but they'll still pick an Italian organized crime family over mine. I need to be sure involving your connections doesn't wind up playing into Salvatore's hand and giving him more information than he needs, whether he's connected to this or not. I'd rather the four of you go to my mother's friend and stay with her and her husband until my family can sort out a better solution."

When the woman arrived, I was unprepared for a Moroccan. Jorge's mother met Noor Idrissi while going to college in California. There was something familiar about her, but I still haven't put my finger on it.

"Jorge, I don't want to endanger anybody else. Isn't there somewhere else we can go that doesn't draw more people into this?"

"Noor is married to Hisham Azizi."

I take a step back, unprepared for Jorge to name one of the wealthiest financiers in Frankfurt who's known for ties to Moroccan organized crime. There're always whispers he's some type of crime lord disguised by his refined custom-tailored suits. I've met him a couple of times, and I've always been slightly awed by his entire aura.

He's not flashy.

He's not menacing.

He's just there. He fills whatever room he's in with charisma.

It's no surprise so many people accept his investments or want to work with him. There's a sophisticated nuance to him.

The kind where I'd trust him with my millions, but I'm not sure if I'd trust him to buy me a drink or trust him not to put a bullet through someone's heart.

"Will you go there with us, Jorge?"

"No. I'll see you settled there, but it's best if I remain here. That way I can visit if I need to, but I can also meet with my brothers or cousins when they arrive. I can't be seen coming and going from their home too frequently. My mother and Noor have been photographed together many times over the years at various events. I'm certain plenty of international law enforcement agencies have photos on file of Noor and Hisham vacationing with us, but that doesn't mean I need to raise any red flags that will draw attention to you. They can get you into their house discreetly."

I hate the idea of him leaving me. It leaves a sour taste in my mouth as I consider the approaching evening. The sun won't set for a few more hours, but just the thought of the unknown out there in the dark and being out of Jorge's reach terrifies me. I feel heat rising along my neck as bile burns the back of my throat and makes my gums sting. It suddenly feels far too hot in here. When I swipe my hand across my forehead, I feel the sweat.

Invisible weights press on me from every direction, and the air is becoming too thick for me to breathe. No matter how deeply I try to inhale, there doesn't seem to be enough air to fill my lungs. I'm growing lightheaded and reach out to hold the dining room table to brace myself.

Jorge's arm slides around my waist. "*Chica.*"

I don't know if he's whispering or speaking at a regular volume, but his voice sounds distant and soft even though he's right beside me. I offer a shaky nod, but panic wells in my chest, spreading out behind my ribs, creating a burn that makes me want to rub my fist over my sternum. My ears are ringing. My vision's tunneling to a narrow focus right before my eyes.

"*Chica.*"

I turn a blank stare toward Jorge, once more shaking my head. I feel the tears welling in my eyes, but I no longer feel like I'm controlling what's happening. My breathing's labored and uncomfortable. He guides me to the sofa, and my mom and sister sit on each side of me while he perches on the end of the coffee table. He takes both of my hands in his, rubbing the outside of them and squeezing them rhythmically.

"Liesel, look at me. Liesel."

"I hear you. Jorge, please don't leave me."

"I'm not going anywhere."

His thighs bracket mine, and I lean as far forward as I can to rest my forehead against his shoulder.

"I won't go anywhere without you knowing where it is."

"No, not good enough." I struggle with each word.

"I have no plans or moves to make until my family gets here."

"No, don't leave me. I—need—you." I stumble over those three words as I sob.

My mom rubs her hand up and down my back. "Maybe Anne should just stay here."

Friedrich's been quiet and unobtrusive since he arrived, but he speaks up. "If being away from Jorge's going to give her a panic attack, I can take Heidi and Gretel to your friend's house. You can stay here with Anne. If anything changes, then you can bring her to us, or I can come back and get her."

Friedrich's offer registers with me, but I have to turn it over in my head a couple times before I understand what he's offering. He's been the rock I expected Bastian to be. Instead, that piece of shit turned out to be a pebble in my shoe.

Jorge grips my shoulders and eases me back before cupping

my face, holding it in place, so our gazes meet. "Liesel, do you want to stay here with me while they go to Noor's house?"

I nod.

I feel incredibly selfish, but as hard as this has been for my mom and Heidi, it's still all new to them. I've been carrying the weight of all of these hidden manipulations for years now, and the incessant danger is pushing me beyond my breaking point. The only thing holding me together is Jorge.

"Jorge, can I really stay here with you?"

Chapter Eighteen

Jorge

"Yes, *chica*. You can stay."

Liesel's panic attack unnerved me since I recognized what was happening all too clearly. I've had more than enough of them to recognize when one's starting. Hers wasn't nearly as bad as it could've been. It made me wonder if she's had them before. The moment I realized what was happening, instincts screamed to call Bastian and have him come back to check on her in case he was familiar with what hers are like. But since she was able to control it, and it didn't wind up being that severe, I'm glad I breathed through my own rising panic.

Sensing she needs time alone with me, the others disappear. Gretel goes into her bedroom to gather her belongings, and Heidi and Friedrich go back next door to pack theirs. Heidi offers to gather her sister's things as well. Once we're alone, I lift Liesel onto my lap. She kicks off her shoes and burrows against me.

"I'm sorry about that, Jorge."

"You never have to apologize for needing me. I promised you I would be here. I'm on your side. I'll protect you and support you any way I can."

"Thank you, Daddy."

She whispers those three words as she turns to look in the bedrooms' direction. Gretel's closed her door, so I'm certain she can't hear us. I stroke hair away from Liesel's shoulder and lean forward to kiss it before kissing along her neck up to behind her ear, I press my lips close to the shell, and my warm breath makes her shiver.

"That's what daddies are for, *chiquita*."

My hand glides down her back to cup her ass. It rests heavily there. Tempting as it is to squeeze, I'm certain she's still sore from earlier. I gaze down at her, and her eyes drift closed as she relaxes fully against me. Her breathing is even and calm now. I'm not convinced she's asleep, but she's dozing. I do my best to avoid disturbing her as I shift and pull my phone from my pocket. With my arms boxing her in and my screen behind her, I text Joaquin.

ME

Friedrich offered help through his connections to the Camorra.

My brother's response comes three minutes later.

JOAQUIN

You knew he would.

ME

Yes, but it surprises me how quickly he made that offer. Can you look into whether that family has ties to Salvatore or if anyone has been speaking to him recently?

JOAQUIN

Of course. It'll take me a little while, but I can
work on that right now.

ME

Those photos freaked me out.

JOAQUIN

I bet they did. We can be on a flight in 20
minutes.

ME

You already gassed up the plane.

JOAQUIN

You saw I included Tío Enrique when I sent
the clean version of that folder back to you.
There was definitely spyware on there. He
ordered our pilots to be on call. He's waiting
for you to ask. But only because he trusts you
have the sense to do that so he doesn't have
to send any of us.

ME

Just you and Alejandro for now.

JOAQUIN

Pablo and Javier can come too.

ME

I don't want to pull them away from their
wives if we don't have to. They're both still
newlyweds.

JOAQUIN

True but Florencia and Madeline understand.
It's not like Pablo and Javier haven't traveled
without them.

ME

I know but those trips haven't been into the
unknown. They were dangerous for sure but
not without some reassurances.

Our texts flow back and forth quickly. As much as I'm typing, I'm doing my best not to disturb Liesel as she rests against me.

JOAQUIN

Fine. I'll speak to Tío and see whether he agrees with you. Regardless we'll be there in about nine hours.

ME

Thank you.

It's nearly an eight-hour flight when there's no headwind. My brother's building in an hour's buffer to get everybody to the private airport on Long Island and get wheels up.

Liesel's eyes pop open when she hears the bedroom door open. She doesn't scramble to get off my lap, but her cheeks pinken as she turns toward her mother. Gretel takes it with aplomb as she watches Liesel and me rise from the sofa.

I stand with Liesel in front of me with my left hand on her outer shoulder. Not only am I trying to be respectful in front of the mother of the woman—I don't even know how to describe my relationship with Liesel—I guess the woman I'm seeing—but I'm also using Liesel to hide my raging hard-on.

Fortunately, I've never been into tight trousers, but it wouldn't take close examination to be able to tell my cock's at attention. The suite's door opens, and Heidi and Friedrich step inside with their belongings. Heidi wheels a small suitcase over to where Gretel still stands near the bedroom doors.

I know we can show up unannounced to Noor, and she'll make space available for us, but I prefer to be more courteous than that. I excuse myself to the bedroom where I make a quick call to let my mother's friend know what's going on and to ask if I can bring the others over. It only takes a few minutes to make the arrangements.

I consider whether to send them without me. It feels rude to do so, but it would certainly be far less conspicuous, especially if these people continue to take photos. I have no way of knowing who else might see these pictures right now. For all I know, whoever this is could also be sending them to Interpol or the FBI. It's one thing to be seen at public events with Hisham. It's another to be seen going to his house.

It's never been overly concerning to us for anyone to see *Mamá* hanging out with Noor or to even have people see us on a yacht vacationing together. It's different when you have questionable guests over to your main residence. That starts to raise eyebrows. I return to the living room after I hang up with Noor.

"Guards will take you to Noor's house. Her husband, Hisham, is there right now. He worked from home today. They have more than enough space for you. You should be well fed and comfortable while you're there."

It doesn't take long for Gretel, Heidi, and Friedrich to say their goodbyes and leave with a set of guards to drive them in one of our SUVs. I pull up the tracking app and show Liesel. We can watch the dot while they head to Noor's house. Relief washes over Liesel's face before she wraps her arms around my waist. It seems so inconsequential, but I knew it would reassure her.

"Are you hungry, little one?"

Our meals never seem to happen at the right time.

"I am. Hunger keeps hitting me in the quiet moments when something goes wrong, and I forget I haven't eaten."

"Do you want me to order you a cheeseburger?"

I waggle my eyebrows and grin. She huffs, then nods.

"Yes, please."

After I've phoned in our order to room service, we both glance at our computers. She looks toward the refrigerator, and I'm certain she's wondering about the box inside. Once she's asleep, I must give it to one of my men to deal with. It can't stay in the fridge much longer. It's already been compromised. They won't dispose of it, but they'll know what to do to store it.

Grizzly is the only word that comes to mind. If I hadn't been around such extreme violence my entire life, it would be enough to send a shiver along my spine. Instead, all I can do is heave an imaginary sigh and move on.

Neither of us really focuses on the TV show I turn on while we wait for our food. Neither of us is chatty as we eat, but we don't mind the companionable silence. Once our trays are cleared away, I extend my hand to Liesel and lead her from the sofa to the bedroom.

"Strip."

The single word command startles her. There's more authority in my voice now than when we came in here earlier for her spanking. It's my Dom voice. She scrambles to obey, pulling her clothes off and hurriedly folding them, unsure where to put them. She holds them in front of her chest as though they're a shield. Her confusion about the shift in my tone is obvious. I've hardened my gaze and watch her. Her gaze sweeps around the room before she deposits the pile of clothes at the foot of the bed.

"Come and kneel before me."

"Yes, Daddy."

Her answer slips from between her lips with no thought. Her gaze darts around, but she refuses to look up at me once she's kneeling. I do nothing but watch her. She fights to remain still, but it's clear she doesn't know what to do. I know she wants to see my face, hoping she can read my expectations. At the same time, she doesn't want to give in to that temptation. She wants to maintain control over her willpower.

The minutes drag on, and her confusion pulsates from her. It takes a solid five minutes before her shoulders relax, practically drooping before her chin tucks, and she sighs. I cup her chin, and my thumb strokes over her cheekbone. She looks up at me.

"Such a good little *chiquita*."

A smile twitches at her lips, but she fights it. She lowers her gaze again and leans her cheek against my hand. I twist my wrist so I can tunnel my fingers into her hair rather than support her chin, but my thumb continues to stroke her cheekbone. I do nothing more than that.

I'm certain her mind is buzzing as she tries to guess what I want or what I'll ask next. The unknown is scary, but the longer I remain a silent presence, the more I feel her relax under my hand. The tension in her neck eases, and her head bobs twice before she lets her chin dip to her chest.

With each passing minute, she relinquishes more control to me, putting her faith in me, knowing whatever happens next, she must go with the flow since she's naked and kneeling before me. Either are a sign of submission in this dynamic. Together, it proves I lead, and she follows. I don't underestimate the enormity of her trust.

"You are so beautiful and strong, *chiquita*. I could watch you all day and all night."

"Thank you, Daddy. I wouldn't mind watching you all day and night either."

"Have you knelt before anyone else?"

"Never."

"Have you ever been handcuffed or restrained? Was the other day your first adult spanking?"

"Yes. I mean, I've had my hands held above my head a few times and gotten some playful swats during sex, but nothing like what you've done."

"Do you have any experience with power exchanges?"

"No, not really."

Her inexperience somewhat surprises me since she fell into our dynamic so easily today and the day before yesterday when I spanked her for the first time. A hint of wariness niggles in my mind since I've never introduced anyone to BDSM or power dynamics. However, I can admit—even if it's only to myself—that it's a wave of pride and ego that goes along with knowing I'm her first.

I'm fucking certain I'll be her only BDSM partner.

I wouldn't be doing a fraction of what I am if this were something just between friends or if I wanted to fuck her and forget. This is absolutely more than that.

I help her to her feet as I consider what needs to happen before we go any further. I unbutton my shirt and strip it off before helping her slide into it.

"I don't want you to get cold, and I find you far too distracting. When we aren't being intimate, you can always push back against what I say or do. You are my equal in every-thing, all the time. But when we're behind closed doors, I lead, and you follow. You follow my commands, but only because you want to. If I ask something of you that makes you uncomfortable or you can't do it, then you need a word you can use that makes me stop immediately. No questions asked, no trying to change your mind, nothing. It just immediately ends.

I observe her carefully as she considers what I'm saying.

"Sauerkraut. Does that work?"

I grin. "Yes, *chiquita.* As we get to know each other's prefer-ences and thresholds, we'll move slowly. Is there anything you can think of that you definitely don't want to try?"

She stares at me wide-eyed before she responds.

"I'm not really into the idea of taboo bodily fluids, but I don't mind sex during my period."

Her cheeks flush, and her gaze darts away.

"I feel the same way. I've spanked you pretty hard, but only with my hand. Are you curious about other implements?"

"Implements?" Her voice squeaks slightly on the last syllable.

"Whips, crops, floggers, spoons, belts, canes, birch."

"I don't know. Nothing that would leave any scars."

I draw her against me, my left hand cupping her ass.

"Look at me, Liesel."

I wait for our gazes to meet.

"I would never forgive myself if I did anything that resulted in permanently marring your skin. It would mean I was careless and disregarded your well-being. It would mean I harmed you. The things we share might hurt, but I will never harm you. I wouldn't deserve your trust and your faith in me if I were so reckless."

"I know, Daddy."

Her response is barely more than a whisper. If we stood apart, I wouldn't have heard her.

"Is there any part of you that's more sensitive to pain than others?"

"Not anywhere unusual from most people, I suppose."

"Okay. Is there anywhere you don't want to experiment with pain?"

"I don't know. I guess not."

"What about hot and cold? Any sensitivities to those?"

She shakes her head.

"I need to hear you, Liesel. When we're like this, you need to speak. I have to be clear on what you're communicating to me. There can be no room for me to misunderstand."

"I'm fine with hot and cold."

"What about sound and light deprivation?"

"I think I'm okay with both of those as well."

Her hands have come to rest at my waist. They're warm

and soft against my bare skin. I'm no man whore, but I've been with enough women to know what I'm doing and have enjoyed myself plenty of times. No one has felt as right in my arms as Liesel does.

"Are there any positions that are a hard pass for you?"

"No, not that I can think of."

"Very good. Do you have questions for me right now?"

"No, but I'm sure I will in the future."

"All you have to do is say your safe word, even if we're not in the middle of some type of scene. If you want to shift our dynamic to us having a conversation between equals, then you say sauerkraut, and we discuss whatever's going on."

"You spanked me because I risked my safety walking in front of the window. Will there be other rules for me?"

"Yes. They'll be about your safety. There'll be guidelines on where you go and how many guards need to accompany you. I won't keep you from doing things or going places. That's not my intention. My purpose with rules for your safety is so you can continue to do all the things you want without coming to harm."

"I can appreciate that. Will there be rules beyond ones for my safety?"

"Perhaps. We'll have to figure that out as we go along, *chica*, and we see what works for us. I'm not looking for a Daddy Dom/Little Girl situation. I won't give you a bedtime or insist you eat your vegetables. I won't punish you if you go out without your coat or want to stay up late or feel argumentative with me when you're frustrated or having a bad day. But perhaps we'll come across things as we get to know each other better, and we decide to make a rule out of them. I don't know. If we do come across something like that, we'll discuss it."

"Thank you, Jorge." She watches me for a moment, uncertain whether she should use my name.

"*Chiquita,* you can call me whatever you want. We might have a budding relationship that includes a power dynamic and BDSM, but I'm not your Dom, even if I'm dominant. You're not my sub, even if you are submissive. You don't have to call me sir or master or anything like that. In fact, I would hate it if I heard you call me master. That's just not how I envision things with you."

"But what if I wanted to call you sir?"

"Why does that appeal to you?"

"I'm not entirely sure. I like the idea of the deference when we're like this. Especially when I'm naked or mostly naked and you're clothed. I'm not somebody who enjoys feeling vulnerable—not that I think anybody really does—but I feel safe with you when I'd feel vulnerable to the world. It's the same as when I was kneeling naked a moment ago. I know how vulnerable I was, but being with you made me feel protected. I wasn't scared. I was intrigued."

I ease the shirt off of her and toss it on the bed next to her clothes. I thumb her nipples before tugging and pinching.

"What intrigues you?"

"The curiosity and uncertainty of what's going to happen next, and that I have no control over it. I don't have to make any decisions. I can just be in the moment, that I'm not protecting myself. I'm not shielding myself from some emotional, intellectual, physical threat. That you'll do that for me, and I can just be at peace."

"That's precisely what I want you to feel."

She bites the left corner of her bottom lip before lowering her gaze to our feet.

"You promised you'd fuck my mouth earlier, and I'd really like to do that now, sir."

I point to the floor, and she lowers herself to her knees.

"And why is that? Do you think you can bring me to my knees by sucking me off?"

"There's a certain feeling of empowerment, knowing I can bring you that kind of pleasure. But that's not all of it. I like the idea..."

She pauses as she gathers her thoughts.

"Take your time, *chica*."

"I like the idea of kneeling before you to do that rather than, say, lying between your legs on the bed or even kneeling beside you on the bed. It's like I'm offering you something. I know you don't expect tit for tat. You're not helping me to get something from me...But I feel so limited by what I can do right now to express my appreciation...To give you control and to give you pleasure through that control—I don't know. It—just... It—feels—exciting."

Her explanation's halting. She stumbles over her words, pausing at the end of nearly every sentence as she continues to think aloud.

"Unfasten my pants, *chiquita*."

She reaches out and grasps my belt. It only takes a moment before my pants are open, and my boxer briefs are pushed down. She wraps her hand around my cock and strokes.

"Take me in your mouth and suck until I come down your tight little throat."

Chapter Nineteen

Liesel

The weight of his cock on my tongue is divine. I'd like to think
—I hope—I give good blowjobs. They don't top my list of most
enjoyable sex acts, but I don't mind them. With Jorge, I'm eager
to do this. If I can make it even a fraction of how good it felt
when he went down on me, then I'll count it as a success.

I've wondered about his dick since I met him, and now I
can see and touch it. Taste it. The man is proportionate. He's
tall and broad shouldered, so his dick suits him. That thought
tempts me to chuckle, but I concentrate as I run my tongue
from his balls to the tip. I flick the slight opening before sinking
my mouth onto it. I draw back slowly, teasing him as I go.

I shift my position to make it easier to take more since my
goal is to make him come without using my hands. I've clasped
them behind my back to fight the temptation to stroke him
while sucking. He doesn't rush me, so I breathe easily. I do my
best to relax my throat and not gag as I push to swallow him.

I've only done that a couple of times with guys in the past, and it was more by accident than on purpose. It never lasted more than a couple seconds before intuitive panic kicked in.

My eyes are closed since there's little to see at this angle, and now I want to concentrate. I think about every blowjob scene I can remember from romance books and porn. I think I'm getting it right from his periodic groans. They're deep and rumble. Uber masculine. They make me feel desirable and appreciated in a way words or even touch can't. It's on a primitive level that seeps into my bones. It's like I'm coming alive for the first time in—I don't know how long.

I work his shaft, licking and sucking until I have to come up for air. I pull back for a moment and finally shift my focus to look up at his face. I release my hands, ready to give in and stroke him, so I can rest my jaw for a moment.

"No hands."

Jorge's fingertips feather up from the crook of my neck to behind my ear. He weaves his fingers into my hair before easing my head forward. I need no more prompting to wrap my lips around his cock. I tease him with how slowly I slide down his dick. With another deep inhale through my nose and a leap of faith, I work to swallow him.

You want to submit, and he wants to dominate.

Show him you trust him more than you can put into words. Show him you're his to enjoy.

Make him come like he did you.

I want this for him and for us. Whether I can swallow a guy's dick was never symbolic of anything to me before. I didn't care whether a guy thought I gave *the best* head as long as they thought I gave great head. I don't think it's the same insecurity which prompted me to sleep with some guys in my past that I now know I could've lived without. It made me feel good about myself at the time. In this moment, I want to prove something to myself as much as I do Jorge.

I want to prove to myself that I can let go. That I can accept that moment where I feel out of control—the urge to pull away or gag when he slides down my throat—and know that I can push through it. That I can be patient enough to do this with just my mouth rather than rushing through this like I do most things—moving from one task to another—everything very transactional. That I can be in the moment and not thinking about what'll come next—what this is a steppingstone to.

Who knew a blowjob was the metaphor of your life?

"Fuck, Liesel. I'm fighting not to come yet."

I keep my eyes closed, so he can't see how I revel in that. He presses my head to him and thrusts a little harder. He'd been letting me do most of the work, just rocking his hips here and there. But now he's fucking my mouth. He's not rough. I'm certain he's being careful with me while shifting the balance of control. He's let me have my turn leading, and now he's back in charge. It's well-timed as my jaw starts to ache from being open for so long.

"You're going to swallow my cum, *chiquita.*"

I hum my agreement. He pulls back slightly to make it easier for me to take his more forceful thrusts. When I open my eyes and look up, I find him observing me. He's aware of my comfort even in the middle of getting off.

"Rub your clit and finger yourself, *chica.*"

I can't focus on my body enough to gain any relief, but I discover I'm dripping wet with arousal. He plays with my right nipple, rolling, pinching, tugging before squeezing my breast.

"Fuck, yes. *Fuuuuck.*"

I taste his cum as the first few jets hit my tongue. I work to swallow as fast as I can to keep from feeling like I'm drowning. He pulls out and jerks off twice, giving me a pearl necklace with the last few ropes of cum. I swipe my finger through it and smear it on the nipple he just played with before pushing up my breast and licking it off. He bends in half and sucks on my other nipple.

I'm unprepared for him to wrap his arm around my waist and lift me off the floor. His other arm comes around me, underneath my ass, guiding my legs to wrap around his waist. He moves with such ease, it surprises me. I scramble to grasp his shoulders. I'm tall and solid. I don't know any other man who could maneuver me like this without it being awkward. Instead, it feels graceful the way he moves me the way he wants.

"I won't drop you."

"I know."

He carries me to the bed and sets me down. He steps back and sheds the rest of his clothes. I pull down the covers then scoot away, making room for him. When he climbs in beside me, I recline. He follows, wrapping his arms around me as he presses his body against mine.

"You had me seeing stars, little one. That was—that was—"

He shakes his head and smiles. I left him speechless!

I cup his cheeks and press a tender kiss to his lips. Nothing exists beyond him as the kiss deepens. I love the feel of his tongue invading my mouth. The way his everything forces me to only focus on him. I open my legs, and he shifts to lie between them.

"I have an IUD, Jorge. Even though I'm on birth control, we used condoms most of the time too. He and I were both paranoid about me getting pregnant before we were ready. As far as I know, I'm clean. I haven't tested since before he and I got together. But we both did back then. I have no reason to question whether his results changed. If he ever slept with someone else, I'm certain he wore a condom. He knows too much about STIs not to."

I don't want to mention another man's name while I'm in bed with Jorge. But he deserves to know.

"I've never had sex without one. I don't date. I haven't had a girlfriend since I was seventeen. I had a couple of regular partners, but they're not romantic. I always wore condoms with both women."

A spark of irrational jealousy spikes through me.

Two?

Sure, I had a live-in boyfriend who I had sex with multiple times a week. But hearing he fucks two women...

At the same time?

"Had, Liesel, not have. Wore not wear."

"Huh?"

"Past tense. They may not know it's over, but it is."

"Are they your subs?"

"When we roleplayed, yes. I didn't have vanilla with either of them. But I don't have contracts with either of them, and they weren't daily relationships. We'd meet for sex. Nothing more."

"Are you friends with them?"

"Friendly. But we don't text or call to shoot the shit. We don't hang out, and they aren't who I'd turn to if I needed something. I will end things with both of them in the morning. I would have done it sooner, but honestly, I haven't thought about either woman until now."

What more can I do than nod?

"Thank you."

I guess I can at least say that much. I've never had a conversation like that. I suppose they're fuck buddies, in a way, but getting glimpses of what a D/s relationship must be makes it feel more substantial than just fuck buddies. But what do I know?

"I don't do random hook ups, Liesel, so I don't have any condoms. I can get some delivered if you want."

"And I didn't have sex in random places, so I don't carry one either."

"I test regularly because I'm a member of a BDSM club. That's where I went with them. I had to provide regular proof that I'm healthy. I tested just before I left New York, and I haven't been with anyone since then. Do you want me to order some?"

"It would be the responsible thing to do."

Neither of us sounds thrilled at the prospect of waiting. I reach between us and stroke his semi-erect cock. The tip's been pressing against my pussy, making me want to squirm. I love the feeling of his lips feathering over my collarbone then up to the crook of my neck. He kisses the side of my neck until he gets to my earlobe. He flicks it with his tongue then tugs with his teeth. My hand moves faster, my hold tighter, as he lengthens against my palm.

"I want to feel your cunt wrapped around me. I want to slide into your smooth, warm, wet pussy and never leave. I want to make you beg then make you come. I want to fill you with my cum and watch it drip from you."

"Fuck, Daddy. Yes. I want to feel so full. I want to feel like you're going to tear me in half because you're so big. I want you to fuck me so hard that I'm sore tomorrow."

I move my hand out of the way, and Jorge pushes up onto his hands. I tilt my hips, and he thrusts into me. I'm so wet that it's easy for him to slide in, but I'm still tight enough that the friction is mind blowing. We're watching each other, and we both register that sublime moment when our bodies become one.

"You've always been mine, Liesel. It was just a matter of time. But now that I'm inside you, there is no denying you belong to me. I will fuck you hard, and I will fuck you often. I will be gentle, and I'll be tender whenever you want."

Does he mean we'll make love and not just be kinky?

"Not just when I want, Jorge."

"I'm not used to vanilla, but I want it with you. Only you."

My chest tightens, and it's not just from the exertion of moving with him as he pounds into me. He keeps offering more of himself than he does with any other woman. I'm certain of it. He may have spanked others in the past, but I doubt it was for their safety. It might have been a punishment but in the context of a roleplay scene, not because he cares about their real-life wellbeing.

"Only me, Daddy."

He shifts to slide his arm under my right leg. He rears back, lifting my leg up to his shoulder as he kneels. He grasps my hips and moves with such purpose that I can't keep up. He pummels my pussy. The angle allows him to slide so deep into me that there's nowhere farther for him to go. He bottoms out, pausing and flexing his abs each time. Then he slides back, and I see how my cream makes his cock glisten before it disappears into me again.

Over and over.

It would be hypnotic if not for the arousing pain from each forceful thrust. His body is a scientific marvel. I see the scars that came from bullets and blades. They're mostly covered by tats, but I feel them as I run my hands over his chiseled body. Knowing how arrogant he can be—no—how arrogant he can come across—it would be easy to think he works out and stays in shape for his ego. Maybe he even believes in the health benefits. I think it's more than that.

The air of danger that's always accompanied him along

with the lifestyle I'm piecing together make me think he's in shape to protect himself. The scars tell me he's mortal and can't outrun a bullet, but I think he's tried. I think he's bareknuckle fought plenty of times and has used his strength to save others. I can only speculate because I doubt he'd tell me the truth if I asked, but my intuition says he lives with far more danger than I'll ever fully know.

Can you live with that?

Can you live with him possibly dying?

Can you live with the danger you'll be in? Things are beyond your wildest nightmares right now. What if this is tame for his lifestyle?

I'll deal with it when I have to. Right now—right now, I want to come.

This isn't the time for more deep reflections. I've done enough of that since the moment I opened my mouth to him. I've been in my head, and I've needed to work these things out. But now I want to just enjoy the sex. I want to enjoy the connection without worrying about the whys and wherefores.

"I'm close."

"Me too, little one. But don't come yet."

"But—"

"I said, don't come yet."

"Yes, Daddy."

Fuck that's hot.

He lowers my leg, and I shake my head in protest. He slaps my tits. *Hard.* The sound rings in the room.

"Don't tell me no, *chiquita.* I'll fuck you however I want."

He pulls out and flips me onto my belly. I push my hips up, ready to move onto my hands and knees. He surges into me with enough force to flatten me. His body presses into mine, and I can't believe how erotic it feels to have him encage me between him and the mattress. My fingers splay before they curl to grab the pillow. He covers my hands with his, and I relax my death grip. His fingers slip among mine. He rocks his hips at an excruciatingly slow pace. I want him to keep jackhammering me.

"You are my *chica*. I will make you come when I'm ready. Or did you forget how badly you want to submit to me? Did you just say all of that to lead me on?"

"What? No. I meant all of it."

"Then your memory isn't very good."

"I want what you want. I just also really want to come."

He chuckles before nipping my right shoulder.

"Do you feel how much bigger I am than you?"

"Yes."

"Can anything get to you without going through me first?"

"No."

"Do I control what happens to your sweet little cunt right now?"

"Yes."

"Then keep trusting me to take care of you, Liesel. If it's too much, safe word."

"I'm just impatient. I trust you, Jorge. I enjoy how you take care of me."

"I know, baby girl."

He rocks faster, and his height presses me into the mattress. I do my best to rub my clit, but I can't get enough friction.

Grrr.

Just as I'm about to get frustrated, he lifts his body from mine. He kneels between my legs, keeping his thrusts deep but much slower. His hands roam over my back and shoulders, rubbing and massaging until I relax. He kneads my ass cheeks, and I sigh.

"Good girl."

He pulls out, and I look over my shoulder. He guides me

onto my hands and knees as he moves to lie beside me. His hands grip my waist, and I straddle his hips. I moan as I slide onto him, yet another position where he's impossibly deep. We move together until we find a rhythm that works for both of us. My clit grinds against his pubic bone as I rock.

"Please, may I come?"

"Yes."

I lean over him, my hands beside his head as I concentrate. The sensation starts within my pussy and moves into my lower belly. Then it explodes.

"Fuck!"

"Fuck, Liesel. I'm coming."

We ride our high together as his hands hold me in place. His fingers will leave marks as they dig into my ass. My heart's pounding as I suck air in through my nose that burns as it fills my lungs. I can't hold myself up since my arms are shaking. He eases me to lie on top of him. I pull my legs up, and my head tucks against his shoulder, sharing the pillow. His hands stroke my ass and back as we both settle.

Fuck. If that wasn't the best sex of my life, then I don't know what was.

"*Chica?*"

"Yes?"

"I didn't know it could be like that."

His voice is soft and almost mystified, like he's unsure what just really happened. I kiss his neck.

"Oh?"

He tenses for a moment, and I realize that was utterly the wrong response. Damn. He thinks it wasn't that special to me.

"Jorge, it's never been like that for me."

It hasn't. It wasn't just the most physically fulfilling sexual experience I've ever had. It was being with him. We knew what each other needed without saying it. The emotional connection was deeper than I've had with anyone else, yet we don't even know each other that well. I'm scared to read more into it, but he felt it too. I thought maybe I imagined it, but it's real.

My phone rings, breaking the mood. I can't afford to ignore it, so I peel myself off him. I hate leaving his arms, but I stretch toward the end of the bed. I pull my phone free and look at the screen.

This is not who I want to talk to right now.

Chapter Twenty

Jorge

I know before she even answers who's on the other end of the call. Her expression tells me everything. Then the fact she puts the phone to her ear rather than on speaker confirms it's Bastian. I keep my expression impassive, not wanting to show how much it irritates me. But an outsider looking in would say Liesel and I are the fucked-up ones in this situation, and I don't really have a leg to stand on to feel pissed that he's interrupting our first post-coital bliss.

"*Hallo?*"

She answers in German and continues on after he greets her.

"I was rushing for the phone."

Fuck, I bet he noted she sounds a bit breathless. I have to wonder what he's saying to her as I sit through the silence. I'm not a fan of silence when someone else controls it. I'm happy being on my own and don't need noise to fill my surroundings. I work best when I can utilize intimidation rather than having to physically mete out justice, so silence is my preferred tool. This might just drive me crazy.

The urge to catastrophize creeps back into my mind. It's been years since I've had to fight the urge so frequently. I feel myself growing anxious as I wait for Liesel to reply. I breathe through my increasing heart rate until I calm.

"Thank you for checking on me, Bastian. We're all fine."

He says something that makes her brow furrow.

"That's none of your business. We aren't together anymore."

Liesel remains at the far end of the bed, and I'm certain it's to keep me from hearing any of her ex-boyfriend's side of the conversation. I've noticed her habit of biting the left corner of her lower lip when she's too anxious to be aware of showing her emotions. I offer her what I hope is a reassuring nod. I see some of the strain leave her face, but she's certainly not as relaxed as she was a few moments ago when she was draped across my body.

"Bastian, we've discovered things about each other we don't care for, and they are insurmountable. You left, and I told you what would happen if you did. That wasn't about having time to cool off. You made your choice, and it wasn't to support me or my family when I needed you. This has nothing to do with anyone else and everything to do with just you. You don't like what you decided, and now you regret your choice, but that's entirely too bad."

She remains quiet for a moment before offering me a reassuring smile. She's placed her trust in me earlier, and now it's my turn to reciprocate. I have to have faith she won't go back to him. Nothing she's said so far makes me think she will, but to my core, I am a realist. I know that when all of this ends and whatever new normal appears, she may decide she acted rashly, and I'm not who she wants after all. As a person plagued with enough self-doubt on my own without various situations adding to it, I am familiar with these niggling questions and uncertainty. Fortunately, I know how to push past them, so I employ all those learned skills right now.

Liesel takes the phone from her ear and puts the call on speaker. I don't know if it's to avoid feeling like she's being rude, or she fears I might think she's keeping secrets, or she wants moral support because of what he's saying now. Hearing his voice on the phone makes my hands fist, a reaction I usually control, but it gets the better of me this time.

"You ended this just so you could fuck that piece of shit mafioso. What? Did you think his dick would be bigger than mine, so you wanted to go for a ride? You're going to regret this choice when he goes back to the States, and you're left behind with nothing and nobody. He's probably behind all of this anyway. You'll have no one to blame but yourself when he gets you injured. Do you think I'll cry over your grave when he gets you killed?"

I can't disagree there's truth to what he's saying at the end. I know there is. Even after this ends, danger will be ever-present in Liesel's life now that she's with me. I observe her expression and body language as Bastian continues. She's tense and scowling off into space. It's clear she hates what he's saying, but I know she's intelligent enough to recognize the partial truths in what he's spewing.

"Bastian, enough. Jorge has nothing to do with this. It was about your choice not to support me and take my side in all of this."

"He has everything to do with it. Even if he's not responsible for this, you chose him first."

"I chose a friend who has the means to help. It doesn't mean I didn't want you there beside me."

It's my turn to look away. That's hardly what I want to

hear. Liesel crawls back to me and cups my cheek and shakes her head. I get what she's trying to convey. It doesn't mean she didn't want him there. It also doesn't mean she did. She's trying to make a point about his failure as a boyfriend. I get that. I remind myself of how conflicted she must feel. This isn't clean cut for her.

I have no one else to consider or worry about. I have nothing to leave behind like she does. I wish it were as simple for her as it is for me.

Could she have chosen me out of convenience? Was the spark of attraction already there, and then her need for my help, coupled with physical desire, be the reason why we wound up where we are? I don't believe so. Sex wouldn't have been the way it just was if that were the case. But it's hard not to question this entire situation.

"Bastian, I won't argue with you over this. There's no going back. I want you to move out. If you refuse, then I want you to take over the lease."

She offers me a tentative smile as she mouths, *I know I'm moving out anyway.*

Could she have already considered and decided to move back to America with me?

"Don't worry, I've already started boxing things up. I don't want to be here the next time you are."

"So, what was the point of this call, Bastian? Were you trying to trick me into admitting something to beg for you when you have no intention of reconciling? Or are you packing because you're having a tantrum?"

"I'm packing because calling was a last-ditch effort, hoping you'd come to your senses, but you clearly won't. You're making a tremendous mistake, and the only mistake made was on your part."

"You've made this about you when worrying about a relationship falling apart is the last thing I need right now."

That makes me wonder if there would have been anything between us if Bastian proved to be supportive. Once more, I wonder if she's turned to me because she doesn't have another option for support, since her mother and sister are just as mired in this as she is. That is a hard pill to swallow if that's the case.

"I won't have a conversation like this with you again, Bastian. You've been an important part of my life for two years. I hope we can get to a point where there's no hostility, since it's inevitable we'll be around each other because of Heidi and Friedrich. I don't want to make them miserable just because things didn't work out between us. But for right now, it would be better if we go our separate ways. I need to focus on one crisis at a time. Goodbye."

"Fine, Anne. Have it your way."

The call ends, and Liesel tosses her phone behind her. Once again, silence fills the room. I want to give her time to work through her thoughts and feelings. I don't know what she wants or needs from me, so the best I can offer is slipping my hand under hers and entwining our fingers. It's the nudge she needed. She inches forward, looking at my lap. I open my arms to her, and she settles against me with a sigh that feels soul-deep. I hate that she needs comforting, but I'm glad she wants it from me. I stroke the hair down her back as she listens to my heartbeat. I can tell it soothes her.

"Jorge, I know parts of that sounded bad. They sounded ungrateful and as though I'm with you merely out of convenience, but that wasn't the case. This isn't an ideal time to begin a new relationship. But this is when life presented me with this opportunity, and I'm not willing to let it pass me by. So, some of those things I said weren't to appease Bastian but were rather half-truths to make a point. This situation showed the weaknesses in my relationship with Bastian. It was already broken. We just didn't know that. It's unfortunate it came to light the way that it did, but it's better I know that now than not. You could've been a woman with the resources to help me, and I wouldn't have fallen into bed with you. Our attraction already existed before everything exploded. He and I would've split up regardless because he just wasn't the man I needed him to be during all of this. He made his choices, and so have I. Let's face it, you and I wanted each other before any of this ever happened. Inconvenient? Yes. True? Also yes. Something was brewing between us all along."

She leans away to look me in the eye and cups my cheek, brushing her thumb over my afternoon scruff. The way she anticipates my thoughts and addresses my worries before they take root surprises me. Surely this proves our connection isn't superficial.

"His choices right now made it easier for me to recognize he isn't the right person for me. Maybe you and I would've connected. Maybe we wouldn't have, but I think it's inevitable this relationship would've ended because having any thoughts of being with someone else shows we really weren't meant to be together. If I could be drawn to you or someone else so easily, then I couldn't be that truly in love with him. What I've felt with you tonight is something I never have before. The ease of being with you was unlike my past. I can't overlook that has to have been a sign. I'm sorry if this hurts Bastian. That certainly wasn't my intention, but he doesn't seem to feel any remorse for the pain he's causing me, so I refuse to allow any guilt to dictate my choices. I wish it could've been different, but it isn't. So, I'm moving forward with us, if that's what you still want."

"Of course it is, *chiquita*. I'll always want it to be us."

When we lapse into more quiet, it's not uncomfortable. Just the opposite. I think we share a sense of peace. The call certainly changed the mood, and I don't know that she wants to jump right back into fucking the night away like I'd originally hoped. The exhaustion slams into me harder than it has in a long time.

Now that I'm able to cradle her against me, skin to skin, without worrying about her family or a boyfriend, I'm allowing the enormity of finding a woman I may spend my life with, along with the dire situation with her father, to catch up to me. Near sleepless nights aren't unusual, but I'm only human. At some point, I always have to catch up. Holding her is the most comforting thing I've ever experienced, so I find the need for sleep pulling me under.

"Little one, how are you feeling?"

"Super tired all of a sudden."

Neither of us suggest postponing sex. Instead, we move together. I slide down until my head is on the pillow. She snuggles next to me; her arm draped over my ribs. My preferred sleeping position is on my side or stomach, but as I doze off, I've never been more comfortable than I am now.

Chapter Twenty-One

Liesel

The sun's peeking around the curtains when my eyes open. Immediately, I know Jorge's already awake. His thumb's grazing the back of my shoulder absentmindedly. I tilt my head back and feast my eyes on the most handsome face and hottest body I've ever seen. He leans forward and brushes such a soft kiss against my lips that I almost don't feel it.

"*Guten Morgen, chiquita.*"

"*Guten Morgen,* Daddy."

Our next kiss is so much more potent. It's the opposite of the one we just shared. This is laden with passion and the unsatisfied need that began last night. He guides me to sit up. I'm ready to straddle him, but he turns me to face away from him as he sits up too. We can see each other in the mirror as I climb on reverse cowgirl.

"Watch us, little one, see what I can see. Look at how gorgeous you are. Not only first thing in the morning, but every moment of every day."

Oh my god.

I'm mesmerized by the erotic scene playing out before me. My tits bounce with every rise and fall. His right hand grips my hip as his left one kneads my breast. He's not as deep as he is when I ride him facing the other way. Without stimulation on my clit, I know I won't come. I think he's banking on that. This is its own kind of foreplay. It's winding us up for whatever he decides will come next. I can't help but be curious about that even though I want to live in the moment and not wish away what we're doing in anticipation for what will come next.

"Daddy, this is so fucking hot."

It's not like I haven't had sex in this position before, but it's the first time I've watched myself do it. It tempts part of me to be critical of what I've always seen as physical flaws. However, it's nearly like an out-of-body experience. I'm watching a porn of two other people moving in perfect synchronicity that are completely enthralled by what they're doing.

I've watched enough porn over the years to know what's good and what isn't, whether it's amateur or professional production. I'd call this top-notch. If I were a mere spectator, this with a vibrator would definitely get me off. We stare at our reflection, not needing to say anything else. I'm just basking in the physical enjoyment. I want to emblazon this in my memory.

I'm certain he could keep going in this position until he comes, but he realizes that isn't what I need in order to get off, that I need something more. He lifts me off of him and lays me flat. He scoots back down the bed before licking my entire pussy from my asshole to my clit.

His tongue toys with my clit before thrusting inside me. My moans fill the room, and I can smell the sex. I'm usually not fond of the scent, but this only adds to the entire experience as he laps me over and over again.

I once bought one of those sucking sex toys out of curiosity to see whether it really could replicate a mouth. It was fantastic on my nipples, but only mediocre on my clit. It didn't always get me off. If that toy manufacturer had designed it based on Jorge's skills I wouldn't have lasted more than thirty seconds.

"May I come?"

"Yes, *chica.*"

This is a slow building orgasm. I can feel it creeping up on me. It doesn't hit me like a raging storm like the ones from last night. This is a gradual ache that grows into a burn, and then it becomes pleasure radiating through me.

Sex is like an existential experience with this man. It makes me question everything I've known in the past, everything I've thought about my own desirability and how I've reacted to other men. I've had a healthy sex drive for more than a decade but being with Jorge is making me wonder if I was really just hibernating. It's almost like a sexual awakening is taking place. Perhaps that's because I'm with somebody I'm truly sexually compatible with. I pray we turn out to be this compatible beyond sex.

He moves up to my chest, straddling me and pushing my tits together. His cock rests in the valley. With each forward glide, I lick his tip. I catch my breath when he retreats. I open my mouth, my invitation clear.

"If I let you suck me off right now, I won't last."

"That's fine. We can do this again and again. I want to make you come just like you did for me. I want it to be as good for you as you make it for me."

"Much of my satisfaction comes from yours. I get a rush out of watching your orgasms, knowing they belong to me."

"They do. Gladly. I feel the same way, Jorge. Please don't deprive me of that right now."

"I want to fill your pussy and your ass, little one."

"I want that too, Daddy. I'm so wet for you that you could use me as lube."

He moves back until he's between my legs, then thrusts into me. I'm like a fucking slip and slide right now. He moves back and forth a few times before pulling out. I wait for him to flip me over, but instead, he lifts my legs, pressing them toward me. He's so careful as he eases into me.

I know he's studying my reactions to every moment he presses his thick cock into my tight asshole. I know he had women he was with, and I know he's into at least some BDSM. It's probably his experience as a Dom that makes him so aware. He gives me a moment to adjust once he's inside of me. It's not like this is the first time I've done this. It's not like past partners haven't been careful with me, but this is just different.

He just studies me like a hawk. I know he's attentive to every breath I take. It makes me feel so incredibly special and cared for that my heart aches a little. To say he's a generous lover is an understatement. When he begins moving, I moan.

"Safe word if you need to, *chiquita*. Never take more than you can, just for my sake. I wouldn't forgive myself if I harmed you, and it will make it hard to trust you if we ever want to do more than vanilla."

"I know. Jorge, thank you."

His thumb works my clit, and I realize he's the first guy I've been with who's just known what rhythm I need. I can't help but wonder if that's a testimony more to his experience with women than intuitively knowing my body. But whatever the reason, I'll take it. It's not mine to reason why. This is one of those times where I'm happy to just go with the flow. As I get closer, his thrusts speed up, and I know he's almost there too.

"I don't know that I can hold on much longer."

"Neither can I. Come for me, baby girl."

I gladly follow his command and tip over the edge into bliss. I feel him come before he goes still. Then he's easing out of me with just as much care as when we started. I squeeze my ass cheeks, but I know a little dribbles out of me. He watches as though he's fascinated by what he sees. Maybe he is. He's done the things he swore he would do. He's come down my throat, across my chest, in my pussy, and in my ass. He helps me off the bed.

With a nod, I hurry out of the room and into the bathroom for a moment of privacy. We'll need maid service to come. It was hardly ideal, him giving up his bed to my mom that first night. But at the time, we were all exhausted. We had house-keeping come in the next day, but none of us loved the intrusion. My guess is Jorge wouldn't have let them in at all during his stay if he didn't need them to. I'm positive he values his privacy above most things. I do too.

When I head back into the bedroom, I find him on the phone, and this conversation seems to be going better than mine did.

"Yeah, come straight here. Liesel and I will be waiting for you. I don't have any news… All right, I'll see you in thirty."

I'm about to meet members of his family under less than auspicious circumstances. It would be intimidating regardless, but this is almost overwhelming. While I was in the bathroom, he wheeled my suitcase in. I'd forgotten all about it last night since we didn't exactly prepare for bed the way you normally would.

"Joaquin and Alejandro are here. They just landed."

"What're they like?"

"Joaquin looks just like me except bossy."

That makes my eyebrows shoot straight up since I could easily describe him that way too.

"Alejandro is the pretty one in the family."

That makes my brow furrow. How could anyone possibly be more attractive than Jorge? I tried checking out his social media after we first met. It was fairly limited, mostly pictures of him working out, but not your typical flex photos. There were also pictures of him out hiking and playing tennis. Several were of him at polo matches, but I never got the sense he played. All of them are carefully curated not to have anybody recognizable in the background. It's as though his social media exists because that's the expectation for somebody his age, not because he enjoys it or feels compelled to overshare with the world.

"I need to check my email, little one, so as much as it pains me to say, you take the first shower. That way I'm not distracted by temptation, and I can get some stuff done before my brother and cousin arrive."

I playfully pout but nod.

"I'll need to do the same thing."

I've taken unexpected days off, but I still have duties to my clients, so I'm checking emails throughout the day. We've told the staff that we had a family emergency with someone in Brahm, and that's where Papa has been. It just happened to coincide with me catching a cold, or so people at the office believe.

The half an hour between Jorge's phone call and his family arriving feels like it was about thirty seconds. He's barely out of the shower before there's a knock on the suite's door. He goes to answer it, and two of the most remarkable men I've ever seen walk in. In an instant, I can tell which one is Joaquin. He couldn't be confused as Jorge's twin, but the resemblance is strong.

And Alejandro—makes any fashion model look like some schlub off the street. Okay. He is the pretty one. Maybe I would've been attracted to him if I'd never met Jorge. But it's everything about Jorge that appeals to me. His looks and his sheer presence. It's different from Alejandro because I don't get a sense his cousin is as introverted as Jorge. It doesn't make him as mysterious as my man.

My man. Fuck if that doesn't sound good.

Jorge greets them with hugs that last longer than most would deem manly. It's obvious how close he is to them. His embrace with Alejandro is just as sincere as the one he shares with Joaquin. If I didn't know better, I'd think he and Alejandro were brothers not cousins. I think they were likely raised that way.

"This is Anneliese."

It still sounds odd when I hear him use my full name. He hasn't done it since we first met, and that was rare. I love my name. I think it's beautiful, but I prefer Liesel with Jorge. I've never loved Anne, but some time in elementary school, it became a default.

"Hello. How was the flight?"

I shake both men's hand, and their smiles appear genuine. It puts me at ease. I wouldn't want to meet either of them as shadowy figures in a dark alley, but they're relaxed and friendly here.

"We're nepo-babies, so a private jet makes travel easy."

Joaquin grins with his self-deprecating comment. I've hated being called that because of my executive position at the family firm. I've shied away from it, but these three men appear to own it. I don't doubt they all contribute to their family's businesses— legal or otherwise.

"Thank you for coming. I—"

A lump forms in my throat. The benefits of a few hours of intimacy with Jorge to forget what's happening slip away. It crashes back down on me when I recall—again—that these men are only here because we need more help than Jorge can do on his own. He pulls me into his embrace and kisses my forehead.

I know he's looking at Alejandro and Joaquin, but I have no idea what their silent communication means. I can see the other men's faces, but I can read nothing from them.

"You matter to Jorge, so you matter to all of us. Not quite the welcome to the family we'd like to offer, but we'll do everything we can."

I tense and feel him do the same.

Welcome to the family?

I can daydream about that, but we live on two different continents. I'm set to inherit a family business I can't easily run remotely. Not without making trips back here every few weeks. That's not the kind of jet-setting I'd like. Could I walk away? After this and what I've dealt with, I think I could.

But Jorge and I haven't spoken about the future beyond saying we want to be together. Considering me a member of the family is a tremendous leap. The idea warms me from my chest down to my belly and out to my limbs. It makes my cunt ache for him again.

"Thank you."

"We should sit down and review everything. Liesel, you need to tell us more about what's happened since the supposed Parisian syndicate approached you. Beyond the bank transactions and emails, did anyone start acting differently toward you?"

Jorge steers the conversation away as we walk toward the sofa and armchairs. He lifts his arm from around my waist to around my shoulders as we settle beside each other on the sofa. The men fill the chairs as though they're thrones when they put their arms on the rests. They cross their left legs over their right, and I have to wonder if that's a family genetic trait because they do it so naturally and identically.

I know my father's secretary was the leak who shared the Diaz Holdings investment intentions, but I don't know that she has the means to pull off a plan this intricate. I know she sold the information to the Kutsenkos because Jorge told me yesterday. How they leaked it from there, I don't know.

Friedrich's revelations yesterday about his family connections would make me question him, but there's nothing he wouldn't do for Heidi. Now that I know the things *Onkel* Clyde's been up to, I wonder if there's something between him and Papa I don't know about.

They've always been super close. As far as I know, they rarely argue and have been happy working together, but I'm starting to realize there's far more I don't know about my family business than I ever could've fathomed. I look over at Jorge before I share my next thoughts.

"How far have you dug for *Onkel* Clyde's clients? Are there ones he could have that I don't know about? It seems like there are more secrets at every turn. Clients Papa and *Onkel* Clyde kept hidden records for, or maybe even ones Papa doesn't know about. Despite being family and having a solid working relationship, this confirms what I've always suspected about human nature. You should never underestimate people's ability for duplicity and ambition. You never know how deep that could run."

All three men nod, and I suspect if anybody understands the truth behind that, it's them. Joaquin is the one who answers my questions.

"From what we can tell, both by your uncle's banking records and investigating his connections with American syndicates, there's nothing new for us to question. We've been aware of everything that's happened within the last couple of years. I planted some information to see if it might draw our Irish rivals out and make them contact him, but nothing's been a go."

"Perhaps it's one of our employees or colleagues' partners, but I can't think of anyone who I could tell you to suspect."

Joaquin nods. "I'll still investigate all of them. You never know who you might find during a game of leapfrog."

A knock interrupts whatever Joaquin was going to say next. He's slightly closer to the suite's door, so he goes over and opens it. Where I'm sitting allows me to see there's a package in the guard's hands. I can't believe we are going through this yet again.

What the fuck now?

I don't want to look as he comes back to us. Nausea washes over me, but I know I have to. Joaquin looks at Jorge, who nods. Joaquin flips open the lid of the box and reaches inside. I think I might vomit. Fortunately, he pulls out a sheet of paper before handing it to me and closing the box. It's in German, and I know Jorge is the only member of his family who speaks the language.

WE HEAR EVERYTHING JUST LIKE WE SEE EVERYTHING.

So, it's an ear. I can handle seeing that even though the thought turns my stomach over. I reach for the box, but Jorge takes it instead. He lifts the lid just enough for me to peek in. But immediately I'm questioning whether that could be my father's. For starters, it looks too big to be his. I push the lid back, and Jorge allows it to open all the way.

"Can I touch it?" I can't believe I just uttered those words, but I need a closer look.

"Let me, *chiquita*."

He glances toward his cousin and brother. I don't understand the warning expression he shoots them. He pulls the ear out, letting it rest flat on his palm. He brings it as close to me as he dares.

"What's that mark on the lobe? It looks like it could be a scarred piercing. Can you turn it over?"

I take the box from him, so he can use both hands. There's definitely a corresponding mark on the back of the ear, so it could be the other healed hole. I look over at Alejandro and Joaquin before meeting Jorge's gaze.

"My father's never had a pierced ear. I don't think this is his. Do you think they're torturing someone else, or could this be from a cadaver or something?"

Jorge's reluctant to answer that, but he shakes his head. "They might be torturing someone else, but since we don't know who this is, I couldn't say whether this is standard intimidation for them or just a one-off. It looks like it's not as fresh as the hand."

He clearly didn't want to explain any of that to me, but I appreciate that he did. Maybe they cut this ear off Papa the very first day, or maybe this was somebody's leftover corpse.

"Jorge, why would they send this and the pig's eye with no new demands? The million euros we supposedly transferred seems to have bought us time. This is intimidating as much as it is revolting, but I'd think they'd want something from me. We haven't progressed past this idle waiting and periodic threats."

"It's to keep you on edge, to wear you down through fear. That'd be when they make their demand. When you're too emotionally exhausted to put up an argument. You'll be so desperate to get your father back, you'll agree to just about anything."

"Is nowhere safe?" That desperation Jorge just mentioned feels like it's about to take hold.

"We need to get Liesel somewhere else. It needs to be somewhere we can better control. There are too many variables here for us to know what everyone is up to."

"I'll make it happen."

Alejandro pulls his phone out and steps over to the workspace. His voice is low, so it's just a soft murmur to me. I can't make out what he's saying. Joaquin pulls out his laptop, and it's only a couple minutes later that he's turning it to show Jorge and me what appears to be phone logs. The three of us move to the dining room table, and Jorge settles the laptop between us.

"I finally gained access to your father's phone records. This is a list of phone numbers he's called within the last two months. I have the actual records that show the dates and times. I wondered if you'd recognize any of these that I haven't been able to identify. About half of them go to burners."

I can see where he wrote that beside the phone number, but there're still ten or so numbers with no information next to them. In this day and age, there aren't too many phone numbers I have memorized anymore. Not when I have contact lists connected to my phone, email, and customer management records.

I shift and pull my phone from my pocket and unlock it. I start to search to see if I've called any of them before. None of them match my call history. I move over to my text messages and then my WhatsApp. It's still coming up with nothing.

"Do you think he could have other phones? If he's getting calls from all of these burners, perhaps he has some of his own that he's using."

"You know your father better than I do, Liesel. Does that seem probable to you?"

"Yes, it does. I never would've said that before this started. But now it seems highly probable. I don't know that he'd keep them at the house. I doubt he's said anything to my mom. We could ask her. My guess is they're in his office, and she knows nothing. If I'm supposed to be out sick, I can't easily slip in and poke around."

Jorge's hand covers mine, and he gives it a squeeze. "We'll send men tonight disguised as cleaners or maintenance. They'll go through the whole office looking for any other devices.

They'll search everywhere, not just your father's office. They'll look in every employee's cubicle or office."

"I have a place lined up for us."

Alejandro walks back over before Jorge and I decide whether to ask my mom. For right now, I'll stick to keeping this among the four of us. I can't believe Alejandro already has a place lined up for us. Who do they know here who can make a safe house appear in less than five minutes?

"*Chica*, we'll move to the safe house. We'll make it difficult for anyone to follow us. Let me go and pack."

He pushes back his chair, and his long strides carry him into the bedroom. That leaves me with an awkward moment of silence before Alejandro cracks a joke.

"Jorge always takes the longest to get ready. He's been proving that since he was born. He was four days overdue when the rest of us either came on our due dates or a couple days before."

I chuckle as I hear Jorge's voice coming from the bedroom.

"Good things come to those who wait."

It only takes a few minutes before he comes back out, but the joke was enough to make me feel less uncomfortable among two virtual strangers. Even if Jorge and I hadn't fucked this morning and yesterday, he still feels like far less of a stranger than he should, considering we haven't spent time together before all of this started. Not in any way that would allow me to get to know him better. But merely sharing the same space has given me insights into who he is. Ones I couldn't possibly get just by going on a few regular dates.

He brings my bags with him too. I'd already put my dirty clothes from yesterday in my suitcase lid's compartment. He only had to grab my toothbrush and zip it closed. He wheels the luggage to the door and leaves it there before pulling out his phone and likely firing off a text. He comes back to join us at the dining room table.

"What about..." I tilt my head to where the refrigerator is.

"We'll have a team come in who'll make it look like we were never here. They'll know what to do."

What more can I do than nod? Within five minutes, the luggage has disappeared ahead of us with Jorge explaining that it'll help us remain inconspicuous if it isn't obvious we're leaving. He admits people could be watching us for real or at least monitoring the hotel. Another set of guards awaits us in the hallway. Jorge, Joaquin, and Alejandro form a barrier on my left side while five more guys surround me on my right side and in front as well as behind me. It looks like it could be a rugby scrum except they're not lifting me over their heads. I'm a tall woman, but I'm still shorter than most of them.

I never thought of Latin American men as being particularly tall or even having that broad a build, but all of these guys look like the enormous trees you'd find in the Black Forest and have shoulders as wide as the Alps. It's rare I feel petite, but I do amongst this huddle. I'm virtually invisible as we travel down the emergency stairwell until we get to the first floor that has access to a service elevator.

We go all the way down to the hotel's underground parking garage. Four of the guards get out of the elevator as another one hits the stop button. I watch as they scout the parking lot. They come back and give us the all-clear. Once again, I'm encircled by what feels like my personal safety detail.

It surprises me when we walk over to a silver VW Jetta. I suppose I expected it to be one of the SUVs I heard Jorge used when he came to meetings at my office. This seems so bland in comparison.

"We want to blend in as best we can. The men will take a couple of the SUVs and go in different directions. Other guards will follow us in similarly average vehicles. Huge SUVs still stand out on the street here. It's not that often you spot four adults in a car together, at least not one that isn't a taxi or rideshare. But we'll take our chances with people seeing four of us in the car because that's less remarkable."

I nod as he opens the rear passenger side door for me. He goes around the trunk to get in before Joaquin climbs behind the steering wheel. Even though we know Alejandro and Joaquin can hear him, he keeps his voice low.

"Normally, I would be the one to drive since I have the heaviest lead foot in the family and am the best at weaving through traffic."

What he leaves silent is he's letting his brother drive, so he can sit beside me. Our hands clasp, and his thumb strokes over the back of mine. It surprises me that we take such a circuitous route wherever we're heading. Alejandro has his phone out, but he doesn't seem to be running a live route. Joaquin takes random turns, even doubling back a few times, but he always finds his way back to the correct road. I know he's doing that to confuse—perhaps lose—anyone who might be following us.

It takes us about forty-five minutes, but we arrive at a fairly rare community. Gated ones just really aren't a thing here. Joaquin pushes in a code Alejandro tells him, and the gate slides open. We travel fairly far into the neighborhood to a spacious home. Alejandro hops out and punches in a code to open the garage door.

He steps aside, then follows the car in. Immediately, the garage door begins to close. I unfasten my seatbelt and reach for the door handle, noticing Joaquin hasn't turned the engine off yet.

"No, *chiquita*, don't get out yet. You never leave a vehicle without one of my family members or men opening the door if I'm not there to do it. You don't get out of a car in a garage until the door shuts all the way. We don't turn off the ignition until there's only a couple of inches between the bottom of the door and the ground."

My brow furrows as I consider what he's saying. They're not just protecting themselves against someone following them in. It could be to protect themselves against someone shooting at them—or hell, even tossing an explosive in. They keep the car running in case they need to unexpectedly leave again. That's not unnerving or anything.

Once we're inside, a man greets us. His accent tells me right away he's one of Hisham's men. He introduces himself and points out where various things are, along with giving the guys a code to a wall safe.

"Jorge, I can't believe how much Hisham and Noor have done for us. We're complete strangers. I'm indebted to him and to everyone who's been helping us."

He cups my face in both hands before pressing one of his gentle kisses to my lips. His right hand trails down over my ribs before wrapping around my waist, pulling me against him.

"Remember, *chiquita*, you're family now."

He whispers in my ear, and it sends a tingle along my spine. I wish he were whispering dirty nothings to me. Those would be so sweet. He eases away from me, and I offer him the warmest smile I can. I love the sound of that.

"Is this Hisham's neighborhood? Are my mom, Heidi, and Friedrich here too?"

"No, he lives elsewhere in a less conspicuous neighborhood, but he owns several properties."

The man explains groceries will be delivered in about an hour. We thank him before he leaves, then we look around downstairs. I yawn and barely cover my mouth in time. I think feeling safer here—not just because the house is in a gated community but because I'm with Jorge, Joaquin, and Alejandro

—puts me at ease, which signals my body to tell my mind it needs the rest.

"Would it be okay if I go upstairs and take a nap?"

"Of course, little one. Sleep as long as you want. I'm going to call my uncles with the guys. I'll come and check on you when we're done."

"All right, I'll see you in a little bit."

Chapter Twenty-Two

Jorge

I'm glad Liesel heads upstairs, so I can talk to my family. I know what I just whispered to Liesel, but I need Alejandro and Joaquin to be a little less obvious.

"I know she appreciates you saying she's part of the family, and that means a ton to me, but we haven't discussed anything that far into the future."

"You're calling her *'chiquita.'* You've never called any woman that."

"I know, Joaquin."

In my family, that's become a sure sign you've found the woman you're meant to be with. None of us have called a romantic or sexual partner that before, but it seems to be a common theme. I've heard my *tío* Enrique call my *tía* Elle that. My next older brother, Javier, calls his wife, Madeline, *chiquita* and *chica*. So does my oldest cousin, Pablo, with his wife, Florencia.

"It just slipped out the first time, but it felt so right, I haven't stopped myself. But seriously, you need to lay off with it. She just broke up with her boyfriend yesterday."

Considering what she and I have done in the last twenty-four hours, it would look like rebound sex to most people. It could have been a casual hookup, but she and I know it's far more than that.

"Do you want to use one of your phones or mine to call the others? I don't want to talk about this anymore."

"We can use mine."

Joaquin's interrupted again by a knock on the door. All three of us draw our guns as I walk toward it. I turn back and look at them with a nod as I holster my weapon. I open the door to Hisham.

"I didn't want to discuss what I've learned over the phone or via text or email. I've used all the channels I have access to, to learn more about your situation, Jorge."

He certainly doesn't mince words. The four of us move into the living room.

"Hisham, thank you for everything you're doing. Not just reaching out to your contacts, but providing two homes for us to stay in. You and Noor have always been dear to my brothers, my cousins, and me. I know you're doing this for *Mamá* just as much as you are for me. We all appreciate it."

"You're welcome. You and your brothers are like our neph-ews. And your cousins are nearly as close to us as that."

He smiles at Joaquin and Alejandro as he speaks. We sit in the living room, and I mentally prepare myself for whatever's about to come. Hisham doesn't prevaricate but launches straight into the intel.

"Clyde's doing some fucked-up deals that're probably the reason his brother got kidnapped."

"How fucked-up?"

Joaquin scowls as he speaks. My mannerisms are so similar

that my expression mirrors his. Alejandro's eyebrows shoot straight up. I don't know if it's nature or nurture that my brothers and I have so many similar mannerisms, but it's genetically fascinating to watch Alejandro. He looks the most like *Tío* Enrique, but his mannerisms and speech pattern are just like his father. The Diaz genes run strong through all of us. We all favor that side of the family more than we do any of our others.

Alejandro expresses the same doubts that I have. "I can't believe Clyde would have anything to do with his brother's disappearance. Do you think he's responsible?"

Hisham's eyebrow twitches as he leans back in his seat. "He's negotiating some shifty-ass backdoor deals that'll get him killed and may have already signed his brother's death warrant. I haven't figured out who but there's money moving between Latin America and Asia. I suspect he's getting help from someone powerful enough to hide this from you until now. I'll keep looking into this. I have a few more strings I think I can pull. I'll give you an update as soon as I can, probably by mid-morning."

He means a rival in NYC. We can try to hide shit from one another, but nothing stays secret forever.

As we all rise, he reassures us he can let himself out. Joaquin, Alejandro, and I take our seats again. We're all mulling over the news in our heads. I glance at the mantle clock. It's only been thirty minutes, but I hear Liesel coming down the stairs. I go to meet her.

"Is there something wrong, little one?"

"No. To be honest, I don't think I can fall asleep because I'm starving."

We haven't had breakfast, and it's approaching lunchtime.

"I know I'm hungry as well."

"Obviously no one's living here, but do you think there might be something I could snack on until the groceries arrive?"

"Probably. You can go and see what you can find. I'm about to call my uncles. My other brother and cousin will probably be on the line too. You can stay with us if you'd like."

She glances toward Alejandro and Joaquin. "I can go back upstairs if that would be easier for you. I'm not a fluent Spanish speaker, but I might understand some of the things you say."

"If we need to discuss anything we feel isn't safe for you to hear, we'll switch to an Amerindian language that's indigenous to the part of Colombia where my family originated a couple hundred years ago. There are probably only about five hundred people in the world who speak the language these days."

"Oh, okay, that must be useful."

She's trying to be tactful. It is. It has its purpose. She heads into the kitchen while I go back into the living room. We decide to use my phone to call *Tío* Enrique. Conveniently, Pablo and Javier are at his house right now. It's not unusual for them to be there in the early morning since we take turns with who comes over to work out in our home gyms.

Our *tío* has the largest gym in the family. It takes up most of his basement, so we hold meetings down there while we work out. I'm certain Javier and Pablo knew we'd call to check in since Alejandro and Joaquin traveled last night. We get through our greetings when Liesel returns to us. She shakes her head as she sits on the sofa beside me.

We go through a quick round of introductions after I add *Tío* Luis—Pablo's dad—to the call. He's in Colombia right now dealing with someone problematic. As he finishes greeting Liesel, I hear somebody's voice in the background. Then *Tío* Matáis introduces himself. He's Alejandro's father.

I can tell their kindness surprises Liesel. I'm certain she probably expected them to sound ruthless and gruff, which they absolutely can and do most of the time, but never around women and children. *Tío* Enrique was always the fun uncle who gave us sugary treats at our sports games.

In a fucked-up turn of events in New York syndicate life, kids from the Four Families—Mancinellis, O'Rourkes, and Diaz—used to play on the same teams or they'd compete against each other. It began with peewee and little league. The Kutsenkos and their Andreyev cousins didn't arrive until middle school and high school, just like my brothers and I didn't move to the States until around the same time.

We played high school sports with them. The others didn't go to elementary school together because of the way school district lines were drawn. However, we all went to high school together with the exception of Pablo and Juan—that fucker.

I hate that he died, but I don't miss him. They grew up in New Jersey, but they still played club sports with us through high school. All of our parents took turns providing snacks and *Tía* Margherita—Pablo's mom—used to bring *tres leches* cakes to games whenever a kid had a birthday party.

Tío Enrique used to get in trouble with my *tíos* for spoiling us. They'd give him a hard time because our mothers would give my other *tíos* "the look." They didn't have to say anything to convey their displeasure and their expectation for their husbands to remind *Tío* Enrique not to spoil us.

My mom was the fun police growing up. She was the one who'd stuff our *piñatas* full of little boxes of raisins and stickers when everybody else's parents let them have candy in theirs. I don't mind the walk down memory lane because, despite losing my father at such a young age, most of my memories are happy ones of a raucous family that loves to tease each other and never needs an excuse to get together to eat.

As I consider the little Hisham told us and what we'll likely discuss, we'll get into things that mean we really need to switch to *Macaguán*.

"Liesel, we're going to talk about other syndicates and their businesses. It's not safe for you to hear this. We'll switch languages, but we don't want to be rude. Is there a TV up in the bedroom, or do you want to look for one somewhere else?"

Her expression tells me her answer before she says anything. "No, I don't mind. I'd rather stay here."

I was holding her hand, but now I wrap my arm around her shoulders. If it wouldn't make her feel uncomfortable in front of my brother and cousin, I'd curl her up on my lap. She leans heavily against me and sighs. I stroke her hair, and I feel her body relax as my family and I pick up the conversation in *Macaguán*.

"*Tío*, do you think we should talk to the others?"

Everybody knows I'm addressing *Tío* Enrique even though my two other uncles are on the call. The others are the leaders of our rival syndicates in NYC. We aren't making progress on our own, so I may need to eat an entire humble pie and ask for help.

"It's definitely looking like we'll need to from what Hisham shared with you."

Pablo jumps in with a question. "Do you think we should wait to hear from him again and see if he discovers anything else?"

"He said he'd get back to the *niños* by mid-morning tomorrow. Maybe we make Maks and the others a last resort. However, we could start fucking things up and seeing who responds. I could start pulling out of investments or teasing ones that'll never happen."

It doesn't matter how old we get, my parents' generation still calls all of us boys. *Tío* Matáis's suggestion is sound. It's the strategy we've used plenty of times to bait people. The Mancinellis, the O'Rourkes, and the Kutsenkos do the same thing.

We wind up agreeing to hold off for a little while longer before speaking to the heads of the other syndicates. We also agree we won't send any money to Gunter's captors. They haven't retaliated against the fake million-euro deposit, and they haven't demanded more. They may not even know it was a phony transaction and are satisfied for now. The less complicated we can make this, the better. If they don't need placating, then there's no reason to bring up their demand again.

I suspect it's never been about the six million euros. If it were, they wouldn't send body parts. They'd go into the Schlossbergs' accounts and merely take whatever they want since they're already laundering money through Liesel's. It's the intimidation to keep control. I don't want to say it aloud, but I fear Gunter's kidnapping came about because they got nervous that my family's involvement with Schlossberg & Sons signaled an impending loss of control. That we'd investigate the company's financials and discover what's been going on.

By the time the call ends, I know Liesel's fallen asleep against me. The doorbell rings, and she doesn't even shift. Alejandro heads over to greet the guy who brought us groceries. Unfortunately, I have to extract myself from Liesel since the man doesn't speak English. I ease her to lie down on the sofa before going over to thank the guy. He explains there are some meals already prepared and hot. That's a huge relief to all of us.

However, it only takes a moment for the three of us to realize a European-size trip to the grocery store will never feed us for as long as this food is intended to last. We usually work out two times a day. I haven't since I've been away on this trip. I've only gotten some runs in and a few trips to the hotel gyms, but we all devour at least three to four thousand calories a day.

I go and rouse Liesel. She's so fucking beautiful when she's drowsy. We head into the kitchen and pull out the food. Once we're seated around the table, Liesel speaks up. From her tone, I can tell this is something that's been worrying her.

"Jorge, what if people followed us from the hotel?"

It's Joaquin who answers instead. "I brought drones with me I can launch if we leave this house. They'll scan the neighborhood for anyone pulling out at the same time as us. Our guards will be with us. The ones who went in the SUVs will have come back in understated cars as well to guard us. We also have a few guys who ride motorcycles. They'll ride interference. They'll maneuver so no one can get too close to us."

She looks over at me. "How do you have a fleet of vehicles at your disposal?"

"It's magic, *chiquita*."

She laughs but waits for a proper answer. I just stare at her. It takes her a moment before she dips her chin and looks down at our food. I hate that this is one of potentially a lifetime of lies of omission.

I can't tell her the SUVs are rented from a legitimate company, but the VW Jetta we rode in today is stolen, and so are the other cars and motorcycles. We'll ditch them before morning and have other vehicles at our disposal if and when we need them.

It's not long before we're done. Alejandro offers to clean up. Then we return to the table with our laptops because we each run our own businesses and have work to do.

Chapter Twenty-Three

Liesel

While the three guys work, I spend an hour mulling over what to tell my *onkel*. I can't keep what's going on from him any longer. Jorge hasn't suggested he's involved, and I have no reason to suspect it on my own.

"Jorge, I have to call *Onkel* Clyde. We've said nothing to him yet. I know we should've. But I don't know—I guess I didn't want him to interfere in case he's part of this, and I know he still could be."

"No, it's time, Liesel. Make the call."

"I'll have to speak German, or he'll immediately suspect something's going on."

It only rings twice before I hear his gruff voice on speaker-phone. It's always that way. I suppose that's why I expected Jorge's uncles to sound similarly, but his greeting is warm.

"*Onkel* Clyde, I need to tell you some things that're very upsetting. Somebody kidnapped Papa four days ago."

"What?!" He explodes; I knew it was coming.

"I went back to the office after lunch, and there was a box with his hand inside. It had his wedding ring on it."

"And you didn't call me immediately?"

"No, I didn't. To be honest, I was too stunned to think very clearly at the time, but I have a friend here in Frankfurt who I suspected could help me. I went to him."

"Jorge Diaz."

I'm shocked he guessed. I look over at Jorge, eyes wide in confusion. He nods and taps the air with his palm, reassuring me.

"Anneliese, I know about the Diazes' potential investment and what was going on. Your father told me about it. The only friend you could have who'd know any way to approach a situation like this would be him. *Hola*, Jorge, I'm certain you're listening."

"Good evening, Clyde."

There's a protracted silence before my uncle speaks again.

"I don't want to imagine where this conversation is going, but I'm glad Anneliese has you. You certainly aren't the first person I'd think of for her to rely on, but you're certainly the best while I'm here in Munich."

"Thank you."

I share an abridged version of what happened with my mother and sister coming to stay with us. I keep my breakup with Bastian short and to the point before I tell him where my mom, Heidi, and Friedrich went.

"Jorge, I'm not shocked you have connections with Hisham. I appreciate he offered all of you sanctuary."

My gaze meets Jorge's. I don't know what to say next, so he takes over.

"Clyde, we know both Anneliese and Gunter have questionable clients. I know what's going on with Anneliese and her Swiss accounts."

There's another uncomfortable silence before my uncle relents.

"If you use this information against us, Jorge...I'm only telling you because I have faith you can help find my brother. We began receiving threats from someone about a year ago. They're the people who've been extorting Anneliese. When she brought it to Gunter's attention, he downplayed it. He didn't want whoever this is to know Anneliese told him anything. He thought we could collect information—insurance—against them to extricate all of us."

None of this sounds like the *onkel* I grew up with. The one with whom I have so many happy memories. The one who used to walk around with my standing on his feet, pretending to be a giant. The man who'd let me curl up on his lap and tell me stories about when he and Papa were young boys. That was a lifetime ago for both of us.

"Who could this be?"

"Anneliese, I honestly don't know. You've sprung this on me, and as you know, it's a lot to take in. I need to consider all the players in this situation."

"*Onkel* Clyde, be careful. I don't know if they might come after you too."

"I know, Anneliese. I'm glad you have Jorge there. Listen to everything he tells you to do. Jorge, do you have family coming, or is it just you and whatever guards you have?"

"A brother and a cousin are here."

That's all he shares. He doesn't mention which ones, and he doesn't admit they've heard this conversation. I hang up with my *onkel*. He took that far better than I imagined, but I'm certain he's reacting now that we're not on the phone.

"How're you doing, *chiquita*?"

"Better than I thought I'd be, to be honest. He's more upset than he's letting one."

"I know he is. He's German. He's genetically programmed to be stoic."

Jorge flashes me a grin before leaning around me to look at Joaquin and Alejandro. They're busy and minding their own business. Jorge slides his hand into mine and leads me up to the bedroom. Once we're there, he shuts the door.

I slip off my shoes and so does he. He scoops me into his arms, and I wrap mine around his neck. He presses a gentle kiss to my forehead before brushing my lips with his. He sits on the bed and places me next to him. We shuffle around until he's sitting against the headboard, and I'm on his lap. He offers me a tender kiss on the lips, and I sigh. I burrow against him, but it doesn't feel like enough for either of us.

"Strip, *chiquita*."

"What? Right now?"

His soft smile reassures me. "I won't fuck you right this minute, unless that's what you want. But strip."

"Yes, Daddy."

I climb off the bed while he does the same. I shed my clothes without hesitation.

"Trust me about this, little one."

"I do. Completely."

Heat suffuses my chest, knowing how truthful I am.

"*Chica,* only my family says that to me. No one else is stupid enough to have that kind of unconditional emotion toward me."

"I can guess why, Jorge. But I know my faith isn't misplaced."

"Do you feel so far over your head that you're drowning, and you don't know how to swim to the surface?

"Yes."

"Give me control for a little while, *chiquita*. Let me take care of you and show you I'm here to do that. Let yourself focus on something other than your fear."

"What do you mean?"

"I've spanked you in the past as a punishment. It can also be for pleasure."

"As a distraction?"

"In this case, it is in a way. It can be so much more. It's about letting me take the lead without you fighting for control over something you can't. All you have to do is concentrate on how you feel when I touch you."

I look at him skeptically, but he knows when I accept this. I'm at least willing to try. I nod and step closer to the bed. He sits on the edge and taps his lap. Rather than sit on it, I lie across it. His hand grazes over my ass, his fingertips like feathers.

What I wouldn't give for him to have one of those right now to see how my body would react to that sensation. React to Jorge wielding it.

Goosebumps rise on my skin. He fills his palm with my right ass cheek and massages, squeezing and rocking. He gradually tightens his hold on me.

"You're mine now, *chiquita*. Mine to take care of and to pleasure. Mine to punish when you lose your way."

I inhale a shuddering breath as he switches to the other ass cheek.

"There are dirty, dirty things I want to do when I fuck you, little one. There are sweet things I want to do as I worship you."

His fingers slide between my ass cheeks, and my instinct is to clench—but only for a moment. I relax, and his fingers inch farther down. He glides his index and ring finger along the outside of my pussy lips three times before he lets his middle finger dip into my cunt—but only to his first knuckle. I moan and shift restlessly. He feels how wet I am already and how much wetter I grow as he continues to tease.

"This fine ass is mine to spank, squeeze, pinch, and fuck whenever I want."

"Yes, Daddy."

I agree without hesitation. I hope my tone tells him I'm being honest and not just responding to dirty talk in kind. He uses the cream on his middle finger to slowly circle my clit as his other hand reaches beneath me to tweak my nipple. He pinches and tugs before rolling it between his index finger and thumb.

"These tits are magnificent. I'll suck and bite and fuck them whenever I want. They were made for my enjoyment, little girl. They're mine just like the rest of you."

Perhaps one day we'll watch a baby we make together nurse from them. I've never pictured that—not even had a hint of an image of that—with another man. Not even Bastian to tell the truth. I would've run for the hills if I had this early in another relationship. Now the thought makes my cunt ache.

He lets go of my nipple, trailing his fingertips up and over my collarbone, then down past my shoulder blades. His whole hand glides along my back until his arm wraps around my waist. His hand rests on my belly for a few seconds; his possessiveness clear, if only implied. As he draws it back, I reach for his wrist and press it against my taught stomach.

"Daddy, please."

I don't know what I'm asking for. The words tumbled out of my mouth. It could be several things. My spanking. His possessiveness. Our baby. The first two for sure, but the third is far too much. Hell, maybe all I want is an orgasm. I turn my head to look up at him, and his gaze is so heartfelt that he might give me all four right now if I wanted them.

He dips the single digit all the way into my cunt. He does

nothing, and I whimper. He draws it out, and my right foot tries to stomp, but only my toes touch the floor. He makes sure his finger's covered in my cream before tracing a line between my ass cheeks until he reaches the place my body hides from him—for now. He presses against the hole, the pad of his finger easing into the tight opening.

"Can you guess how many times I've pictured a plug in your ass? A secret only we know about. One that makes you desperate for my cock every time I put it in. One that prepares you just for me."

"Fuck, Jorge. That's hot."

"That's because you're hot. You've filled many of my nights, visiting me in my dreams and dancing in front of my eyes as I jerk myself off."

"I've—I've—"

"You've what, little girl? Rubbed your clit, wishing it was me? Wishing my cock was sliding into your pretty pink pussy?"

"Yes. Fucking hell, Jorge. Since the day we met. I've wanted you when I shouldn't have. When I wasn't free to have those thoughts, but I did."

He pulls his hand away from my puckered flesh and bring it down on my ass. The sound of his flesh landing against mine fills the room, but he didn't strike me hard. I moan. He lands another and another across both cheeks.

"Tell me your dirty little secrets, *chiquita*."

"I wanted you to fuck me in the conference room. Bend me over or lift me onto the table. Any position if it meant I felt you inside me."

"A place where anyone could've walked in on us."

He keeps the swats light, but he continues to pinken my ass as we talk.

"Yes. I didn't care. I wanted you so much, and you were always close enough to touch but never mine to have. I knew that shadow in the alley was you. I was sure of it. As much as it scared me, I wanted you to pull me into the shadows."

"What did you want me to do?"

"Fuck me against the wall. Shred my panties after you demanded I pull my skirt up for you. I wanted you to take me. As much as I wanted to fuck you where anyone could see us, I wanted it as a dirty secret too."

"Fuck, *chica.* I might come just hearing that fantasy. How did it feel the first time I spanked you?"

"Like the first time anyone besides my family's truly cared about me. That your control was genuinely for my own good, not to be domineering and isolate me."

"What did you feel the second time?"

"Peace. Restitution and reconciliation, I suppose. It's not like I felt unworthy of your attention before that, but—I don't know how to say it—not in English or German. Like—you may have spanked other women in the past, but I got a piece of you no one else has. That my punishment was genuine and not for sexual gratification."

He feels me tense as I explain. He lands a particularly hard spank across my horizontal crack. I yelp.

"That's precisely what it was. You have part of me *no one* has ever had. A part I'm not sure existed before you. Being with you gives me peace I've never known."

He sets a pattern of alternating sides as my ass surely moves from bright pink into a deeper rose hue. He varies the speed and strength he uses. It stings and burns, but it's not the kind of pain my body wants to run from. Just the opposite. I do my best to raise my hips to meet his hand.

"Daddy?"

"Yes."

"What did you dream about?"

"Kissing every inch of you. Tasting you as you come on my

tongue, drinking you like fine wine. Holding you in my arms while I fuck you until you're not sure if you're begging me to stop or keep going. Worshipping your body with a tenderness I never imagined I'm capable of but only feel for you. Falling asleep with me still buried in you. Waking up to you, knowing I'm where I belong. Holding the woman I adore for as long as she'll have me."

"Wait."

I struggle to roll away, so I can look up at him. I reach back for the hand that was on my belly. I tug until it's between us, then pressing against my middle again.

"I didn't walk away from what I had just to walk away from you later. We *will* figure us out *together*. I don't want to hear you talk about us as anything but permanent. I have *never* been this adamant about that with anyone. I wasn't married when you met me because I needed time to know whether that person was the one for me, and clearly, I know he wasn't. I don't need that time with you. Or rather, I've had all the time I need. Hear me now and hear me well, Daddy. If this ends, it's because you let me go. Not the other way around, Jorge."

I settle back on him lap and reach back with my other hand to where his rests on my ass. I try to lift it, and he lets me. I press down to make him spank me.

"We aren't done yet."

I grin, but he can't see it.

"Suddenly, you're in charge, *chiquita?* I didn't get the memo."

His hand cracks across my ass with enough force to push me forward and make me squeak. I'd scream if I didn't want his relatives to know what we're doing.

"Shh, *chiquita.* Those kinky fuckers downstairs don't need to know how I pleasure my woman—not that they'd care. They probably wouldn't even register your screams of pleasure. They'd kill me if I harmed you."

If I weren't so focused on my burning ass and giving him all of my undivided attention, I'd have a lot to consider with that admission. He let it slip, but he hasn't said anything to take it back.

He balances things with a much lighter swat, and I relax completely against him. My body's like a rag doll. He peppers my ass with playful spanks now. He rubs it like he did before he got started. He nudges my legs apart, and he can see the evidence of how aroused I am.

"I thought you might try to rub your clit against my thigh to get off, little one."

"I was focused on relaxing, Daddy."

"When you weren't making demands that tested my fortitude not to stop and fuck you."

We chuckle as he helps me onto my feet. We quickly strip. Once we're both naked, he pulls back the sheet and duvet before getting into bed. He holds his arms out to me, and I crawl over to him, prepared to sit on his lap with both of my legs to one side.

Instead, he guides me to straddle him. His dick's been at attention since the moment he hugged me when we finished the call to my *onkel*. I ease onto him, and we both groan as he slips deeper inside me until my pelvis meets his.

He presses my head against his shoulder, running his hand up and down my back. It doesn't take much to convince me to lean against him. As one hand brushes my back, and the other one cups my ass, lightly tapping it, I release a shuddering breath before my body goes lax against his. I Kegel as we sit together. It's only a moment later that I tremble as I cry. He kisses the top of my head over and over.

"Baby girl, the spanking was to get you to let go of the physical strain of trying to manage everything that's been happening. Despite my help and my family's, I know you feel responsible for your. Your body's been coiled tight with the stress of helplessness and frustration. You let all of that go when you gave me control to do what I wanted with your spanking. Now, you're at ease enough to let your mind relax too. You know I'll take care of you the way you need me to."

"You really get it. You get me."

"I don't want you to get the wrong idea about my proclivities or me. You'd think your tears would kill my hard-on, but instead I'm like a fucking steel pole. It's not like I get off on your misery, *chiquita,* but the need to console you and have us feel like we're one with no ending and no beginning keeps my dick up."

"You'd think crying would make my pussy dry up, but what you described is how I feel too. I know you need to be in control. I know you need to console me as much as I need consoling. When we're like this, there is no end and no beginning. We're one."

"Always, *chica.*"

I believe him. But all of this would be so much easier if we could just find my father. Neither of us is in a rush to get off, but eventually, we both get restless. I lean back, and he sucks my right nipple as his hands guide me to grind my clit against his pubic bone. We've both been aroused for so long that we're coming in a matter of minutes.

"I don't want to rush us, Liesel, but we need to go back downstairs. Joaquin and Alejandro won't care how long we're up here, but I need to check in and see if they've made any progress."

"I refuse to be embarrassed, but it's hard not to be. I also want to know what's going on. I needed this, so thank you."

"Any time, little one."

We share a quick kiss before heading back downstairs. It's only a couple minutes after we join Joaquin and Alejandro that the doorbell rings. All three guys pull out their guns. Joaquin heads to the front door. I have to imagine it can't be anyone with nefarious intent since there are guards staked out around the house, and they've allowed us three visitors now. It's only a moment later that I recognize Hisham's voice. Alejandro, Jorge, and I go out to greet him before we move to the living room.

"I didn't expect to be back here so soon, but I got news less than a half an hour ago. I was in the car at the time, so I came here directly. My informant figured out some of the banking information Joaquin sent over to me. I learned more about the route the laundered money's taking."

I hadn't realized he'd done that, but it must've been while we were all working. I focus on what Hisham's telling us.

"The amounts change for each transaction, but they eventually add up by the time they make it to the bank in Italy. It's being laundered through several small merchants in France, then you, Anneliese, along with the banks in Switzerland and the Caymans."

Both countries prioritize protecting their customers' anonymity, so that makes those obvious choices.

"So, what does that mean now?"

From the protracted silence, I can tell Hisham's said all he's going to. I shift my attention to the other men, and Jorge, Joaquin, and Alejandro all make the same grimace. It's Alejandro who speaks up.

"That means we have some business to take care of back home. We need to call *Tío* and see what he thinks of all of this."

I look around, understanding I can't listen to the call they must make. I'm not sleepy anymore, so dozing against Jorge won't occupy me. I don't want to sit and stare at the walls.

"I'm guessing you don't need me down here anymore."

"There's a TV in the primary bedroom. There are streaming services already logged in."

"Thank you, Hisham."

Jorge wraps an arm around my waist and kisses my forehead. With an audience, we won't do more than that. It reassures me enough to help me get by. I hug him before stepping away. Hisham says his goodbyes and heads out. Alejandro, Joaquin, and Jorge have practically supersonic hearing. I'm certain they don't speak again until after I shut the door upstairs.

Chapter Twenty-Four

Jorge

"From what Clyde told Liesel and me, and from what Hisham just shared, this has to be a major player. At this point, it would shock me if this isn't coming from back home."

My brother and cousin both agree with a grimace. The last thing we want to do is deal with the bratva, mob, or Mafia. We need to figure out if any of them play a role is in this.

It rings twice before we hear *Tío* Enrique's greeting. We give him a rundown of everything that's happened since we spoke to him earlier.

"That's a lot to take in, *sobrinos*."

"It is, *Tío*, and we're still muddling our way through a lot of this, but it's more information than we had when we woke up this morning."

"Do you think any of it is actionable?"

"Not yet. I think we need to plan for how we'll strike these various groups before we're back in the States."

I know that means talking to Liesel about our future, and I don't know how that conversation will go. We may want to be together, but I can't guarantee the logistics of it. It's a precarious tightrope I'm on right now, since I know she won't leave Germany without getting her father back, and I won't leave here without her. I'd prefer her to be in the States, regardless, because I can protect her better there. We have the full force of all of my family's resources in place.

"I assume you've begun planning, Jorge."

I consider my answer, and my thoughts race a mile a minute.

"Not specifically, *Tío*, but I think we need to do more than have *Tío* Matáis test the waters by screwing with their investments. That'll take too long to coax them out. The more I think about it right now, the more I believe we need to act now. All three families have investments here in Frankfurt. Whether they want to admit it or not, the Kutsenkos still have the Heidemann holdings. It's time we let them know we aren't taking their meddling like we're their little bitches."

I recognize the harrumph even if I can't see Javier's scowl.

"That's too obvious. They're probably already expecting us to strike those facilities. They'll think this is just about our deal falling through."

I know my brother has a point, but I push back because we need to keep working through all possibilities before we reject any.

"You don't think they know about Gunter? I'm certain they do. They'll know this isn't just about the deal. They'll know it's about the Schlossbergs. Even if it isn't them, they may know something. This could be the nudge they need to come forward."

Pablo's not usually the mediator—Joaquin is—but he offers

a compromise. "We pick something less obvious than the Heidemann holdings, but we go after something of theirs in Frankfurt. We don't necessarily make it obvious that we're behind whatever happens."

"But it has to be something connected to the Schlossbergs to tease out whether they have anything to do with this."

I don't think Pablo's wrong. I don't even think Javier is either, but we can't just strike them without a specific desired outcome.

"We could take an entirely different approach."

I look over at Alejandro and raise my eyebrows. When no one speaks up, he continues. His suggestion surprises me since it's something that hadn't even remotely crossed my mind.

"We leverage the 'Thieves in Law.' They aren't hiding as much anymore, so they're targets we won't have to search hard to find. At least ten percent of prisoners in Germany are Russian speakers, and that gang continues to recruit within the prisons. It's not like we'll risk catching anyone innocent in our crosshairs. The Kutsenkos may not be directly connected to them right now, but we can force them to be."

"How so?" *Tío* Enrique asks what I'm thinking, and I'm sure everyone else is too.

"We target the Heidemann facilities since we don't want Maks and his family to keep them, but we make it look like it was the Thieves. Let the bratva think the Thieves are trying to expand or retaliating for the bratva's presence, even if it is legal. We snatch the bratva's *avtoritet*—Maks's brigadier or top guy in Frankfurt—and make it look like the Thieves took him. We intercept and steer the communication between Maks and his man. Depending on how Maks and his family react, we'll know whether they have Gunter. We can always send him two middle fingers. If the bratva took Gunter, they'll get the double meaning. If they don't have him, then at least we guarantee some MAD that'll weaken both sides here. It may leave room for us to sweep in and expand."

MAD—mutually assured destruction. If anyone understands that Cold War era scare tactic, it's the Russians. It's the principle that keeps the Four Families from truly annihilating one another.

I glance at my watch. This isn't a job to pull off in broad daylight, and we can't get everything in order by tonight.

"This could work, but we need at least a day to plan and line up everything. We should be safe here, so I'm not worried about Liesel staying here with us tonight or during the day tomorrow. She definitely needs to go to Hisham and Noor's before we start. What about the Mancinellis and O'Rourkes? Do we see how the Kutsenkos handle things, then decide who to strike next? Or do we go for a triple header? The latter will probably spread us too thin."

"Can you each spearhead a mission, *sobrinos?* Or would it be better if all three of you work together?"

Alejandro, Joaquin, and I look at each other as we consider our *tío's* questions. We know we can each handle a mission, but it would mean none of us have as many men as we'd like. This isn't a city any of us know well, so it would be wiser for us to stick together. Alejandro speaks for us.

"If you want us to each lead, we can, but it'll spread us thin with the men we have. Depending on how long the bratva takes to engage, this could last a couple days."

I don't love that idea. "True. That makes me think we do need to divide and conquer. I don't want Liesel and her family in limbo that long. Gunter may not have that time to spare."

"Hisham has somewhere you can take Maks's guy once you have him. He has men who can watch him until you're ready to deal with him."

Tío Enrique is reassuring, but I don't want to wear out our welcome. House guests are like fish. After three days, you want to throw them out. We've descended on Hisham and Noor like an entire school of them.

"He's already doing so much for us. I don't know that we should ask for more."

"I'll make it up to him."

I'll take my *tío's* word for it, so I'm ready to move on to the next big picture. My brother, my cousin, and I will work out details for the attack on the bratva amongst ourselves.

"What about the Mancinellis? Just because the money is winding up in Italy doesn't mean we should assume it's them because they're the most obvious. Joaquin hasn't found any direct links to them, but that doesn't mean they aren't hiding in plain sight. What can we do to them here?"

No one answers me right away. Everyone's weighing our options. I'm getting anxious and second guessing my idea to hit each family here.

Frankfurt may be the banking capital of Central Europe, and all Four Families have dealings here, but that doesn't mean we have to hit them here.

Then again, we don't want to make it obvious that it's us, which is what could happen if we do anything to them back in New York or anywhere else. We don't need to play our hand so soon.

But if we don't get it right here, then we might still show our asses. I'm not convinced we have all the men and means to pull it off here. Alejandro, Joaquin, and I are plenty capable of plotting and executing, but only if we have all the right tools at our disposal. I'm concerned we don't.

My mind is spinning. I usually don't suffer from so much self-doubt these days. Having to make life altering decisions in a matter of moments doesn't leave room for self-doubt.

However, at times like this, when I don't have to make split-second decisions, my anxiety rears its head.

I know the temperature in the room isn't going up, but it feels like it. I breathe through my heart rate wanting to spike. I force away the invisible weight pressing on my shoulders without shrugging them like I want to. I don't need Joaquin and Alejandro worrying.

"Jorge?"

"Hmm? Just thinking, *Tío*."

I have no idea what *Tío* Enrique just said. I glance at my brother and cousin to see if I can get a hint. Instead, I see the exact worry I tried to avoid. Joaquin comes to my rescue when he whispers to me.

"He wants to know if we should make it look like the 'Ndrangheta are causing trouble for Salvatore."

I dip my chin in thanks before I respond to our *tío*.

"That's probably our best bet since they're the largest Italian syndicate in the area. Lorenzo just invested heavily in a hedge fund, basically squeezing out the *'Ndrangheta's* influence. I noticed the *'Ndrangheta's* underboss worked with Gunter about three years ago. We could make it look like the *'Ndrangheta* are defending a past business partner while retaliating against the Mancinellis' expanding reach. If we're going to blow up the Heidemann buildings, we have to do something more subtle with them. We make it look like the *'Ndrangheta* bribed the *Landeskriminalämter* to investigate the Mancinellis, but they'll call off the dogs if the Mancinellis hand over Gunter. If they won't, then we make it look like the *'Ndrangheta* are threatening them with the *Bundeskriminalamt*."

The State Offices of Criminal Investigations handle domestic money laundering schemes if they go beyond the local prosecutors' or police's purvey. Since this would involve a foreign syndicate, the Federal Criminal Police Office could plausibly get involved too. It would be a major inconvenience for the NYC *Cosa Nostra* don.

"I can get started on that right away. It might take me a few hours to get into all the necessary accounts, but I can spoof some emails to get the ball rolling with threats to Lorenzo."

Joaquin can't stand Lorenzo. Like hates him with the fire of a thousand suns because the closest my brother's ever come to dying was when Lorenzo fucking shot him. The *carechimba* hit him six inches from his heart because the fucknut's night vision sucks. He was aiming for Misha—Maks's cousin—and hit Joaquin instead. It was about eight years ago, during a weapons deal between the Mancinellis and us that Misha thought to crash. If we were still kids, my brother would be bouncing in his seat, raring to go.

"Jorge, are you good with that?"

"*Sí, Tío.* I think that's for the best. We can't be too obvious about everything, or everyone'll guess it's us too soon. That still leaves the O'Rourkes though. Do we go for overt or covert with them?"

"Those dumbasses need overt. They can't find their asses with two hands and a flashlight." Javier's practically snarling.

The O'Rourkes may not have been directly responsible for what happened to my sister, but Javier holds any and all mobsters accountable for what happened to his wife. Right now, the O'Rourkes can't even glance in Madeline's direction without Javier losing all his shit.

Pablo often remains quiet during meetings like these. It's not for lack of things to say. He's a scientist through and through. He's a keen observer, and he considers every variable and what order to test them before he forms a hypothesis—or in this case a mission strategy.

"I agree with Javier. If they're involved with this, then they know you and Anneliese are connected, even if they don't know the extent of it. With the way things stand after what happened with Javier and Madeline, if this is them, they should've backed off. Assuming it was them, they never should've taken Gunter to begin with."

"What do you have in mind?" I'm certain he wouldn't have spoken up yet if he didn't have something to suggest.

"They've made inroads into Eastern Europe over the past four years. We know Gunter and Clyde have connections to some wealthy investors in the Czech Republic and Estonia. Make it look like someone snitched to them, and they're pissed about the O'Rourkes targeting Gunter. We know the O'Rourkes have done deals with Clyde before to get product into Germany that's then gone on to those two countries. Pick someone from one of those countries and make it look like they retaliated. We steal whatever they currently have warehoused here and make Gunter the ransom. Make it look like the Czech or Estonian wants to trade. We can even give some of their product back, if they return Gunter. If they don't have him, then we have new merchandise to sell."

I nod my head even though only Joaquin and Alejandro can see me. "We can handle the two missions with the men we have. We can even do both tomorrow night if we start working on the logistics now. If Joaquin begins work on the Mancinellis, maybe we strike gold and don't even need to attack the bratva or mob."

I get a round of laughs. Even if none of them have Gunter, we may still pull off all three attacks just because we can.

After we ended the call yesterday, Liesel came back downstairs. We put a movie on, but none of us were fully paying attention.

We were all lost in our thoughts. We all called it an early night. Once alone, Liesel and I climbed into bed. The moment our bare skin touched, the rest of the world disappeared. Knowing there was nothing we could do to further our search, we allowed ourselves to enjoy making love.

That's the only way I could describe it. We weren't rushed. It wasn't rough. Passionate—so, so passionate—but not fucking. I haven't had vanilla sex in years. I haven't missed it. With Liesel, it was like discovering something brand new. We were completely equals, and that's what we needed. We're still establishing our relationship. Most likely, I'll go back to being the dominant one during sex. We like it that way. But we need to know we're in this together as partners who both give and take.

Afterward, we crashed hard. I needed to catch up on my sleep. I must be alert tonight since our missions are a go. I know today was boring for Liesel, but she worked from the safe house all day. When I apologized for it feeling like we were all sitting around, she assured me she prefers it uneventful.

I caught her staring off into space a few times while we all worked. She hasn't asked any questions because I've shared as much as I can. She knows I wish I could tell her more, but she understands it isn't safe for anyone if I do. If we're going to make this relationship work, this is something she'll have to accept. Better she gets a taste of it now than after we're married.

Joaquin had his portable trifold monitor set up like I did at the dining room table. Alejandro and Liesel both set themselves up in the living room. I purposely picked my chair so I could see Joaquin's screens and Liesel. Joaquin, Alejandro, and I texted what we couldn't discuss aloud. None of us wanted to ask Liesel to spend hours in a bedroom just so we could talk. Not the most convenient method of communication, but I appreciate the guys being considerate.

We dropped her off at Hisham and Noor's before heading out for these missions. I doubt walking away from her will ever get easier. She knows we won't be back until at least morning. I witnessed her glassy eyes, but she swallowed the threatening tears and put on a brave face as we said goodbye. I'm proud of her, even if I hate why she had to. At least, she's with her family right now.

"Ricardo, take your men and sweep the building. Make sure no one's in there."

We do our best to not have casualties of war. We aren't always so lucky, but we have time tonight to make sure. Not a lot of time, but enough.

"*Sí, capitán.*" Yes, Capitain.

"Josue, take your men around to the south side."

"*Sí, capitán.*"

We're lucky that Heidemann Labs and Heidemann BioTech are next door to each other. They're conveniently located for us to take out two birds with one stone. Or in this case, two buildings with one bomb blast.

Without Pablo—our explosives expert—here, Josue is our lead bomb tech. He can set and diffuse just about anything. We're fortunate he came along with Alejandro and Joaquin. The man has never suffered a day of jet lag in his life. From the size of his luggage, you'd think he only travels with a toothbrush, but he always has fresh clothes without a single wrinkle. He's perpetually single—and loves it—so he can travel without much fuss or worry about leaving someone at home. His sister feeds his fish.

Alejandro, Joaquin, our men, and I watch Josue and three other guys jog toward the far side of the first building. We wait for the all-clear to come through our earpieces before the rest of us advance.

"*Stoppen!*"

We knew a guard would spot us. These aren't syndicate men, so we're firing rubber bullets from CO_2 rifles tonight. I aim for the guy's midsection below his bulletproof vest then his shoulder. He falls to the ground with a bellow. If his yelling "stop" didn't alert other guards, his howl of pain did. Men appear from guard huts around the perimeter.

Pop-pop-pop.

The sound of guns firing rounds at the oncoming surge of German guards fills the air, but it's much quieter than regular rifles. We have those with us, but we want to inflict minimal harm to these men. These might not technically be lethal rounds, but they'll do damage at close enough range. We want to disable these guys not kill them. It's not long before we're zip-tying the security team. Three of our guys switch their CO_2 rifles for real ones in case any of the Germans decide to play hero.

"*Las explosiones uno, dos y tres están programadas, capitán.*" Blasts one, two, and three are set, Captain."

Josue's update comes sooner than I expected. He and his men worked without interruption. That means we can get out of here faster. Those I didn't assign a task at the Labs move with me to the BioTech complex. This place is much larger.

We're all dressed in black with dark camouflage paint around our eyes and noses. Most of us are taller than the stereotypical Latino, but we share the common dark eyes. It means with the paint on, along with balaclavas, we're not easily distinguishable. Since our guns do the talking for us, I'm not worried anyone will identify us to the police later. At best, they'll give a general description.

We breach the entrance and round up the guards patrolling the building. There are some late-night custodians and scientists who get gagged and zip-tied before some of our men guide them outside. They join the half dozen people Ricardo's team found in the labs. They get blindfolded once they're escorted out of the building. I trust the men to get them a safe distance from the blast zone.

We studied the blueprints *Mamá* somehow got ahold of for us. She didn't ask why, and we didn't ask how. But she pulled through, and our team studied the entire layout for more than an hour. Josue picked out the best places to put the explosives, so his team gets straight to work when he arrives from the neighboring building.

The minutes feel like hours, but they're not. Time ticks away faster than you'd think. We're at the thirty-minute mark, and we can't spend any longer here. No alarms have gone off, and the cops haven't arrived. But the longer we take, the greater the chance we'll get caught. Just as I'm about to order everyone out, Josue gives us the second go-ahead.

Alejandro, Joaquin, our guys, and I pour through the gates. We sprint the quarter mile to our meetup spot. The guards and other hostages are there, huddled together. Some are crying. If I had more than a token conscience, I might feel badly for them, but I don't. I have more important things on my mind, like getting home to Liesel. I do a quick headcount like a kindergarten teacher on a field trip. Everyone's present and accounted for.

"*Josué, ahora.*" Josue, now.

I give the command, and five seconds later, the night sky erupts in flames like Muano Loa—the world's largest active volcano. Sparks of red, orange, and gold rocket upward with a cacophony of shattering glass and exploding bricks that hammers the eardrums despite the earplugs we all put in. A quarter mile away, and the blasts still rattle your teeth.

There's nothing salvageable. Not a single damn thing.

It would have been nice to acquire the companies, but there are plenty of others to add to our portfolios. I give a mental shrug before I order one of my guys to toss a pair of scissors near the hostage group. We already rounded up their cell phones and smart watches. They won't get those back, but if they can figure out how to snip each other's bindings while their hands are cuffed behind their backs, then they'll get free before emergency services arrive. We'll be long gone.

We pile into the SUVs that are a necessary evil for transporting all of us and our gear. They're hardly inconspicuous, but they do the job. We separate, and half of us head straight to the Kutsenkos' chief German spy. Alejandro leads the other half to the warehouse where the O'Rourkes keep their illegal inventory. Sometimes, they send things through Frankfurt. Other times, it goes through Munich or Berlin. Most often it goes through smaller cities that are less obvious. We got lucky.

It's a silent forty-five-minute car ride while we all catch our breath and cool off. It's not just the balaclavas that overheat us. The bulletproof vests, Kevlar helmets, and the weight of our weapons adds up until it's nearly stifling.

Better too hot than too dead.

I inhale deeply before the mask and helmet go back on. It took restraint not to wipe the sweat burning my eyes. If I did, I'd smear the paint. So fucking tempting.

Mind over matter.

It's been drilled into me since I first started training with my uncles, brothers, and cousins at fourteen.

The half dozen men with Joaquin and me spread out. We're in a modest neighborhood that's hardly memorable. We know the Russian guy's single. His wife left his ass with the kids about ten years ago. He shouldn't have been fucking his secretary. So utterly cliché. The woman left him once he lost most of his money in the divorce. Sucks to be him.

"I wish Pablo was fucking here."

With our earpieces in, Joaquin whispers to me on our secure channel. Our cousin's the one who speaks Russian in the family. It would be fucking useful right now as we surround the property.

"We can always call him. He's better than any app."

"I suppose your German will do."

My older brother elbows me and grins. I give him an internationally crude hand gesture.

When everyone's in position—Joaquin to my right on the back patio—I give the signal. I swing the mini battering ram into the door, and the door bursts open. I toss the home invasion tool aside, and I storm inside.

We all keep low, crouching as we progress forward. It comes as no surprise when bullets sail over our heads as our target shoots first and hopes to ask questions later. He's got real bullets, and this time, so do we. I pivot and aim into the living room, taking out his kneecap.

"*Hör auf zu heulen wie ein kleines Mädchen, du Dreckskerl.*" Stop crying like a little bitch, you piece of shit.

I lunge forward, far closer than he expected. My fist strikes his left cheekbone, and his head snaps back. If he were going to live to see tomorrow, he would wake up with whiplash. Since that's not happening, he'll just have to survive the ensuing pain. I drag him to the dining room chair Joaquin pulls out for him. My brother holds our prisoner's head in place, so he has no choice but to look at me. I keep a healthy distance, so he can't spit in my face.

I launch my interrogation in German. Joaquin can't understand me, but we've played these roles so many times that we don't need verbal cues to know how to work together.

"Why did Maks take Gunter Schlossberg?"

"What're you talking about?"

"You and your goons took Gunter Schlossberg from his office nearly a week ago. You sent his daughter body parts. Why?"

The guy tries to ignore me. I kick him in the shin of his wounded leg. He howls with pain.

"Don't make me ask things more than once."

I withdraw my knife from my pocket and embed it in the bullet hole in the guy's leg. It matches Joaquin's knife that I know is tucked away in his right pocket. We've carried ours since we each turned twelve. It's that fucked-up tradition among the Four Families. We may have played sports together, but once each of us turned twelve, we got a knife. We'd go from being teammates to enemies every week. Now we're still enemies and almost never teammates.

"I haven't spoken to Maks in a couple weeks. I haven't had a reason to."

"That doesn't mean he didn't give you orders months ago. My patience wears thin."

My brother grabs a fistful of his hair and yanks back as hard as he can. The Russian's neck arches as he screeches in pain. I slam my fist into the guy's nose. Blood gushes, and I give him another kick in the shin for good measure.

There's something he isn't telling us; however, doubt creeps into my mind that he doesn't know anything about Gunter. He may know something about Liesel or me. I exchange a glance with Joaquin. I suspect he feels the same way.

"You have a couple of choices. You can speak now without us coercing you, or we can slowly hack you into pieces that could go down the garbage disposal without a problem. Which do you think is the better choice?"

The man chokes from the blood pooling in his mouth—

shitty postnasal drip. It's a good thing I'm standing to the side because he spits a wad of gunk before he speaks.

"Just kill me."

"Oh, that's not a choice. That's definitely happening, so you don't get to count that as an option. Either tell us what we want to know, or we'll coerce you with a few friendly nudges."

I put my knife to his left earlobe. Joaquin lets go of the Russian's head and steps around the chair to stand parallel to me. He fishes out his knife and flicks it open. Before the man can suspect what'll happen next, Joaquin has his arm turned and slices diagonally three times on the guy's inner wrist. They aren't deep enough to kill him, not even over time, but they are enough to make a mess.

"You can either tell me what we want to know, or you'll die looking like Van Gogh."

I use my knife to carve a chunk off his earlobe before I pry his mouth open.

"Do you want to eat your own flesh, or do you want to tell me what the fuck is going on?"

True fear enters his eyes, and the defiance dwindles. Stupidly, it still outweighs common sense. I don't think he believes I'd make him into a cannibal, certainly not one who would eat a chunk of his own flesh, but I've been known to do some fucked-up shit in my life. There's a first time for everything. I'm certain he's figured out we're *los Diaz*. He knows our reputation.

"I'd speak up because right now I can't hear you."

The only thing we hear are his howls of pain. I curl my lip in disgust.

"Stop being a pussy. This doesn't even hurt that much. Not compared to what it'll feel like if you keep refusing to admit what you know about Gunter Schlossberg."

"I know nothing. I swear."

My brother and I take turns as we work our captive over for the next fifteen minutes, but we're just getting his denials. Joaquin and I stand off to the side, letting him rest for moment. When we decide the fucker's break is over, I kick the guy in the *huevos*—eggs is a way more fitting term than balls or nuts. That definitely wakes him up.

I press the tip of my knife just below the man's eyeball again. This time I do it a lot harder. It's enough for him to take me seriously. Joaquin returns to his position behind the guy. He puts his knife to the top of our captive's hairline. He angles the blade to make the Russian understand the threat. I grab hold of his wrist, prepared to slice it like my brother did to the other one. But for now, I don't move the blade's tip away from the man's face.

"Maybe I should do exactly what you did to Gunter. Maybe I should hack off your entire ear and pop out your eyeball. Maybe—rather than slitting your wrists—my brother should just hack off your hand."

I keep pressing the tip incrementally harder until I break the skin. I'm certain his vision's already blurry.

"You won't do any of this shit. It's far too messy."

My brother and I laugh.

"Like we give a fuck about that. We have connections, so it'll all get taken care of."

Joaquin's blade presses hard enough against the man's upper forehead to break the skin. At the same time, my brother pulls the man's hair, and I'm certain he thinks my brother's started to scalp him.

I say a prayer of thanksgiving that Liesel isn't anywhere nearby to listen to even a hint of this. It would just add another layer of trauma to this entire fucked-up week. It would mean she hears what the monster in me can do to someone. I'd give anything to keep that away from her.

"Look, you're going to die regardless. Like I said earlier, you can decide whether it's a clean kill, or we hack you to bits and run you down the garbage disposal. It'll take us a long time with just these little knives to carve you up. It'll be death by a thousand cuts. What are you in the mood for tonight?"

Our gazes lock, and I know he realizes I'm not all bluster. I bite.

"I know who you are. Maksim ordered me to watch you, so I know you've been following a woman. I reported this to the *pakhan*, but he didn't tell me to do anything else. He commanded me to observe and stay out of the way. I don't know why you're stalking her."

"You accuse me of stalking? What the fuck are you doing?"

He coughs up blood, and it dribbles down his chin.

"I get it, but I don't know anything about Gunter Schlossberg besides he's the woman's father. He isn't my assignment. You are."

"What have you told Maks?"

"That you stay outside her office and watch her. You've been inside a few times."

"And after work hours?"

The man gives me a stare that isn't a poker face one. It's a "Don't tell Maks I haven't followed you night and day." Lazy motherfucker.

I step back for a moment and cross my arms. I make sure my shirt sleeves pull tight against my biceps as I do. I dip my chin, and my brother releases the guy's hair and pulls his knife away, leaving a shallow cut as he does it. I flex my pecs right before I drive my fist into the guy's left rib cage at the same time Joaquin nails the guy's right ones. Once more, he howls in pain, doubling over from it. I grab hold of the guy's injured earlobe and yank until it looks like I'll practically rip the ear right off.

If he was too lazy to follow me after sundown, then I'm certain Maks hasn't made information flow in both directions. Our captive might be a senior guy here in Frankfurt, but he isn't more than a midlevel guy in the bratva hierarchy. He likely oversees the legit deals and some street level hustles, but he's no mastermind. Maks doesn't have confidants who aren't related to him, so the man's run out of usefulness.

As Joaquin and I observe and assess him, we know we've come to that point where he has no more information to give. We can torture him for the sake of it, or we can end things. We won't get more out of him, and I have better things to do like getting cleaned up and being with Liesel—something I can't do yet, but it's what I want. I know Joaquin feels no personal connection to this guy, so continuing his torture appeals to neither of us.

Joaquin moves his blade to the guy's throat. He begins to press and pull, making the man presume he'll be practically beheaded. Instead, I chop off both middle fingers.

"Hold your hands up and say cheese."

The Russian's nearly passed out, but he follows my command. I snap a photo for Maks. We might send the fingers to him, or we might just threaten to. If the Kutsenkos are involved in Gunter's disappearance, they'll get the significance. If they aren't, then it's just a mutilated fuck you.

I pull the gun from my lower back holster and put it directly between our captive's eyes. He looks up at me, and I match his gaze before I pull the trigger. Blood and other shit splatters, but it's nothing new to any of us. I hate saying how desensitized we are, but it is what it is.

As soon as we finish with the Russian, one of our men brings us fresh changes of clothes. Joaquin and I take advantage of the bathroom and shower. We scrub ourselves, ensuring we take no biological evidence with us. While Hisham's team comes to the Russian corpse's house to make it look like none of us were ever there, Joaquin and I climb into an SUV to ride over to our next destination.

My brother has his laptop, so he's plunking away on the keyboard as he hacks into the email account of the "Thieves in Law" shot caller. I'm sitting next to him, so I can see his screen. I read along as he types.

"Where should I say the exchange happens?"

"Tomorrow evening at Grüneburgpark. Just before sunset. It's a public location, so his men aren't likely to come with guns ablaze. Hell, it'll force me to be civil too. Drop some Thieves' names who'll supposedly be there."

We decided to send the fingers to Maks's *boevik*—guys who carry out illegal operations, and, in this case, second-in-command—to prove we're serious, and Joaquin attaches the photo to incentivize Masks to make sure someone shows up. I observe as my brother finishes the email and shoots it off to Maks.

Joaquin spent time hacking prison records yesterday to discover who the Thieves' main players are. Now he's looking up the tracking devices our men dropped on these guys' vehicles. Most of them are at their homes or work.

He's about to snap his laptop shut because nothing interesting turned up, but Maks's response pops up as a notification. I skim it before reading it more closely. Joaquin looks over at me, and we shrug at the same time as we frown. I'm the first to speak.

"Nothing about that email leads me to think Maks ordered Gunter's kidnapping. He's too ambivalent. We know him better than just about anyone outside his family. The only people who know him as well as we do are the Mancinellis and O'Rourkes. This isn't him playing it cool. He's not threatening the Thieves or giving them carte blanche. He's letting them do their thing."

"Could he really be giving them enough rope to hang themselves?" Joaquin's ruminating, but I don't think he believes that.

"No. He's told them they can do what they want as long as they don't fuck up. We know that fuck up means encroaching on the Kutsenkos' business. He even thanked them for taking out the Heidemann buildings. He really didn't want us to have them. He'd rather no one did."

"Do you think he already knows it's us? Why isn't he at least pissed about his *avtoritet*?"

I consider that. "Maybe he knows it was us. Maybe he doesn't. I bet he knows his operative did a shit job surveilling me, so he was fine to let him go. Let's be real. The man was completely expendable to all of us."

"Was this a loss for us?"

"No. We wanted those holdings, but we didn't need them. Maks can't sell them to anyone else, so he's the one who took the loss. Fuck him."

"We're no closer to knowing where Gunter is."

I don't need Joaquin's reminder. "I know. I can't help but feel like a failure for that."

"*Manito*, we still have the other two families to strike. This isn't on you. You and I have worked as long and as fast as we can. You're doing your best to look for him and comfort Anneliese and her family."

"Doesn't mean I don't feel that way, even if it isn't rational."

"You care about her. You're also a worrier by nature, even if you've learned to control it."

What if I fail so badly Liesel doesn't want me anymore? What if...

"Enough with the what ifs...Don't give me that look. I know you."

I nod to my older brother. Maybe he's gained more wisdom than I have in that whole twenty-one months he's been alive longer than me.

"All right. For now, the bratva's a dead end. We have to leave it at that and move on."

We regroup with Alejandro and our other men at the O'Rourkes' warehouse. The ones who went with us to the Russian's place stood guard around the neighborhood while we worked the fucker over. Alejandro's men stood sentry waiting for us here. My cousin is a fucking ghost, so he's the one who scouted. No one's better at reconnaissance than him. For being the biggest one in the family, he can be the least noticeable. Fucking inconceivable until you watch him.

"What'd you find?"

Alejandro, Joaquin, and I are on the frequency that's locked and for our family's use only. We're speaking *Macaguán* instead of Spanish. I don't know where this conversation will go, so while Alejandro's guys know the answer to the question, we may not want them to know whatever comes next.

We've divided to conquer. We each have a side of the building, and Josue's leading men on the fourth side.

"There're at least fifty kilos in there from their Amazon labs. Pedro tested it. Shit quality like usual. They're getting ready to load the trucks. Ten guys on lookout, five packing, two drivers, and four in the office shooting the shit."

We control everything coming in and out of Latin America, especially what's manufactured in the rainforest. The O'Rourkes, along with the Mancinellis and Kutsenkos, know they only have labs there because we allow it. We'd rather the enemy we know—who won't fucking blow up endangered flora and fauna—than the ones we don't.

They also know there's a set quota on how many labs they can each have—three. When they try for more, we set up controlled burns. Usually, they remember not to bite the hand that feeds them. They also haven't mastered the quality control we have. The Mancinellis are a distant—like light years away—second to us. I have no problem saying as much.

"Only Luca is close to Pablo's skills. Even then, he's like a kid with a toy chemistry set. The O'Rourkes' knuckles still drag too much for them to have anyone who can handle the formulas. The fucking Kutsenkos—fucking apes too—ought to put their KGB-level spying skills to some real use. Maybe then they'd learn how we replicate our shit rather than learning which ones of us are having flan for lunch."

We can own our own stereotypes. Though, only *Tío* Luis likes flan. I can't stand the mushy, slimy texture. If I want a dessert that wiggles, I'll have Jello.

Joaquin looks at me since I'm leading this mission. "What do you want to do with it? If it's shit, do we want to burn it or sell it but pass it off as theirs."

"I certainly don't want our name associated with poor quality. Burning it is a waste though. It's probably going to Clyde anyway. We can give it to him for free."

Fifty kilos isn't that much. We can grab it and go fast. We'll divvy it up among all of us and carry it in our go bags. As long as no one's stupid driving back to Hisham's, the police will be none the wiser. It'll be out of our hands before noon.

"Who're we blaming?"

I point toward a motorcycle in the parking lot next door. "Hell's Angels. They can take it up with the locals here or the branch back home."

None of the O'Rourkes are in a motorcycle club, but they

have plenty of affiliated members. Let them spin their wheels—shitty pun intended—while they sort it out. For all the fucks I give, Dillan can pick a fight with the largest chapter in Oakland. California's nice this time of year for a visit.

"Then let's get on with it. We've been here long enough. I'm not getting a good feeling about being here any longer."

Alejandro's intuition is just as sharp as the rest of ours. When one of us gets a tingly feeling that something's about to pop off, the rest of us listen. The three of us switch our radios back to the main frequency. I give the first command.

"*Mascarillas puestas y tapones para los oídos puestos.*" Masks on and earplugs in.

I inch along the wall to the open bays where the two trucks are parked. I use my cell phone camera as a mirror to show me inside the warehouse. The men who must be the drivers are smoking what smells suspiciously like a product they likely didn't buy from their bosses but rather stole.

I don't know how Alejandro got a powder sample out of there for Jesus to test because almost all the bricks are in boxes. Then again, he and his men waited more than an hour for us. I see some mobsters on patrol, but they look like they're on more of a Sunday stroll than alert. If they were, they'd have spotted us by now.

I pull the clip from the smoke grenade and toss it inside. Tear gas explodes, and a moment later, I dash inside. I lob another farther into the warehouse, catching all of them by surprise. With our gas masks on, the polluted air doesn't bother my team. We launch our attack from all directions. Alejandro and his men head to the office. Joaquin's team goes for the guards. My team takes out the drivers and grabs the boxes with the product.

We're in and out far faster than the previous half of tonight's mission. It's real guns and real bullets for this campaign. There's no stunning or capturing the men here. They're syndicate men. They know—knew—the risks. By the time we're done, two men from my side have knife wounds, and one had a bullet graze his thigh. Nothing that requires more than the stitches Joaquin and I'll give them once we get away. He, Javier, and I are all trained paramedics. Our skills come in handy far too often.

Once we're certain we've left no witnesses, we retreat to the SUVs. Turns out there wasn't just some white powder waiting for us. My guys found some leafy greens too. The shit those two fuckheads were smoking.

"Torch it?" Alejandro's looking back over his shoulder as we arrive at the vehicles.

"No. One big fire tonight is enough. No need to risk the authorities connecting the dots. We did a good enough job with the smash and grab, plus there's no one left. We did what we set out to do. You leave the calling card?"

"Yeah. Wheeled the bike into the middle of the floor myself. I spotted a pair of scissors on a desk when I tossed the office, so I even cut out a little angel from printer paper. Left it next to the bike."

"Artsy."

I grin at my cousin. The man can't draw a line with a ruler. The best he can do is color by numbers.

"We can't all be Fernando Botero."

He's a famous Colombian painter and sculptor known for his rather—uh—voluptuous— figures. That's probably the most tactful way of putting it. His art is a bit too whimsical for my taste, but I sure as fuck can draw a shit ton better than my cousin.

My brother and I each climb into the back of an SUV with a stabbing casualty each. We'll do what we can while in moving vehicles. It's a good thing we both have surgeon-like steady hands. Before putting on gloves, Joaquin and I switch our frequencies over to the one Alejandro joins us on.

"Thank God Hisham and Noor own the house next to them and have no renters right now. The guys can go straight inside. We need to clean up before Liesel and her family see us."

Luck hasn't been on our side since I got here—except for meeting Liesel. But at least we have that going for us. We have a place for the guys to stay. Before dropping Liesel off, we decided we should all relocate to Hisham and Noor's until this is over. Now none of the men have to drive to the safe house for their shifts. The shorter the distance between our men and us, the better.

"I can't wait to get this shit off my face. I call first shower."

Alejandro's not just naturally the pretty one. He's the one who actually takes any kind of skin or hair care seriously. Alejandro and the word metrosexual don't go in the same paragraph—not even the same conversation. But he's the most particular of us. I have sensitive skin and need the special shaving cream, or I break out. My cousin has actual contact allergies to shit. He has to have special camo paint, or he winds up with more than just hives. They're practically blisters.

The house has two full bathrooms, so it'll be like conveyor lines for showers. But everyone learns to be fast and to tidy up after themselves—that includes disinfecting all surfaces in between turns. The men will work out who's responsible for burning all the clothes, so we leave no evidence behind.

By the time we arrive, all three guys who got injured are patched up. Everyone implicitly understands the hurry I'm in to get next door. Normally—despite Alejandro's claim—my family and I would be among the last to clean up, putting our men ahead of ourselves. But they all insist I take one of the first showers. I scrub myself until my skin's red and my scalp tingles. Then I'm into fresh clothes.

Hisham has a guard outside the front door since it's barely dawn, and the neighbors are unlikely to notice. The guy greets me before knocking. It's another guard who opens the door. I appreciate the precautions our family friends take.

"Jorge?"

Liesel spots me immediately and dashes to me. Finally, she's in my arms again, but I have to let go far too soon.

Chapter Twenty-Five

Liesel

As much as I want to know what happened, I don't. Jorge's back in one piece, and short of my father coming home, that's what matters most. I peer over his shoulder as Joaquin and Alejandro come through the front door. All three men have wet hair, and Jorge smells like he just stepped out of the shower.

After seeing amputated body parts, I force my mind away from why they needed to clean up before coming back here. As long as he isn't hurt, I know deep in my heart that I don't care what he and his family did. I don't care who they might have hurt or what laws they broke.

I just don't give a shit.

If you asked me even a week ago, I doubt I could rationalize what I am now. But my father wasn't missing, and I didn't fear death around each corner. Whatever Jorge has to do to survive and to bring my dad home is fine with my conscience.

I suppose that makes me a horrible person. I suppose it makes me amoral.

I have no fucks to give.

The Liesel who existed before meeting Jorge doesn't exist anymore. It's not his fault. It's whoever targeted my family. I'd already changed when I accepted being part of a money laundering ring and taking orders from an anonymous syndicate. My father's kidnapping and torture just sealed the deal.

I'm stronger for being with Jorge. The weight of the world's still threatening to crush me, but at least I'm shouldering it with a backbone of steel. He's helping me see I'm more resilient than I imagined. I'm not weak anymore, and I'm not giving in to these faceless fuckers.

I don't have a bad boy or violence fetish, but knowing Jorge is an apex predator of sorts is hot. He's more than a Rottweiler. He's lion; a king of the jungle. Without a doubt, I know I'll always feel protected and safe with him. Even when we're not eyeballs deep in the shit, he'll make me feel cherished and valued. I can't explain my certainty, but it's there unlike in previous relationships.

"Did Hisham go out?"

Jorge's question pulls me back to the present as he lets go of me and looks around, spotting my family. We tried to doze in the living room while the guys have been gone. None of us could face going upstairs to sleep. Neither my mom nor I wanted to be alone, and neither Heidi nor Friedrich wanted to leave us alone.

"Yes. He and Noor did nearly two hours ago. He said they had something they needed to see to."

Jorge just nods. I think he knows where our hosts went. I already know better than to ask.

"They're wrapping up some stuff for us."

That as much as I'm going to get. They reassured us that they had extra guards posted around the house and the neighborhood. I wish we were in gated community like at the safe-house. But I trust Hisham and Noor despite barely knowing them.

What choice do I have if I want any peace of mind while Jorge's gone?

"Let's join the others, *chiquita*."

I nod—begrudgingly.

"What happened? Did you learn anything? Do you know where he is yet?"

My mom clamps her mouth shut before she full-on peppers them with questions, but we all want to know the answers. I shift my gaze from Jorge to his relatives. I already know we'll get a fraction of what happened, but I pray they can give us something.

"Gretel, we've ruled a few things out. But we don't know where he is yet."

"You were gone for hours though." Heidi's fighting tears of disappointment as she speaks.

"I know it's not fair to ask for your blind faith while giving you so little information, but we need you to trust that we're making progress. It's not safe to tell you more than that."

"Were you doing something illegal?" My mom's whisper is barely loud enough for any of us to hear us.

All three Diaz men stare at her. I'm already far too familiar with that expression. The resignation that settles on my mom's face tells me she knows the answer, but she makes no protests. I shift my focus to my sister. She's darting her gaze back and forth among them before she looks up at Friedrich.

He's the same kind of stoic that describes *Onkel* Clyde. He pulls Heidi closer to him; both arms are already wrapped around him. She buries her face against his chest, and her shoulders rise and fall. She silently cries. I hate thinking it, but it's better than her asking questions the men won't answer.

We've all settled in seats in the living room. Joaquin leans forward in his chair, his forearms resting on his thighs.

"We wish we had more to tell you. For right now, everyone needs some sleep. We're all exhausted. We know it was impossible for you to relax while you waited, but it's the best thing we can do."

My mom's stare is a million miles away as she heads upstairs. Heidi and Friedrich soon follow her, my sister's boyfriend carrying her as she silently cries. Jorge slips his hand into mine, and we bring up the rear. Joaquin and Alejandro remain downstairs despite what Joaquin said about them being exhausted too.

"They'll sleep down here. Joaquin's practically an insomniac anyway, so I'm sure he'll check a few things before passing out one of the sofas."

"Are they guarding the front door? Do they not trust Hisham's men?" I keep my voice down, not wanting anyone to overhear me.

"We definitely trust the men. It's just what we do when we're somewhere other than our own homes. At least two of us are the first line of defense when we're protecting our family."

Our family.

It warms me all the way to my toes that they consider my family and me as part of theirs. All three men have since the beginning. It speaks to the deeply ingrained sense of loyalty, honor, and duty they possess.

Once we're inside the bedroom, we both get undressed and climb into bed. I wrap myself around Jorge's side, resting my head on his chest. His fingertips trails along my back as he hums a lullaby.

My tears begin with a slow trickle before they're flowing. I've tried so hard to keep them at bay, but the cumulative effect of the past week slams into me now that I'm in Jorge's arms again. I only cry when he's here for me to lean on. Around him, I don't have to be strong for anyone else.

When I shudder a sigh and the tears slow, my mind reaches the point of releasing control. We move at the same time, wrapping my hand around his semi-hard cock. It lengthened when he saw me naked just like I grew wet when I saw him. Neither of us acted on our bodies' reactions at first. But now we know what we need.

It's the same thing we did after he spanked me. It's not sex. It's deeper than that. When he's fully hard, I straddle him and take him into my pussy. Instead of just humming, Jorge sings to me.

"*Duérmete niña, duérmete tú, antes que venga el currucutú. Duérmete niña, duérmete tú. Antes que venga. El guanaguana. Qui-qui-ri-qui.*"

When we come to the end of the song, I kiss his neck and lean back.

"What does it mean?"

"Go to sleep child, go to sleep, you, before the screech owl comes. Go to sleep child, go to sleep, you, before the black skimmer bird comes. Caw, caw, caw, caw. My mother sang it to my brothers and me."

"I never would've imagined you have such a rich voice. It's like listening to honey."

He chuckles, and his cock flexes inside me. I moan and rock my hips twice before I settle.

"Thank you, *chiquita*. I sang in a boys' church choir until my voice broke. Then in college, I sang in an acapella group."

"Like in the movies?"

That really makes him laugh. "Hardly, but it was the only time I didn't feel uncomfortable being in front of people. I actually minored in vocal performance."

I sit up and cup his face, kissing his forehead, the tip of his nose, and then his lips.

"You're truly a Renaissance man. Is there anything you can't do?"

"Well, besides when I'm singing, I loathe being the center of attention, even though sometimes work forces me to be."

As I study his expression, I know he means more than just presenting before boards or interviewing them. Sharing something that makes him so vulnerable completely calms me. I feel like I can tackle whatever the next conversation will be.

"Tonight was about luring out whoever's responsible. We focused on the most likely suspects, but we didn't get anything definitive. I don't want to beat a dead horse, *chica*, but I'm going to anyway. I'm sure you must've thought about previous clients when all of this started. Was there really no one at all? Not even a twinge of concern? Maybe, just maybe, there's something you haven't thought of yet."

"There were the Kutsenkos, but they were always strictly business, and everything I learned looked like the deals were above board. We had some California tech guys who wanted to invest through crypto. I wasn't entirely convinced at the time, and I'm not convinced now that the assets were legally obtained. I'm not sure they were theirs to spend, but all of the profit they made from those transactions got reinvested back into their company. I didn't question it too hard. There were three Spaniards who used us about a year and a half ago. However, all three of them are now in jail for tax evasion that they were already committing, but we never knew about."

"I—"

"Jorge! Jorge!"

We hear Jorge's brother thundering down the hall.

"*¡Joaquín, no entres!*"

I'm certain he's telling him not to come in since we're

in a position neither of us wants anyone else to see. We hear his hand twist the doorknob, but at the last minute he stops.

"Jorge, get downstairs. We found him."

"What?" I look at Jorge not wanting to get my hopes up.

"My brother found your father. Let's go."

We hop off the bed and struggle to balance in our scramble to get our clothes back on.

"How, Jorge? How did they do it?"

"I don't know, but we'll find out in just a moment."

Jorge flings open the bedroom door, and we run back to the living room. He grabs my upper arm to keep me from falling down the stairs. It shocks me to see Hisham with them. I never heard him or Noor get home. I glance toward the stairs, and he reads my mind.

"She went to bed."

Joaquin turns his laptop toward us. "We picked him up on the CCTV as they tried to get into your office building."

We can all see Papa looks in pretty good shape. He's upright and walking on his own, but I suspect there's a gun pointed at his lower back, even if the camera doesn't show it. The cameras are on the opposite side of the hand he lost. We watch them enter Papa's office and look around, but they come out empty-handed. Joaquin taps on the keyboard a couple of times and brings up the cameras in the underground parking garage.

"What're they doing?" I point to men moving across the screen.

"Those are our men. They're putting trackers on whatever vehicles those kidnappers are using. Joaquin, Alejandro, and I need to leave again."

"Okay, but do we tell my family anything?"

All four men shake their heads like they're synchronized

swimmers performing a routine. Jorge brushes the back of his fingers against my cheek.

"No, not yet. Not until we have confirmation that what we saw is an accurate feed, and we can get your dad back. Tonight's already been long for them, and I know they don't feel like we accomplished anything because there's nothing we can tell you. I don't want to get anyone else's hopes up yet."

"All right."

My mind's too much of a jumble to do more than nod and barely mumble my thanks. Despite still having little to go on—or at least, I think they still have little to go on—who knows what no one's telling me—our relief is nearly palpable.

"What do I tell everyone when they wake up? Do we wake them now?"

"We let them sleep for now. Tell them the truth when they get up. We got called away, but you know none of the specifics."

I sigh with resignation. I know Jorge, his cousin, and his brother are doing the best they can. I just don't look forward to facing my mom and sister. Friedrich won't be any easier.

"Anne?"

I turn toward the stairs and find Heidi, Friedrich, and my mom on the landing. So much for not waking them. It was likely Joaquin calling out to us now that I think about it.

"The guys are going out again."

Jorge squeezes me hand. "We've made progress, and there's possibly more information. We're going to investigate."

As my family comes downstairs, Hisham speaks to Joaquin, and Alejandro makes a call. I think he's speaking to their men. Jorge says his goodbye to me. He eases me against him as he presses his lips to mine. He can't linger over the kiss he gives me because there's no time, and it's not the right place. We whisper to each other, not wanting to share any more than what we have to during what should be a private moment.

"Daddy, come back to me. Be careful."

"I will, *chiquita*. My first priority is you and everything that keeps you safe and makes you happy. Nothing is keeping me from coming back to you."

I love you is on the tip of my tongue, but it's way too soon to say that. I've had hours and days to mull over my feelings for him. I know my feelings for Jorge came on strong from the get-go, but it's because I weighed the circumstances and decided. I don't expect him to be in the same place as me. I don't want to say it and make him uncomfortable. I certainly don't want to say it and not have it reciprocated. I do the best I can.

"Jorge, I care about you more than anyone in the world."

"I care about you that way too, Liesel."

I don't want to doubt whether my words can be true when I just broke up with someone. I pray Jorge takes them to mean what I intend. We exchange one more kiss and then he's headed out the door. I huddle with my family while Hisham speaks quietly to his wife, who just joined us.

Now we wait.

Chapter Twenty-Six

Jorge

I slip into the driver's seat.

"Where're we going? I need directions."

We're headed to the Bahnhofsviertel—Station District— near the central train station. It's a high-crime area in Frankfurt. The type of place where someone getting beaten to a pulp or left out to suffer after dark is less questionable than in other parts of the city. It's known for high drug use, and there's a red-light district there too. It's worse at night with parties, but it isn't a desirable destination during the day either.

Alejandro enters the destination in the stolen car's GPS, and I take quick glances. The police can track the car if they want, but we'll ditch this one tonight. It's not even the same one we used earlier.

"Looks like it'll take us at least half an hour to get there. Though—with the way you drive...*Para bola.*"

It literally translates to "to stand ball," but it means pay attention. Alejandro fucks around and grabs the "oh shit handle" above his door's window.

"Be glad I haven't killed you yet. And I'm not the one who's been in three rollovers, *primo*." Cousin.

"None of those were my fault."

I snort. "You were driving all three times."

"Rolling my Wrangler while off-roading is a rite of passage."

"You keep telling yourself that about your little Toy Tonka."

I was in the car for that one, and it really wasn't that bad. It just sorta—toppled...Then rolled twice. We got it back on all four and were no worse for wear, though he needed a new windshield. There's a reason they aren't made out of glass.

"You nearly killed me though." Joaquin brushes his finger over a scar over his left eyebrow.

I'm certain Alejandro's rolling his eyes at my brother. "You shouldn't have egged me on to see if I could beat Seamus in that drag race. He was the dumb fucker who skidded into the turn and took out my tail end. He started to roll and pushed me over the edge. He totaled his car. Mine just needed cleaning off."

"Both of you were fifteen and didn't have permits! You're both lucky your moms never found out. You woulda been hiding behind *Tío* Enrique while praying the rosary, and Seamus woulda been hiding behind his grandfather doing the same damn thing. Saoirse's just as terrifying as *Tía* Catalina."

We don't discuss the third time because Juan was drunk in college, and Alejandro went to pick his dumbass up. Juan thought he was funny, yanking at the steering wheel. Alejandro's car swerved on a patch of ice and rolled twice before slamming into a median. He took the blame for that because he was behind the wheel along with two broken ribs and a broken nose.

Juan was already in trouble for underage drinking once he got home. Juan always managed to slide by despite *Tío* Luis and *Tía* Margherita knowing what a little shit he was. There was always some loophole or technicality. It's why he made a good cop for us on the NYPD payroll—until he fucked all the way up, and Maks couldn't forgive or forget.

Our stroll down memory lane helps pass the time. It only takes us twenty minutes to get to our destination. It might not have been a land speed record, but it was better than what the nav said. I pull over two blocks away on a one-way street. Our men pull up at the end of the block. There are no working streetlights, so that's why I stopped here.

"Capitanes, aquí tenéis." Captains, here you go.

One of our men brings our go bags. They have what we need. Not only tactical gear and spare street clothes, but also fake passports and driver's licenses, and a few thousand dollars in several currencies. We have an extra cache of weapons in each. Joaquin, Alejandro, and I put on jeans, t-shirts, and sweaters after our showers. We're in sneakers rather than dress shoes like we usually are. None of us enjoy suits, so we take any chance we can to wear comfortable clothes. Our men are already dressed in all black.

All of us suit up with our Kevlar vests, helmets, NVGs— night vision goggles, extra knives in our belts, and pistols strapped to our thighs. We each have our rifles slung across our chests. On missions like this, we have Velcro badges on the back of our vests that say *polizei*—police. We have them in seven languages. As long as no one looks too long, it'll confuse them. We don't have the letter and number IDs that usually go on the back of German police bulletproof vests. That's what really gives us away.

We move into a formation with Joaquin to my right as we lead. He has the CCTV feed on a small tablet strapped to his vest that he's carrying in his left hand. The screen's so little, I'm not sure how he can tell what anything is, but he always does.

Right at the corner, then across the street, and three buildings down.

My brother tells us all that through hand and arm signals that aren't standard military. We don't need to give our plans away to anyone who can understand those. We're more covert that way. Lessons our grandfather taught our dads—even mine and Alejandro's, who were his sons-in-law. In my family, in-law is only what outsiders say. There's no difference. Once you're family by blood or by marriage, that's all that matters.

We have a dozen men with us, so we spread out. Six split off, three going in each direction as they creep around to the back of the building. The rest of us hunker down as we wait for them to give us an update. It comes through our earpieces.

"No hay puertas aquí atrás. Las ventanas están en el segundo piso. No hay acceso." No doors back here. Windows are on the second story. No access.

"Regresar."

I give the order for them to come back. We use a tool that looks a lot like a crowbar to force the door open silently. There's no light, so we all flip our NVGs down. I enter first since I'll never send anyone ahead of me when I command a mission.

My woman's family, my mission to lead.

Joaquin follows me in. We both have thermal imaging binoculars, so we peer in different directions once we move the NVGs out of the way. Annoying, but both are necessary. We look at each other and shake our heads. I point to a stairwell that goes up and down. Our men know what to do without verbal or hand commands. Four go downstairs with Joaquin, four remain on the ground floor with Alejandro, and I take the last four upstairs.

"*Nada.*" Nothing.

I hear Joaquin's hushed voice in my ear. I'm almost to the top of the stairs with my men behind me, rifles at the ready. I'm the next one with an update.

"*Tres.*" Three.

I can't tell from the heat-seeking binoculars whether any are Gunter. My men and I move toward the door, making room for Joaquin and his men to pass us. They go up to the next floor.

"*Duos. Subiendo.*" Two. Going up.

We all wait for my brother to give us a report from the last story.

"*Nada.*"

I breathe a little easier while Joaquin and his team come back down a floor. Alejandro and his men join me. He sticks with me while half his team goes up to join Joaquin.

"*Tapones para los oídos puestos.*" Earplugs in.

I give everyone a chance to slip them in. My brother and I have devices to burst the doors open. I know Joaquin's ready when I hear him practically whisper.

"*A las tres.*" On three.

It's on my count. "*Uno, dos, tres.*"

The moment the doors swing in, Joaquin and I lob our flash bangs inside. I know his works because even with earplugs, I can hear it. We'll only use our smoke grenades if we have to.

"*¡Él está aquí!*" He's here!

It's one of the men with Joaquin. The men with me still sweep the expansive space. I don't know what it once was, but it looks like a flop house now. Only one man looks intelligent enough to know what the fuck is going on, but we won't underestimate the others. Rather than killing them on the spot, we zip tie them. I check in with the men upstairs.

"*¿Cómo está él?*" How is he?

"Ambas manos." Both hands.

What the fuck did Joaquin say?

Leisel spins around on the sofa as I enter the house. He eyes widen as she watches me help her father inside. Her expression screams it's one of the most joyous moments of her life. She and Heidi sprint to their father, and his arms engulf them probably the same way they have since they were little. I bet he was a bear of a man back then; he still is now.

The sisters look at each other as tears stream down their faces, but they let go sooner than we probably want. Their mom's desperate to hug him too. Leisel steps back and reaches for me but gasps.

"Papa, your hand!"

"I'll explain everything, but—"

Gretel practically throws herself into Gunter's arms, and he wraps them around her, lifting her off the ground. The hand we thought he lost is precariously close to her ass as they kiss in a way that makes me think Heidi and Leisel have never seen— in a way they could've gone their entire lives without seeing. Liesel's nose curls instinctively just like her sister's. They look away. Heidi clings to Friedrich as I pull Liesel against me.

She inhales my scent. Each breath filled with my cologne seems to calm her.

"Daddy." She exhales the word before she kisses my neck.

"Baby girl, I'm here."

"You're not hurt, are you?" She tries to pull away.

"Don't you dare move, or else everyone here will see how hard my girlfriend makes me."

"Girlfriend?"

"Soon-to-be fiancée, not-too-far-in-the-future wife. Is that better?"

"Infinitely."

Gretel and Gunter finish their kiss with a gentle peck. Then Gunter looks at the rest of us.

"I'll explain everything, just let me catch my breath." He kisses Gretel's forehead.

Leisel and I hang back for a moment as my body calms enough to be presentable. We continue to whisper.

"I want you by my side, *chiquita*. Always. We'll figure out what that looks like, but I won't let you go."

By my side.

I mean that to the bottom of my heart. I've never meant anything more. I can't imagine letting Leisel go now that I've found her.

"I don't know what'll happen with our work or our families in the days to come, Jorge. I don't know when I'll go to New York, but to the very depths of my soul, I know I'll follow you wherever you go."

We gaze into each other's eyes, and I see the depth of my feelings mirrored in hers.

"You ready to let me lead because you know I want you as an equal—a partner."

"You've guided me through all of this, been at my side the entire time. You could've commandeered it all and told me nothing. But you haven't. You're dominant with every breath, but you're not domineering. You may exert that dominance during sex, but it's confidence and steadfastness outside of sex. It's what I need."

As I stare down at her, I know I'm falling in love. I'm not convinced I'm there yet, but I think that's merely a matter of time. It's like the foundation is in place, and the walls are nearly built. It just needs the roof on top. Then we can make that house into a home—together.

It's not until Joaquin leaves the kitchen with a silver tray holding a silver teapot and traditional small Moroccan glasses, and Alejandro follows with a tray with heaping plates of cookies and pastries, that I remember there are other people here. I even forgot her family despite hearing their voices.

As we walk into the living room, she stretches to whisper to me some more. "It's sweet to watch Joaquin and Alejandro wait for Noor to tell them where to put the trays. I'm certain I heard one of them say, '*Sí, Tía.*'"

"Don't tell anyone, but the men in my family are just giant teddy bears." I wink at her.

The living room furniture is a combination of European and Moroccan. There are armchairs, but there are also banquette sofas that line three walls with vibrant, beautifully embroidered pillows.

"Now that Papa's back, the colors seem so much richer in here. Everything was a haze before that. I didn't notice it until now."

"I take it for granted since I've been here so many times, but I get what you mean."

Alejandro and Joaquin take the armchairs while the couples sit close together but on separate sections of the sofa. Leisel and I share one with Noor and Hisham, with her parents sandwiched between Heidi and Friedrich and Liesel and me.

Liesel's arm's wrapped around mine, and our hands are clasped together. It doesn't go unnoticed by her father. I breathe easier when he doesn't look surprised. Just the opposite —it's like he expected it. He's aged significantly in the past week, but he still looks so much like he used to. He has his arm around his wife, who has her hand resting on his knee.

"I can't get over the fact you have both hands! I'm struggling to understand." Leisel leans forward as she stares at her father's undamaged hands.

"Papa, what happened?" Heidi asks the million-dollar question.

"I believed I was meeting Clyde for lunch, but I discovered these men spoofed his number and used some tech program to mimic his voice. When I left the office, they grabbed me."

"No one noticed you trying to avoid getting in their vehicle?" Heidi's got plenty of questions, so everyone lets her ask the same ones we all have.

"No one noticed the gun they had to my kidney. I didn't go willingly, but neither did I want to anger them enough for them to kill me at the destination. There were four of them who encircled me, so I wasn't breaking free. They were going to force me into the vehicle whether I wanted to go or not. Once they had me in there, they put a sack over my head and zip tied my hands. I'm not a small guy and neither were they, but somehow they crammed three of us in the backseat of the car. There wasn't enough room for me to struggle against them."

"Papa, they sent a box to the office that day."

The words burn my ears as I hear the pain in Leisel's voice.

"I know, *mein Honigbienchen.*"

Liesel looks up at me then at my relatives before she explains. "My little honeybee. He's been calling me that since I was a toddler. He said I would buzz about, chattering to everyone but never stopping anywhere for long. Definitely not my personality once I got into school, but the name stuck."

She looks lovingly at her father before she nudges her chin and looks down at his hand.

"They took your ring. Did they tell you why or did you guess?"

"They forced me to see them put the ring on a stranger's hand, then place that in the box. I don't know if it came from a corpse or some other hostage somewhere. I didn't ask, and they didn't offer. I'm fine with never knowing."

From the way Gretel and Heidi nod along with Liesel, I think they're fine with ignorance is—maybe not bliss—fine.

"They forced me to log into the office security, so I watched you come back from lunch. Then I saw Jorge arrive. They didn't expect that. It made a couple of them panic, but it was a massive relief to me. Jorge, while you and your family were always one step behind them, you were stepping on their heels. I suspect their arguing amongst themselves is why you found them. They couldn't agree about whether they should move me to another location. They got careless."

Liesel squeeze my hand. "How'd you find him? Joaquin mentioned the CCTV earlier but didn't really explain."

I smile but tilt my chin toward Joaquin, the pride clear in my voice. "My brother did it."

"With Anneliese not in the office working long hours or to recognize anything out of the ordinary, I suspected they'd go back at some point. If they were watching the office, they knew we had your computers. But I knew there was the possibility—especially after we—"

Joaquin glances at me, unsure how *my girlfriend*—I've never been more excited about those two words—wants to proceed with confessing we bugged the office. Gunter's gaze swings to me, and the scowl speaks louder than any verbal threats he could issue. Liesel glances up at me and sees I'm taking it in stride. My expression's neutral without appearing disinterested. I hear how she breathes easier when Joaquin continues.

"I figured if there was still anything at the office, they'd get desperate to find it before anyone else could. I kept monitoring the CCTV around the office building and what I could see in the lobby and hallway. I didn't watch it as a live feed the entire time, so I'm lucky I happened to be on my computer when I was."

"We're so lucky." Liesel's gratitude shows in her voice and expression as she looks at the man I hope will one day be her brother-in-law.

"Once I knew who to watch, I followed them through the city on the security feed."

"Should I ask how you got into the city's police system?"

"You should not, *Herr* Schlossberg." Joaquin's answer is clipped but not rude.

"I'm grateful you did. I nearly had a heart attack when you burst in. I didn't know what to expect, but it certainly wasn't orders given in Spanish. I was dazed from the percussion grenade. They're louder than you think from the movies. It took me a moment to piece together that it must've been Jorge or another Diaz."

Liesel leans her head against my shoulder, and I rest mine on top of hers.

"What about the other boxes? Did you know they sent more things to us?" Gretel's voice wobbles, and I know she's fighting back tears.

"No. What else did they send?"

"A pig's eye and someone's ear." Heidi looks almost green when she shares that.

"A pig's eye?"

"It looks very similar to a human one if you don't know what to look for." I'm softer spoken with that explanation than I usually am.

"Ah."

We wait for Gunter to say more, but he looks too disgusted to add anything. Who knows what else they did to him? Perhaps that was revolting enough to turn his stomach over, or maybe it was the least of the kidnappers' tricks.

There's still something we need to know, but he hasn't shared.

"Papa, who were they?"

I'm eager to hear Gunter's answer to that question because we didn't learn much while we were at the abandoned building that was little more than a flop house.

"I don't know, Anne. They got a call from someone, but the conversation was too vague for me to guess who or what it was about."

Gunter shrugs with frustration since he knows he's not offering much insight. Everyone's exhausted at this point, and it's clear he has little more to offer. I doubt the man's slept well in days, so we leave off where we are, and all agree to pick up the conversation in the morning.

Liesel and I look at each other, unsure what will happen with the sleeping arrangements. Hisham and Noor weren't here early when the Heidi and Friedrich, and Leisel and I went upstairs.

I know Leisel and I would prefer to be together, and I'm sure Heidi and Friedrich feel the same way, but we're both unmarried couples in somebody else's home. It only takes a moment to allay our fears that we'll be separated when Noor lets us know there's a room for each couple.

Once I close the door behind us, I pull Liesel into my arms. She wraps hers around my waist and presses her cheek against my chest.

"*Chica—*"

"Shh, Daddy, just for a moment. I just want to listen to your heart. The rhythm is so steady that it's comforting to me."

I'll happily hold her forever if it means I can make the rest of the world disappear and let her feel safe. We must stand there for close to five minutes before she pulls away.

"Daddy, I'm tired, but not sleepy."

I'll take that as a hint that she feels up to sex right now. I know I certainly want to bury myself inside her and forget about everything for a while.

"Strip, *chiquita*."

I lead Liesel over to the bed before I turn to where our suitcases sit. We left them at the safe house, so I don't know who brought them here. Frankly, I don't care. I'm quick to open mine and withdraw five ties. As I examine the frame further, I realize it's truly European. While king-size beds exist, they're not as common as full-size or queen.

"Stretch out your arms and your legs as wide as they'll go, little one."

Fortunately, since Liesel is so tall, it makes it easy for me to bind her wrists and ankles to the bed frame's side railings. It's a bit of a stretch for my ties, but I'm able to do it using the wider end to wrap around her wrists and ankles to protect them, while the skinny part of the tie easily wraps around the metal bars along the side edges. I use the fifth tie as a blindfold.

I'd wished the last time we experimented with BDSM elements that I had a feather to tickle her with while I edged her. I recall what I have in my Dopp kit. I have sensitive skin, so regular shaving cream doesn't work well for me. I actually use an old-fashioned shaving powder that I mix with water and use a brush to apply.

I go back to my suitcase and pull out my shaving kit to find that brush. I know she wonders what I'm doing now since she can't see me. I stand away from the bed, enjoying what's in front of me. I have a glorious view of her wet pussy. The longer I stand watching her, the more it glistens as her excitement builds.

Her nipples stand at attention. The air is just cool enough to harden them without it being cold. Her tits are magnificent. They're just the right size for me. A little bit more than a handful each, but plenty for me to play with. I feel like a kid in a candy store.

I can't wait to get started. I head over to the bedside and put the shaving brush on the table. I kiss her left cheek and down along her neck, over her collarbone and shoulder, along her bicep, to her forearm, to her wrist. I travel my way back up her body, repeating those motions.

Then I kiss the valley between her tits, and I smatter kisses around the circumference of her areola. Then I'm licking it. I flick her nipple as I suck. I go back to kissing her breast. I lean farther over the bed, using my height to my advantage as I repeat the same attention to her other nipple. I press her tits together, and titty fucking her is such a temptation right now, but I want to edge her instead.

I kiss down over her belly, moving farther to the left to kiss her ribs. When I come even with her belly button, I press smacking kisses on the silky skin surrounding it until I reach it. I swirl my tongue, dipping inside, then flicking it. I move back along the satiny surface, making a diagonal line from her navel to her hip. I graze my teeth along the soft flesh, and now I leave love bites along that path.

I move diagonally again, except now I'm headed toward her smooth mound. I keep leaving marks with my teeth and suction from my lips. When she removes the blindfold, she'll see I've marked her. It's territorial and possessive as fuck, and she moans with each one. She tries to lift her hips to offer her cunt to me, but she's tied too tightly for her to do much since she can't use her feet to leverage herself.

When I get to her pussy, I kiss around her outside nether lips. I even press a kiss to her clit. Then I draw my tongue along the groove where her leg meets her hip. After that, it's kisses along the inside of her thigh. I leave more love bites as I go.

My tongue flicks the back of her knee before I press a kiss

to her kneecap. I kiss along the inside of her calf then nibble at the outside of her ankle. It's a quick kiss on the top of her foot and then flicking my tongue across her instep.

I watch goosebumps rise on her flesh as I edge her. I work my way back up to her pussy where I finally pay proper attention to her clit. I suck on it as my tongue licks her over and over. I abandon the sensitive bundle of nerves to lave her opening. I dip my tongue inside and purposely slurp her cream. The sound causes her to tremble.

On the quietest whisper, I hear her name for me. *Daddy.* She repeats it in a soft chant, begging for me to move things along, but I'm not ready to stop edging her yet.

I grab the shaving cream brush and move around to the other side of the bed. I'd hate to ignore one half of her. With the lightest touch I can manage, I trail the brush along her body following the same route I did with my kisses on her left side. Her brow furrows as she tries to figure out what causes the fluttering sensation over her skin as I move the brush in small circles.

My touch is as gentle as I can be, the soft bristles barely feathering her skin. Her trembles increase. As I move down her ribs, I discover just how ticklish she is as she attempts to shy away, even if only for a moment.

The brush makes her entire body jerk when I graze her clit with it. Her legs shake as I move from her inner thigh all the way down to her instep. I bring the brush back up the inside of her leg and run it along that crease between her leg and hip as I once again lean over her. If I weren't such a tall man, it would be impossible for me to reach her cunt without climbing onto the bed.

"Jorge, please. I need you."

"You have me, *chiquita*."

"You know what I mean. I need to feel you."

"Your wish is my command."

I untie her right hand before I straighten and guide it to wrap around my cock. I show her how I want to be stroked. Once she knows that's what I desire, I release her hand. She continues on, her blindfolded face turned toward me. I know she can't see what she's doing, but her tongue swipes over her lips in a clear invitation for me to mount the bed and straddle her face. She opens her mouth wide, her tongue pressed flat, but I make her release me.

Tempting as that is, I'm not looking for her to pleasure me. At least not yet. I want her to continue being the sole focus of my attention. I pull away, and she moans in frustration.

"Please, Jorge. I need you. I don't know that I can wait much longer."

My soft chuckle makes her hands fist. I finally crawl onto the bed from the foot of it. I slide my hands under her thighs and bring them up to the outside of her hips. Lying flat on my belly, I worship her cunt, licking, nibbling, sucking until she's begging in English and in German.

"Daddy, *ich brauche dich. Ich kann nicht* stand it. My cunt aches *damit du mich erfüllst.*" Daddy, I need it. I can't stand it. My cunt aches for you to fill me.

As I drive her closer to an orgasm by playing with her cunt, she switches to what I suppose would be Germlish, German-English. Or is it Engman, English-German? Whatever it's called, she's switching between languages mid-sentence. I relish driving her wild like this. When I move up her body, I release her other wrist but keep her legs still tied to the bed.

"Put your hands above your head, little one, and don't move them. If you do, I'll bind them together."

"Yes, Daddy."

She does as she's told, crossing her wrists and grabbing hold of the pillow. I thrust into her hard, then I don't move. My body screams at me. Edging her is edging me too. She might not have touched me other than to stroke me a few times, but I didn't fist myself while I lavished her with my kisses.

The need to move now that I'm inside her practically overwhelms me, but I love feeling her squirm beneath me as she tries to gain friction against her clit or encourage me to move. When she whimpers with frustration, I draw back, then thrust hard. As much as my dick's telling me to jackhammer her cunt, I ignore that need.

Instead, I move slowly as I withdraw, then thrust forward. Between each, I hold my body still as I rest my weight on my outstretched arms. I love looking down and seeing my cock glisten each time I pull back, then watching her abs contract with each of my thrusts.

"Please, Jorge, let me come. *Ich bin so nah und doch zu weit weg*. Please." I'm so close, yet too far away.

I lower myself onto my forearms near her head and whisper in her right ear. "I love the sound of your voice as you beg."

She continues in her blend of German and English. Fortunately, I speak both.

"I need you to fill me, Jorge. Let me feel your cock pounding into me. Every time you pull back so gradually, I feel so empty when you get to the tip. My cunt is burning for you. It's excruciating. Please, Daddy. Please let me come."

I hear that note of genuine frustration, and I don't want to ruin this by making her unsatisfied. I grind my pubic bone against hers and flex my hips, not pulling out far, but just giving myself enough room to press forward and rub her clit with each slide in. She's so wet that there's not much friction anymore, but I still love the feeling. I move inside her so easily now.

"Your cunt belongs to me, little one. It feels like home. Somewhere I long to be and never want to leave."

"Oh, Daddy, yes, yes. I want to be that. I want you to stay

inside of me. It feels like bliss being connected to you, like it's where I'm always meant to be."

With two more thrusts, her head tilts back.

"Please, Daddy, may I come?" She blurts her request in English rather than begs.

"Yes, baby girl, let me feel you squeeze my cock."

She shudders beneath me as she comes, but I'm not nearly done yet. When she's only panting, I shift to kneel. I lean back and brace myself to untie her ankles. Thank goodness she's still blindfolded because it's not my most graceful movement since I have to pull out almost to just the tip to reach. Once her legs are free, I press her legs back, moving her knees toward her shoulders, easing her strained joints. Then I wrap them around my waist and thrust hard.

I pound into her over and over before I draw her right leg up to my shoulder. Again, it's a blessing she's so tall because I can place her foot over my shoulder. She flexes it, her heel pressing into me. Her hands grip my waist, and I slide the blindfold off. I want to watch her expressive eyes through all of this. We're moving together so fast and so hard that the bed bangs the wall twice.

I roll us, not wanting anyone to hear what we're doing. A steady cadence of the headboard hitting the wall will easily give it away. She rides me, rocking just as fast as I pounded into her. It doesn't make the bed any quieter. We both pause at the same time and smile. I sit up.

"Wrap yourself around me, *chiquita*."

I move to the edge of the bed and walk to the wall beside the door to the bathroom. I press her back against it as we move together, her hips rocking to meet each of my thrusts. I surge into her over and over until I can barely stand it any longer. I want to make her come at least once more before I get off.

"Daddy, I'm close again, please." She sticks with English.

"Come, *chiquita,* I can't wait much longer. I need to come too. I want to feel you."

"Yes, Daddy. I want to feel it drip on my thighs, knowing you've claimed all of me. Daddy, I want your cum."

We're possessive. It's not just about her orgasm and the dirty talk about my coming inside her. I know she wants to be the only one who gets it, that my cum belongs to her. I love that side of her. I believe neither of us fears the possessiveness will stifle either of us. Just the opposite. I feel loved when she says things like that. I believe she knows my possessiveness comes from my desire for her and for her safety.

I groan against the crook of her neck as I shoot my load deep inside her. I growl as my dick twitches in her pussy. Her heels dig into my lower back, and her thighs squeeze my lower ribs as hard as I think she can. Our kiss is sloppy as we devour one another. We're both drenched in sweat, so I carry her to the bathroom. I reach for the nozzles and turn the shower on.

"Good idea, Daddy. I think we both need to freshen up before we go to bed."

I lower her to her feet once the water is the right temperature, and I've stepped into the shower. There're shampoos and body wash along with a bar of soap inside the shower. I pour shampoo into my hand and rub it along her tresses. I don't know that I've ever used that word to describe someone's hair, but as it hangs down her back, it seems like the right one. I lather it as I massage her scalp.

She reaches past me to the shelf and grabs body wash. With just her hands, she trails it over my arms and shoulders before skimming along my chest and underarms, over my ribs and waist, then my taut belly. When she gets to my cock, she reaches between my legs and cleans my *huevos,* then she strokes me. I harden again. It only takes a moment for me to be at full attention.

She's quick to wash me off as I continue to massage her scalp. She drops to her knees, pouring a little more body wash into her palm. As she takes me into her mouth, she glides her hands on the outside of my legs, then works her way up the inside, her thumbs pressing into my muscles as her nails trail up my thighs.

It's incredibly erotic watching her and feeling how she now teases me. She angles herself to take me as deeply into her mouth as she can. It's bliss all over again. I tilt my head back, letting the water run over my hair and face as I groan.

"If you keep doing that, *chiquita*, I'll come down your throat."

She hums her agreement. Her hands grip my ass as she presses me to slide deeper into her mouth. I move slowly, not wanting her to gag as the tip of my cock brushes the back of her mouth. She swallows, trying to take me down her throat, but it's too much at this angle, and she can't do it. It doesn't stop me from coming hard. I let go of her hair and press my palms against the shower wall to brace myself.

"Fucking hell, *chiquita*. Goddamn."

When I finish, she releases my cock with a popping sound. I guide her back onto her feet and help her rinse the suds from her hair. When the water runs clear, she reaches for the shampoo, and I'm happy to return the favor as she massages my scalp while I'm kneeling. I lick along her cunt before focusing on her clit. I work it over and over again.

It's my turn to grasp her ass, helping her to balance. With my head leaning forward, the water rinses my hair clean. I don't want her to get cold, so I guide her to take a couple steps forward, so the majority of the water runs over her. Her soft mewls keep my body heated. I slide three fingers inside her and work her inner pussy wall. My other hand presses against her belly, and I can feel my fingers working her.

Once more, it's a blend of German and English. "*Bitte*, may I come?" Please.

I nod my head rather than answer with words. Her fingernails graze my scalp, then cling to my shoulders.

"Holy hell, Jorge. Each one gets better and better."

Her amazement is clear in her tone. I rise as I pull her close to me. We share a languid kiss as our hands run over each other. As I turn off the water, she reaches for towels. We dry off and head back into the bedroom. She opens her case, as I walk back to mine. We both pull out pajamas, but neither of us puts them on. Instead, we lay them at the foot of the bed. I pull the covers back, and she crawls onto the bed. I gesture for her to move over.

"*Chiquita*, I'll always sleep closer to the door."

She glances over at it and nods. "But that makes you the first target, Daddy."

Exactly.

"It also means I can get to the door faster without having to climb over you or go around the bed."

Once she's settled, I turn back to my clothes and retrieve my gun. I check it one last time before placing it on the bedside table. She curls up alongside me when I'm in bed. We're soon asleep, but it's only an hour later before my eyes pop open.

I lay beside Liesel for a moment as I try to figure out what woke me. There's soft knocking coming from the front door. Our bedroom looks out over the front yard. I ease my arm out from underneath her neck, then climb out of bed. I rush to pull on my pajama pants tucking my gun beneath the tight elastic waist. I'm pulling my t-shirt over my head as I walk to the door.

Joaquin, Alejandro, and Hisham meet me in the hallway. It surprises me to see Friedrich as well. I understand why my relatives and Hisham are such light sleepers, but I didn't expect

Friedrich to be as well. He just nods as the five of us head downstairs.

Four of us have our guns drawn. Hisham goes to the door, his gun lifted and ready to fire if he needs to. He looks outside before his head tilts to look down. He lifts a box that's similar to the previous ones we've received.

"How did this get to you if you have guards along your street?" Alejandro's wondering the same thing I am, and I'm sure the others are too.

"That's a good question I don't have an answer to right now."

We move into the dining room which is in the opposite direction from the stairs leading up to the bedrooms. He puts the box on the table and looks over at me. Even though it was delivered to his house, he defers to me. I flip open the lid as all of us peer inside. There's a tongue sitting there with a note next to it. I withdraw the paper and unfold it.

SPEAK NO EVIL.

That's all that's written on there.

"That's human."

Four of us nod in agreement with Friedrich. Joaquin's brow furrows as he speaks next.

"If we rescued Gunter and killed the men who had him, whoever sent this knew Gunter was kidnapped but doesn't know we saved him."

I was just thinking that too. I glance back over my shoulder in the direction of the stairs, picturing Liesel sleeping in our bed. Then I look back into the box before I think aloud.

"If we killed the kidnappers, then who is doing this? Shouldn't whoever hired the mercenaries discovered they're dead and Gunter's gone? It's been several hours. You'd think whoever hired the men would be in communication with them. Has the employer been sending the packages rather than the kidnappers, and they don't know Gunter's with us?"

Alejandro shakes his head. "Maybe they know. They could want us to think there're still more captors. Gunter knew about the cadaver hand because they made him watch them slide the ring on its finger, but he didn't know about the ear or eye."

Friedrich leans in a little closer. "But to what avail if Gunter is here? Are they threatening to take him again? They must know that's pointless if he's here with you. Do they want to take Anne or someone else in their family?"

They all know Liesel is my special name for Anneliese. No one else has used it. I flip the lid closed since none of us need to look at it anymore. None of us have answers to those questions, so Friedrich poses a different one.

"What are you going to do with that?" He looks between Hisham and me.

It's Hisham who responds. "I can take care of it."

Friedrich looks like he has more to say, but he's clearly weighing his words. "I admitted to my connections to the Camorra earlier because I wanted to help. It's not something I can hide from Heidi much longer, considering the current circumstances. But there's more to my role than I shared."

"Your role?" Joaquin's natural suspiciousness fills his words.

"I'm more than just friends with a senior member's son. I'm mostly out, but I was an active member while I was a teenager and in college. I insisted I be released from my obligations when I met Heidi and knew I wanted to be serious with her."

I narrow my eyes at Friedrich. "It's not like you can just turn your back and walk away. There was a price to that."

"I started as a mule, then worked my way up because I'm an excellent negotiator. My best friend's cousin fucked around and messed up a ton of shit for a major deal I'd worked months on with members of an Albanian mafia. My best friend's father leads our branch of the Camorra. That syndicate is more like an organization of clans who are often rivals in Campania, especially around Naples."

I suppose he's explaining the politics for our sake and Hisham's. None of us are unaware of how Italian syndicates work.

"It may have been his nephew, but he had no problem commanding me to kill the guy. I made it a show. I proved that while I may want to leave, I'm still loyal and am still a Mafioso even if I don't work as one day-to-day. It was a violent death, but it was the price for me to get out."

His gaze sweeps the group before he continues speaking.

"I'll make some more calls. I fear this isn't about Gunter, Anne, or any of you so much as it might be about me. It could be my connections, and they've targeted Anne and Gunter because they know they'll be my future in-laws."

He pulls his phone from his pajama pocket and unlocks it. We watch as he taps the screen a couple of times, then puts his phone to his ear. It shocks me when he speaks Italian instead of German. He sounds like a native. I don't know if his branch of the Camorra has passed Italian down generation to generation or if someone in his family is a recent immigrant to Germany from Italy, but he's fluent enough that I'd never guess German was his first language. His English is flavored with a German accent, but his Italian isn't.

The rest of us stand around and listen to the one-sided conversation. In my family, it's only Pablo who speaks fluent Italian, so I don't understand Friedrich. He sounds annoyed for part of it, then is back to normal. The conversation draws on, but he's listening to most of it. His expression grows grimmer by the minute until he hangs up. He drops his phone into his pocket as he sighs.

"You won't like this any more than I do." He's shaking his head as he speaks.

"What did you find out?" Joaquin's mind is probably already jumping to what he might have to dig into further.

"It's a turf war. It's the Sicilian *Cosa Nostra* and the Venetian *Mala del Brenta* against my family's branch of the Camorra and the 'Ndrangheta. If you don't know, they're from Calabria. Their name means bravery—manly virtue."

He scoffs at that last part. None of us interrupt him as he explains more about the Italian syndicates. But as he watches the rest of us, he realizes we don't need the history lesson.

"It's the enemy's side, not mine. This has been quietly brewing for years, but it's come to a head. I guess they decided to go after my future sister-in-law to draw me back in. When things didn't progress the way they wanted, they went after Gunter too. I don't know yet why your investments were the tipping point, but I suspect it has something to do with a balance of power. Not so much you gaining more, but someone losing what they have or not gaining what they want."

"And why would they want you involved?" There's a sharper edge to my voice than I intended.

"Because I'm an attorney. They want access to some of my clients. They thought targeting Anne would force me to help them."

"How long have you suspected this?"

"Since I arrived at the hotel."

"Why didn't you say something sooner?"

His gaze hardens into that of a man who's killed before. It's not defensive; it's unyielding.

"Because finding Gunter alive was more important than finding out why. Because I have a family to protect and loyalty to honor. But now I have no choice but to trust you not only with the Schlossbergs' safety but also this information about my family."

I consider what he says before I respond. "This must be a proxy war. My guess is Salvatore Mancinelli is up to his elbows in this. He's probably funding the *Cosa Nostra* and *Mala del Brenta* since he's related to both."

The Carosis run the *Mala del Brenta* in Venice. Salvatore's nephew, Carmine, married Salvatore's wife's niece, Serafina. His wife, Sylvia, was a Toretta before she married into the Mancinellis. They're one of the main *Cosa Nostra* families in Sicily. Her sister's married to the *Mala del Brenta's* don. It's both sides of Salvatore's family.

"It appears my clients have Italian investors—the Torettas and Carosis. They expect a return on their investment. My clients are the ones laundering the money and using Anne as a front. If things fall apart, then she's one of the people left to take the blame. The money's winding up in Venice and Palermo. I'm to go against my family and help the *Cosa Nostra* and *Mala del Brenta* if I want them to leave Anne alone."

I shake my head since my earlier assumption appears wrong. "Maybe the Mancinellis hands are clean in all this after all. But Salvatore's going to be more pissed than he has been since Luca, Carmine, and Gabriele sucked Anastasia into their little scheme."

Salvatore's nephews Luca and Carmine, along with Carmine's best friend Gabriele, fucked up royally when they tried to do a deal with the *Cosa Nostra* and bratva in Chicago. Niko Kutsenko's now wife was collateral damage. The New York Mafia's heir and their worst sinner both wound up with Salvatore beating the snot out of them. Gabriele was no angel either. All three were banished for several months to a vineyard in Sicily for hard labor.

"Friedrich, I need to know your clients' names."

"Fine, Joaquin."

My brother bolts up the stairs, taking them two at a time after Friedrich agrees to his request. It's only a moment later before he's running back down them with his laptop tucked under his arm. We all pull out seats at the dining room table. I push the box away from us since none of us wants to look at it, even if the lid is closed.

Joaquin asks Friedrich questions about who's involved from his family and any names he might know from the other three Italian syndicates. Then he works silently. There's nothing for us to discuss until we know more. So, the only sound amongst us is Joaquin's fingers on his keyboard. When he looks up, he meets my gaze. Then, Alejandro's. Clearly, neither of us will like what he discovered.

"This is some fucked-up shit. It's not Salvatore at all. It's the O'Rourkes helping out the Torettas and Carosis, and the Kutsenkos are helping your family and the *'Ndrangheta*, Friedrich."

"The who?"

He genuinely looks perplexed, so I explain.

"The Kutsenkos run the Russian bratva in New York. Back in the mid-nineties, the Camorra laundered money for the New York bratva in exchange for gun running. Looks like they resuscitated that relationship. Apparently, the Kutsenkos want to not only piss off the O'Rourkes but Salvatore as well."

I consider what this means to the underworld's politics in New York and their wider international implications. It's Hisham who drums his fingers on the table as he speaks.

"Why? What're the Irish and Russians really going to gain by getting involved in an Italian turf war?"

Joaquin crosses his arms as he leans back. "They're fighting over Europe. One wants to expand even more into Eastern Europe, and the other wants to compensate by increasing their influence in Western Europe. Not only that, I think it truly is to piss off Salvatore, but that's not our problem. Too bad, so sad for him. We need to deal with the Russians and the Irish first."

Alejandro leans forward, his arms resting on the table. "What about Friedrich's clients who passed money through Anne's accounts. We still need to deal with them on Anne's behalf."

I clasp my hands as I lean forward in an almost identical position to Alejandro.

"We need to go back to the U.S. to figure this out."

Chapter Twenty-Seven

Liesel

I wake from a deep sleep, and I'm disoriented for a moment. I know it's Jorge in bed beside me, but I'm unsure where I am when I first open my eyes. Then I remember we're at Noor and Hisham's.

"Did you sleep okay, *chiquita?*"

"Yeah, actually, really well. I'm surprised I did."

"It's the relief from your father being back and exhaustion catching up to you with one less thing to worry about. Your body and mind needed the rest."

I tilt my head to look up at him as he gazes down at me.

"I don't doubt that's most of it, but a lot of it is sleeping next to you. I'm safe here, and I know it. I can relax fully when I'm around you."

He draws me over him to straddle his waist. I guide his cock into me and lean forward. We lie like this for a moment before I rock my hips. His hands guide me into a rhythm as he thrusts up and down, driving himself deep inside me. I sit back, my hands resting behind me. This is the deepest he's ever felt. Our gazes lock and neither of us wants to look away.

There's something spiritual about this. It's not just fucking to get off. It's not even just gentle fucking. It feels like we're making love, and it's more moving than anything I've experienced before. It's like our souls are telling us we've met our mate. That there's no questioning whether we're meant to be.

He sits up and wraps his arms around my waist as I rise and fall on his cock. Our kiss is languid as we both pour emotions into it that aren't even about sex. Our movements are slow and quiet. The bed barely moves. This time's the opposite of how we were last night. There's nothing frenetic about this.

"Come, Liesel, whenever you want. You don't have to ask."

"Thank you, Jorge."

Neither of us uses an endearment, perhaps because we've never been more equal during sex. I crave this intimacy we're creating together. It's not long before I moan as I feel that sensation begin deep in my pussy before it spreads.

"I can't last any longer. Come for me, *chiquita.*"

"I am, Daddy. I'm coming right now."

This time the terms of affection are loving. It's not about him being more dominant and me being more submissive. We truly are equals in this. When our bodies cool from the ecstasy, we kiss each other's shoulders.

Even though we showered last night, we both know we need to do it again. When we step under the water, we embrace and hold each other, unable to get enough kisses. I feel his cock pressing against my lower belly. He's getting hard again, so I ease my hand between us and stroke him.

"Are you sure you aren't slipping little blue pills every day, Daddy?"

He chuckles. "Hardly. I don't need any enhancements when I have you. I can't get enough of you."

With one more kiss we move apart, and I turn around sticking my hips out to him. He grasps them knowing the invitation, then slides into me. He wraps an arm around my waist as his other kneads my tits. Once again, he's just rocking as the anticipation builds for both of us. I press my hands against the wall, but when my fingers bend as though they'd claw at it, he leans back. Both hands cup my ass as he moves faster and harder.

"Rub your clit, baby girl."

I happily do as he says. My head tilts back for a moment before it drops forward, my chin tucked nearly to my chest as we move together. The force of his motion rocks my hips along with him. I do my best to press back as far as I can each time he bottoms out in me. This is a quickie, and we're both coming soon. Once he withdraws from me, we hurry to finish the shower.

"Liesel, something happened last night, and we need to go downstairs to discuss it with everyone else."

I freeze midway through buttoning my shirt.

"What could've happened last night while we were sleeping?"

"While you were sleeping."

"What?" My brow furrows not understanding.

"I woke to a knock on the front door. I slipped out to check what was going on. So did all the other men except your father. A box arrived with a tongue in it, but obviously it wasn't your father's since he's here."

"Was there a note like last time?"

"Yes, it simply said 'speak no evil.'"

"What the fuck? Why is this still happening if Papa's here with us? Are you sure he is? Are you sure no one took him in the middle of the night?"

Panic bubbles in my chest and makes bile burn the back of

my throat.

"Yes, I'm positive he's still here. Hisham peeked into your parents' room just long enough to know he was there before we all went back into our rooms."

We're both dressed now, so we head downstairs. Immediately I can tell Heidi and Friedrich must have argued. She won't look in his direction and isn't talking to him. I take a seat next to my sister and shoot her a look. She turns her head and glares at Friedrich, who sits across the table from her. Then she leans to whisper to me.

"He decided to share a monumental secret with me this morning. Turns out he's more than just friends with someone in the Camorra."

My gaze darts to Friedrich before it returns to my sister. I keep my voice low to match hers.

"Just how much more?"

Even though I'm speaking softly, it's Friedrich who answers. "I may as well just come out and say it to everyone since more than half of you already know. I'm still a member of the Camorra. I don't serve them day-to-day, and I left that life to be with Heidi. I don't want it near her, but it seems as hard as I tried to keep it away from Heidi and your family, it's permeated our lives here in Frankfurt. What's going on involves my branch as well as three other syndicates."

"Three?!" I can't help but blurt my question.

"Yes, my branch is working with another Italian syndicate against two others that are allied by marriage and now by blood."

I look to my other side and gaze up at Jorge. He's okay with what has to happen next. We don't have to speak to communicate. He knows I need to confirm my family's suspicions about him. As I watch him, he shifts his gaze to Alejandro and Joaquin, his brow furrowing. I turn my attention to them since they're sitting beside each other. It's almost imperceptible, but they dip their chin. I look back at Jorge, and he offers me a sad half smile.

"*Mutti*, Papa, Heidi."

I look at each one in turn. I study my parents' expressions, and it's almost resignation on them. When I look at Heidi, she eyes me suspiciously.

"Friedrich's not the only one with ties to a syndicate. Jorge and his family are in one too or rather I should say they run one in New York."

My hand rests upon the table, and Jorge covers it, his fingers sliding under mine until our hands rest palm to palm. He's reassuring me as he goes into a little more detail.

"It's not just in New York. Our role is larger than that. It's why I've been able to do what I have and why my brother and cousin can help us."

I stare at my parents, and neither of them says anything. Heidi and I speak at the same time.

"You're okay with this?"

We've been doing that since we were kids because we're so much alike. Both of our parents nod, but it's Papa who speaks up.

"We figured out Friedrich's connection ages ago because of some of the business he referred to us. His clients were all legal but barely toeing the right side of the line."

My mom offers Jorge a smile before she picks up where my dad left off. "Jorge's command of the situation immediately reassured me of who he is. It was more than just confidence from wealth and being a powerful businessman. It was far more than that. Once he said he had the resources to help, I knew what that meant. Papa and I don't love the danger that goes along with either of you being involved with your boyfriends, but it's obvious how you feel about each other."

My mom's gaze locks with mine. Neither Jorge nor I have declared our feelings beyond saying we care very much about each other. My mom's basically acknowledging Jorge and I are in love or at least are almost there.

Heidi leans forward, but she says nothing. She must think better of it. I turn my head toward her, and she looks at me. I'm not sure what she's thinking, but I assume it's similar to me. She shifts her attention to Friedrich, and I do the same with Jorge. Whatever expression she's giving Friedrich must be one that says either she forgives him or she needs him.

He pushes back his chair and walks around to our side of the table. He slides into the one to her left. He angles his chair to be as close to Heidi's as he can. He wraps his arm around her shoulder, and she leans against him. Jorge kisses my temple and squeezes my hand.

I don't love where the conversation goes next as Jorge explains more. "Liesel, we're still not sure about who targeted you. We have some ideas, but we're not positive. We know this war among the Italians targeted you for the money they could launder through your accounts. They used a winding path to get the money to Italy. It didn't start or stop where we expected."

"What does that mean?" I'm trying to keep up, but where the hell did any Italian syndicate come from. I remember Hisham explaining the route the money took, and I don't recall it having anything to do with Italy.

"The money originated here, then went to France, Switzerland, and the Cayman Islands. It's final destination was Italy. Palermo and Venice. It's not Friedrich's family or their ally. It's the other side because they couldn't get the money they need to pay for this."

"Why did it originate here? I still don't understand why they involved me."

It's Friedrich who jumps in, sounding ashamed. "It's clients of mine who did business with the *Cosa Nostra* and the *Mala del Brenta*."

All I can do is stare at Friedrich. It's not like I don't know how money's laundered. Even before I became part of this insanely long chain, I knew about it. But I've never heard of money going through so many hands. That's just more opportunities for something to go wrong from a law enforcement agency or one party's greediness. Jorge draws my attention away from Friedrich as he strokes the back of my hand.

"Friedrich fears they used you to force him back into syndicate life, but not on his family's side. They know your practically family, so my guess is they assumed they could use you, and Friedrich would do nothing to stand in their way because he wants to protect you."

It's way too much to digest. I shift my focus to Friedrich, and he looks like shit. Guilt makes him not want to meet my gaze, but I don't blame him. I'm certain he didn't ask for any of this. Not clients who duped him. Not a family who's in a syndicate. Not endangering me since I'm his girlfriend's sister, and I was his best friend's girlfriend. This is a massive weight he bears on his shoulders, so I won't make it worse.

"So where does that leave us?"

I suspect I know the answer, but I want to hear it from Jorge.

"I need to head back to the States since that's where at least one of the parties involved in this is from."

"What about us?"

He stares at me for a long time not saying anything while I await an invitation to go with him. As the seconds tick toward a minute, I realize Jorge's nervous that I'll feel rushed into this or that I'll reject his offer. His anxiety isn't just from being the center of attention among strangers. I think it plays out even when he's with friends and family.

I think it's when he's not in control of a situation. I wonder if that stems from him watching his father's murder at such a young age and feeling like he had no control over what happened to his dad. Or maybe it's because none of his family had control either. Could this be some type of survivor guilt that's lasted with him two and a half decades? I keep my voice soft and low even though everyone else can hear.

"Do you want me to stay here for now or go with you?"

I see the relief in his eyes with those last three words.

"I'd prefer you came with us, but I understand if it's too soon."

"Can we pack my apartment today?"

He beams and nods. "If that's what you want, Liesel."

"I'd have to do it anyway, but this is certainly a far better reason."

"We need to take off today. The sooner, the better. With the number of men we have here now, plus my brother, cousin, you, and me, we won't all fit in Alejandro's jet that he, Joaquin, and their men traveled in. We'll need our family's one to come over too. Between both, they can transport us back. It'll be at least five hours before we're ready to take off. We can go to your place now if you'd like."

I nod, then shift my focus to my parents to see their reaction from everything changing so quickly and the monumental implications to this. Neither of them appears surprised. I wonder what my mother said to my father last night. Heidi's shoulder nudges mine, and I look over at her. She's wearing the same shit-eating grin she has since we were kids, and she had a secret she couldn't wait to share with me.

"*Mutti* and I can go over and pack up your stuff later if you can only take a small amount. We can ship whatever you want and either store or get rid of the rest."

I match her infectious smile. "You just want to raid my kitchen for that mixer and air fryer."

She shrugs unrepentantly.

"Thank you."

My family knows I mean more than just Heidi's offer for our mom and her to go and pack up my place. I look over at Jorge.

"Can we go after breakfast?"

"If that's what you'd like, sweetheart."

That's a new one, but it's an endearment that's appropriate in public. I nod, and we're soon filtering into the kitchen to grab plates for breakfast Noor cooked. I'm certain she heard our conversation, and any parts she may have missed, Hisham will fill in later. We save her the effort of having to plate and serve everything, and I'm sure she appreciates that since I doubt she expected such a full house.

It's not exactly a cheery meal, but we discuss the different things in New York I'll get to see. None of us actually say it's a permanent move for me, but it basically is since my family's offered to ship things.

My father says he'd like to rest, and my mother agrees she could do with some more sleep. Heidi and Friedrich are going to talk more before Friedrich makes a few additional calls. Alejandro, Joaquin, Jorge, and I head upstairs to pack up the few things we took out of our cases. Once Jorge and I have zipped up ours, he comes to stand in front of me and takes my hands.

"*Chiquita*, when we get to New York, I'd like you to stay with me while this is still being resolved. I will likely have to travel, and I'd feel better with you somewhere that has security protocols already in place. But once things are resolved, if you'd feel better with your own place, I understand."

"I'd like that, Daddy. I'd feel better if I were somewhere you know is safe. But..."

I pause, unsure of whether I should share my thoughts. That fear of rejection Jorge must have experienced earlier wraps itself around me. He cups my face before pressing a quick but soft kiss to my lips.

"*Chiquita*, you can stay as long as you want. I'm in no hurry for you to go anywhere that doesn't have a bed we'll share every night."

I nod as best I can with his hands still cupping my jaw. "That's what I want too, Daddy."

Jorge grabs our cases and wheels them out of the room. He carries both downstairs. It's weird to think I'm moving out of an apartment I shared with a man for six months and who I was with for two years in order to move to a new country and live with a man I've barely known two months and have only really been with for a week. When I think of it like that, it's absolutely insane. But it feels right.

I hemmed and hawed about living with Bastian. I wasn't sure I was ready to share my space with him. But it felt like we were ready and the logical next step. It was an easy transition when we moved in together. Despite my nervousness, it ended up working out well until it didn't. I wonder if things will go as smoothly with Jorge.

Jorge, Alejandro, Joaquin, and I take one of the large SUVs since there'll be trunk space for a few suitcases. Jorge explains to me how much room there'll be for my luggage when they factor in everything else that'll need to go in the cabins and holds of the jets. It's not just the space but the weight limits.

When we arrive at my apartment, it shocks me to find Bastian there. I assumed he'd be at work. My gaze sweeps the living room, kitchen, and dining room. Everything's just as I left it. He's packed nothing. He stands from the desk where he works when he's reviewing case notes.

"What the hell are you doing here?"

I feel Jorge bristle, but he says nothing. It's not that he'll leave me to deal with Bastian on my own. I can tell he knows anything he says will only antagonize Bastian more. I walk farther into the living room, and Joaquin closes the door behind us.

"I'm here to get some of my things."

"And what? You felt like you had to bring your guard dogs with you."

"Don't be like this, Bastian. They came to help, and that's it."

Bastian stalks across the living room until he's standing in front of us. Jorge shifts just enough that if he needs to, he can step in front of me.

"Bastian, don't make this harder than it needs to be. We'll pack up my clothes and be out of the way. My mom and sister will get the rest of my stuff in a few days, but I warned you already that you need to leave. I'm not keeping the lease on this place."

Bastian leans toward Jorge's face. The last thing I need is for this to devolve into a fight since there's no way Bastian would win, even if it were only him and Jorge without Alejandro and Joaquin here too. It would be a bloodbath even though I'm certain none of the men would let it go that far.

When I step in front of Jorge, his hands immediately go around my waist. He's gentle but moves me out of the way. He leans in to whisper to me, and I clench my ass as his warning rings loudly in my ear.

"Never step in front of two men who're ready to fight. Do that again, *chiquita*, and I'll spank you."

Bastian gasps since I'm certain he heard Jorge, but I merely look up at him and mouth, *Yes, Daddy.* Alejandro and Joaquin step forward, placing themselves in front of Jorge and me without even touching Bastian. They convince him to back away until he reaches the sofa. Joaquin leans toward him until Bastian sinks onto a seat. Joaquin's and Alejandro's expressions clearly tell Bastian it would be wise for him to not try to get up.

Jorge and I head into the bedroom. My suitcases are stored at the bottom of one of the closets. Most European homes aren't that large, but many have more than adequate storage. This apartment is just like that. I point to things and give Jorge directions as he packs one large case, and I pack the other.

By the time we're done, all of my clothes are in those two cases. I lift my teddy bear I've had since I was born out of a drawer. It's not like I look at him or touch him every day, but it's always been reassuring to know I have him since he was my favorite. My *tante* and *onkel* on my dad's side gave it to my mom during her baby shower, and I apparently gravitated to it from the very beginning.

I close the case I packed while Jorge does the same. He walks over to mine and lifts it off the bed before I can. He always helps me with my luggage without giving it a second thought. Then he goes back to the one he filled and lifts it down. As we wheel the cases out of the room, Bastian's expression shows he finally understands I'm serious. He knows my entire wardrobe must be in those cases.

"You're really going to go—with him."

"Yes, Bastian. You knew that when I arrived."

"Were you fucking him even before we broke up?"

Jorge practically snarls, and Alejandro's and Joaquin's hands fist as Bastian leans forward to stand. He notices the men's reaction and realizes staying seated is his safest bet.

"No, Bastian, I was not. I remained faithful to you until you failed me. Instead of cheating, I broke up with you. I may have been attracted to Jorge from the moment I met him, but I had no intention of acting on it. But he's the man I've needed all along, and you only proved that. You pushed me into Jorge's arms. It was inevitable you and I would've broken up, even if I didn't wind up with Jorge. If I could have thoughts about another man, then I never should've been with you. We didn't have a future together once I realized that. I may be angry and hurt by you, but you don't deserve someone who can't give their whole self to you. You deserve someone who only wants you and doesn't doubt her feelings toward you. Goodbye."

Jorge walks over to Bastian and stares at him until Bastian shifts in the seat. He leans forward, forcing Bastian's back to press against the chair. Jorge's hands land on the armrests, boxing Bastian in. Alejandro and Joaquin stand on each side of Jorge, their arms crossed and flexed. If I were Bastian, I'd be pissing myself right now.

"You get to live because Liesel hasn't asked me to change that. You get to keep your hands as they are because you save children when you perform surgery. Your face won't show any signs we've ever met. But in your mind—" Jorge taps Bastian's right temple. "—remember I can find you anywhere. There isn't a fucking place on this earth where you can hide. Come near my woman again, and I will make sure only God and I know where you end up. Stay away."

Bastian's face flushes with anger, but he remains quiet. The only smart decision he's made since I asked him to come to the hotel. Alejandro takes a suitcase Jorge was wheeling, and we leave. When we get to the ground floor, I stop Jorge.

"I'd like to go into the office and see about breaking my lease."

I speak to the property manager who observes Jorge, Joaquin, and Alejandro in the lobby, along with the large suitcases. When I explain my ex-boyfriend and I broke up, and I'm moving out, he understands why I'd like to stop the rental agreement. I'm not sure if the three men waiting for me intimidate him into honoring my request without argument, or he simply takes pity on me over the breakup. He agrees to end the contract within a week rather than require the thirty days' notice.

I reassure him my mother and sister will be there in a couple of days to sort out the rest of it and to clean. I forewarn him that he may need to convince Bastian that he must leave, that I've already tried. I suggest that if Bastian wishes to take over the lease, then he should be able to do that. Since the property manager knows Bastian as well as my family, I think they'll work something out. Bastian is no longer my problem. If he doesn't want to comply, then oh well.

We head back to Hisham and Noor's house. It surprises me when Noor tells Jorge and Joaquin that she's spoken to Luciana.

"Your mama asked me if the three of you have been eating properly while you've been away. I said all three of you look to be just as healthy and fit as you always have. She's so proud of all of you, and she can't wait to meet Anne properly."

I look forward to getting to know her too.

I glance up at Jorge. He's beaming at Noor after what she shared. I slide my gaze over to Joaquin and Alejandro, and I see their expressions match. It's clear the brothers love their mother and that their cousin's very close to his aunt as well. I recall the elegant woman I met at the restaurant weeks ago, and a moment's worry flashes through me that perhaps I won't live up to her expectations for her son.

As though he perceives my worry, Jorge slides his arm around my waist and kisses my forehead. "I'm certain *Mamá* will steal all your attention from me. I shall be very jealous."

I giggle, and he gives me a quick kiss on the lips. Friedrich gains our attention.

"I spoke to my father, and we've lined up a safe house in Essen for your family. Clyde and his wife and children will meet us there. We need to go to our own places and pack as well, but we wanted to be here when you returned to fill you in. We'll be in Essen for at least a few weeks until we're sure everything's resolved."

I glance over at Heidi. "What about your work? Can you really take off that long?"

"I have the vacation days, so it wasn't too big of an issue."

"Thank goodness."

I notice Alejandro is speaking quietly on his phone. He hangs up just as Heidi finishes.

"We have men who can go with you to your places while you gather what you need."

My family and I thank him for arranging that. I definitely feel much better about them going with armed guards. Joaquin and Alejandro head into the dining room with their laptops, explaining they have work to do. My parents, Heidi, and Friedrich take off, and Noor needs to go to her office in town. Hisham walks down the hallway to his study. It's a beautiful day outside, so Jorge and I head out there and sit together on a swinging bench.

"I know you said you'd prefer to stay with me, but what about work? You're essentially giving up your job to follow me, unless you intend to fly back and forth between here and New York whenever you have client meetings. You certainly don't have to fly commercial."

I shake my head as my eyes widen. "I can't imagine the expense of that."

Jorge cocks an eyebrow as if to say, "We're rich." I just nod.

"Actually, as I consider it more, I realize what the outcome of all of this could be. The Frankfurt office may close. I don't know whether Papa wants to continue working or not. I don't know if my parents would even want to stay in Frankfurt. This has been a deeply traumatizing experience. I assume *Onkel* Claude will carry on the business and who knows, perhaps my parents might move to Munich to be closer to him, or my father just retires."

I shrug and sigh as I continue to ruminate aloud on what this means for my family.

"I don't know what it would look like because *Onkel* Clyde's children are the same age as Heidi and me, but they've taken no interest in the family business."

Jorge appears thoughtful before he responds. "Alejandro's father, my *tío* Matáis, is our financier in most situations. He's who you were originally going to meet with, but he had to be somewhere else, so I filled in. I think it was in the stars for that to happen."

"I think so too."

"Since *Tío* Matáis handles all our legal endeavors, perhaps you'd like to work with him. I know he'd like to spend more time at home with *Tía* Catalina. Perhaps you could help split some of the travel with him or cover the accounts he has when he must travel."

It surprises me that Jorge suggests I work for his family, even if it's on the legal side. Bringing me into the family business is a huge commitment. Perhaps even more so than he and I living together. His arm's around my shoulders, just like it usually is when we sit beside each other. He gives it a squeeze.

"Just think about it."

Chapter Twenty-Eight

Jorge

As I sit with my arm around Liesel on the swing in Noor and Hisham's backyard, I can finally breathe for a few minutes. I'm relaxed knowing we're headed home soon. Even though we haven't resolved anything, at least I have an explanation and targets for my anger once we're home. It took everything in me to only issue Bastian threats when I wanted to tear him apart. If Liesel hadn't been there, I might have. I truly don't know that I would've had the restraint to do nothing if it were just my brother and cousin with me.

I can channel my waves of rage toward the responsible parties rather than feeling flustered and frustrated like I have this entire time. I push off with my feet every few swings, and I wonder if one day Liesel and I might sit like this when we're old and gray, watching our grandchildren play in our yard. That makes me consider where we might live.

There're two neighborhoods adjacent to one another. They've become syndicate Switzerland. Couples from all Four

Families live there. It's practically become an underworld compound. It's where most of us grew up. We moved into that neighborhood when *Mamá* brought my brothers and me to the U.S.

The Kutsenkos and their Andreyev cousins didn't move into the neighborhood until the oldest, Maksim, married and had twins. Then his brothers and cousins followed him—of course, because they're an eight-tentacle octopus. Where you get one, you get all the others with only one brain amongst them. Their mother moved into a home once the brothers were out of the house and could afford to buy her the property there. Before that, they'd grown up near Brighton Beach, a Russian enclave.

Pablo, his parents, and his brother lived in New Jersey. But he and Florencia recently purchased a home in that neighborhood. Javier and Madeline did the same thing. They live a couple streets over from *Mamá*.

All the Mancinellis, except for Carmine, grew up there too. His parents had a home farther out in Queens along the coast. Carmine's parents got married at nineteen when his mother got pregnant with him. Paola's and Cesare's fathers forced them into the marriage, then basically exiled them to a beautiful, sprawling home far away from everyone else. However, Carmine and his wife, Serafina, now have a home in the neighborhood too.

As teens, we generally stayed away with our own groups of friends, but every once in a while, our paths would cross. There was one particular time where it exploded in our faces. All of my generation's members of the Four Families wound up at the same high school party. We were keeping to ourselves until Maria Mancinelli's friend tried to approach Joaquin because she had a crush on him. Joaquin was a senior when the girls were freshmen.

He was flattered by the attention but not interested. It was super noisy, and Maria misheard what Javier said, thinking my brother claimed the girls were flat-chested bitches. Instead, Javier basically told Joaquin *Tío* Enrique would flatten him like a dead dog if he went anywhere near girls so much younger than him.

Maria told Carmine and Gabriele, who then called over the rest of their family. The Kutsenkos and Andreyevs heard and thought my brother insulted a girl, so they got involved since they *love* to fancy themselves every woman's knight in shining armor. Fucking hypocrites to the nth degree. Then the O'Rourkes chimed in, egging on both sides.

It turned into a syndicate melee with guns and knives. Everyone who wasn't in a syndicate took off in different directions once the fight broke out. At least we waited until the outsiders fled before we drew those weapons. We barely got out in the nick of time when we heard the sirens. It was actually Maria who got us all off the hook with the cops. She recognized some officer whose father was in the Mafia. She explained who was there and why the fight happened. Before we knew it, the cops were gone.

All the syndicate members hid in nearby yards or behind trees at a park, waiting to see what would happen. The outcome was all Four Families' leaders were absolutely livid. The old bratva *pakhan* tortured the Kutsenkos and Andreyevs, just like he'd done while training them. Don Salvatore, *Tío* Enrique, and Liam O'Rourke—the mob boss—lit into their respective family members. It was apparently a jumble of languages among all the men; native tongues mixed with English.

None of the leaders had been that angry in decades. Probably the entire time they'd led their families. I nearly cringe remembering that, but I don't want Liesel to misunderstand.

"You seem deep in thought, Daddy."

I reach across my lap to clasp Liesel's hand then draw them onto my thigh. "Just remembering something from high school about a fight that broke out among members of the Four Families."

"Four Families?"

"Yes. One of the Mafia wives in New York named us that. It's the families who lead the mob, the Mafia, the Cartel, and the bratva. *The* Irish mob are the O'Rourkes. *The* Russian bratva are the Kutsenkos. *The* Mafia are the Mancinellis. *The* Cartel is us."

Her lips turn down, and her head tilts away from me. "Do you really have that much to do with each other?"

She's already admitted to her family that I'm in a cartel. It's time for me to explain what that truly means.

"Unfortunately, yes, *chiquita*, we do. You've seen how we sometimes have overlapping clients and deals. It's hardly our preference. We also own rival businesses and generally try to fuck each other over as frequently as we can."

"What does that look like?"

I remain silent. Her brow furrows at my piercing stare.

"Jorge—"

"Liesel, this is something that'll always be part of our relationship. There's a lot I'll never tell you. I can't. It wouldn't be safe for you to know if I did."

"As in safe from these rivals?"

"No, not so much from them. I mean not safe if law enforcement detained you or arrested you."

She swallows as she considers what I've just said.

"*Chica?*"

She looks like there's more she wants to say, but she's weighing her words. I hate that there's anything she's uncertain about between us or uncertain she can say to me. My thumb glides over the back of her hand, hopefully offering her some reassurance.

"If we marry, could they make me testify against you?"

"Supposedly, no, but there're certainly ways they can work around that. They can make you testify about my family members or even about members of rival syndicates, hoping to back you into a corner where you'll divulge things about me."

Her eyes water, and my heart breaks. Is this too much for her? Her free hand rests on my chest as she twists to look at me.

"Jorge, I can't imagine anyone doing that to me, putting me in that kind of position. It hurts my heart to think somebody would attempt to make me betray you. I would never do that. Even if this doesn't work out between us, I wouldn't do that to you. And after all your family's done to help me, I would never do that to them. But considering what you've said two other families have done to me, I'll sing like a fucking canary to get back at them."

"I appreciate that sentiment, little one, but the less you know, the less likely you are to be trapped in the middle. Even if you wanted to help my family like that, I never want you in that position. It's too dangerous. I don't fear the other syndicates retaliating if you testified against them, but they would target the rest of us. It's better if you simply have nothing to do with any of it. That also means not only will I lie by omission—keeping things from you, giving you these blank stares—I'll also tell you outright lies. I'll look you in the eye and make up some story that doesn't even remotely resemble the truth. But again, I'll do it to protect you and my family along with the people who rely on us for their safety and their jobs. It'll never be about just me. If I could tell you the truth and avoid being deceptive, I would."

She stares at me for a long moment, and I notice her eyes

drift to my shirt collar, then back up to me. I'm not sure at first why she did that, then it dawns on me.

"Liesel, you will never see me come home with lipstick on my shirt or smelling of another woman, and not because I changed first. You will see me in clothes I didn't leave the house in because I *needed* to change for other reasons. There are very few limitations to what I'll do to protect you and the people I love or have a duty toward. But infidelity is a line I will *never, ever, ever* cross. There will always be another way. I couldn't do that to you. I couldn't live with the shame of that. And my family would castrate, then murder me, my mother being at the front of the line with a rusty knife. Cheating is just something that never happens in my family. It's simply too dishonorable and too hurtful to consider."

Now's the time I need to admit to at least one of our business endeavors.

"One thing I can't and won't keep from you is that my family owns several nightclubs, bars, and strip clubs. Because I'm an accountant and Pablo just got married, I've been managing them right now. I'll pass that responsibility on to Joaquin. Alejandro travels too often for it, but there will be times I still need to go during the day because I'm responsible for payroll and maintaining all the accounts from various vendors. None of us go for entertainment, not even before my brother, cousin, and *tío* became involved with their soulmates."

"Soulmates?" She sounds curious and perhaps hopeful.

"Absolutely. The women who've fallen in love with the men in my family couldn't be better suited to their man. They're the perfect matching half."

She watches me intently as I explain. I cup her jaw and lean forward to brush a whisper of a kiss against her lips. I pull back just enough, so I can speak.

"I believe you're mine, *chiquita*. I wouldn't be sitting here with you, divulging all of this if I didn't believe you were the other half of my heart. We've been attracted to one another from the beginning, but the way I feel around you is unlike anything I've ever felt toward another person. I dated in high school and even a bit in college and grad school, but I knew it would never be serious because none of those women were ones I wanted to be with forever. I didn't allow so much access and knowledge of my family. Instead, I kept them all at arm's length. Most complained I was too emotionally distant for them to want to continue a relationship with me. Some I missed more than others, but I was never brokenhearted about any of them. If we don't work out, I'll never force you to stay, but it would devastate me."

I know it's too soon to tell Liesel I love her. I'm not positive she's there yet, even though I'm confident she's my romantic soulmate. I believe we'll be compatible, but I'm not positive about that either. She's not rushing to agree with me about how I see us. So once more, I don't want to make her feel backed into a corner or face the rejection of her not reciprocating.

She slides her hand along my stubble until her thumb and fingers slide around my ear. Her nails gently graze my scalp as her thumb rubs my cheek.

"I rather like you with this more than just a five o'clock shadow."

I haven't shaved in a couple days, so my beard's growing in. Fortunately, it's always been even growth, not in patches.

"Jorge, I want to spend the rest of my life being the one who enjoys touching your beard. My emotions are still a jumble, but I'm clear about that. I don't know how best to describe them. However, certainty is there. I haven't had that with any man in my past. If I had, I'd be with them. I wouldn't have been drawn to you. I understand what you're telling me about your duties. I know you can never leave this lifestyle."

"You're right, but it's more than just a lifestyle, Liesel. That almost implies I want things this way. I don't. None of my family would pick this if we were given a choice. If any of us attempted to leave, we'd make ourselves targets to the rest of the syndicates. My family would never agree to that, so it would make them targets too. Our lives are only safe because we stick together. Family is everything to us, to our very core, and from that, loyalty, honor, and duty drive us."

I watch her reactions as intently as I do when I'm conducting an inquisition on someone. I don't want to miss a single blink, flinch, or twitch of a smile.

"Not only would it be impossible for any of us to extricate ourselves safely, we also know what life would be like for the people who rely on us if another family led. None of us want to create that kind of hardship and misery for people who have very few means to provide for themselves or protect themselves without us."

"I never considered it that way, Jorge. I can guess what things your family does that're on the wrong side of the law. I'm certain most people wouldn't view your situation the way you described it. They'd probably look down on you and deem what you do not just illegal, but immoral. That you have a choice, but I understand now that you don't. Nothing about you that I've gotten to know makes me believe you enjoy what you do, but I can't deny how I've benefited."

"There's nothing I wouldn't do for you, *chiquita*. If that means using the resources and means I have, then no one will stop me."

As we gaze into each other's eyes, I feel like there's still more she wants to say. I wonder if she wishes she could share the same sentiments I have. Perhaps she's as nervous about revealing her feelings as I am. If that's the case, hopefully, the right time and place will come along soon, so we can both be confident enough to do that.

"Jorge, what does a typical day look like for you? You mentioned some of your businesses, but is there anything else? Are there any others?"

"Yes, quite a few. Normally, I get up and meet my family to work out. More often than not, it's at *Tío* Enrique's in New Jersey because he has the biggest gym since he has the largest basement. But we still take turns since all of us have home gyms. Most of us squeeze in a second workout sometime in the afternoon or evening. Some days, I stop by *Mamá's* to see how she's doing and if she needs anything. Joaquin and Javier do that too. At least one night a week, my brothers and I have dinner with her. Madeline joins us now, and I hope you will too. Most Sundays, we get together as an entire family for lunch or dinner. During the week, I share at least one meal—sometimes two—with my cousins or brothers. It's mostly lunch since our work overlaps so frequently. Now that *Tío* Enrique, Javier, and Pablo are in relationships, they don't have dinner with others as often. *Tía* Catalina and *Tío* Matáis almost always have dinner together. That's the same way for *Tío* Luis and *Tía* Margherita when *Tío* Luis is home. I look forward to having dinner with you most nights, *chiquita*."

There are a lot of people in my family, and I know how confusing it is. But Liesel seems to remember my family tree, and it feels good to know she's taken enough interest to learn how we're all related.

Her smile is one of relief. It saddens me to know she's leaving her family and all her friends here behind for me. I've never really done that. I went away to Rhode Island when I attended Brown for undergrad and to Connecticut when I went to Yale for grad school. However, I was close enough to easily come back to New York to see my family or to help with any missions where they needed me.

"*Chica*, you might appreciate talking to Florencia since she recently moved back to the States. She was there for college and grad school then worked for a few years before returning to Colombia when her mom got cancer. She'll understand what it's like for you since you're returning after so many years. I assume you still have friends there from grad school. Maybe you could reconnect with them."

"I can do that?" She sounds shocked that I'd agree to—let alone suggest—she be with people outside of my family.

"Yes, little one, you can socialize with whomever you want. I ask that you be discreet in what you say to other people, and I hate asking you to lie like I will, but it might be necessary. The only thing I'll insist upon is a safety detail for you. Wherever you decide to work—if that's what you want to do—we'll establish a routine with regular guys as your guards. But if anything deviates from your routine, then I want one of the men in my immediate family with you if I can't be there."

"Someone from your family? Is that going to inconvenience them?"

"No. It's always been that way, even with *Mamá* and my *tías*. The men and I often have bodyguards too. There's no one I trust with your safety more than the men in my family. I'd prefer there always be a man with you purely for size, speed, and strength. But if a situation ever happens where you're only with *Mamá* or my *tías*, you can trust they'll protect you as though you're their own child. The women in my family are—"

I consider how to phrase this without freaking her out.

"Jorge?"

"The women in my family are well trained to this life. *Mamá*, *Tía* Catalina, and *Tía* Margherita grew up in cartel families. It's all they've ever known. *Tía* Elle has syndicate connections. Florencia's family was cartel adjacent—if you will—in Colombia. Madeline's past relationship and her sister's marriage have brought her into syndicate life before she became involved with Javier. Her sister—"

I want to run my hand over my face since we're about to get into even more complicated family trees.

"Yes?"

"Madeline and Laura grew up next door to Pablo. They were practically his sisters. Laura married the head of the Russian bratva, Maksim Kutsenko. Maksim is my brother's brother-in-law."

Liesel's eyes widen, and her jaw drops open.

"How does that work for family holidays?"

I grimace. "Madeline and Laura's parents will take turns for Thanksgiving, Christmas, and Easter. Whichever couple isn't hosting goes to the other family, but only the couple. So, Maks and Laura will sometimes come to my family for the holidays, but the rest of Laura's in-laws will do their own thing. Just like there will be times when Javier and Madeline will go to the Kutsenkos for a holiday, but only they go. Laura's best friend and her best friend's sister married brothers in the Mancinelli family. It gets even more complicated since they go on double dates."

"Don't the men—um—well—" She's flustered, and it's rather adorable.

"No, the men don't try to kill each other when they're with their wives and children. However, there's no guarantee something couldn't happen when it's just the men together. We're all too senior to target each other anymore, but that doesn't mean there aren't situations where one of us could get hurt or worse. It depends on how things evolve or unravel. Either. Both."

I shrug since there're still times where things get violent

among families. There was a shootout a couple of years ago where my family and the Mancinellis' paths crossed with a foreign syndicate. That syndicate now has ties to the O'Rourkes and Mancinellis through marriage and us because of *Tío* Enrique's position as *jefe de jefes*.

It's a good thing the Four Families aren't connected by combined blood at this point, or it would be majorly incestuous. As long as none of my generation's children wind up together, we should be safe that the bloodlines don't cross over too many times. But who knows? Maybe that would be the best way for all of us to extricate our families from this fucked-up life. I can't imagine that or look that far into the future.

"You told me about working out and eating with your family and payroll at the strip clubs. What else do you do on a normal day?"

I'm glad we're moving back to an easier topic.

"After I get home from my morning workout and get cleaned up, I usually check the markets since Asia and Europe have already been open for several hours, and the U.S. is just starting their day. I'm not just a CPA but a licensed broker as well. After that, I'll deal with any correspondence or paperwork needed for the companies I own which include three accounting firms where my name isn't on the letterhead. But if anybody asks, they'll easily discover I own the companies. I'm also our family's accountant for the casinos we own in Atlantic City, Vegas, and Reno. We own a few in European cities and Tokyo. I'm a heavy investor in a luxury car line with manufacturers in Asia, so there are times where I must travel for meetings there too. Mostly I'm home every evening by eight even if I have dinner with someone in my family."

"That's your mornings and a little about your evenings. What about your afternoons?"

I suspected she would ask that, and that's where things get more uncomfortable to discuss.

"My afternoons often involve family business in our communities."

I give her that blank expression again, and she's already picked up on what that means. However, there's a greater risk someone from another family will speak to Liesel and shit all over us.

"My brothers and I are known as *Tres J's*. Our reputation stems from our early childhood in Colombia. After *Papá* died, we became targets for local street gangs. We had to protect ourselves since some members wanted to build their reputations on killing the *jefe de jefes'* nephews. We also protected our mother when we believed we had to. We were too young to understand *Mamá* was better equipped than most to not only defend herself but to retaliate."

I don't need to share how my brothers and I had all stabbed and killed before we reached double digits. It wasn't until my brothers and I were in college that we learned just how *Mamá* sought her revenge after *Papá* died. If people think my brothers and I are psychopaths, then Lord only knows what they would say about our mother. After my father's murder, she made a very clear point that hell hath no fury like a widowed woman.

I can't tell Liesel any of that, but I can share things from when we left Colombia.

"When we all moved to the States and closer to *Tío* Enrique, who isn't just the head of the Colombian cartels but is also the strongest, most powerful *jefe* in Latin America, we thought we needed to protect ourselves with the same reputation we needed in Bogotá. We were so young, we didn't know any better except that we needed to protect each other."

I need to explain this to Liesel before anyone from the other families pollutes her mind about us.

"We aren't the men people believe us to be except for when we have to play the roles our family's responsibilities necessitate. I have anxiety that flares at the most inopportune times, but thank heavens for the medication I take. Javier is an introvert and misanthrope through and through. He just doesn't like other people and would rather be by himself or now with Madeline and our family. And Joaquin is painfully shy. They think he's the laziest man in any syndicate because he's practically a recluse whenever he can be. Nobody ever believes these things about us, but it's true."

"I've seen hints of that anxiety. You can always come to me if you need help." Liesel brushes a kiss on my cheek before sitting back to continue listening.

"Because of the reputation we've developed and our duties to our family, we're the shit stirrers."

That's as much as I can say without admitting to crimes. As *sicarios*—enforcers—we cause problems for local businesses, then force them to pay protection money against the threats they don't realize come from us. We also handle a number of the low-level members who need a little reminder that they work for us and not the other way around. Pablo is our head enforcer, but I can't tell her that. I definitely can't tell her that my brothers, cousins, and I are *sanguinarios*—the blood thirsty ones—the "Blooddrinkers," as some would call us. Others call us butchers since we're the ones who handle—dispose of— people who make poor life choices.

"Pablo oversees our legitimate operations in New York, so he's also a *jefe* in his own right because of our local endeavors. We all have roles, *chica*, and mine often fill my afternoons."

I hate it, but I'm certain she'll figure out much of it over time just like Madeline and Florencia.

"So, you're usually just a regular businessman. That seems so normal."

Liesel's assessment makes me smile as I nod. If that's her takeaway from what I just explained, then her ignorance is bliss.

"Jorge, I do have one question. I know you explained you can't leave, and that all makes sense, but how was Friedrich able to walk away?"

"He's not a member of the ruling family of his branch in the Camorra. His father is probably a senior member, and from the sounds of it, he was well-connected to the ruling family. However, he wouldn't have the same responsibilities as his best friend did. I'm certain they can and have called upon him to go back to Essen or wherever they want to send him, and he's had to fulfill obligations. He'll never explain that to Heidi."

Liesel merely nods, but I see the sadness in her eyes. She accepts what I've told her and how I've described the life she'll have. But it seems like she's sad for her sister, even though Heidi will have less to do with syndicate life than Liesel will. It makes me wonder if she's hiding her emotions about our future better than I thought.

"Jorge, I accept this life that I'm walking into. It's not like I've been part of a syndicate before, but you know I've had questionable clients. It wasn't by choice, and I didn't realize the extent of it, but I've essentially worked for one of them. I supplied information to the people extorting me and didn't stop the money passing through my accounts. I know who and what you are and have since the beginning. However, this comes as a monumental shock to Heidi. She's never dealt with anything like this, and that's not what she signed up for with Friedrich."

"Do you think it will cause a rift they can't overcome?"

"I don't know. It depends on whether she can get past the secret he kept. They've been together a couple of years, and I doubt his role would've come out without everything that's happened. I don't know if she can live with lies of omission and bald-faced lies. I suspect she can because she loves Friedrich, and I think they're soulmates too. I just don't know for sure. I hope they can because they're good together. They make each other happy."

"I hope for that as well. If something that's hard for you to understand or accept comes up, I hope you'll talk to me about it, Liesel. But if there's something you don't feel comfortable sharing with me, then I hope you'll go to someone else in my family. They'll accept you because you're important to me, but I'm confident they'll also accept you for you. How could they not?"

I give her the most heartfelt smile I can, and I hope she knows it's genuine.

"I can agree to that, Jorge. I'm certain there will be times when I need help. It's good to know I have somewhere to turn."

Chapter Twenty-Nine

Liesel

It's been a long-ass day, but we're finally in New York. Jorge and I spent a long time outside this morning, sitting on the swing, even after that heavy-ass conversation we had. I'm relieved we did since I feel like I've truly made an informed decision about coming here with him and not wondering if I just did it out of necessity.

Saying goodbye to my family was gut wrenching, and there were tears streaming down all our cheeks. But in the end, we parted with smiles and well wishes. I dozed a bit on the flight, but I tried not to sleep too much. I've learned the best way to fight jet lag is to not sleep on the flights in either direction. I do my best to stay awake until a reasonable time at my destination, go to bed, crash hard, sleep eight to ten hours, then wake up at a normal morning time and get on the local clocks. It's worked well for me in the past.

It was tempting to actually sleep since the jet had a private cabin with a bed. It also tempted Jorge and me to do far more than him leaving me to rest. Perhaps if it had only been his brother and cousin there, we might have. But a few of the guards were on the flight too. We were both too embarrassed to do more where they could overhear us.

"*Chiquita*, I'd like to show you something if you're up to it."

"What is it, Daddy?"

"It's a surprise. It's here in the building."

"Okay."

We've just gotten to his penthouse and dropped off the luggage. We head back into the hallway to a flight of stairs. I can already see they start and end on this floor. His condo is the only penthouse. We climb up to the roof, and he opens a door leading directly into a greenhouse. The air isn't stifling like you might expect.

What lies before my eyes is absolutely breathtaking. There's an array of flowers unlike anything I've seen before. It's almost like a miniature Amazon, but there are also roses and tulips, and other flowers you wouldn't find there. When I look to the left and peer down one of the rows of flowers, I spy a vegetable garden.

Jorge intertwines his fingers with mine and leads me to the right. The scents are almost overwhelming. It's as though I've stepped into a perfumery like the ones I've been to in the south of France. I marvel at everything I see.

"Jorge, do you grow all of this? Do you have two green thumbs?"

"I do. I find botany relaxing. Some people might watch fish to lower their blood pressure, but being among my plants has that effect on me."

"How did you discover that?"

His expression takes on a faraway look I've come to recognize whenever he talks about his father.

"*Papá* had a garden in the backyard where he'd grow

vegetables for us. It was pretty much everything we could possibly need, but he had a smaller area where he grew lavender for *Mamá*. I used to love digging in the dirt and finding worms we could use when *Papá* took my brothers and me fishing. There was something about the feel of the cool soil between my fingers, and I loved how happy it made *Mamá* whenever she went out to the garden after *Papá* died. I did my best to take care of it."

"Weren't you only eight or nine?"

He nods but doesn't answer. As I watch him, his Adam's apple bobs. I think he might be too choked up right now to answer me. Instead, he leads us down a path to the left. We wind through a patch of sunflowers that are almost as tall as I am. They come up to mid-chest on me. In the center of the greenhouse is a fountain.

I hear the water bubbling, and it sounds like a babbling stream. I notice the water feeds into the irrigation system, so it's not just for appearances. There's a lounger near the fountain. Beside it is a small table with a stack of books. This must be somewhere Jorge truly comes to relax. I shift my focus to him when I sense he's watching me.

"Do you like it, little one?" There's a note of uncertainty in his voice.

"Yes, it's incredible. I love everything that I see. Would you mind if I came up here sometimes without you?"

It's definitely relief I see now. He wanted to ask me to join him, but he worried I'd say no.

"Of course. You don't need my permission. Hell, half of my family raids my vegetable patch without me knowing. I'll come up to get something, and the vine or bush will be picked nearly clean."

"Do you think you might be able to bring a second lounger up here? It's as close to serenity as I've ever seen."

He beams at me, and it's pure joy I see in his eyes when I tell him I'd like to share this space with him. "That's how I feel about it, too. Have you ever done any gardening?"

"A little, but I certainly wouldn't say I have a green thumb. I don't kill my plants. I just don't make them flourish like this."

"Any time you'd like to come up here, I'd be happy to share this with you."

We walk over to the vegetable patch, and his expression quickly turns to a playful scowl.

"Jorge?"

"Yeah. Javier definitely decided payment for his help keeping my plants watered was to pick off all the peppers and tomatoes. I'd hoped to use some tomatoes for the dinner I planned to cook you tonight."

"You were going to cook dinner?"

"Yes, *chiquita*, I do manage to keep the wolf from the door."

"The wolf from the door? What does that mean?"

"It's an idiom I learned from an English friend. Maybe it has something to do with the three little pigs, but I don't know. It just means to keep from being hungry."

"Ah, I'm pretty good with British idioms since I went to university there, but clearly I either need a refresher, or there are some I never knew. Daddy, remember though, I'm German. We don't do peppers like you do in Latin America. We have some spicy foods, but probably nothing like you're used to."

"I meant bell peppers, but that's good to know. If I set you ablaze, it won't be with peppers."

"Really? What would it be with?"

He waggles his eyebrows. "My tongue or my cock, of course."

I'm sure my cheeks are radiating as much heat as those spicy peppers I don't like. I have no idea why that comment out of all the ones we've shared makes me blush, but it does.

He gathers a few vegetables in his arms, and we head back downstairs. We're efficient in the kitchen as he points to where things are, and I help him make dinner. What would've taken him an hour to prep alone is in the oven within twenty minutes. It's something small and probably unremarkable, but it makes me feel like we're a real—a normal—couple.

We've just cleared the table and are in the middle of doing dishes when his doorbell rings. He glances at the security monitor, so I look too. I recognize Luciana. Jorge hurries to dry his hands before answering the door. I giggle along with Luciana when Jorge lifts her off her feet as he hugs her.

"*Mamá.*"

There's nothing short of relief and happiness in his voice with that one word. I realize it's been more than a month since the last time he saw her. Nothing about him screams mama's boy, except for right now as he kisses her cheek and gives her an extra squeeze before putting her back on her feet. They don't let go immediately until she pats him on the back. Then they step away from each other. This side of Jorge confirms what I suspected between showing me his greenhouse and seeing him with his mother.

I'm certain now I've fallen in love with him. It hasn't taken that long, but it's been long enough.

I dry my hands as well and step out of the kitchen.

"Anneliese, it's so nice to see you again."

She offers me a hug that's nearly as good as my mom's. Immediately, she feels like someone I can rely on. I suspect there'll be many times when I do. At least now, at the beginning, as I learn to navigate life in New York and as—I guess—a Cartel woman.

We let go of each other, and the three of us walk into the living room. Luciana takes a seat in the rocker recliner as Jorge and I sit on the rocking loveseat. The living room furniture is certainly designed for comfort. While much of the decor is rather minimalist, it's still a very welcoming space. I can tell that not just the garden is Jorge's reprieve from life outside his front door. It's relaxing for someone who contends with anxiety. It's a good thing he has these spaces.

"*Mamá.*"

Jorge's clipped word sounds so aggrieved my head whips over to look at him, but he's staring at Luciana.

"What did your brother do now, Jorge?"

Luciana's tone is one I'm sure she used countless times with Jorge and his brothers, but when they were much younger.

"Javier stole all my peppers and tomatoes. Make him give them back, *Mamá.*"

"You really think I can convince your older brother to give those back to you? He's probably already eaten all of them."

"But, *Mamá*, it's not fair."

"Jorge, didn't your brother come over here to help you? Didn't he water your plants and make sure everything was okay upstairs?"

"Yes, but, *Mamá*—"

"Don't you think it's only fair to share with your brother since he helped you?"

"He could've asked, *Mamá*. He never asks. He always takes my things."

I listen to the conversation going back and forth. Jorge could sound petulant and childish if I didn't know better, but it's clearly a running joke amongst his family. He's playing the role of the youngest brother so well I can't help but giggle. Luciana appears utterly unimpressed by her son's antics, but I see the twinkle in her eyes as they talk.

"*Mamá*, you never take my side. You always take my brothers'."

"*Gordito*, all of you say that, and all of you know it's not true."

"Are you sure, *Mamá?*"

Luciana cocks an eyebrow and gives him a look that makes him appear indignant. As much as I try to stifle my laughter behind my hands, I sound more like I'm choking than anything else.

"See how it is, *Mamá?* Even my girlfriend sides with you. It's not fair."

"Well, now you have someone else to kiss your boo-boos and make it all better, *gordito*."

His eyes widen, and I'm positive he's blushing.

"What does *gordito* mean?"

"Chubby little boy. All three of my sons were born with the roundest little cheeks. I've always called all of them that."

I have tears practically rolling down my cheeks as I laugh even harder. If I thought Jorge's day sounded pretty normal earlier, this is like Twilight Zone normal. What alternate reality have I stepped into where a Cartel narco-trafficker is being teased by his mother? And where said narco-trafficker is complaining to his mother about his older brother stealing his toys—or vegetables in this case?

Jorge wraps his arm around me and mutters to me, but I'm certain Luciana hears him. "I thought you were on my side."

"Oh, I am, but I absolutely love this."

He kisses my temple and smiles at me. I don't think any of this was just for my benefit. I suspect the conversation would've happened anyway, even if I weren't here, but it certainly puts me at ease.

"Anneliese, I don't know whether Jorge has said this or not, but if he has to travel over the next few months, I'd very much like it if you'd come to stay with me. I'm sure you don't know too many people here in this city, and I know how overwhelming it is to move to a new country. I did it when I went to UCLA and then again several years later with *Tres J's*."

It surprises me to hear Jorge's mom use that term for her sons. I figured it was a nickname or something people outside the family used for the brothers, perhaps in more of a derogatory way than as an endearment. Perhaps it's both, depending upon who's using it.

"I'd like that very much, Luciana. Thank you. It's been a while since I've been in the States for more than just a couple of days and business meetings. I'm not that familiar with New York, especially outside of Manhattan."

None of us acknowledge my ignorance of Cartel life and what it would mean if Jorge's away from home. I appreciate that it goes unsaid, but at the same time, the offer is there.

"You're welcome over anytime, especially without Jorge. The boy still eats me out of house and home. His brothers aren't any better. I swore up and down when they each left home, my kitchen would no longer be a cafeteria, but it still is."

"Jorge mentioned all three of them have dinner with you at least once a week and stop by at least once each. That must be a massive grocery trip every week for all three of them."

"It is, but that doesn't stop them, and sometimes they bring Alejandro and Pablo. I can never keep enough food in the house for them. It's only gotten worse with age. You've seen how big they are. They all have hollow legs."

My face hurts from smiling so much since Luciana arrived. The conversation continues for another twenty minutes as mother and son catch up, not exactly skirting what happened to my family but not going into detail. I'm exhausted but happy as she says goodbye. Jorge shows me the main bedroom and helps me unpack as he makes space in the dresser and closet.

"Your mom is amazing."

Jorge looks over at me as he lifts a stack of t-shirts out of one drawer and places them in another.

"She really is. I couldn't ask for a better mom. We haven't always seen eye to eye, and I didn't love all of her rules. When I was a kid, she was definitely strict, but I've never doubted everything she's ever done is out of love."

"I suspect she's very protective of you and your brothers still."

"Absolutely."

He pauses for a moment and assesses me. I wonder what he's thinking because he's definitely weighing whether he should tell me.

"*Chiquita*, when my *papá* died, *Mamá* made sure the men who did it paid for their sins. She ended the threat to all of us, so those men could never hurt anyone again. *Mamá* also made sure the man who hired them did too. She sent one of his *huevos* in a box to his wife with a handwritten note that said, 'If I can't have my man, neither can you.'"

What Jorge shares stuns me. The elegant woman who teased her son and made me feel so at home has a violent streak I never could've imagined. It should shock the shit out of me and scare the piss out of me. Instead, I respect her even more, and it relieves me to know she's like that if I'm to stay with her when Jorge's not around.

"Liesel, you need to know all of the syndicate mothers are like that. In the O'Rourke family, Breda, Saoirse, and Siobhan are *not* to be underestimated. Before Siobhan's son, Dillan, became the boss, it was the sisters' older brother who led their family, and before that it was their father. When their brother, Donovan, tried to make their sons go on a mission younger than they agreed to, Breda ordered a hit on one of Donovan's men. She made sure the guy was in intensive care for weeks. She didn't have him killed, but he was never the same afterwards.

She did it to remind her brother and everyone else that he might have been the head of the family, but his sisters' hands were the ones who turned it. Galina, Alina, and Svetlana are the bratva mothers. They survived growing up in Russia, and their husbands were all KGB before becoming bratva."

That last bit isn't as descriptive, but it tells me all I need to know about the bratva mothers.

"The Mancinelli women are like the O'Rourkes. They all grew up in Mafia families and married Mafia men. Maria Mancinelli is close to my age. Her uncle's the don. Her father's his *consigliere*, or chief advisor. Her oldest brother is the underboss, and her second oldest brother is the *capo dei capi*, or captain of captains. Her husband's one of the senior most *capos* along with her third brother and their cousin. The best shooters out of all four families, until *Tía* Elle joined ours, were in that family."

I'm not certain what to say at the end of that story. I mull over what he's just shared, and I'm struck by a realization that fills me all the way to the marrow of my bones.

"Jorge, you need to know that even though I don't have the history your mom has or the mob, Mafia, and bratva women, I'm no different from them. If we have children, I won't think twice about protecting them the same way. You say there are no limits to what you'd do to keep me safe, and I don't doubt for a moment that would extend to any children we have. I feel the same way about you, but I admit the thought of anyone harming our children creates such a visceral rage in me even you wouldn't talk me out of whatever I'd want to do."

He stares at me for a long moment before he nods. "*Chiquita*, the one thing I would ask of you, God forbid that situation should ever happen, is that you speak to me first. Not because I'll try to talk you out of it, but to ensure your safety. Let me work alongside you. If our children were ever in danger, I couldn't bear risking you too."

"That's fair, Daddy."

I can live with that. I'm standing by the closet, and he walks over to me. He slides his arms around my waist, pulling my back to his chest as he kisses my neck.

"I love seeing your clothes hanging beside mine, *chiquita*. It looks so natural to have them there."

"And I love knowing you made space for me to share your dresser too. It really makes this feel like home rather than just a place I'm visiting."

"I think I need to show you just how at home you are in our bed, little one."

I turn toward him, and he takes my hands loosely in his. He walks backward to the bed as he draws me with him.

"Daddy, can we be more adventurous tonight?"

Chapter Thirty

Jorge

I stare at Liesel for a moment. "What kind of adventurous?"

"You know I like it when you spank me. Can we use something besides your hand?"

"We can, but I've never brought a woman here, Liesel. I don't have toys or implements I recycle on women. I don't have any paddles, crops, or whips."

I'm adamant she knows I wouldn't use anything on her that I've shared with another woman. I think it reassures her, and I'm certain she prefers it, even if it's inconvenient.

"You have belts."

"No, absolutely not. I will not lash you with a belt the first time you receive a spanking with something more than my hand. We will build up to that unless you do something that risks your safety or someone else's. Then it'll be a punishment, and you won't enjoy anything about it. I'd rather not associate your first memories of a toy or implement with a punishment, but I will if I have to."

I feel the shiver running along her spine. She could shy away from the dominance in my voice and the threat of corporal punishment. Instead, she leans into it. I don't know that she wants to test my promise, but it arouses her to think of me commanding her like that.

I tug her closer and inhale. I yank her t-shirt over her head and shove her bra out of the way. I latch onto her nipple and suck so hard she yelps. When I pull back, I slap it.

"You like the idea of me punishing you. You want it even more than you did the spankings I gave you in the hotel. I smell your arousal, Liesel. It makes me want to lick your cunt until you come on my tongue."

"I'd be embarrassed by the first half of what you said, Daddy, if the second half didn't set my pussy ablaze."

"*I will undress you.*"

Because I have control of this situation and of her. But we both recognize it's because she allows it. She doesn't doubt for a moment that I'd stop the instant she told me to. I'm only doing this because she consents. Oh, how she consents. I can practically hear her thoughts since her face is so expressive.

Yes, please. Right this fucking moment, please.

I unfasten her jeans and push them down her hips. We both took our shoes off at the door when we came back from the greenhouse. She steps out of her pants before I toe the jeans and fling them aside.

"What the fuck are these, *chiquita?*"

"Panties, Daddy."

"Do you think you should be wearing them?"

"Um—no?"

"You may wear a bra because I know it would embarrass you not to. But you will *not* wear panties again. When I want to see, touch, taste, or smell your cunt, you will *not* have anything in my way. I may not be so demanding as to insist you only wear skirts and dresses, but you won't put any more layers between your cunt and me ever again. Am I clear, *chiquita?*"

"Yes, Daddy."

Fuck this is hot.

"You will throw all your panties away in the morning. If I find any, I will burn them."

"Will you go commando for me?"

I wrap my hand in her hair and tug until she's looking up at me. I reach around her and unfasten her bra, stripping her of it as I speak.

"Do you want every person within ten feet of me to know you keep me hard morning, noon, and night? That just the thought of you makes me want to drive my cock into your mouth, pussy, or ass. That when you're near me, I'm like a wild beast barely kept in his cage. If you want anyone and everyone to see my hard-on, then sure, I'll go commando."

"No. It'll make people stare. Then I'll assume they want what's mine. I'll scratch their motherfucking eyes out and cut out their tongues."

Her eyes widen at her declaration. It's a good thing I can read lips, even when they're barely moving because I understand what she says more to herself than me.

Where the hell did that come from?

I stare at her for a moment before I slap her other breast. I trail the tip of my tongue from her shoulder to just behind her ear. When I nip at her earlobe, it must sting. I tug until her head tilts toward my lips.

"Promise, *chiquita?*"

"Yes."

"Good girl. I like you feisty and possessive. On your knees."

"Yes, Daddy."

I unfasten my pants and push them, along with my boxer briefs, low enough for my cock to spring free.

"Lick it all."

My hand's still in her hair, so I control her head. I push down but not hard enough to hurt her neck. She obeys my command, flicking her tongue along the ridge on the underside. I groan, adding more pressure to her head.

"Do you know how good you look licking my cock?"

"No, Daddy. I don't."

"It's about the most erotic thing I've ever seen, *chica*. Suck."

She slides her mouth down my length, taking as much as she can. She sucks harder when I groan again.

"Fuck, baby girl. I love to listen to you speak because you're brilliant. I love watching you suck me off because you're sexy as fuck."

She works my cock for a couple minutes, but she squeals in surprise when I lift her off the floor. I place her on her belly on the bed, facing me, before I guide my cock back into her mouth. She's called my body svelte before. Whatever it is, I take advantage of my height to spank her ass. I'm not gentle. I crisscross it until it must prickle and feel like a torch's been lit next to it. She keeps sucking my dick the whole time.

"Let go and stand in front of the mirror."

I have a full length one beside the dresser, closer to the door than the window. I turn her, so she has to look over her shoulder to see her ass. She sees the faint outline of my hand in a few places. She knows I'm walking to and from the bathroom, but she appears too mesmerized to watch me, even as I get naked too.

"This, just like your tits and pussy, is mine. Come here."

I walk past her to the armchair in the corner near the window. She follows me, slightly trepidatious since she sees her hairbrush in my hand. I have something in the other one that she can't see; it's just clear my hand's wrapped around an object.

"Straddle me."

She follows my directions and eases herself onto my lap. She takes too long.

"Unless I tell you to do something slowly, I expect you to obey immediately."

"Yes, Daddy."

Does she sound as breathless and horny to herself as she does to me?

What I have in my hand is small enough that I can completely hide it in my curled fingers. She has no idea what's coming. My thumb rubs her clit with just enough pressure to leave her frustrated. I know she wants to squirm, but she knows I won't allow it. Being at my mercy, wondering what I'll do next, consumes all her attention. I don't want her think about anything else because that's what she needs right now.

She's not wondering about her family.

She's not feeling guilty for how things ended with Bastian.

She's not scared about being in a new city where she only knows my family and me.

She's not worried about where she'll work.

She's not terrified more people will come after her or her dad.

She can just focus on the here and now.

She knows I'm giving her that.

I understand without her asking. I know she feels out of control, so I'm showing her that I have it, and I'll use my control to take care of her.

Can anyone who doesn't long for this push-pull, give and take, dominance and submission fully understand this? Do most people consider this nuts?

I haven't considered it much, to be honest, because I've been into BDSM since I was in college. But what I'm sharing with Liesel is far beyond just the acts. It feeds my emotional and physical needs on such an elemental level—a level I didn't know exists. Now I desperately need this with her, and I think I always will. This isn't just about the crisis we're still in the midst of. This is far deeper within me.

I open my hand, and she spies one of her smallest hair ties. She explained while we were unpacking her toiletries that it's a tiny rubber band from a package she used the last time she grew out bangs because they would annoy her.

I rub her clit harder and faster until she can't keep from shifting, her sore ass pressing against my steely thighs. I tilt her hips forward and wrap the rubber band around her clit.

"You will tell me the moment this goes from uncomfortable and unfamiliar to concerning or painful. Whether you use the safe word or not. Do you understand me, Liesel?"

"Yes, Jorge. I promise."

The seriousness in my voice makes her respond in kind. I'm certain the sensation is odd. A more intense version of what she's felt when I've pinched her clit in the past. From her expression, there's a throb that makes her want more, not less.

"Lie over my lap, *chica*."

My tone isn't gentle per se. It's just not as demanding. I help position her.

"Yes, Daddy."

"What's your safe word?"

"Sauerkraut."

"Good girl. Hold onto my ankle or put your hands on the floor if you're tempted to reach back."

"I know."

Before she can wonder if I'll ask if she's ready, the back of her hairbrush lands across her ass.

"*Heilige Scheiße.*" Holy fuck.

Whack.

"*Verdammt, das tut weh.*" Motherfucker, that hurts.

"Breathe through it, Liesel, or I stop."

"Yes, Daddy."

She inhales, and I feel her body relax. I don't think she'd noticed how rigid she'd gone.

"The more you tense, the more it'll hurt, little one."

"I'll try."

My hand sweeps over her ass before I rub away some of the burn.

"I know you will, *chica*. You're being so brave."

I swat her ass two more times on each cheek—right, left, left, right. Her back arches, and she grabs my ankle to keep from reaching back. I can guess what she's thinking right about now.

Why the fuck did I ask for this?

The next one lands on the underside of her ass, right in the middle. Her thighs squeeze.

"Your needy little pussy likes how it feels when you do that. Is your clit begging to rub against something as it grows more and more sensitive? Do you need me to fill you with my cock?"

My questions make her moan.

"Are you aching for any kind of relief to how empty you feel right now?"

Her body relaxes over my lap as she focuses solely on how badly her pussy needs my attention. That's why she's unprepared for me to spank her with the bristles. It's not as hard as the other ones, but it makes her yelp, nonetheless.

"Your ass looks delectable, *chiquita*. Red with white dots now."

"If you say so."

I guide her outside leg over one of my knees, opening them wide to me. She screams when the back of the brush lands against her exposed cunt.

"Daddy!"

If that wasn't bad enough, I pluck the rubber band from her clit. The rush of blood back into it is nearly too much.

"Fuck. I'm seeing stars. It's like my body no longer belongs to me."

As I move her how I want, her confession slips out as though she didn't mean to share it aloud. She goes along with what I demand. Her mind's likely scrambled from myriad sensations. Before she knows it, she's straddling me again, and I surge into her.

"*Scheiße*, Daddy!" Fuck, Daddy!

She doesn't even know what language to speak or think in. She grasps my shoulders and holds on as she rides me. I thrust over and over, rocking her hips, making her clit grind against my pubic bone.

"Do you want to come, Liesel?"

"Yes. So badly."

"Ask."

"Please, may I come, Daddy?"

"Yes. Five...Four...Three...Two... Now."

Her orgasm erupts.

"Daddy!"

"Yes?"

She pants as she speaks, but I understand every word. "That's probably—the most powerful one—I've ever had—and —that's saying something—since the ones you've given me—far surpass anything—any other man—or you—have before. I've never—had one on command—like that."

She rides me, not realizing she compared me to her past. I take it as a compliment, if not a challenge to keep rocking her world.

"Daddy, I have a sudden urge to pee that I've never had before during sex. I'm fighting it. It's so strange."

It must pass because her face relaxes. But then there's a stream of liquid dripping from her.

"Did I—did I just squirt?"

"Yes."

My voice's ragged when I answer. She was looking down at my now wet lap, but my tone jerks her attention to me. She sees I'm barely holding on. I doubt my gaze has ever been so intense.

I stand then carry her to the bed. She's barely on her feet before I spin her and press her against the bed. I spread her ass cheeks, and she knows what's coming next. She relaxes as the tip of my cock presses against her rosebud. As I slide my lubed cock—her cunt did that for me—into her, she bares down to make it easier for me to enter her.

Then I'm squeezing her ass cheeks, pulling them apart and pushing them up. She clenches the sheets, prepared for me to pound into her. Instead, I'm slow as I try to be incredibly gentle while I move within her. I'm sure she feared I might lose control and fuck her like a sex doll. From her expression as she looks over her shoulder at me, maybe she almost wishes I would. To be desired that much...

But I don't, even though I want her that intensely. I'm careful with her because as strong as my desire to fuck her is, my desire to never harm her is far stronger. I let go of her left ass cheek and glide my hand up her damp back. The heel of my hand presses into knots as I travel between her shoulder blades and up to her shoulder. I grip her as I draw back then ease into her, rocking against her.

"Fuck, baby girl. I'm going to come."

Before she can say anything, I pulse within her. I feel the spurts of cum, and she clenches around me, milking my cock.

"I want to fall asleep inside you, *chiquita*. Buried to my balls with my cum trapped in there."

"Figure out how to get us onto the bed, and you can do whatever the hell you want as long as you're inside me."

Soon a wave of sleepiness sweeps over me. I'm certain she must feel the same.

"It's been a long day, *chiquita*. We both need some sleep."

"I know. I can barely keep my eyes open."

We're hardly graceful as we climb onto the bed. We both reach around for the covers and draw them over us. We wind up laughing until I spoon her. I brush hair off her shoulder and kiss it.

"Are you okay, little one?"

"Far better than okay, big one."

I chuckle. "That was amazing, Liesel. I've never—"

"Neither have I. I've never squirted, and I've never—I don't know. Surrendered?"

"Being in control of anything has never felt that special. Your trust in me—it's everything to me."

There's a pregnant pause, like we both want to declare our feelings, but neither of us do. Instead, we settle against each other. I don't know when she falls asleep, but I pass out hard still buried in her.

Chapter Thirty-One

Liesel

Sometime during the night, Jorge slipped out of me and out of bed. He woke me this morning, and I could smell the fresh soapy scent on his skin. We've fucked in the past, and I think you could almost call how gentle he was in my ass last night making love. There's no doubting that's what we just did this morning.

He bound my wrists together before using a tie around my tits to press them together. Then he used two more ties to secure my calves to my thighs. He claims I looked amazing. I suspect I looked like he'd hog tied me. But the way we moved together. The way we looked at each other. It was just different.

Last night created physical responses I'd never had before. This morning created emotional ones I didn't know I could have. I've made love in the past, but this was like my very soul was part of it.

Now I lie draped across Jorge's chest. We'd probably catch

our breath much easier if I weren't lying on top of him, but I'm so incredibly comfortable. My head's high on his shoulder and his arm's wrapped around me. His hand rests on my ass while the other holds me between my shoulder blades. He seems in no rush to make me move.

"*Chiquita*, what did you think of last night and just now? It was definitely more than just the ties I used when we were at Hisham and Noor's."

"I liked it all a lot. I've never been restrained before being with you, and you spanking me was the first time I'd ever done that as well. I mean real spankings, not just a few taps."

I feel him tense beneath me. I know he loathes any reference to my sexual past. I'm not thrilled to share it either, but I want him to know my inexperience, so he can teach me safely and properly. He talked me through everything this morning, and it made it easier to appreciate the closeness this dynamic creates.

"I'd like to try more if you'd like that too, Daddy."

"Very much, *chiquita*. There are more things we can do here, but if you'd really like to explore BDSM, then we can go to a club."

"I'd definitely enjoy that."

"There's one in Brooklyn I know of. It's not as luxurious as ones in Manhattan, but we'd have far more privacy. There are members of all Four Families who are shadow owners of various clubs. It's useful for us to go unnoticed while having access to member lists. We all pretend as though we're the only ones with investments in those clubs, and we pretend as though those are well-guarded secrets, but they really aren't. It also means every once in a while we run into each other. Things have shuffled around since other couples are into the same things we are, *chica*. For our wives' and girlfriends' sakes, we try to make sure our memberships don't overlap as much."

I push up to meet his gaze. "I definitely wouldn't want to run into members of those families while I'm there with you." *Or women you fucked in the past.*

"I think there are even some silent agreements among the couples on which nights they go, so they don't run into each other. This one in Brooklyn is much quieter."

I don't think I want to know how he knows that. He strokes my ass, and I notice I clenched just like he did a moment ago.

"If you think it'd be better than if we were to run into—someone...Sure."

"*Chica*, I'm one of those silent investors and members of the Manhattan clubs. I've never been to the one in Brooklyn as a member, but I own it."

He gets it without me having to spell it out. I suppose he'd feel the same way if the shoe were on the other foot.

Strip clubs and BDSM clubs. I don't know what to make of these revelations. I have pangs of jealousy, as I think of Jorge around beautiful, naked women and places that exist purely for sexual fulfillment. I don't quite feel inadequate, but I definitely feel a little insecure since he's already into BDSM and clearly has had past partners who know what they're doing.

He kisses my forehead and offers me an understanding smile. I like how I don't have to spell everything out to him. That we're on the same wavelength about so many things. It makes all of this new stuff easier.

"*Chica*, we both have pasts, and I never want mine to hurt you. That's why I'll happily go to a club I've never been to before and why I'll pass the management of the strip clubs to my brother. Yes, there will be women dancing when I go to do payroll. The clubs are open nearly twenty-four hours, but I've always gone directly into my office to run payroll or the storerooms to check inventory. I don't hang out with the women or on the floors. I have general managers who oversee the day-today functioning of those clubs. I hope you can believe me when I tell you there's no woman more beautiful to me than you. Why on earth would I want to look at or touch another woman when I'm with you? I don't want anyone else, and I would never risk losing you for something so foolish and worthless as that."

There's an adamance in Jorge's tone that's unwavering. I use both of my forearms to help prop me up. I'm careful not to dig my elbows into his chest, but I want to see his face. His expression matches his tone. There's a no-nonsense air to it. One that shows he believes what he says so deeply that it's irrefutable.

I stretch and press a quick kiss to his lips before I settle again. I can't get my arms all the way around him because he's lying on his back, but I hug him as tightly as I can.

"Thank you for explaining all of that to me, Jorge. I admit I wondered."

"I don't blame you for that, little one, and you're being far more understanding and reasonable than I would be if the situation were reversed. I don't doubt I would be far less gracious about the situation and likely far more demanding if it were different."

I chuckle and kiss his chest. I don't believe he's exaggerating in the least.

Once we were up and finally out of bed this morning, Jorge and I had brunch together at his place. I noticed last night that his fridge was stocked with fresh food. He explained it was likely Javier or Madeline who stopped by to make sure there was stuff for us to eat, so we wouldn't have to worry about groceries or going out to dinner or even ordering in.

We've just pulled up to Enrique's house in New Jersey. I don't know that the word house is even adequate. Mansion even feels like it describes a place smaller than what I'm seeing. There's a wall around the property that must be at least twelve feet tall. It's in a gated community with a gate at the driveway. Men in all black with bulletproof vests and rifles were at a guard house by the gate, and I see more of them patrolling the grounds. My eyes must be wide as saucers as I lean forward while looking out the windows. It's unnerving to know his uncle feels he and his wife need this level of protection.

"This is—um—a lot to take in."

"*Chiquita*, it's precautionary. *Tío* Luis and *Tía* Margherita live in a gated community here in New Jersey, but their property isn't gated like everyone else's who lives in a house rather than a condo."

"Why is that?"

"Part of it is because they're in such a residential area of New Jersey. It's not where most people would expect a senior Cartel member and his family to live, but much of it is my *tío's* reputation."

As I glance at the house before looking back at Jorge, I try to imagine what that reputation could be.

"Jorge, what do people think about your uncle that makes him more terrifying than Enrique?"

"It's not so much that *Tío* Luis is more terrifying than *Tío* Enrique, but *Tío* Enrique's position makes him a greater target than *Tío* Luis. *Tío* Luis's nickname is *El Espíritu Santo*, or the Holy Spirit. When he visits someone in Latin America, they know *Tío* Enrique sent him, and there's no redemption for however they fucked up."

I stare at Jorge, blinking like a beached fish. I know he won't explain more than that, but he's made it clear one uncle serves as the executioner for the other. I don't doubt Jorge's killed more than one man in his life. I don't doubt it was justified because it was surely an "us or them" situation. I don't think he merely goes around killing people for shits and giggles. But for a man to have the moniker "the Holy Spirit," that understandably strikes fear in just about anybody.

Jorge already explained to me about not getting out of a vehicle without one of the guards, one of his family members, or him opening the door for me. But it still makes me jump when a man standing beside the window reaches for the door handle. He holds it wide open for me, and I glance at Jorge.

He nods his agreement—permission—I don't know what to call it exactly. Even though we're behind two gates, I'm relieved to know he deems it safe for me. I stand, and the guard closes the door behind me. Jorge walks around the hood and slides his arm around my waist before leading me to the front door.

"It's impressive, I know, but you have to remember we're an enormous family that spends a great deal of time together. All of the houses have enough room for everyone to stay there. Sometimes we get home late or have to leave early."

That's another veiled hint. I understand those are probably times when he'll want me to stay with Luciana.

"Part of the house is also *Tío* Enrique's office. There's space for him to work in his study which is large enough for my *tíos*, cousins, brothers, and me. There's also another room where he can meet with men who work for us."

I nod because I don't know what else to say to that. It makes sense, but there doesn't seem to be an appropriate response. When I look up at Jorge, I can tell he doesn't expect one from me.

There are plenty of other cars in the driveway, so he opens the door using the punch pad next to it. He already explained to me that once upon a time there was an open-door policy to most of the homes. However, more of the men have found wives and girlfriends, so that's no longer the case. Now they call or text each other as they go through community gates and then again as they pull into the private driveways. It only took me a moment to realize this rule existed to avoid anyone walking in on the couples during intimate moments. He's implied all the couples, even his *tíos* and *tías*, are just as lusty as he and I are.

We hear several voices as we step into the foyer. It nearly overwhelms me as I consider all the people I'm about to meet. A flash of nervousness sends a shiver along my spine.

"*Chiquita*, everybody already knows your situation, so you don't have to explain any of that. Just be as outgoing as you're comfortable with. If you'd rather remain quiet and observe, no one will think less of you for that."

"Thank you."

He gives my hip a squeeze as we head into the living room. *Holy shit.*

It's like being in a house of mirrors. The family resemblance among the men is mind boggling. There's only one man who doesn't look like the rest of them, so I assume he's Alejandro's father. There's also one Latina who doesn't resemble the other two, so that must be Jorge's *tía* Margherita.

I look between Alejandro and the man who must be his father. They're standing exactly the same way but in opposite parts of the room. Their expressions are so similar, yet Alejandro looks like a younger version of the man who must be Enrique. So much so you'd assume Alejandro was Enrique's son, if not for his matching posture and expression to his father, Matáis.

Luciana and her sister, Catalina, resemble Enrique and the other man who must be Luis. He and Enrique could almost be twins except Luis's hair is slightly lighter than Enrique's. While he's clearly an extremely muscular man, he's a little leaner than

Enrique. If Jorge hadn't explained Catalina's a year older than his mother, I would believe they were twins.

The man who must be Pablo is standing next to Margherita. He's a carbon copy of his father. The only way to tell them apart is Luis has some gray around his temples, and they have different tattoos showing on their arms. It appears from here that the only feature Pablo inherited from his mother are his eyes—they're dark hazel rather than brown. Otherwise, she got no say in him because even Pablo's posture matches his father's.

I knew Jorge and Joaquin looked similar, but now that I see a man with a blonde woman standing beside him, there's no way I could confuse him for anyone but Javier. I get why they're called *Tres J's* and not just because that's the first initial of their names. They could practically be triplets. They're all the same height, same build, same hair color, and same eye color. I'm certain from the back it's difficult to differentiate them. Their faces are just different enough to be able to tell one from another but not by much.

The blonde woman looks close to my age. She comes to greet me along with Javier. As my gaze sweeps the room, I suspect the others are waiting for Jorge's brother and his wife to greet me first. The men's tight embrace reminds me of when Joaquin and Alejandro arrived in Frankfurt.

"Hi, I'm Madeline."

"Hello, I'm Anne. It's nice to meet you."

"You, too. I know Javier's been just as excited to meet you as I am. We've been curious to see who's willing to put up with Jorge."

The brothers let go of each other, and Jorge embraces Madeline.

"I'm not the one who wound up with Oscar the Grouch over here."

Jorge tilts his head toward Javier. His next older brother scowls at him, and I admit he does remind me a little of the puppet from the children's TV show. I used to watch it when I was in elementary school to help me learn English along with the classes I took. Javier offers me a hug as well. It's not quite as warm as the one Jorge and Madeline shared. But I think it's because Javier wishes to respect me since he's uncertain of whether I'd welcome the embrace. When we step apart, Joaquin comes over to join his brothers.

"It's uncanny, isn't it?" Madeline's voice is soft as she speaks to me, but I hear the laughter in it.

"It truly is." I can't stop staring.

"It makes me wonder when Javier and I have kids whether they'll look more like his side of the family since the Diaz genetics are so dominant."

I consider what Madeline says, and a wave of curiosity and a sense of excitement surprise me because I'm now picturing children with Jorge. Dark hair and dark eyes are dominant genes. Since no one in his family has blonde hair or light eyes, I doubt any children we'd have would possess those recessive traits. Same thing for Madeline, whose blonde hair is a couple shades darker than mine, but not by much.

I observe the brothers together in what I'd call their natural habitat. They appear so relaxed, yet there's something about them I can't quite put my finger on. Madeline nudges my arm.

"Don't be fooled by their resting bitch faces. They're really not that bad. Even mine, who's the prickliest one of the three of them."

I can't help but laugh since Madeline's hit the nail on the head. None of them appear exactly unwelcoming or unfriendly, but none of them seem the type who'd strike up a conversation with a stranger or want a stranger to talk to them.

I recall what Jorge told me a while ago about Joaquin being

shy. That surprised me considering how outgoing he was with me. But Jorge explained Joaquin was comfortable with me from the beginning since he knew I'm so important to Jorge and because Jorge trusts me. If that hadn't been the case, Joaquin would've been far more reserved.

He also shared with me that Javier's the most introverted. He's the most suspicious of them, but that's not what made him enjoy his solitude before he and Madeline got together. Instead, Javier simply enjoyed his own company and would spend hours assembling Lego sets. Even though they can now order them online, it's a tradition for the brothers to go to the store together to pick up new special edition sets for Javier. Jorge shared that when they were younger and lines still formed outside stores for the special edition sets, they'd camp out together.

That story warmed my heart as I pictured three brothers hanging out and enjoying each other's company and supporting each other's hobbies so much. I could imagine Heidi doing that for me and me doing that for her, but neither of us was ever into anything so deeply that we'd want to.

Introductions to everyone else follows, and by the time we sit down together, I feel welcomed by everyone. Even though Madeline introduced herself first, I find myself gravitating toward Florencia. I think it's because she and I are both newly arrived in the U.S., as well as this family. Madeline's been so kind to both of us, making sure we feel part of the family and know where everything is.

It surprised me at first, but Jorge reminded me Madeline grew up coming to this house since her family used to be so close to Pablo's. Madeline's family used to alternate Sunday dinners with Luis and Margherita. Apparently, Pablo's younger brother, Juan, used to be best friends with Madeline's older sister, Laura.

I didn't get all the details, but something happened between Juan and Laura that severed the bond between those two families. They're now merely neighbors who coexist side by side. I suspect whatever Juan did to Laura led to his death. Jorge gave me no details about that, and I haven't dared ask for them. I figure if and when I should know, I will.

At the end of dinner, the men gravitate to each other. Soon they're in the kitchen doing the dishes. It's nice to see a stereotype obliterated when the men wrap aprons around themselves to protect their tailored suits. I notice Enrique's wife, Elle, is in the kitchen with them. At first, I thought it might be because this is her home too, but she's involved in a conversation with the men. She stays in there and out of their way while the men clean up around her.

I glance over at Luciana, who's talking to Madeline and Margherita. Catalina and Florencia are talking to me—or rather talking around me—as I stare at the kitchen. Catalina saying my name draws my attention back to her. I'm embarrassed that I was ignoring the two women.

"It's not that the women always do all the cooking, but when we do, the men always do all the cleaning up. As moms and wives, we've instilled it in the men that if they can make the mess, they can clean up the mess." Catalina's smile is infectious, just like her sister's.

"I'll be sure to remember that."

"Absolutely. We've drilled it into our sons so well that none of them have dared get housekeepers. They're generally all very tidy, but they know none of their parents would allow such laziness that they couldn't clean up after themselves in their own homes. Once in a while, they'll have somebody come in if they've hosted a family party or if they've been out of town long enough for dust to accumulate. But don't let my *sobrino* fool you. He should have dishpan hands and know how to scrub a toilet."

As humorous as her tone is, I know she's not exaggerating.

"I'll be sure to remember that too."

I force myself not to look back at the kitchen, but I still wonder why Elle is among the men when none of them are laughing anymore. It appears like a very serious conversation. It makes me wonder if it's work-related or perhaps if it has something to do with me.

If it does, then why is Elle there?

Jorge made it abundantly clear women and children are meant to be kept away from Cartel dealings. I don't necessarily feel suspicious, but my curiosity is certainly heightened. In the car on the way back to Jorge's—or rather—our condo, he explains without me having to ask. It's a bit unnerving how he often reads my mind.

"Liesel, *Tía* Elle's family history is about as complicated as mine. She knows things most people wouldn't about Cartel life because of her upbringing."

I wait for Jorge to say more, but he offers nothing else. It's basically what he told me the other day. I test the water.

"Your mother and aunts also grew up in syndicate life, but they weren't part of that conversation."

"No, they weren't, though I know my father often involved my mother more than he probably should've. He trusted no one's opinion more than *Mamá's*. I suspect the same is true for *Tía* Margherita and *Tío* Luis, and *Tía* Catalina and *Tío* Matáis."

"So, will they explain everything to their wives when they get home?"

"Perhaps some, but not all."

I want to ask more, even demand a full explanation now that Jorge's opened the door to this topic. But it's a test. Not one he's giving me, but one I'm giving myself to accept these half-truths and half-explanations he warned me about. I have to be okay with not knowing everything. He's explained as much as he can, and I know he could've said nothing or come up with a lie.

This situation is so different from anything I've experienced in the past. If I'd been with another boyfriend who refused to tell me anything about what he was up to, I wouldn't have trusted him. It would've caused trouble between us. Yet, I accept what Jorge's telling me and not telling me because I understand he's doing it with the best of intentions to protect me.

At the same time, he's telling me what he can, so I don't feel entirely excluded. He's doing his best to find middle ground, and I appreciate that, even if I wish I knew more of what's going on.

We're headed to Enrique's for a second time in two days. I wasn't prepared to return so soon after being here last night, but apparently the men have a meeting. Jorge confided it's about my situation and me along with trying to figure out exactly what happened with my father. It's an even greater surprise when Jorge guides me to the dining room where Florencia's sitting with a man, and papers are spread in front of them. It's jarring when Jorge calls me Anne as he makes the introductions.

"This is Randolph McKenzie. He's an immigration attorney who's been working with Florencia to get her papers in order for work permits and a green card. I thought it would be a good idea for you to speak with him as well."

An attorney with an Irish last name? That's a question for later.

"Oh—yes—I suppose that's a good idea since I'm technically here on a tourist visa. The last time I lived in the States, I was here on a student one. I hadn't thought about this."

It's another heavy weight on top of the mountain of them from the events of the past nearly two months of knowing Jorge. I suppose in the back of my mind, I knew I'd have to sort this out since I agreed to come to America with Jorge. I assumed it was a permanent move. It was easier to believe that than to go back and forth in my mind about whether I should do this. I just leapt headlong into it. Seeing an immigration attorney makes all of this very real.

I don't have any doubts or reservations. It's just a reminder of what a massive decision I've made to not only leave Germany and my family, but to come here to be with a man I haven't known very long. An outsider looking in would likely say I'm certifiable or at the very least impetuous and naive. I've had moments of those thoughts throughout all of this, yet I'm able to silence them easily before they can become doubts. My certainty that Jorge is the man I'm meant to be with far outweighs my worries of what someone else might think.

"*Chica.*"

Jorge's voice is soft beside my ear. His hand was on my waist, but it slides down to my hip, precariously close to my ass. Whenever it's there, it's just as reassuring and delightfully possessive as it is when his hand rests at my lower back. It's often there when we're walking together, if his arm isn't around my waist or my shoulders, or he's not holding my hand. When his hand is at my lower back, it feels protective, while the hand near my ass is affectionate. I love both.

"Are you all right? I know this is a lot. I thought it would be a good idea since he's already here to speak to Florencia. I thought the two of you might like some moral support, so neither of you feels alone in all of this. I also thought it was practical to get the ball rolling sooner rather than later and to have you meet with him since I needed to be here anyway. But if this is too much and not what you want to do, then you don't have to meet with Randy."

Randy and Florencia are discussing something again now that introductions are done. I know it's a courtesy since Jorge began speaking to me.

"It's a lot to take in, but I'm not opposed to it. It's smart to get the paperwork in order sooner rather than later. I'd hate for there to be any complications that force me back to Germany."

"Randy will help you navigate what the best options are, whether it's a work visa for you to set up an American office of Schlossberg & Sons or you working for *Tío* Matáis, or having me as a significant other being your sponsor."

"I don't know if a boyfriend is enough, Jorge. I thought it had to be a spouse. That's the way it is in the movies at least."

"For a green card, it does have to be a spouse. Randy is clever and knows immigration law as though he were born to it. He knows how to find any loophole we could possibly use for me as just a boyfriend. More likely than not, he can make it work through employment rather than any personal relationship."

I observe Jorge closely as he explains some potential options. I don't think he'd propose to me merely for me to get a green card, and I wouldn't accept a proposal just for one. Neither of us would enter a marriage for a document, but it's important we both understand all of the options and implications.

"I'd like to hear what Randy has to say."

"All right, little one. I'll be in *Tío* Enrique's office. If you need anything, it's down the hall. But it would be best if you called or texted rather than just come and knock on the door."

I look down the hallway in the direction he points. I understand he means only knock on the door if it's an emergency. Otherwise, don't go where I could potentially overhear something I shouldn't.

Yes, Daddy.

I mouth my response, so neither Randy nor Florencia can hear. He gives me a quick kiss on the cheek before pulling out the chair next to Randy. Florencia's on one side of the attorney, and I'm on the other. Then he disappears down the hallway.

Chapter Thirty-Two

Jorge

I worried I ambushed Liesel yesterday by having her meet with Randy. However, it worked out for the best. She got to know Florencia better, and I think they're on the way to being thick as thieves. She gained a lot of insightful information from Randy and even began filling out some paperwork to get residency established.

We headed home after that, and she napped for a bit while I caught up on work. We had a wonderful dinner in the garden and moved over to the loungers set up by the fountain. I had a second one added across from mine, and then a double lounger placed between them. It was a clear night, so we shared the double lounger and watched the stars.

After that, we headed back down and soaked in the tub together. Her back was a maze of knots, so I gave her a massage that turned into a back and front one while she rode my cock. I woke in the middle of the night to the pleasant surprise of her lips wrapped around my dick. It was the best blowjob I've ever gotten.

Right now, she's asleep at our condo while I prepare for the mission at *Tío* Enrique's. It's not like we skulk around, but for meetings like this, it's better when we gather after sundown. Our comings and goings are less noticeable.

The guys and I began plotting in our *tío's* kitchen the night Liesel met my extended family. *Tía* Elle is involved in this because of her connections. She can get information even Joaquin can't. I noticed Liesel watching us as the men did dishes, and *Tía* Elle—consulted. I'm certain she wondered why my *tía* was involved and none of the other women were.

Tía Elle called in some favors in Venice, Naples, and Palermo to learn more about Friedrich's clients. We're adding more security to what Friedrich's providing so neither side in the Italian syndicate war can go after Gunter. The douche—the CEO of the firm that hired Friedrich's law firm—basically runs his money laundering like a Ponzi scheme.

He robs Peter to pay Paul by passing money through all those different hands to make it look like each subsequent deposit or investment is built on the previous ones, but really, it's all the same money. The Italians caught wind of this and decided to put him to work for them.

The *Cosa Nostra* hired him for his expertise, so he had no personal stake in extorting Liesel or kidnapping Gunter. Turns out he met Liesel at Friedrich's firm's Christmas party nearly three years ago. Friedrich volunteered to take care of him, and I agreed. I'm not asking for an explanation, and he's not offering one.

Tonight, we're focused more immediately on the O'Rourkes and Kutsenkos who targeted Liesel and Gunter, even if indirectly. We've decided to go after the O'Rourkes' whiskey distillery in Ireland. We want to ensure they understand just how long our reach is. If they want to fight a proxy war with the Kutsenkos, then they can go for it, but they're leaving my woman and her family out of it. Losing a major source of their revenue will remind them why *Tres J's* has the reputation we do.

We stir shit up and fuck you over with a motherfucking smile.

Joaquin hasn't stopped digging since before he arrived in Frankfurt. He learned it wasn't Maks and Dillan—the bratva and mob leaders—who liaised with the different Italian factions. It's Pasha and Finn. They're their respective family's accountants like I am.

Apparently, a few months ago, they had the same genius idea to commit some insider trading with the same company. It wound up bankrupting the company, having the SEC up their asses, and both of them losing a shit ton of money. They're using the feuding Mafias to get back at each other without getting their hands dirty. I don't give a fuck about their squabbles, but I give a fuck about them hurting Liesel and her family.

The Kutsenkos are about to have their westward expansion in Europe upended. My family doesn't just speak Latin American Spanish. We all speak Castilian too, so Spain's looking ripe for the taking. Since Portugal is right there next to it, we'll take from them there too. We'll remind him he picked the wrong *hombres*—men—to fuck with. To remind the bratva they're not the only ones who protect what's theirs, we're going to steal all the construction site materials Maks has secured on a property in Long Island.

We're not just taking the steel beams and lumber. We're going to take the heavy equipment as well. It's going on a ship to Germany directly to Friedrich's family. We're buying more allies in Germany and Italy. The enemy of my enemy is my friend and all of that.

It'll put a dent in whatever funds Pasha planned to send to the *Cosa Nostra* and *Mala del Brenta* behind Salvatore's back. I wouldn't want to be Don Carosi or Don Toretta this Easter. There's a litany of confessions for them to make before that holy day. They better pray Salvatore's feeling forgiving.

Joaquin's face lights up as his computer dings. "*Tía's* contact came through."

My brother's barely slept since the flight back from Germany. He runs off less sleep than all of us, but right now it's even less than usual. I'll make sure Javier stays out of my garden long enough for my oldest brother to have his pick of everything. He'll grab some vegetables, but he'll probably take half my heliconia rostrata—hanging lobster claw, an indigenous plant to Colombia I smuggled into NYC. I grow them for *Mamá*, and he loves nothing more than to swoop in, cut a huge bouquet, and give them to her before I can.

I fucking hate being the baby of the family. It's a fucking rip off.

We've decided what we're going to do to the bratva and mob, but we need to coordinate all of these attacks, so no one has a chance to warn the other.

"When can you get everything in place, Jorge? I hate that I have to leave for Colombia in the morning."

I shift my focus to *Tío* Luis, who's been silent alongside *Tío* Matáis. I recognize my *tío's* tone. It's restrained anger.

"We can start everything once Madeline, Florencia, and Liesel are taken care of. I want Liesel to stay at *Mamá's*."

Madeline's going to go there too, and Florencia's going to Pablo's parents' house. This is the first time Liesel will experience me going on a mission. Madeline and Florencia have already gone through it with Javier and Pablo, but that doesn't mean they're any more prepared for the fear Liesel will undoubtedly experience.

It's not like any of us believe we're immortal. It's not like any of us outgrow the fear that something could go wrong—that today could be the day we breathe our last. But we learned to compartmentalize those emotions.

I know it's horrible being the person left behind. Talk about feeling out of control. I don't envy *Mamá*, my *tías*, or the other women in our family when they have to sit by and watch us walk out the door, then wait to discover whether we'll come home. It's not easy knowing we put the women in our family in that position. We all struggle with guilt from that since none of us want to cause them pain, but when duty calls, we have no choice but to answer.

We already decided what we're doing to the O'Rourkes and Kutsenkos, but we have to hammer out the logistics. I already feel guilty about leaving Liesel, but now I'm asking my brother and cousin to do even more for me.

"Alejandro, Joaquin, are you sure you don't mind going to Ireland? You just got back from Germany with us."

Alejandro chuckles. "I'll be sure to enjoy a few drams of that whiskey before it all goes poof. Joaquin and I are unattached, so we may as well enjoy the single life along with a single malt."

My cousin thinks he's far funnier than he is, but I appreciate his willingness, along with my brother's, to take another international flight when we've barely been home.

Joaquin's more restrained when he chimes in, but I know he doesn't resent helping me. "We'll set off once we finish here, that way we can arrive in Ireland with time to get our bearing."

I nod as I sweep my gaze around the room. I want to rub my hands together like some Machiavellian cartoon villain, but I restrain myself.

"Everything kicks off tomorrow night. It'll be late here in New York but early in Ireland. We have to ensure our attacks are simultaneous. Otherwise, word'll get out, and Pasha will alert Finn or the other way around. The last thing we need is them working together against us."

Tío Matáis and *Tía* Catalina are the most outgoing in our family, but my *tío* usually remains quiet during these planning meetings. It's not that we don't need or want his opinions, but his role in the family is to look like his nose is clean. He's brutal and lethal like the rest of us, so he goes on missions when he has to. But tonight, he's been more of an observer. Now he gives the fatherly advice we're all used to.

"Bedtime, *niños*. All of you have early mornings, and two of you have long flights you can sleep during." Boys.

Liesel barely noticed when I slipped into bed last night when I got home from *Tío* Enrique's. We spent the morning together, but I had things to coordinate this afternoon. Alejandro and Joaquin took off for Dublin shortly after the meeting finished last night. Once Alejandro and Joaquin got settled at their hotel in Ireland, they jumped on a video call with the rest of us, so that took up a chunk of the afternoon. We ran over all the details one last time for tonight's multiprong attack.

Liesel and I had dinner together tonight in the garden before I took her to Queens. She took everything in stride when I explained as much as I could but left out most of the details. I believe it relieved her to go over to *Mamá's*, so she didn't have to face any of this alone. Even so, I hated taking her over there, knowing it was possibly the last time I'll see her.

She was dry-eyed when I walked out the door, which is more than I can say for myself. I was definitely wiping my eyes as I headed out to the SUV. There might've even been a few sniffles. It's the first night we're spending apart since all of this started.

It's not just about missing out on sex. It's the idea of not holding her while we sleep. It's the idea of not being the last person she sees at night, then the first person in the morning. Same for me. I don't mind being around my family, and I'll always enjoy their company more than most people's. But I'd much rather be under the covers with the most beautiful woman in the world. There's no one more attractive to me than Liesel.

I wish I could make this magically disappear or finish it with just a snap. That way I'm not leaving her to worry about my safety, and I'm not worried about how she's handling all of this. Instead, I'm slipping out of the driver's seat of one of our SUVs.

I, along with my brother, cousin, and *Tío* Enrique, are dressed in our black tactical gear. We have our bulletproof vests on with our Kevlar helmets and NVGs. It's like when we staged the raid that freed Gunter. I have a rifle slung across my chest and a pistol strapped to each thigh. I have knives in each front pocket, and one tucked in my right boot.

The two dozen men with us all have earpieces in, set to a frequency we can all hear. If my family and I need to talk privately, we'll switch to *Macaguán* on our own frequency. We're totally fine with the language's endangered status since less than five hundred people speak it. It's like Welsh and Navajo during World War Two. No one's cracked its meaning, so it keeps my family and me safe.

"Paco, take your men to the far side. Cut the alarm cables and fencing. Get it open wide enough to let the bulldozers through. Javier, take your guys to the left. We need the girders and lumber loaded on that semi. *Tío*, you and your men come with me to get the cranes and smaller equipment. Pablo, you good with the devices?"

"Yeah, *primo*."

My cousin's a trained chemist and biologist. Short of a PhD, there are few people better trained in chemistry than my Harvard, MIT, and Cambridge-educated cousin. He could devise chemical, biological, and probably nuclear devices if we needed them. I wouldn't put it past his knowledge or skills. Tonight, we just need his explosive ordinances. He's no pyro, but he likes to make things go boom.

Even though *Tío* Enrique is the *jefe de jefes*—the most powerful Latin American alive—he follows my orders on this mission. I'll always defer to his advice, but he lets me lead this mission because it's about avenging Liesel. When my brothers, cousins, and I first started going on missions, we all feared not protecting him well enough. We'd lay down our lives for one another without a thought, but we believed *Tío* Enrique had to come before anyone else. He disabused us of that idea quickly.

On nights like tonight, he's a regular *toro*—bull—like the other men. I'm the brigadier since I'm heading this brigade. There are various other titles I could have, but that's what we use during missions of this size and scale. During our smaller mission to rescue Gunter, the men called me *capitán*. There are more men tonight, and they know I'm overseeing all that happens here, as well as, what's going down in Ireland. It's not a promotion but a recognition of this operation's magnitude.

Our *halcones*—falcons—have been in the area since this morning. They're our eyes and ears, surveilling this construction site for any bratva members. Four *sicarios*—hitmen—enforcers—what I often am—already took out the bratva guards just before we arrived. It's why no alarms are going off. Our *sombrillas*—umbrellas—or protection squad—not to be confused with hallucinogenic mushrooms—are staggered around the perimeter to make sure no one interrupts us. Our *balcaceros*—gunrunners—make the best drivers, so they're behind the wheels of our semi and tractor trailer.

"On my mark."

My fingers countdown from three before I point toward our target. We break off into our assigned groups and get to work. We've trained for jobs like this for years. Our men move with near synchronicity that comes from having things drilled into us. *Tío* Enrique is a hard task master no one wants to disappoint.

We've pulled off heists like this before, so no one doubts their role. We complete each task in near silence, only speaking to give commands as the heavy machinery's loaded onto the tractor trailer. Hand and arm signals suffice to get the lumber and beams onto the truck.

"*Directo al puerto*." Straight to the port.

We need to get to the Port of New York before the Kutsenkos and their Andreyev cousins intercept us. We have the container ship ready since we own it. Everyone who isn't riding in the semi or trailer piles into the SUVs. They're customized vehicles that have reinforced undercarriages to protect us from IEDs—improvised explosive devices. They're bulletproof from top to bottom and all the way around. The tires could be practically shredded, and they'll still roll.

Much like the irony that almost all of us went to high school together, the Four Families get our vehicles customized at the same shop. If the two neighborhoods are syndicate Switzerland for where we live, then the guy who owns the shop is our retail syndicate Switzerland. We're on our best behavior if we unfortunately run into rivals there. None of us want to lose our relationship with our car guy. He's that good.

The only way to tell our vehicles apart are by the hubcaps. He customizes those too. We need to differentiate them since there are times when more than one family is bolting from a situation that escalates too much. We aren't going to memorize license plates that rarely get used twice, so we need something easy to identify to ensure we get in the right town car, limo, or SUV.

From where we are on Long Island to Port of New York, in theory, should be about a fifteen-minute drive. Despite it being the middle of the night, there are still road closures from daytime construction. It takes us half an hour. I take the time to call Joaquin. I have it on speaker, so Pablo, Javier, and *Tío* can hear too. It's a rare occasion for *Tío* and Pablo to ride together much like a king and crown prince usually wouldn't.

"*¿Cómo te fue?*" How'd it go?

"*Perfectamente.*" Perfectly.

"*¡Por el amor de Dios! ¿Estás borracho?*" For fuck's sake! Are you drunk?

"*No peor que Alejandro.*" No worse than Alejandro.

I hear my cousin in the background. "*Cállate. Estoy inten-tando dormir.*" Shut up. I'm trying to sleep.

Trust the two of them to snag a barrel or three of the whiskey. They'll claim it's a finder's fee or their price for an early morning's hard work. They're safe, and they're done. That's what matters to me. I can tell they're on the plane as we continue in Spanish.

"Did you have any problems?" *Tío* Enrique isn't amused.

"No, *Tío*. They definitely weren't expecting us. It's their fault it was so easy. The factory guards were barely rent-a-cops. Completely unprepared for the dozen of us who swarmed the place. They were so unprepared we didn't off them. Bound and gagged them until we were done. Dumped them naked a block from the warehouse and factory since it's still burning. We were in and out in half an hour."

The plan was for them to break into the distillery and

attached warehouse. They were to break open all the casks and let the whiskey spill everywhere. It's good shit and high proof—like a hundred-forty, so very flammable. A smooth burn going down your throat, and a roaring fire when a match is lit next to it.

"Sleep it off, *sobrinos*."

"*Sí, Tío*."

Both Alejandro and Joaquin answer, and they both sound as drunk as the other.

We've been back at *Tío* Enrique's for the past hour. *Tía* Elle had a buffet waiting for us. It was far better than the sandwiches we usually toss together when we wind up at one of our bachelor condos to debrief. Javier, Pablo, and I briefly spoke to their women after the mission to let them know things were progressing the way we wanted.

The irate calls start just when we expected them. Before I can hold Liesel again, we have to deal with a very pissed-off Salvatore on the other end. *Tío* Enrique puts it on speaker as we all gather in his office.

"What the hell, Enrique? What did you think you were doing sticking your nose in a fight in Italy? You have no business getting involved. You way overreached on this one."

I guess he found out about the ship on the way to Germany. Someone at the docks must have told him. The Mafia and mob take turns running them. It depends on the way the wind's blowing whether we're kissing one ass or the other to get shit in and out without customs officers harassing us. Working at night means we get around our rivals and law enforcement.

"*Cabrón*, be glad I didn't do far more than I did. I merely gave the Camorra an upper hand with some free gifts. If that happens to inconvenience your family, then so be it. I could've rained down holy hell on those involved. Consider my restraint a sprinkle gift for Maria and her baby."

"How the hell is this a gift? What the hell is a sprinkle anyway?"

Tío Enrique chuckles. "Apparently, it's a party people throw after the baby is born. The women in my family already sent baby shower gifts to Maria, so this is ours to Matteo."

"I still don't see how any of this is a gift, Enrique."

"I didn't blow anything of yours up, Salvatore. You should've intervened and ended all of this once you knew the Torettas and Carosis targeted a woman. You definitely shouldn't have stood by the moment you found out Jorge was involved with Anneliese."

There's a long silence, and I wonder if Salvatore muted the call while he talks to members of his family despite how late it is. There's a strong probability he's meeting with his brother and nephews just like *Tío* Enrique is with us. Salvatore's voice is brittle when we hear it again.

"I suppose you expect me to say thank you, don't you, Enrique?"

"It certainly wouldn't be amiss. I could've taken this far more personally than I did since you sat back and watched. However, since you didn't actively participate like the O'Rourkes and Kutsenkos, I figured I'd go a little easier on you. But you know better than to believe my graciousness will last long."

"And I suppose you expect me to thank you for that as well."

Tío Enrique merely chuckles again. It makes lesser men want to run.

"I suppose we live to fight another day, Enrique."

"*Adios, cabrón.*"

"*Ciao, faccia de cazzo.*"

Testicle face. *Caremonde*—face of a penis—is the Spanish equivalent.

Both men have been leading their families for more than three decades. They haven't lived to be in their late fifties by acting purely out of spite and impetuousness. Salvatore knows when to back down and give someone else the win if it means his family doesn't lose in the long run. I'd count yesterday and today as successes.

The O'Rourkes and Kutsenkos won't be far behind, but *Tío* Enrique will field those calls too. This isn't over with them. Not even nearly. They'll retaliate against our retaliation. It'll be just another normal week in paradise. I'm not even worried about that right now. That's a problem for another day.

"*Mis llaves*, I'm ready to see Liesel."

My keys. It's weird Colombian slang, but it means close friends. We call a group of close friends our *llavero* or keychain.

Javier pushes back his chair as he speaks. "I'll head over to *Mamá's* with you. I want to see Madeline too."

He and I will ride together to Queens while Pablo doesn't have far to go from *Tío* Enrique's to get to his parents' since they're in Jersey too. I'm certain he's as eager to see Florencia as I am to see Liesel and Javier is to see Madeline. Joaquin and Alejandro will go home to their places, or they may crash here a while longer since they're both exhausted and jetlagged all over again. *Tío* Enrique is already walking out of his office, likely to find my *tía*.

My brother and I are wiped, so it's a quiet ride in a town car together. I punch in the passcode to the door and let us into *Mamá's* house. Javier goes directly to the alarm system and turns that off before resetting it. We both go up to the bedrooms we've had since we were tweens and moved to the States. It surprises me to find Liesel sitting up with the bedside lamp on.

She pushes back the covers and scrambles off the bed as I kick off my shoes and slip off my button down.

Then we're clinging to each other chest to chest since she's naked. There was time for her to pack an overnight bag, so she has pajamas and a robe lying across the foot of the bed in case someone else woke her and she needed to get up. The tsunami of relief that crashes over me nearly makes me stagger backwards. It's not just the force of Liesel's hug.

I lift her off her feet and smatter her face with kisses before our lips meet. We can't get enough of each other. I realize her relief is just as strong as mine. I carry her to the bed, and she straddles my lap as I sit. We work together to unfasten my pants and push them out of the way enough for to free my cock. Then she's sliding down it, and we're kissing again.

"I'm so glad you're home, Daddy. I've been worried sick the whole time."

"I have too, but I promised you I wouldn't let anything get in the way of being with you."

She cups my face. "You've been telling me that since the very beginning, and I've always believed you."

Her gaze searches mine, and I wonder if something happened while I was gone. Sitting together like this—with her warming my cock—is the bond we need after the expected but hardly wanted separation. The physical connection makes our emotional bond stronger.

"Liesel?"

"I have my own good news."

"Oh?" I can't imagine what it'll be, but we've been apart for the better part of two days and have barely spoken.

"I spoke to Papa and *Onkel* Clyde while you've been gone. I even called Randy to see if this idea is viable. I'm going to continue working for Schlossberg & Sons, but I'll start that New York office we talked about. It means I should be able to stay here with you without too much trouble. I'll have to travel some, at least in the beginning, but in the long run, we'll be together most of the time."

"That's excellent news, *chiquita*. I couldn't ask for better than that and having you in my arms."

The backs of her fingers brush over my stubble, up to my cheekbone, and along my temple.

"Maybe I can think of one other thing, Daddy, that might be even better to hear."

I twirl a lock of her hair around my finger. "I can think of something too."

We speak at the same time.

"*Te amo.*"

"*Ich liebe dich.*"

I love you.

It doesn't matter which language we say it in. It's sweet that we both defaulted to our native tongue the first time we've said it aloud.

We laugh that we spoke at the same time, saying the same thing but in different languages. This time our kiss is imbued with all that love we feel. There's as much affection as there is lust. It's a blending of our souls and a promise of the life we'll build together. It still hasn't been that long despite all that's happened since we met. But I've never meant anything more in my life than the silent pledge that goes along with my declaration. I think Liesel feels the same way. I think it's been on the tip of our tongues since nearly the beginning, but there were obstacles to overcome first.

I've done a lot of shitty things over the years. A few I even regret. But nothing has made me feel redeemable more than those three German words. I feel like one of my roses in my greenhouse.

I'm in bloom.

If I ever said that aloud in front of anyone in my family—man or woman—I'd never live it down. But it's true. Cartels and roses hardly go together most of the time, but I suppose they do tonight.

"I love you, Daddy."

"I love you, *chiquita*."

Epilogue

Liesel

"*Papá*, it's simply not fair that Cristoph's going on his first mission, and you won't allow me to go either. *Tía* Elle's going. I can't believe you're not going to at least consider what I have to say."

I'm smirking at Jorge as I stand behind our daughter, who's livid. Just as I suspected years ago, my genes had no say in what our children look like. Jorge's facing a mirror image of himself, except this one's about to erupt like a volcano.

"I've already explained to you, Elise, why your brother gets to go and you aren't."

"He's younger than I am, *Papá*, and since *Tío* Enrique, *Tío* Luis, and *Tío* Matáis are too old to go, you could use the extra hands."

I practically snort as I attempt to stifle my laughter. Our daughter spins around and glowers at me. Elise and Cristoph Diaz. Our two oldest children have German first names, which makes for an interesting combination with a Colombian last name and coloring. It confuses people even more when they meet our other two children, Mariana and Isidora.

"I wouldn't let your *onkels* hear you say they're too old. All three of them can still put the rest of you to shame. They may not go on missions anymore, but I'd still wager on a bunch of men in their mid-seventies who can lift more than you and run faster and longer than you, *Häschen*." Little bunny.

"Fine, I'll give them that, but you're still allowing Josue, Andrés, Santiago, and Esteban as well as Cristoph, to go. They aren't nearly as useful as my *hermanas* and *primas* are." Sisters and female cousins.

Jorge and I exchange a glance. Our daughter's not entirely wrong. Our daughters and nieces have proven themselves very adept with technology. It's not just Joaquin who can hack just about anything. The five girls got pissed off at their brothers and cousins three Christmases ago because of the boys' machismo. The guys claimed they were real men since they'd all grown taller and stronger than their sisters and cousins.

The girls decided to show them there's more to life than brute force. The girls got together and hacked all of the boys' savings accounts and transferred the money among themselves, then spent it to buy their own Christmas gifts for each other. It was almost too brilliant for us parents to complain about.

However, we still had to force them to return the money to their brothers and cousins. Jorge and I, along with the other parents, still get a chuckle out of it. But right now, Jorge's trying to avoid the sparks from the live wire standing in front of us.

"*Mija*, nobody's doubting you're intelligent enough to be helpful on these missions. However, nothing changes the fact you're not as big or as fast as the boys, and you're not as big and fast as the men we'll face." My daughter.

"But I'm an even better shot than Cristoph."

I'm both proud of our daughters and rue the day *Tía* Elle

taught all the girls how to shoot alongside the boys. She's still the best shot in the family, and our daughter is one step behind her.

I try to step in and diffuse the situation.

"Elise, you have exams in the morning, and you can't be half asleep during them from being up all night. You can't risk not making it home in time."

She mutters in German, even though she knows Jorge and I understand her. She thinks we can't hear her.

"*Das ist Schwachsinn.*" That's bullshit.

Jorge inhales, his shoulders going back as his chest broadens. He's upset with Elise, but he's not doing it to intimidate her. Madeline warned Florencia then me that *Tres J's* can't help it. They just have resting bitch face.

"Now you're not only not going, but you're grounded for three weeks. You can hand over all your devices to *Mamá.* You'll get back what you need for school. You know better than to swear."

"*Es tut mir Leid.*" I'm sorry.

Her apology is heartfelt, and she knew the moment she spoke her thoughts aloud that she'd erred. She also knows it won't eliminate her punishment. However, she's still not deterred from her argument.

"I bet Mila and Petra will get to go."

All of the syndicate couples of Jorge and my generation eventually bought homes in the same two neighborhoods, and we've raised our children here just like they were. The youngest generation didn't go to elementary and middle school together, but they're at the same high school. The same rivalries that existed among Jorge and the other men now exist in this generation too.

Elise's on the same club soccer team as Mila Kutsenko and Petra Mancinelli, who're both a few years older than her.

They're thick as thieves and best friends during team sports. But in sports with individual events, they're more competitive than the boys could ever be.

It's Jorge's turn to try to stifle his laughter, but he chokes. "*Mija*, there's not a chance in hell that Maks or Luca will allow their daughters to even consider this. You should be glad I'm so much more forward-thinking than they are, since I've allowed you to help us strategize. I guarantee Mila and Petra aren't even in the same house as the men in their families."

He pulls our daughter into his arms and strokes her back. I see her relax against him, even if she doesn't want to admit his hugs still comfort her the same way they have since the day she was born.

"You know we can't allow you to go on missions, even if you were strong enough and fast enough to keep up, because it would open the door to all the women in the Four Families being targets. Not all of the women and girls want to do what you want. All of them may be trained to defend themselves, but if I allow you to come, then it makes your sisters and cousins targets. People outside the Four Families will see it as open season on women and children. That's bad enough for us, but our family will not bear the responsibility of making women in the other families vulnerable too."

"But *Tía* Elle—"

"No. *Tía* Elle came to this family with skills already, but you know she's never in the thick of missions. She doesn't engage in hand-to-hand. She keeps her distance and maybe one day—when you're fully an adult—that might be a possibility too. But for right now, I simply won't allow it, whether you agree with me or not. My first and greatest responsibility is to protect you, your *mamá*, and your siblings, so I won't willingly endanger you. That's non-negotiable. I love you, *mija*, and that will never stop. My protectiveness will never go away."

Elise huffs but nods. She hasn't pulled away from Jorge, and she returns his squeeze. She inherited my build and is as tall as I am and just as sturdy. But even in his late forties, Jorge is still massive. He has the body of a man half his age, and there's no denying I love it just as much as I did when we met. I may not look the same as I did before four children, but he's never once made me doubt he believes I'm the most alluring woman in the world.

Elise offers Jorge and me a kiss on the cheek before she heads into Pablo's office. He's increased his duties more and more as the older generation retires. Enrique will be the *jefe de jefes* until his last breath, but Pablo is now more than just New York's *jefe*. He runs most of Latin America with his cousins beside him. He'll listen to Elise's suggestions not just because he's an indulgent first cousin, once removed but because she's brilliant. However, she won't talk him into anything either.

"You know that's your daughter, *chiquita*."

"Mine? Oh, no, Daddy. That is you through and through."

Jorge shakes his head. "She might look like me, but that's your personality."

"Hardly. I'm much more willing to compromise than you are."

Jorge scoffs as he wraps his arm around me and leans in to whisper in my ear. "The only compromise I'm willing to make is that we're headed home in five minutes instead of ten."

"How is that a compromise?"

"Because my cousins will get my attention for five more minutes. I could make us leave right now. If they try to take longer than that, I'll drag you up to our room here and have my way with you."

"That's a compromise I can live with. It would mortify our kids, but it wouldn't surprise anyone our age, *Meine Liebe*." My love.

We laugh, but we're soon kissing like we always have. Like we can't get enough. Like our life—the one we've built together —depends upon being one. Like it's the air we need to breathe and the food we need to live. There will never be enough kisses or moments spent making love—a good hard fucking never goes amiss either.

"*Te amo, chiquita.*"

"*Ich liebe dich, Daddy.*"

"Fuck the five minutes, *chica*. Everyone's busy right now. We won't be missed."

Jorge sweeps me into his arms and takes the stairs two at a time despite his age and my weight. We don't care that someone will likely figure out what we're doing. We're pretty sure we conceived Mariana here, and she wouldn't be the only one of her generation conceived in someone else's home. Our brothers, sisters, and cousins—we don't use in-law in this family —are just as bad as we are.

My husband—my one great love—bends me over the bed. I lift my skirt—I haven't worn panties in nearly twenty years—as he unfastens his pants. Then he thrusts into me.

"Fuck, Daddy."

"That's right, *chiquita*. Who's fucking you?"

"You, Daddy."

"This is going to be hard and fast. You're going to squeeze those sweet thighs together and keep my cum in you when I'm done."

"Yes, Daddy."

He lands a spank across my ass, but he's careful not to make it too loud. He pounds into me, and I claw at the bedding. He's right that it's fast. I'm begging to come within a couple minutes. He pinches my nipples through my shirt, and my orgasm explodes. I feel his cock twitch as my cunt squeezes him, wanting to hold him in place. He kisses my neck.

"Aren't you glad I had no boundaries and followed you around Frankfurt?"

"Aren't you glad I let you spank me?"

I look over my shoulder, and we kiss with as much passion as the first time we did in that hotel room all those years ago.

A bachelor party was the last place Alejandro De Santos Diaz expected to meet the alluring woman who was most certainly not what she seemed. He came to Chicago to celebrate and left when his revenge was done. He assumed she remained there, so he's unprepared to discover the mysterious beauty in NYC. What is Vita hiding in *Cartel Protector?*

Would you like an additional steamy scene from Jorge and Liesel? Continue reading!

Bonus Epilogue

Liesel

We make our way inside, and the place is incredible. You'd never guess it's a sex club. It's in a brownstone in Brooklyn. You enter through the front door, and it makes me wonder what the neighbors think. The interior is dark; the walls painted black. In what would be the living room and dining room, there's an expansive lounge. They converted the kitchen into a bar where people can sip their drinks while watching the exhibitionists in the lounge. The music's low, just enough to keep conversations among the patrons private without disturbing the neighbors.

"They own the buildings on both sides."

"You read my mind."

"I wondered the same thing the first time a member at another club mentioned the place."

"Are they just empty?"

"I guess."

He leads me to a man with a yellow band around his arm. It has the letters DM in black stitching. Dungeon Master or

Dungeon Monitor. Whatever this place calls them. They monitor everything and make sure everyone plays nicely. Jorge told me always uses a pseudonym when he goes to his regular club. I watch him write it on the form.

"Mr. and Mrs. Gonzalez, where would you like to start?"

The DM looks at us expectantly. When neither of us answers, the guy looks around.

"Neither of you have been here before. I didn't realize. Would you like a tour?"

Jorge watches me, and I nod. We will speak as little as possible while we're in public. When the guy steps away from the table he stood beside, he notices our guards—two of a only half a dozen men Jorge would ever trust with this assignment.

"Gentlemen, I'll be with you in just a moment. You can start filling out the forms. Couples only need one."

I nearly choke trying to stifle my snort. I look back at them, and with only their mouths visible beneath their half masks, I can tell they aren't as amused as I am. Jorge comes to the rescue.

"They're with us. They won't scene or watch."

"We can't allow—"

"Yes, you can."

Jorge's tone makes the guy freeze. He stares at my husband before darting a glance at me. He takes in my husband's size, then he does the same with our guards. He thinks better than to argue. The four of us follow the DM in silence as he gives us a tour. Rather cliché, but the basement has the most hardcore stuff. There are levels of bondage that I've never seen before, not even in porn. Jorge keeps his arm around my waist and even shields me from some of it. I won't yuck on anyone's yum, but compared to what I imagine trying, it looks disturbing to me.

We head back up to street level, and the DM explains the rules if we want to engage in anything in the main room. Again,

Jorge looks down at me. He'll defer to what I want. I chose the lace up the front vest for a reason. I also have a garter belt and thigh highs on despite not having panties. I wouldn't have to be completely naked if we decided to scene in here.

I almost switch to German, but I catch myself.

"Maybe later."

We finish the tour by going upstairs to the converted bedrooms. They're themed, and they vary in styles. There's the classroom, the doctor's office, the kiddy playroom, and traditional room with the implements on the wall and a St. Andrew's Cross taking up half a wall. There are also some unique ones, like one that has an ocean view painted on the wall and lounge chairs spread around the room. It makes me wonder if we'll get a honeymoon.

Jorge leans sideways and brings his lips to my ears.

"Pick anywhere in the world, *chiquita*. Tell me how many weeks you can be away from work."

"Weeks?"

"Weeks, little one."

"Yes, Daddy. Let me think about it."

We keep our voices low, so no one could recognize them. There are a couple rooms already in use with curtains drawn. The people don't want to be watched. There's one that's in use, and people watch through the window. It's a creepy ass basement.

Each unto their own, Liesel. Each unto their own.

"Is there something you'd like to start with?"

The DM looks expectantly at us. I look back toward the stairs, then I look at the door to the resort room. I point to it, and the guy nods. He wasn't chatty, thank God. But he also picked up on us not being talkative, either.

"Do you want to be watched?"

"No."

Jorge's decisive, and I agree. If we want voyeurs, we'll go downstairs. We make our way back to the resort room, and our guards mill around in the hallway. I know their routine from other places we've been to together. They'll always have their eye on our door, but sometimes they'll pretend to—or maybe they really are—watch a couple through open curtains. Sometimes they stand somewhere and appear like they're waiting for someone. They've sworn they won't watch us if we allow curtains to remain open or been in main rooms. I believe them.

Jorge closes the door behind us.

"Strip, *chiquita*."

"Yes, Daddy."

I take off the vest and skirt, but I hook my thumbs in the garter belt and look at Jorge.

"As fucking hot as you are in those, I want you naked. I want every inch of you bare to me. I don't want anything in the way of what I crave."

"Yes, Daddy."

I'm quick to take off the garters and thigh highs. He knows how I feel about bare feet on public floors, so he says nothing about my shoes staying on. Once I'm not standing, then I'll kick them off. It's just a quirk, I guess. He indulges it.

"Relax on one of the chairs."

Relax? I'm way too eager for that. I follow his directions and recline against one of the lounge chairs. I hear him gathering things and moving a table near the chair, but I don't know what he has.

"I'm going to lower the back, then I want you to roll over."

I do as he commands. He soon has my wrists and ankles cuffed to links on the chair. They're there for this purpose. I hear the lid of something pop open. Then I feel oil trickle down my back and between my ass cheeks. I turn to look at Jorge, and he's taken off his t-shirt and is only in his jeans. His abs ripple as he kneels beside me.

"*Sie wollen sich doch nicht verbrennen, meine Dame.*" You don't want to burn, ma'am.

I smile at him as I lick my lips.

"Are you my cabana boy, Daddy?"

His hand lands across my ass, and I wiggle it, encouraging another one.

"Do I look like a boy, *chiquita?*"

"Definitely not."

I focus my gaze on his cock, which presses against his pants. He's hard, and the temptation to reach out and pull him free then suck him is tremendous. But with my arms restrained that's not an option. I open my mouth wide instead. It surprises me when he indulges me. My tongue laps across the head of his cock as he pours more oil onto my back. I slide my mouth down his shaft, and his groan makes me wetter.

The moment his hands start to massage my shoulders and back, I suck in a breath. I practically swallow him in the process. He grunts and thrusts his hips forward. The more he rubs my back, the more aroused I get. The more aroused I get, the harder I suck on him. This is why he indulged me. He knew.

His right hand travels back to my shoulders while his left hand kneads my ass. His fingers slide between my ass cheeks, grazing over the puckered hole. He circles it, coating it with the oil. I press my hips up as best I can, but his hand presses me down. He pinches for good measure before both hands glide along my arms.

"Make me come, Liesel."

I redouble my efforts, and it's only moments later that I taste his cum as it shoots down my throat. I lick him clean before I lick my lips.

"Thank you, Daddy."

"I think it's the other way around, little one. Thank you."

His oiled hand wraps around his cock and strokes. Our eyes lock, and he knows how jealous I am. It turns me on to watch him, but I also feel robbed when I'm not the one touching him. His dark eyes sparkle with amusement. He stands and moves toward my feet.

"Now that I can concentrate..."

If that was Jorge unfocused, then God save me tonight. When I rolled over, I spotted the things he grabbed and put on the table. Before he walked to the end of the lounge chair, he grabbed a butt plug we brought from home that's almost the same girth as him. In other words, fucking big. I can't see behind me, but I hear the lid of a bottle pop open, and I wonder if it's the same oil or just regular lube.

He kneels on the chair on one leg. His tongue trails from my left knee up to my pussy. He kisses it over and over before I yelp when a riding crop slaps it. Where did he get that from?

He chuckles, then he's spreading my ass. I relax as I feel the butt plug press against my hole. It's well lubed, and I've done this before, so it slides in with little resistance. Immediately, it feels different. I clench, and that only intensifies the feeling.

"Daddy?"

"Yes, little girl?"

"Did you just frig me?"

"Yes."

Fucking ginger. That's what must have come out of the bottle. The inside of my ass burns, but it's not excruciating. I know he didn't use that much. He put more of the regular oil on than the ginger, but fuuuuck.

"Why, Daddy?"

"How do I wish to punish you? Let me count the ways."

The riding crop swishes in the air, and I brace for it. I can't not squeeze my ass when the leather bites my flesh, and that just sends a shot of pain up my ass. I feel it in my pussy too, and I moan.

"It's not a punishment if you enjoy it, Liesel. You questioned my safety protocols."

I argued pretty adamantly that we didn't need guards with us tonight. He warned me that we would go nowhere if I didn't agree. It took too long for me to come around to the idea, but I was embarrassed.

The crop lands across my ass.

"You're still learning the risks we face. I won't suffocate you, but I will be by your side when shit goes wrong, Liesel."

He nails my right horizontal crack, pushing my ass up. I know he enjoys watching it jiggle as it drops. He brings the crop down three more times.

"You could put yourself in danger if you don't have a detail, and I will never accept that. I have never stopped you from being your own person. I don't expect you to agree to everything I say. I don't want you meek. But I want you to fucking stay alive."

"I'm sorry, Daddy."

"I know you are, *chiquita*. I don't doubt that. I'm making sure you remember how sorry you are."

He releases my right hand.

"Play with your clit, Liesel. But don't come."

"Yes, Daddy."

I slide my hand between the chair and my pussy. I watch him lay down the crop and pick up a flogger with little metal studs.

"Use your safe word if this is too much."

My emotions are welling inside of me, and I'm suddenly apprehensive that I won't be able to take it. He puts the flogger down and releases my left hand. He helps me to kneel and sits where I was just lying.

"Baby, it's all right to be nervous about this since you've never experienced true BDSM."

"I just want to make the most of this. I don't want to get it wrong."

"There's no such thing as getting it wrong. It's whatever we want to explore together. Baby, once your punishment is done, we move onto your fantasies. All right?"

"Yes, Daddy. Are you going to let me come tonight?"

"Many, many times. Until you beg me to stop."

"Is that a punishment?"

Orgasm denial is one form of punishment, but overstimulation can be, too.

"No. Orgasms will never be a punishment. I may not let you have them, or I may make you wait. I'll probably make you beg for them regardless of whether it's a punishment. But I will never pervert your pleasure."

"I love you, husband."

"I love you, wife."

He kisses me, then stands. I lie down again, and he refastens my left wrist.

"I'm going to give you twenty lashes, Liesel. You voice and expression tell me you feel guilty about disagreeing with me. I knew that before we left the house. I need you to always trust me implicitly about your safety because I will never take it for granted. You mean the world to me, Liesel. There's nothing I won't do for you. No one is ever coming between us. You are mine, and I am yours. *Fertig*." Finished.

"Yes, Daddy."

"Count them."

I inhale, and Jorge waits until I settle. Then the tiny spikes rain down on me. They're like ice rain hitting my skin. Cold and harsh, but they won't hurt me.

"One. Thank you, Daddy. May I have another?"

"Yes, *chica*. You're such a good girl."

It's the same thing he could say to his dog or a small child, but it doesn't sound like that. There's pride in his voice.

"Two. Thank you, Daddy. May I have another?"

And so it goes as the thongs swish through the air, then crack against my lower back, ass, and upper thighs. I try so hard not to contract my muscles, knowing the ginger will only increase the burn, but I can't help it. It's an involuntary response. I feel so full with the plug, and I've gotten so close to coming three times that I feared I wouldn't stop myself.

"Fifteen. Thank you, Daddy. May I have another?"

When nothing happens, I twist as best I can and look over my shoulder. I gasp, then giggle.

"How'd you get Little Jorge here?" It's a vibrator he got me after his first trip to Boston.

"You stepped away from your purse to go to the bathroom before we left. I slipped it in there."

He starts the vibrator I named after him. We've played with it a few times, and he knows the settings I like and how to slide it into me to hit me where I crave it most.

"Pinch your nipple again. Keep your hand out of the way."

I obey, twisting my hips to allow my hand to slide up my ribs, and he turns on the toy. He swirls it around the moisture at the opening of my pussy. Then he presses it into me. I writhe, and the lash comes down again.

"Sixteen." I pant two breaths. "Thank you, Daddy." I pant one more. "May I have another?"

Oh, fuck me, fuck me, fuck me. Please fuck me.

I squeeze my eyes shut and suck in a breath. I try to kick my feet, but I can't. When I clench, not only does it squeeze the butt plug with the ginger on it, it presses the vibrator against my G-spot. When I shift my hips, the rabbit ears on the vibrator rub my clit.

"Daddy!"

"Safe word, Liesel."

"No."

I cry with a hoarse voice. I won't stop. I can take it, and I want to. But it's so much right now.

"Anneliese."

"Don't call me that, Jorge."

He brushes hair from my sweaty temple, and I see his concern. When I glare at him, he relaxes and nods. He steps back to where he stood before.

"I'm sorry, Liesel."

"Daddy, you don't have to apologize. I just don't like it when you call me that. It feels like you're a stranger or a real Dom."

He leans over and kisses my left ass cheek.

"Four more, *chiquita*. You can do it."

"I know, Daddy. May I have another?"

He lands the last few, and I sigh. His hands are slick with more oil when he caresses my ass. It surprises me how he's naked when he climbs onto the lounger and brings his body down over mine. He reaches between us and withdraws the plug and the vibrator. I gasp when the vibrating tip presses against my ass.

"I'm going to come in your ass before we leave tonight, baby. But right now, I need to be inside your pussy. Do you need a moment?"

"No. I need you."

I'm pleading, and he gladly gives me what I desire. He thrusts into me, his chest pressing into my back. His long arms drape over mine so we can hold hands. His fingers lace with mine as he thrusts over and over.

"I want to make you come, Liesel. Tell me what you need."

"Just keep doing this... God, it feels good... You're so deep... Fuck... Just fuck me."

He obliges, surging into me over and over.

"May I come, Daddy?"

I'm gasping each word. My heart feels like it's going to break free from my chest, but it has nowhere to go with Jorge's weight pressing me into the chair. I love the feeling of being trapped between two immovable objects. I feel safe and protected. I feel dominated. I feel loved.

"Yes, *mi amor*." My love.

"Call me that again, Daddy."

"*Mi amor. Meine einzige Liebe.*" My only love.

I love the blend of Spanish and German. It's so us. I have another flash of regret that I've experienced this with someone before Jorge. But the way I loved Bastian is nothing like what I feel for Jorge. It was love built an illusion, and that's why I knew it wouldn't last a lifetime. I outgrew it. With Jorge, I know our love will grow together.

Thank you for reading Cartel Rose

Sabine Barclay, a nom de plume also writing Historical Romance as Celeste Barclay, lives near the Southern California coast with her husband and sons. She loves her days at the beach soaking up way too much sun, a good Netflix binge, and a strong hot chai. Her heroines are independent women who can defend themselves but love their Alpha heroes who want nothing more than to protect their soulmates in her Mafia Romances. She's Gen Y/Oregon Trail and loves creating engrossing contemporary romances that will make your toes curl and your granny blush.

Subscribe to Sabine's bimonthly newsletter to receive exclusive insider perks.
www.sabinebarclay.com

Join the fun and get exclusive insider giveaways, sneak peeks, and new release announcements in
Sabine Barclay's Facebook Dubious Dames Group

Do you also enjoy steamy Historical Romance? Discover Sabine's books written as Celeste Barclay.

The Cartel Brotherhood

Cartel King
BOOK ONE SNEAK PEEK

ENRIQUE

She's going to fall off that fucking ladder.

I slow my pace to a jog as I approach a house with a woman far too high on her ladder, leaning far too much to the right as she tries to fish something out of her gutters. She's got to be about five-five to my six-three.

I could reach whatever she's fishing around for. She's more likely to fall off and break something. I should mind my own business and keep going with my run, but there's no way I'm doing that. I wouldn't if it were a woman of any age, and I wouldn't if it were an elderly person, either.

If it were a guy my age, maybe I'd let him deal with it, but for her—there's something in how she's reaching. Some frustration I can feel even from here. I approach slowly as I walk up the driveway. I'm only halfway to her when a humongous dog comes bounding toward me.

451

No wonder there's a baby gate across the entrance to her open garage. The massive beast doesn't bark, but he growls. It's a Mastiff, much like the one Laura Kutsenko has, except this one is a different color and easily weighs about fifty pounds more than her giant companion. I wonder if this one is as much of a love bug as Laura's. At least, that's what she's always claimed. The woman on the ladder speaks to her dog, giving him a command.

"Hush, Constantine. Lie down."

The dog immediately obeys, but he inches closer to the baby gate, still growling at me. It's only then that the woman notices me. She grips the ladder as she jerks away. I hurry over and grab the ladder, tempted to demand she come down from there.

"Who are you?"

If anybody's going to do the demanding, apparently it's her. Not that I can blame the woman, since I'm a complete stranger.

"I'm Enrique. I saw you as I was running. You looked a little wobbly up there."

"Well, I was okay until I was startled—but thank you."

Dismissive is the only way to describe her now. I don't blame her for that either. She's a woman in a precarious position with a strange man looking up at her. Now that I'm certain the ladder won't fall over, I step away. I don't need to look like a perv staring up her shorts.

"Would you like some help? I can easily reach whatever you're going for."

Cartel Viper
Cartel Prince
Cartel Rose
Cartel Protector
Cartel Devil

Do you also enjoy steamy Historical Romance? Discover Sabine's books written as Celeste Barclay.

The Ivankov Brotherhood

Bratva Darling
BOOK ONE SNEAK PEEK

LAURA

As I sit across from the four Kutsenko brothers, I press my lips together to keep from drooling. No four men should be so strikingly handsome. Not all from the same family, anyway. I fight a valiant battle against letting my gaze drift toward the eldest, Maksim, whose ice-blue eyes bore into me. After years of negotiating billion-dollar investment contracts while facing countless ruthless businessmen, I've learned to keep my expression studiously blank. But it's a true struggle today. Instead, I focus my attention on the squirrelly lawyer sitting across the conference table. While he's disingenuous with each comment, he's a good negotiator. But I'm better. How cliché am I?

While I feel Maksim watching me, I focus on Dmitry Yakovitch as he continues to argue the merits of the venture capitalist company I represent, RK Capital Group, merging with

Kutsenko Partners. What he means is the merits of Kutsenko Partners acquiring RK Capital Group, then stripping it and making it another money-laundering shell corporation. While most people in New York have little awareness of the Russian mafia, I do. The Kutsenko brothers' names appear on no titles or deeds anywhere in New York City, but it wasn't difficult to determine which shell companies likely belong to them. Their assumption that I'm unfamiliar with them is proving beneficial to me as they continue to whisper amongst themselves in Russian. I think they may even believe they're convincing me that they don't speak much English.

The senior partners of RK Capital Group know who I'm negotiating with, though they may not know I'm aware of these Russians' more nefarious operations. They've given me the go-ahead to agree to a merger with an eventual acquisition, but only for the right price. A price to the tune of twenty billion dollars. Considering an investment firm like Goldman Sachs is worth nearly one-hundred-and-twenty billion dollars, my clients' asking price appears reasonable.

"Mr. Yakovitch, I shall stop you now." I raise my left hand, pen caught between my index and middle fingers. When I have his attention, I lean back in my chair and casually twirl the pen over my index finger and thumb. "Fifty billion is my clients' asking price. You know that. Your clients know that. RK doesn't oppose the merger. What they oppose is the insulting offer you've made. It's nearly noon, and I'm hungry, Mr. Yakovitch. I have a delicious ham sandwich waiting for me. I even have three chocolate chip cookies waiting for me. If we aren't going to make any progress, I shall let you go, so I can move onto my eagerly anticipated lunch."

I cant my head just enough for me to appear as though my gaze rests solely on the opposing attorney's face, but I can see each

Kutsenko brothers' reaction. My face battles yet again against showing my emotions as I fight not to smirk. Their muted but surprised expressions confirm what I already know.

"Please tell your clients to make a reasonable counteroffer, or I will conclude this meeting and enjoy my ham sandwich and cookies."

Dmitry glares at me before turning to Maksim and his three brothers. In rapid Russian, he doesn't interpret my suggestion. Oh no. There's no need for that. I can't catch every word because his voice is too low. But I catch something along the lines of "The bitch refuses to budge. What now? A fucking ham sandwich. More like a stick up her ass."

Maksim swivels his chair to look at his brothers. In Russian, he says, "Fifty billion is ridiculous. She's not so stupid or naïve not to know that. My guess is they'll settle for twenty billion. We offer fifteen."

"That's barely better than what we already offered," Aleksei, the second-oldest brother, argues. "She'll be eating the fucking sandwich and dipping her cookies in milk before we walk out the door. We need the buildings."

"We offer twenty, Maks," Bogdan, the youngest, insists.

As I watch the brothers discuss, their voices barely lowered, I pull my lunch sack from the black leather satchel by my feet and set it beside my laptop. It's a ridiculously pink floral bag with an embroidered monogram, the L and D overlapping. It's an empty prop, but they don't know that. I watch as five sets of eyes narrow. I offer a smile that would appear innocent in any setting other than this meeting. It's patronizing, and I know it.

Bratva Sweetheart
Bratva Treasure
Bratva Beauty

Sabine Barclay

Bratva Angel
Bratva Jewel

Do you also enjoy steamy Historical Romance? Discover
Sabine's books written as Celeste Barclay.

The Mancinelli Brotherhood

Mafia Heir
BOOK ONE SNEAK PEEK

LUCA

This asshole is pissing me off. We've been going around in circles for five minutes, and the longer we stand out here, the greater the likelihood someone will spot us. I have a sixth sense about these things. It's why I'm still alive at the ripe old age of thirty-one.

"Espinoza, enough already. Either sell to us or don't, but we set the price. Your tequila is good, but it isn't nectar from the gods."

I'm watching Carlos Espinoza, some lackey for the Mexican Culiacán Cartel, try to maneuver me into paying more than the agreed upon price. I know it's so he can skim off the top.

"It's as close as you're going to get. You've upped the order, so the price per case goes up."

My uncle, Salvatore Mancinelli, is the New York don. He negotiated this deal, and I warned him it was a bad idea. But what do I know as his underboss and heir? I'm not backing down.

"Haven't you ever heard of a bulk discount? The more I order the better the price should be. No one else around here is buying from you. You know we're your only choice in three out of five boroughs. You aren't going to the Bronx because you won't get more than pennies there. You aren't going to Queens because you don't want to run into the Colombians. You aren't going to Manhattan because then you face the bratva along with us. And what are you going to do in Staten Island? Sell to us anyway? We control Staten Island and Brooklyn when it comes to liquor stores, so take the money and go."

"Luca, there are plenty of liquor stores in Brooklyn that aren't owned by Italians. I'll go there."

We aren't friends. He's patronizing me by using my first name. Fuck him and the horse he rode in on. I have other solutions for this shit.

"And I'll just take what I want from them for free. That's not a half bad idea. The deal's over. Take your shit with the worm in it and go."

"Motherfucking racist. Not all tequila has a worm in it."

"You're selling Mezcal. It's known for the fucking worm. I wouldn't start calling me names, you *penche hijo de puta*." Fucking son of a bitch.

He has twenty-five crates of stolen tequila that he's trying to offload because he knows he can't sell it at his own liquor store.

"What did you call me?"

Carlos takes what he thinks is a menacing step forward, and his two bodyguards do the same. Not smart. Neither of my two bodyguards nor I react, but the three men in each of my cars open their doors. They won't do more than that. It's just a reminder that the Culiacán can try, but the *Cosa Nostra* still run New York City.

"This is the third and final time I say this. Sell or leave."
Every head turns toward the liquor store's back door as it opens.
A gorgeous blonde steps out, and I wish I had the time to
appreciate her beauty, but she's about to die. Carlos and his
men draw their guns and pivot toward her. My men pull their
weapons too, but we keep them pointed at the Mexicans. The
woman stands like a deer in the headlights for a second before
ducking behind the industrial garbage dumpster like a frightened rabbit. Three shots hit the metal almost at the same
moment. That's all it takes for my men and me. The two bodyguards standing with me aim for a guard each, and I set my
sights on Carlos. We squeeze our triggers, and the men fall.
Screeching tires tell me Carlos's driver takes off. I hear more
gunshots as at least one soldier in my cars tries to shoot the
escaping vehicle. Glass shatters, but the sedan keeps going. I
hear more tires squeal as one of my SUVs takes off and chases
the guy. I holster my gun and wave my men to do the same.
I inch forward toward the trash can, but I see the shadow shift.
The woman bolts from the other side. She's still the frightened
rabbit, but I'm the fox pursuing her. She's fast, I'll give her that.
But she has to be at least a foot shorter than me. My legs are a
lot longer and cover a lot more ground with each stride.
She weaves among the cars, most likely believing it's harder to
hit a moving object. She isn't wrong, but I have no intention of
shooting her. I push myself harder and pounce as she darts out
and tries to cross the last stretch of parking lot to reach a better
lit area near a bus stop. I lunge.
"Stop running, *piccolina*. I won't hurt you."
I wrap my arms around her and pull her back against my chest,
but I'm quick to spin her around and put space between us as I
grasp her arms. Of course, she fights me.
"If I wanted you dead, I would have shot at you, too."
"It doesn't mean you won't kill me after."

She's breathless as she continues to struggle. I almost let go to take a step back, insulted at what she implied. But I can't blame her. If I were a woman, I'd be terrified of the same thing.

"I'm not going to rape you. I'm going to talk to you."

"Talk? You are not a man who talks if you just killed a guy."

"To keep him and his men from killing you. I told you, if I wanted you dead, I would have shot at you too. And I wouldn't have missed."

She stops struggling against me, but her eyes continue to dart from one place to another, trying to find somewhere to flee. I know I can keep her in place with only one hand, so I release her left arm. I still have a firm hold on her right one, but I haven't held it nearly as tightly as I could.

"I'm Luca. I know you figured out you interrupted something you shouldn't have. Did that man know who you are?"

"Yes."

"What about his driver? Would he know you?"

"Yes."

"Do you have a name?"

"Yes."

"*Piccolina*, we won't get very far if yes is all you can say. Are you willing to answer me with more than one word?"

"No."

I knew that was coming, and I grin. I can't help it. I wasn't wrong about her being gorgeous, but I doubt she wants to know that's what I think. At least, not if I want her to know I won't assault her.

"Fine. I have more than twenty questions I can ask that you can answer with one word. Do you work at the store?"

"Sometimes."

Ah, an improvement.

"Did Carlos know you were still working?"

"No."

"Do you have a car, or do you take the subway or bus?"

She raises her chin and remains silent. Smart but counterproductive.

"The subway or the bus will get you killed. You're too easy to find and follow. Do you have a car?"

"Yes."

"Can you stay with someone instead of going home?"

She refuses to answer.

"If that man knew you and you sometimes work in the store, then he knew where you live. If he found that out, so will someone in his cartel."

"I know. Let me go. The longer I stand here, the more likely someone is to come back for me."

"No one will touch you while I'm here."

"Arrogant. If he shot at me, he would have shot at you."

"And he would have died, anyway. What's your name?"

"Jane."

"Look, I know you won't get in one of my cars and let me drive you somewhere. In most cases, I would say that's a smart move. But you did nothing wrong tonight except for leave work at the wrong time. I know that, and you know that. But the Culiacán won't see it that way, *piccolina*."

She freezes for no more than five seconds before she trembles so much that I can see it. I don't know what drives me next, but it's the same instinct that's made me call her little girl three times. I pull her to my chest and tuck her head against it. I stroke her hair down to her shoulders, rubbing my hand up and down her back. This is the most inopportune moment to notice she isn't wearing a bra. I will my body not to react.

"What does that mean?"

Her voice is barely more than a whisper, but I know what she's asking.

"It means little girl."

"I should be insulted, but the way you say it..."

"It has nothing to do with your height. I know you're not a child."

God, do I know she's not. She feels amazing. Her tits are soft as they press against me, and I can see she has the most delectable ass. I'd love nothing more than to cup it and squeeze until she goes up on her toes and begs for me to wrap her legs around my waist and fuck her. For fuck's sake. Stop, you disgusting asshole. That is not what you need to be thinking about.

"Why didn't you shoot me? Whatever you were talking about, if it was with a Cartel member, then it wasn't completely legal. Carlos didn't want me alive to talk about seeing you together. Why are you letting me live?"

"I told you. You did nothing wrong but try to leave work. He should have checked the building before starting the meeting. That was on him. The only thing I take issue with is you leaving by yourself and walking into a dimly lit parking lot. I suspect you do that often, and that's too dangerous. Jane Doe, I don't hurt women."

Mafia Sinner
Mafia Beauty
Mafia Angel
Mafia Redeemer
Mafia Star

Do you also enjoy steamy Historical Romance? Discover Sabine's books written as Celeste Barclay.

The O'Rourke Brotherhood

Mob Boss
BOOK ONE SNEAK PEEK

DILLAN

I hate meetings like this. I don't need to wear pants from some shitty off-the-rack suit that are too tight to *try* to make my dick look bigger. I'm secure in my cock size, and I don't need to show how big my balls are for people to know I run this part of the city. I loathe strip clubs too. I'm past the point where naked women make my jimmy do jumping jacks. I can appreciate a hot bod and gymnast level strength, but it does nothing for me. These douchebags? They're practically ready to come in those cheap arse pants. Why am I here? I keep asking myself that. Seamus and Shane are doing just fine with these negotiations. I'm just here to look good. I'm the muscle today. Or rather my name and my position. Who the fuck thought— way, way back in the day —that giving the mob hierarchy nautical names was a good idea? Fucking Skipper. This isn't motherfucking Gilligan's Island. None of these numb nuts are the Professor, even if they think they're fucking Mr. Howell.

But who is that? If this is *Gilligan's Island*, then she's Mary Ann.

I glance at Seamus, but he's focused on the Albanian he's trying not to lose his shite at. Shane smirks at me when I dart my gaze to him. I cock an eyebrow as the waitress walks over. She's definitely not a dancer. She has too many clothes on. But you can barely call the pieces of thread she's wearing clothes. She's got on a bikini top that's barely more than pasties, and the skirt she's wearing would make my Catholic grandmother do somersaults in her grave.

It's the standard uniform for this place, but somehow it doesn't look right on her. Not because she doesn't have a banging body because she does. Not because she's a butter face— but-her-face —as in great bod, not so great face. She's beautiful in a super understated way. That's part of what makes her look out of place. She has next to no makeup on. I think those are even her real eyelashes. The natural beauty is drawing way too much attention.

"'Scuse me."

She tries to step around Zef Hoxha, the *kyre* of the Albanian mafia here in New York. When he reaches out to grab her wrist, I'm out of my seat with my hand around his. He never gets a chance to touch her because my hold is so tight he can't bend his fingers. I keep squeezing until it must feel like I'll snap the bones.

"No touching."

Zef drops his arm as much as my hold allows. I let go and stare at him before I tilt my head toward the waitress. I narrow my eyes, and he knows what I expect.

"I apologize, miss."

"That's all right, sir. Here's your drink."

She's polite as she hands him his glass. Unfortunately, to put down the rest, she has to bend forward, giving everyone a view of her glorious cleavage. Tits and arse are what sell here, and she has them in spades. I'm certain it's why my cousin hired her. If I sit down, everyone will know I'm just as guilty as these fuck nuts because she's made my dick do something that hasn't happened in a strip club since I was like twenty-three. I'm now thirty-three.

Mob Boss
Mob Star
Mob Princess
Mob Saint
Mob Bride
Mob Knight

Do you also enjoy steamy Historical Romance? Discover Sabine's books written as Celeste Barclay.